Sign up for our newsletter to hear about new releases,
read interviews with authors, enter giveaways, and more.

www.ylva-publishing.com

WICKED THINGS

EDITED BY JAE AND ASTRID OHLETZ

TABLE OF CONTENTS

INTRODUCTION

IN 2013, WE PUBLISHED OUR first Halloween anthology, titled *When the Clock Strikes Thirteen*. Seven authors of lesbian fiction served otherworldly and supernatural stories. Everybody involved had a lot of fun. We were surprised and happy when a project born out of love for a holiday we don't even celebrate in Germany (where we live) became a surprising success: *When the Clock Strikes Thirteen* became a hit with readers and was even a finalist for the GCLS awards.

The decision to repeat the experience wasn't a difficult one. This time, we bring you fourteen stories about werewolves, vampires, ghosts, lunatics, and other beings that will keep you glued to your seat.

Enjoy the read and never stop dreaming...

Astrid Ohletz & Jae

SpiritQuest, LLC

Andi Marquette

"She's a little weird," Mike said.

Mandy looked up from the counter and the video camera she was futzing with. "And you're not?"

Allie grinned at him from her pile of extension cords. "There is that."

Mike shrugged and took his cigarettes out of the left breast pocket of his shirt. He had a thing for retro cowboy shirts with faux pearl snaps. Today's was black with silver piping. He had recently changed the color of his Mohawk from green to purple. It made him look like some kind of tropical bird, and with his rangy frame, the effect was even stronger.

"There's weird, and then there's cool weird. I'm in the latter category. I mean, we don't even really know where she's from." He stood and dug a Zippo lighter out of his front jeans pocket. "Think about it. She just showed up—what? A month ago?"

"People come and go all the time in this line of work," Allie said. "We've taken other volunteers on outings, and some weren't local."

"Yeah, but we usually have a bit more info on them."

"She agreed to the waiver. We have all the info we need."

"And she knows a lot about the paranormal," Mandy said. "I mean, a lot. And she's up on local history."

"Maybe she's a rival ghost hunter and she's been sent here to spy on us." Mike flicked the lid of his Zippo toward Mandy. It made a loud clicking snap. "Or she's with the government, and we're all on some kind of watch list."

"For researching the paranormal?" Mandy scoffed.

"Look what they did in *The X-Files*." He waved a hand dramatically. "The government is always up to shit. Right, Allie?"

"Don't drag *me* into this."

"Come on," he prodded. "You have to admit, Sky's kind of mysterious. And strange. She's got government spook written all over her."

"So the government has nothing better to do than spy on some poor-ass ghost hunting operation like this?" Allie gave him a skeptical look.

"You never know what they're doing. They spy on everybody. Maybe some crazy antigovernment people are using ghost hunting as a front."

Allie laughed. "Dude, you really need to stay off those conspiracy sites on the Net. I know it's hard to believe, but not everything you read on the Web is true."

"This from someone who tries to record paranormal activity," he shot back, though he was laughing, too.

Allie snorted. "Why would the government send such an obvious lesbian to spy on ghost hunters?"

"Um, hello?" Mike indicated himself with a flourish and then gestured at each of them. "Because we're the gayest ghost hunters in town. Maybe in the nation. Screw SpiritQuest. We should change our name to SpiritQueer."

"That makes us sound like a gay cheerleading squad," Mandy said, laughing.

"Ain't nothin' wrong with that." He spun on his heel and with an exaggerated sashay, circumvented the several boxes he'd been digging through in his search for battery packs and left via the back door, giving them both a little huff as he did.

"I think she's nice," Mandy hollered after him. "And cute," she added under her breath, though Allie heard the comment anyway.

She raised her eyebrows. "You think everybody's cute."

"And?" Mandy set the camera aside. "What's wrong with that?"

"Nothing. But if you're planning on putting your swerve on her, don't do it while we're on the job."

"What, like tracking ghosts in dark buildings in the dead of night is supposed to make a girl feel all romantic?" She reached for her can of Coke and the sleeve of her baggy sweatshirt caught on one of the video cameras she had yet to check. She carefully disengaged it before she picked up the can.

"Two words," Allie said. "Jessica Stillwell."

The flush on Mandy's neck accentuated the olive tones of her skin, even under the fluorescent lights. "Whatever," she muttered. "That was an accident."

"Yes, when people trip on a staircase, they always end up with their lips on someone else."

"Fine. That one time."

"Make it the only time. Off the job, I don't care what you do." Allie finished wrapping the heavy orange extension cord around its plastic holder and set it next to the three cameras Mandy had already finished checking and placed on one of the myriad shelves behind the counter, all with neatly handwritten labels signaling what the shelves were for.

"She's not weird."

Allie looked over at Mandy, who had just finished another camera.

"She's just intense. And tuned in." She handed the camera to Allie.

"You're saying she sees dead people?" Allie asked teasingly.

"I don't know. But she does seem more tuned in to that, don't you think? There are people out there like that. Maybe she's one of them. Plus she is really knowledgeable about the paranormal."

"Which makes her perfect for ghost hunting." Allie placed the camera on the "checked" shelf with the others. "Three more for this job, I think."

Mandy murmured agreement and started on another camera. The back door clanged shut and Mike reappeared in the doorway to the storage area. His cheeks were slightly reddened from the cold.

"Okay, I figured out the real reason she's weird," he announced.

"Do tell," Allie said without looking up from the inventory sheet on the counter.

"She's intense."

Mandy nodded. "I was just saying that. And being intense isn't necessarily weird."

"Please, girl. You're only saying that because you think she's cute." He made a dramatic gesture with his hand.

"I don't care how weird she is." Allie gave them both her parent glare. "As long as she helps out, takes this stuff seriously, and plays well with others—living or dead—she can hang out with SpiritQuest."

"Oh, yeah. Totally." Mike nodded emphatically, as did Mandy. "She seems to work best with you, though. And I don't mind chasing ghosts with Miss Thing, here. Plus, you won't have to worry about me tripping into a liplock with her." He cut his eyes at Mandy and smirked at her answering glare.

"Be glad I kind of like you," she said.

"Sweetie, I know you do." Mike fluttered his eyelashes, then turned to dig through a box. "So what else did you find out about the latest gig?" He directed the question at Allie while he rummaged.

"Hold on." Allie left the counter and went to the long utilitarian table against the wall that served as desk space. She picked up the big white binder and flipped through it to the section she wanted. Allie was always organized—to the point of accusations of "anal retentive" from Mike and Mandy—and she created separate binders for different parts of the state. Within each binder were sections for each of the different locations they'd gone ghost hunting, with photos, full reports, and references to the associated computer files.

"Halstead House."

"It sounds like it should be totally creepy." Mandy put another camera on the shelf. "Gothic. And perfect for our Halloween outing."

"Built in 1889 with money Charles Halstead made in the Pikes Peak gold rush," Allie continued. "Charles's adult son Frederick took up residence in 1896. Frederick's wife was Lillian and their sons were Edward, Charles, and Frederick, Junior. Daughter Lily." Allie flipped another page. "Family with money, known around town, doing all that stuff people from the upper echelons are supposed to do."

"High class parties," Mike said. "Must be nice."

"The sons all lived reasonably long lives," Allie continued. "Lily, however, did not. Born in 1902, died 1928." She stared at the photo from the newspaper article she'd printed out from microfiche. It detailed the circumstances of the accident that had killed Lily Halstead. In the photo—a professional sitting, taken from the torso up—she was dressed in a dark 1920s-era blouse that must have been the top part of a dress, since women didn't wear pants much during those years. At least not "proper" women. She wore a matching hat and her eyes bored into Allie's even from the crappy print-out, a little smile on her lips that made it look like she knew something nobody else did.

"She was mad hot," Mike said over her shoulder. "And I don't even like girls that way."

"It's so sad that she died so young." Mandy had joined them. "And now she's stuck at the house."

"So the rumors say." Allie flipped the page to the anecdotes that detailed the strange occurrences at the house, which was now a tourist attraction. "Objects being moved. Furniture, too. Especially in what used to be the parlor, which, apparently, was one of Lily's favorite rooms. She liked to entertain there."

"Did she have any boyfriends?" Mandy craned her neck to see the page.

"No mention of any. She wasn't married, either."

"Sounds les-bish to me." Mike pointed at another photo of her. "I mean, seriously. Not just mad hot. *Smokin'* hot. And there was lots of experimenting going on then. All those sassy flappers getting a little somethin' somethin' in the back of a neighborhood speakeasy."

Allie laughed. "Great story, dude. If only it were true."

"Hey, it could be. You never know. The love that dare not speak its name was getting spoken a hell of a lot. And I'm betting Miss Smokin' Hot here did some talking with the ladies, if you know what I mean."

Mandy giggled while Allie studied the photo Mike had singled out. In this one, Lily stood next to a gorgeous car of the era, her foot placed jauntily on the running board. The car's driver's side window was open, and Lily rested her right hand on the door, her expression a grinning challenge with hints of mischief. She was dressed in a light-colored dress that came down to her knees, dark shoes, and a dark coat. A Twenties-era tight cap adorned her head, tilted just so. Allie had written the photo's date underneath. It had been taken the year before Lily died.

"I mean, twenty-five in this photo and back then, if she wasn't married yet...leaning les-bish," Mike said. "Just sayin'."

Mandy smacked him playfully on the arm. "Has anybody seen her?"

Allie nodded. "The current caretaker—remember Mary Clement?—claims she has. Most recently a month ago."

"Uh-huh. She only shows for the ladies." Mike nudged Allie's right arm with his and Allie smiled.

"What were the circumstances?" Mandy asked.

Allie flipped to the page with the description of the incident. "Late afternoon. Mary claims she was checking the downstairs areas of the house after the last tour had gone through and she thought she heard someone talking in the parlor. She says she leaned her head in and looked around and didn't see anything at first, but as she turned to go, she saw something out of the corner of her eye and she looked back and she says she saw a woman."

"So what makes her say it was Lily?" Mandy again, leaning in closer to read over Allie's shoulder, which made her breasts press into Allie's arm.

"Mary says she's not sure what made her do it, but she said Lily's name, like she was asking if that was who it was and the woman said yes."

"Mary actually *heard* her respond?"

"So she says. Totally clear."

"Then what happened?" Mike, leaning in just as hard on Allie's right.

"Lily—if it was Lily—stood there for a few seconds, then disappeared. So Mary says. She was freaked out about it on the phone, and it's been a month." She flipped to the next page. "There have been other alleged sightings of a woman about Lily's age around the grounds. All the descriptions say the same thing. Youngish, pretty, wearing 1920s-style clothing.

"So why did she stay behind, I wonder." Mandy moved away, much to Allie's relief. As much as she liked Mandy, she wasn't too keen on having a coworker's breasts all up against her arm. "And if that is her showing up, she clearly hasn't reincarnated."

"The age-old question my dear," Mike said in an overblown British accent.

"For all we know, *everybody* stays behind." Allie closed the binder, choosing not to engage Mandy's latest obsession with reincarnation. "Let's finish up. We need to be ready to go tomorrow afternoon."

Mike sighed heavily and dramatically but went back to his boxes while Mandy returned to the counter. Allie set the binder back on the desk, thinking about Mandy's question. That was why she did this work, she figured. To find out if there really were ghosts and why they stayed. She went back to the inventory sheet.

"Hi."

Allie practically jumped out of her jeans. "Shit." Her heart pounded. "I didn't hear you come in."

"Sorry about that." Sky motioned toward the doorway to the foyer. "I saw you in here and tried the door. It was open. Got everything under control?"

"I did, until you scared the piss out of me." She'd have to get on Mandy's case for not locking the front door before she left. "Anyway, yes. We're good to go. Is your schedule okay to come with us?"

"Wouldn't miss this one for the world," Sky said fervently and smiled. From comments she'd made over the past month, Allie knew Sky was really interested in this particular outing. And not for the first time, Allie felt she'd seen her somewhere before she showed up asking to come along on a couple of jobs. She always wore jeans, motorcycle boots, a dark tee, and a black leather motorcycle jacket. And Mandy was right. Sky was cute, in a rakish butch kind of way. Not too tall, not too short. Dark hair and eyes, though sometimes, in the right light, her eyes looked sort of blue.

"So what do you know about the Halstead House?" Allie's heart had stopped hammering inside her chest and she leaned on the counter. Sky had provided some great historical information about the last two jobs they'd done.

Sky slid her hands into her jacket pockets. "Been there a few times. Classic Queen Anne architecture and design. Frederick Junior lived in it until 1973, at which point he turned it over to the historic trust. He tried to preserve a lot of the nineteenth-century touches, though parts of it were modernized for him. He was a lifelong bachelor." Here Sky gave a knowing smile. "Though he had several close gentleman friends over the years. If you know what I mean."

So there was at least one possible strain of gay in the Halstead household. Maybe they *should* change their name to

SpiritQueer and go gay ghost hunting. "What do you know about Lily?"

Sky didn't answer right away and instead stared off into space. "She died young," she finally said, and Allie thought she detected sadness in the words. "Accounts say she was vivacious—the word they used at the time—charming, adventurous, a social butterfly. Engaged in philanthropy, especially for less privileged women and children. Again, descriptions from the times." Sky paused. "She liked to drive. Fast. At least as fast as the vehicles of the time would let her." She stopped and stared off into space again for a few moments. "When she was killed, she wasn't driving, though. She was a passenger."

Allie remembered the newspaper articles she'd read.

"The driver survived," Sky said.

"Rebecca Sanford," Allie supplied.

"Yes. She never forgave herself. Didn't drive for years after that."

Allie shot her a look.

Sky seemed to catch herself. "So the accounts say," she added, a little hastily. "The whole family was devastated, too."

Allie pulled the cuffs of her flannel shirt over her hands, which had become cold in the past few minutes. "I got the impression that Lily didn't marry or have any kids."

"Back then, you'd better hope you were married before you had kids," Sky said with another smile. "At least in the upper classes. But in this case, no, she never married. And no, she didn't have any kids out of wedlock."

"Did she leave anybody in particular behind?" Allie crossed her arms to help warm up.

Sky regarded her for a few seconds. "Rebecca."

"Oh, my God. Seriously?" Allie felt stupid for saying that at Sky's expression. "I mean—shit, that's an even sadder situation than I thought. How do you know?"

"Letters they wrote."

"Letters? Where?"

"Private collections," Sky said, vague. "I know a few people."

"You'll have to hook me up with some of these private collections."

"Remind me later."

"So are there any photos of Rebecca?" Allie hadn't seen any in the newspaper accounts.

"Yes. Frederick Junior left a few behind in the house. Pictures of Rebecca with Lily." She raised her eyebrows. "Nothing sordid," she said, and it sounded like she was teasing. "So I understand that some people say they've seen Lily around at the house."

"You think it's possible?"

Again, Sky waited a while before responding. "Sure. But sometimes people see what they want to see, and there are photos of Lily all over the house." Sky had a tendency to stand perfectly still, almost to the point that it was like she wasn't even breathing.

"Power of suggestion, you're saying?"

"Maybe. And if a spirit doesn't want to be seen, it won't. If it does, it will."

"What do you mean, if a spirit wants to be seen?" Allie was sure the hair on the back of her neck was standing straight out and a chill shot up her spine.

"People assume that spirits can't manifest in a corporeal sense and that they're struggling to make themselves heard or seen." She cocked her head. "That's not the case. Most can manifest physically. They just choose not to."

Skepticism washed the chill away. "So what proof do you have of that?"

Sky grinned. "Research. And a lot of anecdotal evidence, since there's not much grant money out there for people who want to coax spirits into manifesting and prove that the line between life and death isn't absolute." She swept her gaze around the dingy, cluttered office space that SpiritQuest occupied as if to emphasize her point about money. At least the front room didn't look as bad with the overhead fluorescents off. Mike had brought in some floor lamps a few months back and Allie had turned all three on after he and Mandy left for the evening.

"So if that's true, why don't they want to manifest?"

"Think about most people's reactions to seeing their dead relatives or friends walking around in plain sight. It would probably cause mass hysteria."

She had a point, and Allie nodded slowly. Sky leveled her gaze at Allie, and her eyes, for a brief moment in the softer light of the floor lamps, looked almost blue. "Some among the living are able to deal with a full-on manifestation. But not many."

Allie frowned. "Assuming that it's true that all these ghosts are out there choosing not to manifest, why do they do little creepy things?"

"Because the living want to believe. They like not thinking of death as an absolute. The little things are teasers, and keep people engaged in remembering."

"Okay. I'll buy a bit of that. Have you seen a full manifestation?"

Again, Sky was silent for a few moments. "I like to think I have."

"So basically, you're telling me that ghosts choose to manifest or not but you don't have any proof of this and you're not sure you've even seen a full manifestation."

Sky shrugged, and the movement seemed exaggerated because she'd been standing so still. "If I told you I had seen full manifestations, would you believe me?"

Allie laughed. "Okay, you've got me there. For all the ghost hunting I do, I'm actually pretty skeptical."

"I know."

"So why do ghosts stay behind and not cross over or whatever it is we're supposed to do when we die?"

"That's a matter of personal spirit preference," she said with a little quirk at the corner of her mouth.

"There's nothing mystical about it? Like they had unfinished business or something?"

"If they did and they want to stay behind to see how it plays out, they will. So no, there's not really anything mystical about it."

"Okay, then are there any conditions on death? Like, are you tied to a specific place or stuck where you died?"

"Spirits tend to manifest in places that were familiar in life. Sometimes they'll connect with a specific living person, usually someone they knew and loved."

"So can they go anywhere, at any time?"

"Depends. Spirits use energy that connects to something or someone that they had ties to in life, even peripherally. Sometimes, they can gain entry somewhere that they weren't all that connected to in life through a living person. I'm not sure how that works, but it does." She pulled her hands from her pockets. "I've got to go. I'll meet you at the Halsteads' tomorrow."

"Okay. We should be done setting up at ten. Come by earlier if you want to watch that part."

"Thanks. Not sure, though. Anyway, I'll let myself out." She turned and went through the doorway into the foyer, which had been constructed in such a way that Allie couldn't see the front door from her current angle. She exhaled and rubbed her hands up and down the sleeves of her flannel shirt. The chill of the autumn night had managed to permeate the office. And Sky's creepy theories probably helped with that, too.

Mandy and Mike were right about Sky's intensity. She wondered if Mandy might also be right about Sky being "tuned in." *Please*, Allie remonstrated herself. How the hell would Sky know what a ghost wanted or didn't want? Or how a ghost could travel? Next, they'd be SpiritQuest Travel Agency or something. Totally nuts. And there Sky had been, talking like she'd had conversations with ghosts. Like she hung out with them all the time, having coffee or beers or whatever.

Sky was probably a little crazy, Allie decided, but in this line of work, that was generally okay. At least she did her research about the places they were going to visit. A lot of research. She seemed to know quite a bit about the Halstead House. Allie picked her keys up off the counter to go lock the front door, after which she'd text Mandy a cranky reminder to make sure the damn door was locked after hours. She stuck the key in the lock, but something wasn't right.

"What the hell?" She turned the doorknob and pulled. The door was already locked. She unlocked it and locked it again, testing it. Sky didn't have a key. So how—? Wait. Hadn't Mike said last month that he'd had some trouble with the lock? That was it. She was a little weirded out by Sky's paranormal talk, and that, coupled with what she at first thought was a locked door, gave her the heebie jeebies. Sky had been right about that, at least. People did tend to manufacture things in their minds. She checked the door again and went to gather her things so she could set the alarm and leave out the back.

Allie dialed the number Mary Clement had given her first thing the next morning. A man answered.

"Hi. This is Allie over at SpiritQuest confirming our appointment for tonight."

"You'll be wanting Mary, then," he said. "Hold on." It was a landline, and he set it down on something with a clunk. Allie heard voices in the background, and then the phone receiver was picked up.

"This is Mary."

"Hi, Mary. It's Allie at SpiritQuest."

"Hi, there. We are confirmed for tonight. And I'm so glad you're coming. I think Lily was here again yesterday." She said it with some excitement.

"Really? What happened?" Allie picked up her coffee and sipped as she moved her iPad aside. She'd chosen a table in the back of the café, away from the front door and the counter so she could have some privacy and hear better.

"One of our visitors saw her out back, by the gazebo. There have been several sightings of her there, but this one was such that the visitor attempted to talk to her. She was curious about Lily's historical clothing." Mary laughed a little nervously.

"So Lily was—um, corporeal?"

"Oh, yes, according to the visitor. She appeared to be as solid as the rest of us. That aren't ghosts, anyway."

"What was Lily doing?"

"Sitting in one of the chairs we keep on the patio by the gazebo. Then she got up and stood by the rose bushes we have back there. I'm told she really liked roses."

"Did she respond to the visitor?"

"She apparently waved and went into the house. The door was propped open. That's when the visitor came to me. She wasn't scared, just excited that she saw what she was convinced was a ghost, since she found no sign of Lily anywhere inside, and someone dressed like that would surely stick out."

"Did she say anything?"

"Not that the visitor heard. Most of the sightings I'm aware of don't mention that. There was one, however, a couple years ago, who seems to have had a full conversation with her. She's been back a few times."

"What?" Allie gripped her phone harder. "Who was that?"

"Well, I can't recall her name. But she was interested in local history and said she was working on a research project about the Halsteads. She was particularly interested in Lily and said she did some ghost hunting as a hobby. I do recall that she had some interesting insights about Rebecca Sanford."

"Do you know if she ever completed that project?" Maybe it was available in a library somewhere and Allie could track down the researcher. The Halstead House might just require more than one session of ghost hunting.

"You know, I don't. I wish I could think of her name."

"Was she local?"

"I don't know. She was last here about four months ago."

"And you don't know her name?"

"Well, she didn't really say. Let me think about it. Maybe something will make me remember more details."

"Okay," Allie said, trying not to sound disappointed. "Anyway, Lily's ghost sounds friendly, at least."

"Oh, she was quite the charmer in life, all the sources say. Always friendly and kind. Not one of those overbearing wealthy people. No reason to think she'd be different now, is there?" Mary laughed, with genuine amusement this time.

Allie leaned back in her chair and watched as a group of teenaged boys entered, most wearing skinny jeans and skateboard sneakers. "I guess not. Speaking of sources, do you happen to know if there's a collection of Lily's letters that's accessible to the public?"

"Her brother Frederick donated what he had of her papers to the Western History collections at the downtown library. They're included in the main Halstead files."

Allie hadn't had time to really delve into the collection. "What about Rebecca Sanford? Is there a collection related to her somewhere?"

"Well, I don't know. I suppose it's possible."

"Do you know if Frederick ever talked about her?"

"He may have. I think his journals are included in the Halstead collection downtown."

A little prickle worked its way down Allie's spine. "What do you know about her?"

"Not much, but she and Lily were very close, the sources say. There were even a few rumors about their relationship being more than friends." She didn't sound disgusted or judgmental, much to Allie's relief.

"Is there somebody downtown who is really familiar with the Halstead collection?"

"That would be Gareth Ordwell. He's usually there weekdays. Just call the main number and ask for him."

19

That was good news. She liked Gareth. "Thanks, Mary. I will. And we'll see you later this evening."

"You're welcome. I'm looking forward to seeing what you find out. Bye, now." She hung up and Allie brought the archive's number up on her phone's contact list. She called them enough, you'd think she'd have it memorized by now. She'd dealt with Gareth when doing research for some of their other cases. Short, with twinkly blue eyes and a beard that made him look like Santa Claus, if Santa ever developed a penchant for tweed.

"Hi, is Gareth in today?" she asked when her call was answered.

"He is. I'll transfer you," said the guy on the other end. "Can I tell him who's calling?"

"Allie, from SpiritQuest."

"Hold on, please."

Allie waited for the call to get put through. It rang three times, and she was disappointed that she'd end up playing phone tag with him, when he finally picked up.

"Allie! How's our intrepid band of paranormalists?" he asked in his New England-tinged accent. He always sounded like he hadn't spoken to her in years and was so glad she was finally calling.

"Good. Listen, we're going to the Halstead House tonight—"

"Oh, that's a goodie. I wish I had known. I would have loved to tag along on that one."

"Our schedule's on our website. Just give us a call if there are any you're interested in."

He laughed. "Does this mean I'll have to get one of those newfangled computers?"

Allie grinned and took another sip of coffee. Gareth was totally tech-savvy. He just liked to pretend he was a curmudgeonly archivist. "Use your granddaughter's smartphone."

"I'll be sure to handwrite her a note to ask permission."

"Speaking of handwriting—Mary Clement over at Halstead says you're up on the Halstead collection."

"Well, I did catalogue it," he said, preening. "I know a thing or two about the materials therein."

"Great. Are there any letters to Lily in it? Specifically from Rebecca Sanford?"

"Oh, my," he said. "That's a sad story. Rebecca was driving in the accident that killed Lily."

"Yeah, I know. Mary says that there were rumors they were more than friends."

"Oh, my, yes. Not a rumor. They were. Frederick—Lily's brother—discussed it in his journals."

Allie sat forward and called up the Notes function on her iPad. She braced her phone on her shoulder so she could use both hands to type. "Was it something he mentioned often? Or just in passing?"

"Oh, no. Quite a bit. Rebecca and Lily met in 1924 at a social function. Some gala. I can't remember the details off the top of my head. Frederick was quite the gadabout, and a delightful writer and recorder of events. From his description of the soirée, Lily was completely enamored with Rebecca from the first time she saw her. He wrote that Lily waxed incessantly poetic about Rebecca's lovely blue eyes." He chuckled, then dropped his voice conspiratorially. "Frederick and Lily were cut from the same cloth in terms of attractions. According to his journals, she confided in him quite a bit."

Allie didn't bother trying to correct her spelling as she typed Gareth's information on the touchpad. She wished she'd brought her portable keyboard. She'd have to correct this later and add it to the SpiritQuest files. "Who exactly was Rebecca?"

"You mean who were her people?"

"Yeah. Was she from the upper crust?"

"Not the circle that the Halsteads ran in. They were extremely well-heeled. But Rebecca came from a solidly upper middle-class family. Good reputation. Her father was a professor—math, if I recall Frederick correctly—and her mother was educated, too. She ran in art circles, and Rebecca was an artist herself. Painting. Some of her pieces are in the art museum. The Halstead House has one, as well. I haven't been there in a few years, but the last time I was, it was hanging in the parlor. She had a Van Gogh-ish approach. The one there is a landscape in the south of France. She and Lily spent some time there."

"Wow. What happened to her after the accident?"

"We're not entirely sure what happened right after. The reports say Rebecca was terribly injured and it took some months for her to recover. Physically, at least. Frederick didn't write much in the year right after. My sense is, he was absolutely devastated by Lily's death and may have self-medicated with alcohol. The whole family was derailed for a time, from the gossip columns in the local papers." He stopped, as if gathering his thoughts. "His journals indicate that he and Rebecca stayed in contact off and on through the years. So he didn't seem to blame her for what happened."

Allie's fingertips stung, she was pounding so hard on the screen. "Did the Sanfords leave any papers behind?"

"I think they're in the collections at the university where he taught. His wife's are at the art museum. Some of Rebecca's may well be, as well. I'll make some calls. You've gotten me interested in this story again."

"Oh, that reminds me. Mary says that someone a couple years back actually spoke with Lily in a sighting. She says it was a woman who was working on a research project about the Halstead family. Any thoughts about that?"

"Hmm. We get local history buffs and genealogists asking about the Halsteads, so if anybody came in working on that, it wouldn't stick out."

"She would have been really interested in Lily and she would have had some information about Rebecca."

"No, sorry. Doesn't ring a bell. If it was someone who actually said she'd spoken with Lily, well, *that* would definitely stick out. So if she was here, she didn't mention that."

And why would she? People would think she was crazy. Hell, Allie thought it sounded a little crazy. "When did Rebecca die?"

"Sometime in the 1980s. I want to say 1984, but don't quote me on that. I'll check that, too. She ended up in the Portland, Oregon art scene, so there might be a collection of hers up there. I'll see if we can track her papers down."

If she left any, Allie thought. "This is great, Gareth. Thanks so much."

"You know I love talking history. The best kind of gossip. I'll call you when I know more. And let me know how tonight goes."

"I will. Bye." She hung up and took another sip of coffee, which was now cold, but she didn't care. She typed in what Mary had said as well, then thought for a bit. She wanted the names of these alleged private collections that Sky claimed held letters between Lily and Rebecca.

Why would Sky hedge about that? Mike was right, in a sense. She was weird and mysterious. Allie had already done a search on her, but "Sky Adams" didn't have an online footprint. It was like she'd just appeared that day last month out of thin air, interested in going along on some outings. Specifically, the Halstead House. That one interested her the most, though she'd gone on two others with them over the past month and proved herself pretty knowledgeable, as Mandy had noted.

No electronic footprint. Didn't seem to have a phone or other devices. That was pretty spooky, in the government agent sense. Or she was running from the law. But why would a fugitive participate in paranormal outings? Perfect cover, Mike would argue. Allie finished her coffee and stood. Sky would make a cool character in a comic, she decided. She could be a new incarnation of The Shadow.

She tossed her empty coffee cup into a nearby trashcan, picked up her iPad, and headed for the door. Tonight, she'd ask Sky a few more questions.

Allie tested the battery pack on the last video camera. They'd set this one up at the top of the main staircase, directed at the landing. Several reports indicated that both staff and visitors had experienced cold spots while ascending to the second floor. She made sure it was focused on the landing, some twenty steps below. Satisfied, she paged Mike on her walkie talkie.

"Super agent Mike," he responded.

She smiled. "Landing cam ready to go. What's the word on the parlor cam?"

"We figured out how to position it to get most of the room. There's one corner that doesn't show, so hopefully Lily won't hang out there."

"Word is she wasn't the shy, retiring type," Allie said. "I doubt a back corner was her style."

"Unless she wants to mess with us. Over." The walkie-talkie cut his laugh off.

"Are we all good, then?"

"Ready to rock n' roll. All cams up. Mandy's still checking the thermal cam by the front door."

"Let's meet downstairs in five. Over."

"Roger." He signed off and Allie went down the wide hallway to Lily's bedroom. They'd set up the other thermal cam here just inside the doorway. The door was partially ajar and Allie pushed it fully open to make sure it didn't bump the camera. The overhead light was still on. They wouldn't do a full lights-out until Sky arrived, and then they'd operate in the dark. Which was dumb, when she thought about it, because ghost sightings happened at all times of day. Operating at night, however, ensured less noise from the surrounding areas and within the house itself.

"Okay, Lily," she muttered. "If you're still hanging around, it would be really cool if you decided to manifest tonight." She stood looking around the room, which held a huge four-poster bed whose headboard was against the left-hand wall. A light-blue canopy covered it, and one side of the bedding had been turned down, expecting a woman who would never sleep there again. The bed wasn't 1920s-era, and Allie figured it was left over from the nineteenth century. It might not even have been a Halstead bed, originally. Fred Junior might've gotten rid of all of that and the historical society might have acquired this one for the look of it because this room still held nineteenth-century touches.

The fireplace in the wall opposite the bed and framed in dark wood had been modified. The heater in the part that should've held logs looked like it might be from the 1950s and Allie wondered if it still worked. The room wasn't too cold, though houses like this, with their high ceilings and tall windows, were usually drafty.

Bookshelves on either side of the fireplace were filled with books, but some of the spines looked modern. Allie wondered which of the older ones Lily might have liked. Maybe adventure stories like Tarzan or something. Maybe she snuck pulp westerns and science fiction into her bed at night when her parents weren't looking. And maybe as she grew up, she used the big leather chair next to the bookshelf, over which a reading lamp stood, its lampshade decorated with brocade and tassels. And maybe she sat and looked out the window onto the expansive backyard and thought about Rebecca.

Allie glanced at the bed again and flushed, a little embarrassed thinking about Lily in it. "Sorry," she said to no one. "Didn't mean to think about that."

She cleared her throat, feeling stupid. Ghosts weren't telepathic, after all. What Sky had said about Lily, however, made Allie want to be a little more respectful of her, if only because she felt she knew a bit more about her personally.

"Ready?" Mandy asked from the doorway. Allie jumped.

"Yeah," she said, hoping Mandy hadn't noticed. "Just wanted to check the cam angle."

Mandy came in. "I like this room. It feels good." She was wearing another of her ubiquitous sweatshirts under her fleece jacket, this one from Wellesley, probably a leftover from one of her flings. She was also wearing her "ghost huntin' shoes," as she called them. Black high-top Converse sneakers decorated with sparkly cartoon ghosts.

"I'm sure Lily would have appreciated that comment." Allie pointed at the Mel Meter that Mandy carried. "Did you do preliminary readings?"

"Yep. No magnetic or heat weirdness. Mike's got the EMF. Take the Mel." She handed it to Allie and looked around. "That bed is some kind of sexy."

Allie rolled her eyes. "This is work space."

"Just an observation," Mandy retorted. She moved to the bookshelves and scanned the titles. "Interesting mix. I started reading this ultra-cool book on reincarnation this morning. By a guy named Ian Stevenson. He did all these studies on kids, because kids apparently remember past lives better than adults."

"Reincarnation is a little harder to hunt than a ghost. Although KarmaQuest sounds kind of fun."

Mandy giggled. "Wouldn't it be cool if somebody came to this house and it was Rebecca, all reincarnated? And Lily manifested? What a great love story that would be."

Allie shrugged. Maybe it hadn't been a good idea to tell her coworkers what Sky had said or what she'd found out earlier that day. "It'd still be sad. After all, Lily's a ghost. She can't get any action from the living."

"There's a whole genre of erotica that says otherwise."

"Are you serious?"

"Totally. Paranormal erotica."

Allie laughed. "Why does it not surprise me that you know that?"

Mandy snorted. "Your life is richer because of me." She looked at the bed again. "Wonder if it would be cold, to get busy with a ghost."

"Okay, just stop."

"What? It might be a legit question. And fun research, at least." Mandy turned her attention to the framed photographs on the mantle. "Bet that's Rebecca," she said, pointing at one.

Allie joined her to look. Lily was in this image, wearing another dark-colored dress and sitting in a chair outside somewhere. Probably the house grounds. Another woman sat next to her, smiling, and Lily was smiling back at her. Lily's companion in the photo was also wearing a dress, but in a lighter shade. Her hair was dark, and the style framed her face in a way that accentuated her cheekbones. Neither had hats on.

"They're sitting pretty close," Mandy said.

"That could be anyone," Allie said.

"True." Mandy leaned in. "She's cute. And this is trippy, but she looks kind of like Sky."

The hair on the back of Allie's neck stood up again. "No, she doesn't. She has dark hair. That's all. Probably isn't even Rebecca."

"Yeah, you're probably right." Mandy straightened. "Okay, let's get this party started."

"Guys," Mike yelled from the first floor. "Are we going to have our tribal council or what?"

"Coming," Mandy called back. She bounded out of the room and Allie turned to the photo. Mandy was right. The dark-haired woman did look a little like Sky. She turned the light out and left the room, thinking about the photo and what Sky had said about Rebecca never forgiving herself. She checked her watch. Sky would probably be here in about fifteen minutes and then they could get started. She joined the others in the wide hallway, near the front entrance.

"Okay," Mike said, putting on an official air. "Old house. Old floors. Creaky. Try to stay on the runners in the halls and the rugs in the rooms. Tread softly so we don't get our own readings. Chief?"

"Same protocol as usual," Allie said. "Sky and I will start out back, by the old carriage house. You and Mandy start with the driveway. Lily was into cars, after all."

"Les-bish," Mike said with a grin and Mandy laughed.

"Not a word Lily probably knows. Keep it standard." Allie checked the Mel Meter's battery readout. "You two take the second floor once you're done out front."

"Cool," Mandy said. "The bedroom." She wiggled her eyebrows up and down.

Allie shot Mandy a look and her smile faded.

"Sky and I will start in the kitchen," Allie continued, "and do the rooms on this floor. We'll check the parlor a few times, since that's where Mary says she saw Lily. Mike, make sure you check the staircase regularly. Go up and down a few times, see if you can pick up any changes in temperature."

He saluted. He was wearing a light jacket over another retro western shirt, this one red and blue plaid. He had cuffed his jeans so most of his Doc Marten boots showed. He liked his blue pair for outings and he was also wearing his lucky baseball cap. Allie wondered how he had managed to stuff his Mohawk under there, and then it occurred to her that her team might be a little superstitious.

"Mandy, check the hallway every fifteen minutes when you're inside. We've got the laser set up to detect anything moving down it toward Lily's room. You guys might want to just hang out in the hall for a while, see if that brings anything out."

"Okee dokee."

"Let's do this," Mike said with a fist pump.

"Lights are out upstairs. Let's go lights out downstairs. When we've got that done, take your initial posts."

"Roger." Mike handed the EMF reader to Mandy. "We'll take the front half; you get the back on your way out."

Allie nodded and walked down the wide corridor to the kitchen. She had her walkie-talkie clipped to her belt and the Mel Meter in the pocket of her jacket, which was flannel lined but light enough for easy movement. The lights in the parlor, library, and dining room were already out, but the kitchen light was still on. She turned it off and used her pocket flashlight to cross to the back door. This part of an outing always got her adrenaline going, excitement mixed with a little bit of fear. Who knew what kinds of other things besides a playful spirit were lurking out there? She checked her watch. The luminescent hands showed a little after ten. Hopefully, Sky would show up soon. As skeptical as Allie was, she didn't like to do an outing as a single.

She went outside and kept her flashlight on so Sky could find her. The moon hadn't risen, and it was one of those crisp, clear fall nights that seemed to accentuate every sound.

"Hi," came Sky's voice out of the darkness. Allie didn't start, because she'd been half-expecting it. Sky had a habit of appearing like that.

"Hey. We just started. Everything okay?"

"Fine. I was just checking around in the front."

"Did you see Mike and Mandy?"

"No. Were they supposed to be out there?"

"They will be." Allie pulled the walkie-talkie off her belt. "Mike? You guys outside yet?"

"Yeah. Just now. Mandy's running the EMF around the front and by the old driveway."

"Okay. Sky's here. We're going to check back here."

"Gotcha. Out."

In the light from Allie's flashlight, she saw that Sky was dressed as typical Sky. At least she'd be warm in that leather jacket, though she never zipped it closed.

"So reports suggest that Lily might manifest back here," Allie said. She clipped the walkie-talkie to her front pocket instead of her belt, which would make it easier to pull and access.

"She liked the grounds," Sky agreed. "Especially the area by the gazebo, and the roses."

The most recent sighting had put Lily there, too. "Was that in the letters?" she asked as they headed across the lawn toward the gazebo and its separate patio. It was like an island in the backyard.

"Yes," Sky answered, maybe a little too quickly.

"We saw a photo in Lily's room, on the mantle. There was a dark-haired woman with her. Do you know who that was?"

Sky was silent so long that Allie thought she'd disappeared. She turned around and shined her flashlight where she'd last heard her, but Sky wasn't there.

"Might've been Rebecca," came Sky's voice, to Allie's right and slightly ahead of her. Allie hadn't heard her pass. "She had dark brown hair."

"Were they about the same age?"

"Lily was a couple years older." Sky was standing on the gazebo's patio to the right of the structure. A metal table and chairs that had seen better days were to Sky's left as she looked at the gazebo. Which of those chairs was Lily's at the most recent sighting? One was positioned so it looked at the back of the house. Somehow, Allie figured that was Lily's spot.

"So what got you so interested in the Halsteads?" Allie joined her on the patio and played the beam of her flashlight slowly over the gazebo.

"I enjoy history. Good fit for paranormal research." She lapsed into silence and Allie kept the flashlight trained on Sky's boots.

"But why the Halsteads? There are lots of families in this area with long histories."

"And they're all interesting, but sometimes something really intrigues you. I'm sure you have certain historical things that really get to you, and others, not so much."

"Why is that, you think?"

Sky laughed softly. "Mandy's reading Stevenson's book about reincarnation. Might be some answers in there."

"Oh, come on. You believe in that, too?" She shone her flashlight beam on the rose bushes that lined the back of the patio.

"You ever have a déjà vu experience? Or feel really drawn to something in your research and you just can't explain why it resonates with you?"

Allie moved her beam to the back of the house. "Yes. So?"

"So why would you be drawn to something in the past that you have no connection to now, unless you had a connection in a previous incarnation, as someone else?"

The chill Allie felt didn't have anything to do with the cool night air. "Is that why you're so interested in the Halsteads?"

Sky was probably going to say she was Lily reincarnated. If she did, she might just be a little too crazy even for ghost hunting. Allie turned, but couldn't make out Sky's form in the gloom. Damn her for wearing dark colors all the time.

"I don't know," Sky said, and it came from Allie's left. She swung the beam in that direction until it hit Sky's jeans. "I do feel really drawn to this family and this house. And I enjoy research."

Allie stifled a sigh. Sky would be a perfect government agent. Imparting just enough information without revealing much beyond that. "Anybody here besides us?" Allie asked after about a minute. "Let us know."

"You don't need to do that," Sky said, and Allie thought she heard amusement in her tone.

"So you always say."

"If a spirit is present, it knows you're here."

"So isn't it kind of polite to acknowledge it in some way?"

"Just say its name a couple of times. And let it know your name."

Allie cleared her throat, nervous. "Um. Hi, Miss Halstead, if you're here. I'm Allie. I hope it's okay to call you Lily. Because we have been." Okay, that made her feel kind of stupid.

It sounded like Sky was smothering a chuckle. "She'll appreciate that."

Allie shot a look in Sky's direction then walked slowly from one end of the patio to the other, keeping her flashlight beam on the stone underfoot so she wouldn't trip. She held the Mel Meter out. It picked up nothing unusual.

"You never said why you do this," Sky said, and her voice was on Allie's left.

Allie stopped at the edge of the patio and played her light over the back of the house before she pointed the beam back at Sky's boots. "When I was a kid, I saw some things that I'm not sure about."

"Such as?"

She hesitated. "You'd call them corporeal manifestations."

"What was the context?"

"I think I saw my grandfather at his funeral. Only not in the casket. He was standing in the back of the church, and he waved at me." She'd hardly ever talked about that, but if anybody would get it, it would be crazy Sky.

"That's not an uncommon manifestation. Some spirits do that right after their bodies die to try to reassure those left behind that although they may not be living, they're still around. Some think that's comforting. Did you?"

"I don't know. I was just a kid and I told my mom that Grandpa was right behind us." She laughed, a little harshly. "That didn't go over well."

Sky made a sympathetic noise. "Did you see him again?"

"A couple of times. And no, I didn't tell anybody after what happened with my mom. Anyway, looking back on it, I think maybe I conjured him myself. Power of suggestion." She moved over to the gazebo. "Did Lily like to sit in here, you think?"

"Yes," Sky said, and her voice was soft, almost reverent.

Allie looked over toward her, wondering at the tone. Her walkie-talkie crackled.

"Got nothing in the front," came Mike's voice. "We checked the porch, too. Taking it inside."

"Okay. We'll probably be in the kitchen in fifteen. Out." She reclipped it to her pocket.

"Have you seen any other corporeal manifestations?" Sky asked from the dark behind her.

"Maybe a few times over the years. A couple on some outings, but I'm not convinced I actually saw them. The brain, as you've said, can make us believe just about anything. Okay, quiet time for a bit."

Sky didn't respond and Allie strained to hear her, but eventually, all she heard was the movement of her own blood in her head. She had the eerie sensation that Sky had totally disappeared, or that she didn't actually exist. She checked her watch. Ten minutes had passed.

"Well," she said, and her voice sounded harsh as it broke the silence. "I guess Lily either isn't here or she's not interested in showing herself. Let's go in."

"Okay," said Sky somewhere to her left and Allie almost sighed in relief that she was still around. She started back across the lawn toward the house, flashlight in one hand and Mel Meter in the other.

"Careful. The bottom step is loose."

Allie froze, and not because the air had suddenly chilled. That wasn't Sky's voice, though it was female. She forced herself to look at the Mel Meter, which was registering red, off the charts. Holy freaking moly.

"Lily?" She said, surprised at how steady her voice was.

No response. What the hell? Allie's heart pounded and she fought an urge to run. Instead, she forced herself to walk normally to the five steps up to the kitchen. "Sky?"

No response from her, either. Where the hell was she?

"Sky?"

"Inside," she said.

Allie hadn't heard the door open. "Dammit," she muttered. Sky hadn't wandered off on their previous outings. "Stay together," she remonstrated.

"Sorry. Watch that bottom step," Sky said. "Not bad going down, but could trip you going up."

Allie stopped. Her skin crawled with another chill. She held the Mel Meter up, but it didn't register anything. She took the steps two at a time, skipping the bottom one. She'd left the inner door open and she shone her flashlight through the screen, looking for Sky's shape.

"Sky?"

"In the kitchen."

Allie sighed her relief and went in. She latched the screen door, then closed and locked the inner door behind her. Her hand was shaking.

"I think Lily's here," she said as she entered the kitchen.

"I think you're right," Sky said, and in her voice Allie heard—what? Excitement? Longing? Sadness? All three? And it creeped her out.

Allie pulled her walkie-talkie off her jeans. "Mike?"

"Yeah."

"Where are you guys?"

"Upstairs in the master bedroom."

"Were either of you out back within the past five minutes?"

"No. Did you see something?" He asked, excited.

"Heard a voice. Wasn't me or Sky. Check the stairs."

"Oh, super cool. Checking. Out."

Allie put the walkie-talkie in her jacket pocket, her eyes on her Mel Meter. The EMF function didn't register anything, but as she passed Sky, the temperature gauge picked up a drop of about five degrees. "What—" She started to point the Mel in Sky's direction.

"Got something," came Mike's voice from her pocket. She grabbed her walkie-talkie.

"Go ahead."

"Major cold spot on the landing. Lasted ten seconds. Mandy felt it again at the top of the stairs."

"When?"

"About fifteen seconds ago."

"See if you can track it down. Out." She was turning to Sky when Mike's yell tore her from the kitchen. "Shit," she said as she bolted down the hallway to the stairs. She stood at the bottom and peered up into the darkness of the second floor.

"Mike? Are you okay?" She shone her flashlight up the stairs.

He appeared above, leaning over the railing, eyes wide but grinning. "Holy shitsky, captain. The EMF just practically blew a fuse and Lily's bedroom door closed. Mandy and I were out in the hall. We heard it. Not a slam, like a breeze does. A soft click, like if you're closing it."

"Did you pick up anything on the thermal cam in there?"

"Mandy's checking it. I thought Lily might be more comfie with chicks in her boudoir than a dude."

"Just introduce yourself first," said Sky.

"Oh, hey." Mike gave her a wave. "Yeah, I did. So did Mandy. This is freaking amazing. Best outing ever. I'm seriously experiencing a major degree of stokage up here." He was talking so fast Allie almost didn't understand him. She shivered suddenly as ice seemed to settle on her skin.

"Cold spot," she announced and Mike shut up immediately, like someone had pulled a plug.

"Mel Meter's registering...and cold spot's gone." She shone her flashlight around. Sky had moved away, and was staring down the hall toward the kitchen.

"Quiet," Allie said. "I think I hear something." In the kitchen? It got louder. Footsteps. Like heels on wood, coming down the corridor.

"Fuck," came Mike's quiet exclamation from above. "What is that?"

"Oh, my God," Allie said. "The Mel's picking something up. Something major." Her teeth were practically chattering as she took a step down the hall. "Lily?" she said softly, and it didn't seem so stupid in these circumstances. She held her flashlight so that the beam pointed at the hall runner underfoot.

"Lily," Sky echoed.

"I've been waiting," said a female voice that definitely wasn't Sky and sounded like the one from outside. Soft, well modulated. Allie stopped, sure her knees were knocking. Lily. Right here. Talking. Holy crazy towns. She somehow managed to hold onto the Mel.

"I know." That was Sky, somewhere in the hallway and to her right. What the hell?

Allie tried to say something, but nothing came out. Her words were stuck in her throat. She thought she heard somebody coming down the stairs behind her, but she didn't turn around. She couldn't if she had wanted to, since she was in the middle of a major freak-out that had pretty much paralyzed everything but her brain.

"I'm sorry," Sky said, her voice soft. "I should have come sooner."

"I wanted you to," Lily said, and Allie's hands started shaking so badly that the beam of the flashlight jiggled on the rug. She didn't want to shine it down the hall, because she was afraid the light would interrupt whatever this was.

"It wasn't your fault, love." That was Lily again. "I tried to tell you. But you were closed. All those years, too closed to hear."

"I was then. And I couldn't bear reminders. But I missed you," Sky said. "So much."

Allie stared down the hall and used her peripheral vision to try to pick shapes out in the dark. She thought she saw Sky's form in the middle of the hallway some twenty feet away, and just to the left, someone else. Another form, standing close to Sky. She clamped her teeth shut to keep them from chattering.

"I'm here now," Sky said.

Oh, my God. What was happening? Allie couldn't differentiate Sky's form from the other. Or maybe there wasn't anybody in the hall and she just thought she saw something.

"No way," Mike said softly just behind Allie. And then the temperature dropped sharply, a cold that went right through her bones.

"Sh-shit," Allie managed through her chattering teeth. The word came out in visible puffs. She wrenched her arm up, and the flashlight beam pierced the hallway, but nothing was there. "What the hell—"

"Guys," Mandy said from the stairs. "Huge cold spot just went by on the landing—oh, my God. Get up here."

Mike grabbed Allie's arm and pulled her toward the stairs and they barreled up the steps, nearly slamming into Mandy at the top. She had her flashlight trained down the hall toward Lily's bedroom and she was staring, open mouthed.

"Lily," Allie said, stunned. In full-blown corporeal manifestation, right down to the slim 1920s navy dress and light-brown shoes. She stood outside her bedroom door, smiled at them—smiled!—and walked right through the wood.

Allie moved first, practically throwing herself down the hall. "Lily, wait," she blurted as she fumbled with the doorknob. "Wait." She got the door open and held her flashlight up, moving its beam in a staccato pattern from one side of the room to the other. "Lily?"

She was gone.

"No way," Mike said behind her.

"Nothing in the hall," Mandy announced quietly.

"Where's Sky?" Allie turned her flashlight on Mike. He looked at her helplessly and shook his head. "Look for her."

Mandy jogged into the hallway. "Sky?" She turned the staircase light on and Allie winced at the sudden flood of brightness. Mandy went down the stairs, Mike right behind her. Allie heard them moving through the house and turning lights on, calling for Sky. She knew as the seconds ticked by that they wouldn't find her. She leaned her back against the wall just outside Lily's bedroom and slid to the floor until she sat facing the staircase, smiling and shaking again, this time from the aftereffects of her adrenaline rush.

Mandy appeared at the top of the stairs. "Allie! Are you okay?" She rushed over.

"Fine. Just need to rest a bit."

"We can't find Sky."

"She's gone."

"What do you mean, gone?"

Allie laughed a little. "She knew what book you started reading this morning."

Mandy stared at her. "What? What are you talking about? I haven't talked to Sky today. Allie?" She sounded worried.

"Later." Allie held her hand out, and Mandy pulled her to her feet. "We'll sort it out in a bit." She moved to the staircase, Mandy's eyes on her, practically as big as plates. "Mike, let's pack up and go home."

"Roger," he said from below.

"Wait a minute," Mandy said. "How could Sky know what book I had started reading?" Mandy asked. "I didn't tell her."

Allie looked back at her, still smiling. "I know." Because Sky had told her that sometimes spirits needed a living person as a vehicle to get into some places. And she, Allie, had served that purpose for Sky.

"I only just told you here, in Lily's room—oh, my God. Sky was there. Sort of." Her eyes widened. "Oh, my God."

Allie laughed again. "Exactly." She started down the stairs, Mandy right behind her uttering a litany of "oh, my God" all the way down.

"Hi, Allie. Good to see you! Let me tell you, since you confirmed that there probably is some paranormal activity here, we've had quite a lot of calls and tours scheduled. We're thinking about partnering with the LGBT Center for a research project about gay history in Denver during the 1920s. Gareth at the Western History collections is very interested." Mary came around the counter and gave her a hug.

"That's great. Really great. Has anybody seen anything since we were here?"

"A couple of people have claimed they saw the door to Lily's bedroom open and close. And someone reported that she thought she heard a woman laughing in the bedroom."

Allie stifled a smile.

"And some have reported some cold spots on the stairs again. We're hoping Lily shows herself again. Too bad you didn't see her."

"Yeah. Too bad about that. But we got some cold spots, too, and the door thing, as we showed you. Plus some interesting shadows. We'll probably come back in the future, though, and try again."

"What fun! If I could stay up late, I'd love to be here for it."

"We'll let you know. Mind if I look around a little? This whole thing has gotten me interested in the history of this place."

"Of course not. Come and find me when you leave."

"Thanks." Allie went up the stairs to the second floor. Several women who looked to be in their sixties were admiring some of the photos in the hallway. They moved past her and went down the stairs. The door to Lily's room was open and a man and woman about Allie's age emerged.

"Great bed," he was saying, and she elbowed him playfully in the ribs.

"Is that all you think about?"

"What? It's a great bed." He nodded at Allie as she passed them and went into Lily's room. She heard the couple descend the stairs and relaxed.

The room hadn't changed since that night a month ago. Wait. The photographs on the mantle had been rearranged. The one she and Mandy had looked at was now positioned in the center. And Rebecca's painting from the parlor now hung above the mantle. It did look a little like a Van Gogh landscape, but the colors were a little softer. More romantic. The light from the windows up here made it look more vibrant than it had downstairs.

"Hey Lily. And Sky, if you're here," she said softly, and it felt and sounded awkward, since she was the only one in the room. Who was living. She cleared her throat. "Um, anyway. We haven't told anyone what we really saw that night. There'll probably be more ghost hunters showing up, but we didn't want to make it worse if they thought there were corporeal manifestations here. Guess that'll be our little secret." She stood, waiting. For what? She wasn't sure. "Okay. Anyway. Just wanted to let you know."

She heard Mary greeting someone downstairs and exhaled, realizing that she'd been holding her breath. She turned back to the door, and as she crossed the threshold, she heard, from in front of the fireplace, "Thank you," and a slight chill permeated the room.

Allie smiled. "Welcome, Lily," she muttered as she went down the stairs in search of Mary. She found her in the kitchen arranging flowers in a vase.

"Thanks, Mary."

"Oh. Leaving so soon?"

"I've got to get back to work."

"Well, stop by any time. Anybody from SpiritQuest is welcome here."

"Great. Thanks. See you." She was halfway down the hall to the front door when Mary called her and hurried out of the kitchen.

"Oh, I meant to tell you, but nearly forgot, with how busy we've been."

Allie waited.

"I remembered who that researcher was, who said she spoke with Lily a couple of years ago. Hold on just a bit." She went over to the glass counter in the front sitting room. When she returned, she held a folded piece of paper. "Someone called last week and said they were part of a local paranormal book club, and the name of it jogged my memory. That researcher had said she was with this group, so I described her to the person who called, and this is what I found out."

Allie took the paper and unfolded it. It was an obituary, and a photo of Sky stared up at her. The name under it was Rachel "Sky" Schuyler. But it could just as well have been Rebecca Sanford, with shorter hair. Allie tried to say something but the words froze in her mouth.

"So sad. Poor thing died not two months ago. Car accident out of state."

"She lived on Adams Street," Allie said, and she understood, now, why Sky Adams had no virtual footprint.

"That's not too far from here. Oh, and did you know that the book club used to meet in the building where your office is now? They were in the process of moving when—" she gestured at the paper. "Well, when that happened." She tsked sadly.

"Can I keep this?" Allie held the paper up.

"Certainly. Are you going to see if you can find out if she finished her research project?"

"Maybe. Thanks again, Mary. See you next time." She went outside, and the afternoon light of a cold November day threw shadows across the snow-mottled lawn. The Halstead House stood in the center of a city block, and unlike the other Queen Annes along this street, it sat on two lots, so it stood out from the crowd. She took her phone out of her coat pocket and dialed Gareth's direct line.

"Hi, it's Gareth."

"Hey, it's Allie."

"And what can I do for you today, m'dear?"

"Did you ever find out when Rebecca Sanford died?"

"Why, yes. I most certainly did. May twelfth, 1984. Born January twentieth, 1904. And she did leave some papers behind. I have queries out to determine what's in the collection. I'll let you know when I find out."

"Great. I really appreciate it. Catch you later. Bye." Allie hung up and read Sky's obituary again. She'd been born November fifth, 1984. "Damn, Sky. Happy belated birthday," she said softly. "Or maybe I should say happy early birthday, Rebecca."

She folded the paper into fourths and put it in the back pocket of her jeans, then texted Mandy to find out if she could meet for coffee. She stopped at her car and leaned against it and looked back at the Halstead House, the largest on this block, still stately with its light gray siding and maroon trim. It really was a great house. Her phone beeped with a text message. She read it and got into her car. Twenty minutes later, she had a cup of coffee at a table next to the front windows and Sky's obituary next to her cup, still folded. Mandy waved at her through the window before she came in.

"Hey, girl. Let me get something to drink," Mandy said as she draped her coat over the chair next to Allie. A few minutes later, she came back with what looked like a cappuccino and sat down.

"Okay. What's up?" Mandy looked at her expectantly. "New case? Though nothing could top that last one. No Halloween ever will top that."

"You never know. Word may be out on the ghost grapevine how awesome we are."

Mandy giggled and stirred her coffee.

Allie slid the paper toward her. "Remember when you said how cool it would be if Rebecca showed up at the Halstead House reincarnated?"

"Yes, I do. And I believe you have said a few times in the past, rather eloquently, that you don't buy that crap. Though somehow a ghost volunteering with us is more believable in your world."

Allie shrugged. "I'm willing to be wrong." She gestured at the paper. "Read it."

Mandy unfolded it and her eyes widened. "Oh, my God," she said. She stared at Allie. "Does this mean what I think it does?"

"I'm guessing yes. It took her a couple of lifetimes, but it looks like Rebecca found her way back to Lily."

"Oh, my God."

"Exactly." Allie picked up her coffee. "Here's to love." She tapped her cup against Mandy's. "And more Halloweens like that one."

A Certain Moon

Elaine Burnes

ANN DUSTED SHELVES THAT WERE already dust-free, plumped previously plumped pillows, and ignored the disdainful look her cat gave her. She checked the clock for the fifth time in the last ten minutes. It was too early for Erica to be punctual, never mind fashionably late. She paced the kitchen, checking the roast in the oven, the potatoes on the stove. Everything was where it should be, except her emotions. Why was she so nervous? As much as she liked Erica, she knew there was no point in getting her hopes up.

They'd met last summer at a book festival in the city—Erica was a writer, Ann an illustrator. Ann had been sitting in the back row of a seminar on genre. As the panelists had droned on about the popularity of witchcraft novels and the role of speculative fiction in deciphering the modern psyche, she had noticed the woman next to her sighing repeatedly and shifting uncomfortably. As they stood to leave, she asked, "Do you disagree?"

The woman appeared startled, then smiled shyly. "Was I that obvious?"

Ann noted the warmth of that smile and returned one of her own. "Well, I wouldn't blame you."

That got them chatting, and they were pleasantly surprised to learn they lived in the same town. Erica introduced herself and put out her hand. Ann responded in kind. Erica's hand was warm, her grip firm.

"What do you write?" Ann asked as they joined the stream of avid readers and wannabe novelists leaving the hotel conference room.

"Romances."

Ann sighed silently. "So you believe in happily ever after?"

Erica chuckled. "Hardly. That's why I write fiction."

That had been the first tick of attraction.

Ann assembled the members of her tiny household. Only the dog, Farkas, came when called. Freddy, the hamster, gave her a blank hamster stare, and Erzsebet remained in her window seat, back to Ann, but her ears were turned, so she was listening.

"Please behave—all of you," Ann pleaded. She understood the ridiculousness of trying to bargain with these creatures, but she was desperate. "This might be my last chance."

Farkas wagged his curly tail, Erzsebet ignored her, and Freddy, standing against the glass wall of his aquarium home, trembled. Resigned, Ann gave Freddy a comforting pat, attempting to cover some of his bare patches with the bits of fur that remained.

The first time the doorbell rang, Ann about jumped out of her skin. It was barely six o'clock, however, and it was only trick-or-treaters. Of all the evenings for Erica's first visit, it had to be this one—Halloween—complete with a full moon. But this was the only evening that worked for both of them.

What was it Erica had said? "I make a point of ignoring Halloween."

That had been another tick. Ann dreaded the day, or rather the evening, but participated for fear her neighbors, though few they were, would think her more strange than she already felt.

"Far too commercial for me," she'd said, to assure Erica, who did not elaborate on her remark.

Ann's nerves calmed till about seven thirty. She'd suggested Erica come after eight, when the Halloween crowd lessened. With each ring of the bell, Farkas spun in circles, barking, and Erzsebet dove under the couch. Aside from the occasional Katniss Everdeen, the kids' costumes presented the usual suspects—vampires, princesses, witches, and other assorted scary creatures. Ann handed out the candy, searching past the costumed heads to the dark street, now white with falling snow, anticipating Erica's arrival.

She paced her living room, reflecting on this new sensation, anticipating someone's arrival. What had led to this?

After the panel at the book festival, Ann hadn't expected to see Erica again, but there she was at the fancy lunch, with an empty seat beside her. Ann, not knowing anyone else at the event, overcame her shyness and asked if it was taken. To her surprise and delight, Erica's eyes lit up.

"I was hoping I'd see you again," she'd said, pulling out the chair. "I was kicking myself for not suggesting this."

Their conversation flowed easily, as though Ann had known Erica all her life. They compared notes on the workshops they'd attended, what authors they were thrilled to see, and found that, at least literarily, they had a lot in common. After the applause died down for the keynote speaker and people headed off to the afternoon events, Ann boldly asked Erica if she'd like to meet for coffee sometime.

That became a habit. Both worked from home, so any time "away from the office," they joked, was treasured. Coffee turned to lunch on Fridays, a reward for a week of work, though Ann found herself sketching Erica instead of what she was hired for, and Erica confessed to daydreaming instead of writing.

Soon, they were spending Saturday afternoons together. Ann enjoyed Erica's easy company, whether browsing the local bookshop, visiting an art gallery, or picnicking in the park. She hadn't dared hope that it might go beyond friendship until Erica kissed her. Just last Saturday. Suddenly, the world had tilted 180 degrees, and Ann found herself unmoored. That a touch of lips could so alter the universe. The emotion of that kiss had cleaved her—hopeful but also hopeless.

In a last flurry of nervous energy, Ann moved Farkas's bed away from the window. If it weren't snowing, she'd have considered locking him outside till morning. She struggled against her impatience to move things along with Erica and her reluctance for it to end, because it would end. That was certain. As certain as the phases of the moon.

She poured food in the dog's bowl, ran the lint roller over the couch and herself for the eighth time, and put on an Ella Fitzgerald album. She checked the kitchen floor for signs of Erzsebet's leftovers and gave Freddy more BrainFood® pellets.

When the doorbell rang, Farkas spun in circles, barking, and Erzsebet dove under the couch. Ann grabbed the bowl of candy and flung open the door.

"Oh," she said, stopped by the sight of Erica.

Tall, dark, and handsome had nothing on this beauty. Snowflakes dusted her short, dark curls, and dimples winked as she smiled, her eyes gleaming. Maybe it was the evening— they'd only met during the day—but Erica at night took on a whole new level of attractiveness. Ann had the weirdest sensation. Her heart soared, like in the movies and romance novels, but almost immediately, she wanted to slam the door shut. Completely terrified. But also elated. She hadn't felt that in a long time. Maybe it would be worth it, all the heartbreak that would follow.

Erica smiled. "Trick or treat?"

"Treat, I hope," Ann said as she stood aside. "Please, come in."

If Ann had been the praying kind, she might have uttered a prayer under her breath as she set the bowl on the table by the door.

Farkas, jumping and barking against Erica's legs, reminded Ann of her manners. She took Erica's coat and they performed a clumsy pas de deux as Ann reached for the hook while Erica ducked out of the way. Coat hung, Ann turned and found herself inches from Erica. Before she had time to think and stop herself, she kissed her. It was everything she remembered, that rush of joy and heat, filled with promise. Erica's lips were cool but warmed quickly. Ann released her while the kiss still counted as chaste. Don't get carried away, she thought.

"Welcome to my humble abode," she said, to ease the sexual tension.

As if sensing her shyness, Erica took a step back. "Thank you for inviting me." Her eyes shifted from Ann to the bowl of candy. "Hmm, Jolly Ranchers, Twizzlers, and Life Savers. You know, you can tell a lot about a woman by the candy she hands out."

"And what does my selection say?"

"No chocolate." She held Ann's gaze. "I would say you must be very highly evolved—no need for emotional crutches."

Ann laughed nervously but didn't look away. "I wish. I'm afraid all this says about me is that I hand out candy I don't like so I won't be tempted to eat it myself. I happen to love chocolate. The darker the better."

"That's a relief." Erica reached into her jacket pocket and withdrew a small, elegant—dare Ann think ring-sized?—box. "This is for you."

Their fingers brushed as Ann took the box, sending a shiver through her. She opened it to find a single, hand-made chocolate truffle from a shop she had admired on one of their walks through town. "Oh my." A drizzle of shiny coffee-colored icing contrasted with the smooth matte surface of the perfect orb. "You know, I think I'll set this bowl out on the porch so the kids can help themselves and we won't be disturbed."

Life may not be like a box of chocolates, but love might be like chocolate—a surprising burst at first, then a slow, sweet addiction.

Erica bent to pat the little dog while Ann made introductions.

"Hello, Farkas," Erica said, letting him sniff her hand. He looked at her with black button eyes, his tongue hanging out. "Is he a Pomeranian?"

"No, a spitz. Very similar, but the face is more foxlike."

"Ah yes, I see." Erica knelt and Farkas rolled onto his back so she could rub his belly. "That's quite the oversized doggy door you have," she said, nodding toward the front door where almost the entire lower half swung on a hinge.

"Oh, that. It, uh, came with the house."

Reality hit as Erica looked around—that door! Ann's guard went back up and the evening might as well have been over at that point. She changed the subject by offering Erica a glass of wine. A timer sounded from the kitchen. Ann bustled about, finishing the preparations for dinner while Erica wandered the small, open rooms, expressing her admiration for Ann's furnishings.

"This is how I pictured you," Erica said.

"How so?"

"Living in a fairy-tale cottage in a fairy-tale wood."

Ann let out a weak "Ha!" and let it go at that.

"Who's the pretty kitty?" Erica cooed.

Ann turned in time to see her bending to pet the feline. "That's Erzsebet. Careful, she bites."

Erica paused, then chuckled. "Well, don't all calicos?"

"Yes. Yes, I suppose they do." The cat wove between Erica's legs, purring loudly. Ann was stunned. "She doesn't usually do that."

Erzsebet flopped onto her side and stretched. Erica gave her a gentle rub. The cat, seeming to come to her senses, flipped back onto her feet and ran through the cat flap in the kitchen door and out into the yard.

"Is she a mouser?" Erica asked.

Such an innocent question.

"Yes," Ann said. "One of the reasons I bought this house was for the big field in back." That, and the remoteness from the neighbors. So far, there were only rumors of strange sightings, nothing certain. Ann didn't want to have to move again.

"Now see, you've never mentioned you have pets," Erica said.

"I'm sorry. Are you allergic?"

"No, I mean that I'm enjoying discovering your secrets." Erica wrapped her arms around Ann and kissed her neck. Ann nearly collapsed. Nerves, lust, you name it. She relaxed into Erica's arms, almost convinced everything would work out.

The kitchen opened into a small dining area. Ann had covered her scarred, garage-sale table with a cloth. She lit candles with shaking hands. The date aspect of the evening caught up to her. She knew she'd crossed the line between friendship and wanting more, but now she teetered on the brink of panic. The kisses. Both of them. Surely this is what Erica wants too, she thought. *Don't overthink this.* But it was hard not to. Erica hovered by the table, smiling, clearly nervous.

"Please, sit," Ann said. *What happened to our easy friendship?*

They settled in to eating. Ella crooned in the background. Erica made soft murmurings and praised the food. After a moment of silent dining, Erica broke the spell.

"So, what should we talk about?"

Silence. Ann swallowed and looked at Erica.

"Well, that was a conversation killer."

"No," Ann said quickly. "I was just trying to think of something we haven't talked about yet. We've covered our jobs, where we live." She took a sip of wine to buy time. "You didn't tell me whether you grew up here or moved here."

"I did grow up here but moved away. Don't kids usually?"

"What brought you back?"

"My grandmother needs me." Erica mashed her potatoes and then formed a small volcano that she filled with gravy. "She's quite...elderly."

Ann watched her move, how her fingers caressed the wine glass. She loved the volcano. It was so subconscious. She could picture her doing it from childhood. "Is it stressful or do you have a good relationship?"

"Oh, we have a great relationship. I love my Gramma, so I'm happy to help her. What about you? Native?"

Ann caught a flick of deflection in Erica's tone. "I've... moved around a lot. I grew up in New England mostly."

"Whereabouts? I've never been there."

"I was born in Salem, Massachusetts."

"Salem. The witch trials?" Erica flinched almost imperceptibly.

"So the story goes. They actually took place in Danvers, before it was Danvers. We didn't live there very long."

"Military?"

"No, just itinerant. Maine for a few years, then Vermont and upstate New York, now here. My dad longed to 'get away from it all,' but 'it all' kept encroaching."

"What'd he do?" Erica leaned in attentively, as though Ann was the only person on the planet.

"He was a carpenter. He built houses."

"Wasn't he sort of helping 'it all'?"

"Good point, but that's not how he saw it." Fact was, he hadn't wanted to move. It was her mother who forced the migrations. "I'm finding small towns are far less away from it all than cities."

"Depending on what 'it all' is."

"True. I like the anonymity of cities but I love the country."

"And your mom?"

"She stayed home with me and—" Ann threw a glance toward Freddy. "They've both passed."

"I'm sorry."

Ann waved her off. "They were older when they had me. They had a good life together." She poured them both more wine. "So what about you? When you weren't here, where did you live?"

"San Francisco."

"I've always wanted to visit there."

"I liked it. It was easy to fit in."

"I'm jealous. I don't think I've ever quite found that."

"That surprises me. You seem quite fit in-able."

"Why thank you." *If she only knew.*

"I mean it. I'm glad to have found you."

Another rush of attraction warmed Ann. "Me too."

Erica seemed relaxed when talking about herself, but Ann could tell she preferred listening. And despite her nervousness about the whole date thing, Ann felt more at ease than with anyone other than immediate family.

"There's something about you," Erica said. "I can't quite put my finger on it."

Please don't ever figure it out.

"I feel…comfortable with you. More so than…anyone."

"I feel the same way," Ann said. *At least for now.*

"I wonder why that is—that some people make us nervous and others, well, don't."

Ann stared at Erica, unsure of what to say. Her heart both soared and sank. Here was someone who felt comfortable with her. Did she dare let Erica in all the way?

Ann moved to clear the plates. Erica offered to help.

"No, I've got it," Ann said. "You're the guest."

"I'd rather be your friend."

Ann swooned slightly then immediately worried Erica meant it—friends only—but if so, she wouldn't have kissed her. Ann decided she really did think entirely too much. "In that case, grab a plate."

They settled on the couch by the fire with slices of the chocolate cake Ann had spent the morning preparing, with its layer of raspberry jam in the middle. Erica took a bite and moaned. "This is *so* delicious."

Ann wondered if she could ever make Erica moan like that.

When Erica offered to add wood to the fire, Ann went to get their bottle of wine from the kitchen. She returned to find Erica staring at Freddy. Ann froze.

"Is he OK?" Erica asked.

"Um, yes. He's just old." She stood by Erica, holding the wine bottle with a death grip on the neck. She was so used to Freddy that she had stopped noticing the scars and stitches. He lumbered, if something so small could be said to move that way, through the woodchip bedding. He had at least one toe missing from each foot. They snapped off so easily and were the devil to stitch back on.

Erica straightened. "If he wasn't moving, I'd say he was dead. Had been for some time."

Ann's heart pounded. Erica gave her a warm smile, returned the couch, and didn't say anything more. Ann shot a glance at Farkas, but he was curled up in front of the fire. Erzsebet was still outside. She relaxed. Maybe I can get through this evening, she thought. Then, maybe, she'd try telling her. It's not like any of it had been Ann's choice.

"Do you believe in reincarnation?" Erica asked as Ann settled beside her.

"Not really. Why? Do you think we knew each other in a past life?"

"I've never believed in that, but some people make me wonder. Like you."

"Your flattery is like a spell."

Erica stiffened. "No," she said. "I didn't mean that. I'd never manipulate you."

It was as though a cold wind blew through the small house. Ann shivered. The logs in the fire shifted.

"Hold on. I was joking, but don't you think there's a certain magic to attraction? Why this person and not another?"

"I don't know what it is, but it's not magic."

"Then kismet, or God."

"Do you believe in God?" Erica asked.

My goodness she asks deep questions, Ann thought. "I don't know one way or the other. Could be. Maybe not. You?"

"It's complicated."

Ann chuckled. "Of course it is. That's why wars have been fought over it."

"No," Erica said decisively. "I don't believe."

So she's an atheist, Ann thought. An agnostic herself, she found a certain comfort from uncertainty. Could be, could not be. She didn't know, couldn't know, so she didn't worry about it.

"Any particular reason why?" she asked.

"Religion, any religion, is nothing more than brainwashing. A way to control others. It keeps people from realizing their own power. Their own god within."

Ann liked the idea of a "god within." Could it be that simple? "Intriguing. I would agree. My ancestors fled the old country to escape the abuse of such power." She wondered how she could blurt out something that had been a family secret for generations.

"Religious persecution?"

"No, more personal." Ann glanced at Farkas, sleeping by the fire. Maybe it was the wine. Maybe it was the beautiful woman beside her, but she felt her guard dropping. *I'll never know unless I try.* "The family story is that an ancestor, a beautiful peasant girl, was chosen by a prince. She turned him down. Rather than be humiliated, he accused her of bewitching him and cursed the family. We were driven out of town."

"A woman stands up for herself, so automatically, she's a witch."

"Torches and pitchforks. The whole nine yards."

"That was wrong." Erica said, like it had happened last week.

"It was a long time ago. Who knows if that's really what happened? Maybe just an allegory—power corrupts."

"It doesn't have to."

"What's to stop it? I mean, maybe that's the benefit of religion. Someone clarifying what's OK and what's not."

"Hasn't stopped religions from being corrupt," Erica said.

"True. My goodness, how'd we get onto such a heavy topic?"

"Must be the full moon. It brings out my serious side."

In the background, Heather Peace sang about fairy tales.

"I like your serious side," Ann said.

"I like all your sides."

"You haven't seen them all."

"I hope to."

Ann leaned toward Erica and kissed her. "I want you to."

The stereo switched to the Indigo Girls. Erica stood and pulled Ann into her arms. As they danced, Ann gave in to Erica's charms, melting into her body, so warm and secure.

At midnight, Ann's great-grandmother's cuckoo clock chimed. She and Erica were lying on the couch together, kissing and talking softly. Ann sighed. "It's late. You probably want to get going, huh."

Erica touched her cheek. "Actually..." She kissed Ann tenderly. "I don't."

"Oh." Ann blushed with desire. "Oh."

"You seem uncomfortable. Should I leave?"

Yes. "No. It's just—it's been a long time."

"Me too."

Before she could talk herself out of it, Ann rose and took Erica's hand, leading her to the bedroom. Their lovemaking wasn't perfect at first, Ann was so nervous. Then Erica apologized and Ann realized that she was nervous, too. That broke the spell, and Ann pushed aside her fears, let the past and the future drop away, and focused on the present before her.

Erica made Ann believe in the healing power of touch— her hands, so warm and soft. Ann felt like she was flying, transformed and released, rising past treetops and clouds and into brilliance.

Later, a sound startled Ann awake. She caught her breath, then exhaled when Erica's arms tightened around her. She listened to her lover's breathing. *My lover. My love.* Neither had said it aloud, but Ann began to hope it might be possible.

The next time she woke, cool air bathed her back as Erica slipped out of bed. *No. Don't go.* "You OK?"

"Just need the bathroom," Erica said. Lit by moonlight, she pulled on Ann's robe.

The only bathroom was off the kitchen. She would have to walk through the whole house to get there. The light of the full moon shone brilliantly through the window, reflecting off the fresh snow. The bedroom door creaked. And so it ends.

This was how it had gone down before: potential girlfriend number one ran screaming from the house (that had scared Ann celibate for two years); number two feigned food poisoning and left before dessert; the third one made it to a second date, but then didn't return Ann's calls; the fourth moved away (Ann thought that had been overreacting, perhaps); and the last one found it kinky, and Ann had to break up with her or run naked through the back field, howling at the top of her lungs.

Ann pulled Erica's pillow to her and cried softly.

After what seemed like hours, during which Ann imagined all sorts of unseemly storylines involving Erica fleeing, dying from fright, or going to the authorities, the bedroom door creaked again and the mattress shifted as Erica slid back into bed.

Ann waited, curious. "Everything…OK?" she asked.

"I'm sorry. I didn't mean to wake you," Erica said, snuggling close, her voice tense with energy. "It was incredible."

"What?"

Erica described how she had found Farkas curled by the fire—not in his bed, safe in the shadow of the corner, Ann lamented—and how the light of the moon was just hitting his face.

"As the moonlight spread, he changed," Erica said, her voice filled with awe. "His fox features elongated, his soft brown coat turned gray and coarse. He grew right before my eyes." She'd sat on the couch to watch. "He grew and grew, until he was the size and shape of a large wolf."

Ann felt faint but stayed quiet.

"He looked right at me, like he remembered me from earlier. His eyes were so intelligent, but there was also a wildness. It was like he both wanted to curl up with me and eat me."

Ann nodded in silent agreement.

"Then," Erica said, "he stretched this amazing new body and charged through the dog door." She paused while she pulled the blanket tighter around them. "Will he be all right?"

Ann was struck dumb. Erica was worried about Farkas? Not terrified of him? "He'll be fine. He'll run through the field, howling till morning, then he'll come home and sleep for a day." Ann paused. "Was...that all?"

"Oh, there are a bunch of eviscerated mice strewn about the kitchen."

"Erzsebet, I'm afraid."

"I figured. She was lapping up their blood and rolling in the gore."

"Oh god. I'm sorry."

"It's OK." Erica kissed her cheek. "Want to tell me what's going on?"

So Ann told her. "At least since my great-great-grandmother's time, Farkas, Freddy, and Erzsebet have been handed down, generation after generation. A beastly bequest. It's the burden of immortality."

"Did it have anything to do with the curse you mentioned earlier? About your ancestor insulting a prince?"

"Yes," Ann said, "but he didn't curse the family, exactly. He cursed the family pets. Farkas became a werewolf,

Erzsebet a vampire, and Freddy a...what? What do you call an undead hamster?"

"Zombie," Erica said, like it made sense.

Ann felt tears well. "You don't mind?"

Erica kissed her neck. "No. Wait till I tell you about the skeleton in my closet."

Ann blinked. Outside, in the dim light of the first hint of dawn, a wolf howled.

She curled into Erica's warm embrace. "Tell me, my love," she whispered.

Walking After Midnight

Lois Cloarec Hart

Liz held out her hands. "C'mon, Gem. Toni and Becca throw the best Halloween parties. You have to come."

Gem scowled. "No. You know I hate parties. I've got a big bowl of miniature chocolate bars, some of which I'll even give to trick-or-treaters. And there's a Boris Karloff retrospective on cable. You've been bugging me about this party for two weeks now, but those are my Halloween plans and I'm not changing my mind. You can just forget it."

Liz shook her head. "All right, I didn't want to have to do this…"

"Do what?" Gem regarded Liz uneasily. Her best friend wore the same expression as when she'd conned Gem into a disastrous double-date two years ago. Her companion had ended up falling-down drunk and slobbering all over her. She'd put the woman in a cab at the restaurant but discovered later that her so-called date had stolen her phone. "If this is another of your brilliant ideas to matchmake, you can just forget—"

"Kate Christensen is going to be at the party, too." Liz smiled triumphantly.

"Kate? Christensen?"

"Yup. You've carried that torch longer than the first Olympian, and it's damned well time for you to stop crushing on her like a teenager and do something about it."

Gem sank down onto the sofa. *Kate Christensen*. They'd attended the same high school and been in some classes together, but Gem had spent those grades worshipping from afar. Even all these years later, she still remembered each time Kate had casually greeted her or nodded in her direction. She cherished the memory of the day that Kate had asked for history notes. Their hands had brushed when she'd handed them over. "I...I..."

Liz sat down beside her and patted her back. "Just say yes. You've been coasting on threadbare memories for over a decade. It's time to see if there's anything more than one-sided fantasy between you two."

"There won't be. There couldn't be." Kate was not meant for her. Golden Kate, who had won a full-track scholarship to UCLA, and would've made the Olympic team if not for a broken ankle suffered during trials. Popular Kate, the universal choice for Homecoming Queen, who'd had boys and girls both flocking about her. Brainy Kate, who—when her Olympic dreams were dashed—went to medical school and, much to everyone's surprise, returned to her hometown to do her residency.

"You don't know that. We're not at Hemmingway High anymore."

Gem snorted. "It was easier when we were. At least then everyone knew she belonged with the other jocks—the golden boys."

"She never stuck with any of them long."

"She was with Peter Yancey her whole senior year." Gem remembered every boy Kate had dated, how long they'd gone out, and when they'd broken up. She rolled her eyes. *Obsessive much?*

"He took us all the way to Regionals. Of course he was going to end up with the most popular girl in school. But none of that matters now. It's old news. Kate came back from California with a girlfriend. She's one of us, Gem. There's no excuse anymore for not asking her out."

"No excuse? Are you crazy?"

"I'm not the crazy one here. She's been single and available for over a year. Now's your chance."

"For crying out loud. Kate dates doctors and lawyers and—"

"So what? You're in the medical field. Look at all you two have in common."

"In common?" Gem shook her head. She appreciated Liz's loyalty, but this was ridiculous. "I'm a nurse's aide at Mansfield Retirement Village. I'm not exactly in her strata."

"Stop it. You're running yourself down again. I remember when you wanted to be a doctor, too. All you talked about was joining Doctors Without Borders and traveling to faraway places to help those in need. It was your dream."

"You're right—it was my dream. And that's the problem. I'm a dreamer, not a doer like Kate." *And love is the most unlikely dream of all.* "All those visions of exotic faraway places? Hell, I've never even left this state."

Liz stood up and put her hands on her hips. "You are coming to this party. Toni said Kate's not bringing a date, so you're going to talk to her the same way you'd talk to any other woman."

Gem raised an eyebrow.

"Okay, maybe not like that, because this time you're going to actually open your mouth and say something. And maybe, just maybe, you'll ask her out for coffee. You know that you won't even consider anyone else because you've built Kate into such a fantasy that no real woman could possibly compare, so it's time you either bite the bullet and ask her out, or give up that nonsense all together and let me and Sandy set you up with someone. I mean it, Gem. I'm sick and tired of you not getting on with your life. We graduated high school a long time ago, and it's time you stop reading about love and start looking for it."

Tears stung Gem's eyes, not because Liz's words were unkind, but because they were true. She'd never had a lover, but she did have a vivid imagination and a prodigious appetite for lesbian romance novels. Having seen her friends endure the roller coaster that was all too often love, she wasn't sure that she needed anything more. Real life was just far too messy.

"Gem?"

Gem stared at her hands. "Okay."

"Okay? You'll come?"

Gem nodded.

"Awesome. Meet me at my place tomorrow night. We'll go together." She picked up her bag and walked to the door. "And don't forget your costume."

Gem's head jerked up. "Costume?"

"Of course. It's Halloween, silly." Liz waved and went out the door.

"Oh God, where am I going to find a decent costume in just one day?" Gem scrambled for her laptop and started Googling costume shops. An hour later, after many clicks and calls, she accepted that the only costumes still available were Slutty Nurse, Sexy Pirate, and Dominatrix Cop.

"I can't go in any of those. I'd be laughed out of the party." She slumped and moaned. Any fantasies she might've had about knocking Kate's socks off were long gone. There was nothing remotely flattering to her diminutive form in the available options.

"Maybe Liz will let me off the hook." Recalling the determination on her friend's face, Gem shook her head. "No, she'll make me go if I have to wear a sheet and be a ghost... though that wouldn't be a bad way to hide.... Okay, let's see what I can cobble together from my closet. Maybe something in the vampire line."

Those creatures of the night at least had a romantic aura about them. For a brief moment, Gem imagined looking so suave and sophisticated that she would catch Kate's admiring eye.

Liz opened the door, stared at Gem, and broke out laughing.

Gem's head drooped. She'd felt almost dashing when she left her apartment. Obviously she'd been mistaken.

She'd borrowed her older brother's wedding tux, which—being of a parsimonious nature—he'd acquired from a buddy at a funeral home. The suit was shiny with age, and more virescent than black, but once she'd stapled the trouser legs and jacket arms up nine inches and attached suspenders, it was at least wearable. The cummerbund was somewhat tattered and a repulsive puce, but at least the white shirt, taken from her closet, was presentable.

Finding a cloak had been more difficult. She didn't have the skill to make one, nor the time to find a seamstress. Finally

EDITED BY JAE AND ASTRID OHLETZ

she'd settled on her grandmother's old nursing cape. It was blue, not black, but at least it was red sateen on the inside, even if it lacked the panache of a full-length cape.

Her old Doc Martens, polished for the occasion, completed the outfit, and once she'd gelled back her short, curly brown hair, darkened her eyebrows, and applied powder to her face for the pale, gaunt effect, she'd felt downright noir-ish, despite the thick glasses.

Gem turned on her heel. "That's it. I'm going home. I don't care what you say."

Liz scrambled after Gem, grabbing her arm. "No, no, wait. You look great. I mean it."

"I do not. I look like an idiot."

"You don't, I swear. You're as cute as a button. C'mon. Come inside and we'll have a drink before we go."

Liz tugged on Gem's arm, dragging her inside. "Beer?"

Gem shrugged and looked around before sitting down. "Fine. Where's Sandy?"

"She had to work late, so she's meeting us at the party." Liz handed Gem a cold beer and took the seat opposite. "You really do look pretty cool."

"Yeah, right. You're the one who looks great." Liz was dressed in a flapper's costume, complete with feathered headdress, bejeweled choker, and a black boa. "You're going to blow Sandy away."

Liz grinned. "God, I hope so." Her smile dimmed. "And you, my friend, are not to pull your usual party routine."

"I don't have a party routine."

"Like hell you don't. Every time we convince you to go to a party, you find some corner to hide in and then you leave as early as possible."

"Why not? No one ever notices I'm there, so no one's going to care when I leave."

Liz gazed at her intently. "I care. Promise me you'll make a real effort tonight, okay? Promise."

"I don't know what you want from me."

"I want you to talk to people. I want you to take a chance and put yourself out there a little bit. For God's sake, Gem, I want you to be happy, and sitting at home alone three hundred and sixty-five nights of the year isn't going to do it."

Gem blinked at the intensity in Liz's voice. "Geez, I'm not that bad."

"Yeah, you are, and you're getting worse. If you weren't allergic to cats, you'd turn into one of those cat-hoarding ladies who never leave their house."

"Okay, now that's just an exaggeration. I leave my house lots."

"For work."

"And to hang with you and Sandy."

Liz huffed and pointed her bottle at Gem. "July fourth. You haven't been out with us since July fourth."

"No, that can't be—" Gem's brow furrowed.

"You came with me and Sandy to watch the fireworks over the harbor. And every time since then, when we've asked you to come out with us, you've had an excuse to stay home. You're turning into an agoraphobic."

"Four months?"

Liz nodded. "Four months."

"Huh."

"Lesbians cannot live by romance novels alone. You need to touch a real woman, and soon. If not Kate, then maybe you'll meet someone else tonight. Who knows?" Liz glanced at her watch. "Speaking of which, we'd better get going. The bus will be here in ten."

"You're not driving?"

"Nope. And don't even suggest being the designated driver, because you, me, and Sandy are going to howl tonight."

"You're mistaken. I'm a vampire, not a werewolf." Gem allowed Liz to pull her to her feet.

Liz slung an arm over Gem's shoulders and grinned. "Vampire, werewolf, it doesn't matter. Tonight we're going to find you someone who can make you howl for all the right reasons."

Mounting the stairs to Toni and Becca's house, Gem decided to make the best of the situation. While she had no intention of following Liz's instructions to socialize, this would be a prime opportunity to watch Kate from a distance. Perhaps she would take home a new fantasy or two with which to lull herself to sleep.

Not that she'd ever run out of fantasies. Between the hours of eleven and midnight every night, she and Kate sailed the South Pacific, soared to the stars, skied the Austrian Alps, and rescued innumerable fair maidens from countless villains. They had saved the world so many times that were it not for their modest natures, the UN would've erected massive monuments to them in New York City.

Best of all was the lovemaking. Kate just couldn't seem to get enough of Gem, and was forever seducing her—to the envy of glamorous women and men alike. Sometimes Kate would have to woo her away from another, and sometimes their eyes would simply meet across a crowded room, but always these two soul mates would find each other, whatever the obstacles.

Gem stumbled into Liz's back. "Oops, sorry 'bout that. I think a staple came loose." She knelt to fiddle with her makeshift trouser hem as Liz waited impatiently. "Okay, all better now."

She trailed Liz inside, but stared at her feet and refused to meet anyone's gaze.

"There's Kate. Go say hi." Liz tried to steer Gem towards the fireplace where Kate was holding court.

Gem dug in her heels. "No. Let me do this at my own pace, or I'm leaving right now."

Liz rolled her eyes. "Oh, for crying out—"

Her exasperation was cut off midstream when Sandy pounced on her. Liz whistled as Sandy struck a pose, filling out her Wonder Woman costume in all the right places. Gem grinned. Judging by the look on Liz's face, she'd instantly forgotten all about her mission to hook Gem up with Kate. *Good.*

Sandy winked at Gem and put her glass to Liz's lips. As Liz willingly guzzled the garish green contents, Gem used the opportunity to melt into the crowd. She set course for the most unobtrusive spot she could find, dodging amorous couples en route to the corner farthest away from Kate.

Much to her delight, the location afforded a good sightline to the fireplace and Kate's retinue. Or at least it would have, if she weren't so vertically impaired. Even her boots only added a couple of inches to her scant five feet. It was frustrating to only be able to glimpse the tall, blond pirate queen, who had a burlesque beauty draped over her shoulders and a throng of chattering women around her.

Gem ignored the fleeting pain of seeing Kate's multitude of worshipers. She was too much of a realist to ever picture herself as one of that crowd. Later tonight she would concoct a bedtime story of how Kate immediately divested herself of all admirers as soon as Gem entered the room, rushing over to greet the newcomer—to the dismay of every other woman in the coterie.

Gem hadn't decided if her bedtime story would find her playing hard to get, thereby making her flirtatious lover pay for being so irresistible to others, or if she would coolly accept Kate's adulation as her due and allow herself to be fawned over all evening. She would probably play out both scenarios in her mind, and fall asleep long before she reached the denouement of either version.

For now, though, she had to resolve the height problem. The corner she'd staked out abutted a built-in bookcase. She surveyed the contents by the atmospheric light of flickering candles that reflected from every nook in the room. Spying a large book on the bottom shelf, Gem bent to tug it out. It was an encyclopedia or a dictionary of some kind, but most importantly, it was six or seven inches thick. When she stood on it, her view improved significantly.

Toni and Becca, hosts of the annual shindig, were shuttling trays of hors d'oeuvres out to the hungry partygoers. In the corner opposite her, Gem could see Liz and Sandy nibbling on each other. Here and there, despite the elaborate costumes, Gem recognized friends and acquaintances, but her gaze was always irresistibly drawn back to the fireplace.

To her shock, Kate met her stare, with sparkling eyes and a small grin.

Gem wavered on her book-perch and looked down. *No way was she looking at me.*

She pretended to listen to a group of women nearby, but surreptitiously glanced over out of the corner of her eye. Even though Kate was chatting with the woman hanging on her shoulder, she was still looking in Gem's direction.

Abruptly, Gem slid off the book. Trembling, she knelt to replace it on the shelf and remained huddled on the floor until someone almost tripped over her.

"Hey, what the hell?"

"Sorry, sorry." Gem stood, pressing back against the wall. This time she was grateful that the crowd obscured her vision. Her frantic thoughts matched her erratic breathing. *What should I do? Go now, or wait until she's not looking this way anymore?* It was one thing to admire Kate from afar, but it would be unbearable if Kate was amused by Gem's unmistakable hero worship.

Agonized, Gem stood in her corner, frozen with indecision and buffeted by inebriated guests.

Eventually her customary flight response activated. Determined to escape, she fought her way through the crowd, struggling like a salmon swimming upstream. Gem spied an opening and bolted it for it. Unfortunately the maneuver deposited her in the kitchen rather than the front hallway, but at least the crowd was thinner and she could regroup for another attempt.

"Hey, Gem. I'm glad you could make it. What a madhouse, huh? You'd think we'd have learned from last year, but then, at least the cops haven't shown up this time—well, not yet anyway."

Gem smiled weakly at Toni, who was extracting a pan of cheese puffs from the oven.

"It is a bit crowded. Um, I was just going to—"

Toni slid the hot pastries onto a tray and thrust them into Gem's hands.

"Be a pal and take these out to the living room, will ya? And if you see Becs, tell her we need another case of mix from the basement. Thanks, G." Toni grabbed a towel and hustled over to where a woman had spilled beer all over the counter, the floor, and a fellow guest.

Oh well, I've got to head out in that direction anyway. I'll just dump this on the nearest horizontal surface and get out of here. Shielding the tray with one arm, Gem dodged three guests, did a neat spin around two more, and ended up in the doorway of the kitchen, cheese puffs intact. As she scanned the tray to ensure she hadn't lost any errant pastries during her fancy footwork, someone moved to stand in front of her, blocking the entrance to the living room.

"Excuse me, appetizers en route." Gem started to duck around, and stopped.

Kate stood in front of her with a rakish grin and one hand on her sword. "I see they pressed you into service. Funny, you don't look like hired help, though I must say I wouldn't mind seeing you in a French maid's outfit."

Gem gaped at her. *Did Kate just flirt with me?* She half expected the pirate's image to fade as surely as her nighttime fantasies did, but Kate's blue eyes still twinkled.

Kate looked over the tray and selected a pastry. "Do you mind?"

"Um, no... Please, help yourself."

Kate juggled the hot cheese puff before dropping it back on the tray. "Damn! Those things are hot." She winced as she sucked on her fingers.

Bad brain. Stop that right now. Gem blushed and dropped her gaze. "Sorry. They just came out of the oven."

Kate chuckled. "My fault. I'm always getting my fingers in where they don't belong. Nearly lost a thumb when I was assisting on an appendectomy last week."

Say something, you idiot. Something...suave, amusing... Hell, anything! "I should probably get these out there while they're still hot." *Oh yeah, that was impressive. She'll definitely want to hang around you now.*

Gem focused on her tray and prayed that Kate would just let her by, but no. Finally, unable to bear the silence, she looked up.

Kate was studying her intently.

Gem shifted, trying to think of something to say. *Nothing. I got nothing.*

"I saw you in Riverside last week."

Gem's eyes widened. She often saw Kate in the hospital, but was surprised that she'd been noticed. "Um, yeah, I had to take Mrs. Greenwald over for an appointment. She's a resident at Mansfield, where I work."

"I know. I've seen you bring others over. Hey, how come you never stop to say hi? I'd even buy you a cup of coffee, if you had the time. Not that I'd blame you for ducking hospital swill."

Gem was speechless. A question about why she never dropped in at the White House couldn't have shocked her more.

"What? Can't two old high school friends sit and share a cup of java?" The tone was light, but there was an underlying challenge in Kate's words.

Guests flowed around them where they stood to the side of the doorway, and Gem wished desperately that she could be swept away from Kate. She felt like a fool. None of her books or fantasies had prepared her for this actuality.

Is she mocking me? A rising disquiet gave her the courage to speak. She met Kate's gaze squarely for the first time. "Friends? We barely knew each other in school."

"And why was that?" The challenge was now unmistakable.

Gem couldn't help laughing. That was akin to asking why a bit player wasn't invited to share a superstar's spotlight. Before she could answer, a long arm snaked over Kate's shoulder and a hand stole inside her ruffled pirate's blouse. Gem dropped her gaze from the sight.

"Darling, where did you get to? I've been waiting for my drink for forever. I could die of thirst, you know." The burlesque beauty's words were slurred and petulant, but the air of possession was unmistakable.

With a curt nod, Gem slipped away. She skirted the edge of the room and set the tray on the corner of a hutch. She glanced back at the kitchen doorway. Kate had turned and was propping the burlesque beauty up, but her gaze followed Gem's retreat. When the woman began rubbing herself against Kate, Gem plowed through the crowd to the front door and out into the night air. She was brought up short as she tried to walk away, the door closing on her cape, which she then struggled to pull free before it strangled her.

"Damn it. So much for making a smooth exit."

Gem heaped silent curses on Liz's head as she turned to extricate herself. The mass of people inside had flowed into the front hallway, and she could barely open the door wide enough to retrieve her bedraggled cape. Music, smoke, the noise of a hundred conversations, and the complaints of the women Gem had to nudge back to open the door floated over her head as she tugged free.

She resisted the fruitless urge to attempt slamming the door. Instead, she closed it quietly, adjusted her glasses, and made her way down the long flight of stairs.

She'd barely reached the sidewalk when people began spilling out onto the veranda. Unwilling to deal with any questions about why she was leaving so early, Gem hastened across the street to the cemetery that served as the final resting place for many of the old port's residents from the eighteenth and nineteenth centuries.

A heavy rain earlier in the evening had given way to thick, humid air and a wispy, ankle-level fog, but Gem gave the oppressive atmosphere no notice as she passed under the familiar stone archway. She'd spent her whole life in this southern city, and the Atlantic fogs that regularly rolled in over the port were as familiar to her as her own name. Nor did the thought of crossing through the cemetery faze her. The dilapidated tombstones with barely legible inscriptions were old friends, too.

As children, she and her siblings had played hide and seek, tag, and Red Rover among the acres of ancient oaks, Spanish moss, and granite tributes to those long dead. Later in life, she'd found peace in the quiet beauty along stone paths, as she dreamed of aspirations, possibilities, and love—that most elusive and ephemeral of treasures. It would no more occur to her to fear the cemetery than to fear her own backyard.

Remarkably, the graveyard had never produced satisfactory tales of haunts or restless spirits. Even mischievous schoolboy tales spun on Halloweens past to scare impressionable schoolgirls had failed to stick. The cemetery remained a singularly quiet and uneventful place. There had not been any burials there for more than a century. The old site had long ago run out of available plots, and an expansive new graveyard had opened up on the outskirts of the city.

Now, as her feet trod the familiar paths, Gem considered the events of the evening.

"What a disaster. I know Kate was making fun of me, but why?" Pain seared her heart. It was one thing to know her fantasies were unrealistic in the extreme; it was a whole other thing to find the object of her adoration mocking her. "Oh, God. What if I wasn't as subtle as I thought? What if she noticed me watching her and decided to have a little fun at my expense?"

Tears blurred her vision, and she stumbled over a loose cobblestone. Angrily, she dashed a hand across her eyes. "I don't care. If that's the kind of mean person she is, I want nothing to do with her anyway."

Lost in misery, Gem nearly missed seeing the figure leaning against one of the oak trees, watching her. She almost bolted, but it was a woman, who regarded her with a smile.

"God! You scared the heck out of me."

"I'm sorry. I certainly didn't mean to." The voice was smooth and smoky, redolent of whiskey, cigarettes, and nights spent dancing until dawn. "I heard you talking to yourself."

"Oh, yeah, sorry. I do that sometimes."

The woman shrugged. "No need for apologies. I've talked to myself a time or two. Sometimes we are our own best company, yes?"

"Sometimes." Gem took a second look and gave a shaky whistle. Adrenaline overrode her usual reticence. "Wow! Your costume is great. And do you ever carry it off well. Damn, I wish I looked half as good."

The stranger smiled again and dismissed her outfit with a languid wave. "This old thing? It serves its purpose, I suppose. It is fun to dress up now and then, isn't it?"

Eyes wide, Gem surveyed the slim, elegant figure. It was like the woman had stepped out of Central Casting. She was a dazzling female version of Bela Lugosi. Her high collared cloak swept almost to the ground, and flashes of scarlet were visible when she moved. Her tuxedo was impeccably tailored and fit like a glove. The snowy ruffle of her shirt was so brilliant, it almost glowed. Her shoes *did* glow, the polish on them mirror bright. Her short black hair, intense dark eyes, regal carriage, and subtle, unidentifiable accent all added to her aura of mystery and romance.

Gem approached the woman. "If you don't mind me asking, is that the way the cummerbund is supposed to go? I wasn't sure if the ruffles were supposed to go up or down."

The woman fingered the scarlet silk around her narrow waist. "I believe the original intent of this rather useless piece of material was to have the ruffles up. Perhaps it was to catch crumbs dropped by careless noblemen as they dined, do you think?"

Gem considered that for a moment, then shrugged. "Why not? It's as good an explanation as any." She glanced down at her outfit. "Good thing you weren't at the same party I was. I'd have had to flee in shame."

At the memory of her precipitous exit, her shoulders slumped, and she turned back onto the path. Gem was surprised when the stranger fell into step beside her. *I guess she's going my way.*

They walked in silence for a short while, before her companion asked, "What is your name?"

"Gem St. Claire."

"Is it short for anything? Gemma perhaps?"

"No, just Gem. My mother has a jewel fetish. She named one of my sisters Ruby, and the other—"

"Let me guess, Pearl?"

"Nope." Gem chuckled. "Opal. And she named my brother Cole. She always claimed he was—"

"—a diamond in the rough," they said together, and their laughter rang out through the night.

The humour lightened Gem's depression as they walked along a path that wound through the oldest part of the graveyard. Tombs and mausoleums loomed out of the thickening mist.

"Do you live around here?" Gem asked.

"I did once, but I left a long time ago. I travel a lot, rarely staying in one place for long. But I do try and return once a year or so."

Gem sighed. "I always wanted to travel."

"It is wearisome after a time. I believe it is in our nature to always return to a place we once called home."

"You're probably right."

Wanting to avoid the uncomfortable silences that always seemed to crop up whenever she tried to carry on small talk, Gem waved her hand to indicate the graves on either side of the path and launched into one of her favourite topics—the history of her hometown.

"I was always surprised that this part of the cemetery avoided the ransacking that the Union troops inflicted on the rest of the graveyard. Did you know that soldiers used tombstones to build fire pits, and in some cases they just tossed old bones out and bedded down in the crypts during the winter of 1864?"

Although she understood the exigencies of war, Gem had always felt indignant at the lack of respect shown her ancestors.

"That was a very cold winter. Many of those soldiers didn't survive to see the spring. Some paid for their disrespect with their lives."

That's an odd way to look at it. Gem was sure that starvation and hypothermia were mostly responsible for the deaths among the Union ranks, but she didn't argue. She glanced at her companion. "I never got your name."

"Cleo."

"That's pretty."

Cleo looked down at her, dark eyes amused. "But certainly not as inventive as your mother's choices."

Cleo came to an abrupt halt and took a few steps off the pathway. She jumped up to sit on an ornate old mausoleum and patted the marble beside her. Surprised, but somewhat bedazzled by the glamorous woman, Gem scrambled up beside her, aided by Cleo's strong hand.

"So, what brings you out walking after midnight?"

The sympathetic warmth in Cleo's voice was balm to Gem's ragged emotions. "I went to a party tonight—a Halloween party." Gem fingered her tuxedo pants. "I guess that was pretty clear already."

"You did not have a good time?"

"No."

"Why is that?"

Gem grimaced. "I really don't like parties, but my best friend talked me into going. And, well, there's this woman, Kate…" She glanced sideways, but Cleo's friendly expression didn't change. "Um, I've known her for a long time. I guess the truth is I've had a thing for her since high school."

"And she was there tonight?"

Gem nodded. "She was, with someone else, as usual. I didn't care about that. I mean, I'm used to it and I certainly didn't think I ever stood a chance with her anyway."

"Yet something disturbs you."

Gem stared at the ground. "She...I think she was laughing at me—mocking me, sort of. I couldn't stand it so I took off, and here I am."

"Why do you assume this Kate was making sport of you?"

Gem glanced down at her cheesy costume. "You're kidding, right?"

Cleo tilted her head. "Is she so shallow, then, your Kate, that she would mistake the clothes for the woman?"

"She's not 'my' Kate."

"Then whose Kate is she?"

"Depends on which bimbo she takes home tonight, though my money's on the redhead." Gem looked away. She was embarrassed at the bitterness that spilled into her voice.

"I believe you mistake affairs of the libido for affairs of the heart, my young friend. Just because your Kate may seek to slake her lust with someone available does not mean that she gives her heart so readily."

"Don't call her 'my' Kate. She's not my Kate. She'll never *be* my Kate."

The stranger was silent for a long moment, then she glanced at Gem. "May I tell you a story?"

"Mm-hmm."

"Many years ago and not too far from here, a woman lived with her wealthy husband and three young children. She didn't love her husband, for it had been an arranged marriage—"

"An arranged marriage? Exactly how many years ago are we talking about?"

Cleo chuckled. "Tell me, as a child, did you seek to pinpoint precisely when and where Hansel and Gretel entered the forest, too?"

Abashed, Gem shook her head. "Sorry. Go ahead. You were saying?"

"As I was saying, the woman did not love her husband, but she did adore their children, and was moderately contented with her life. She was aware that her husband took mistresses, but it was the fashion of the time, and she did not protest. However, one day someone new entered her life, and a most unexpected thing happened—"

"She fell in love."

"My dear Gem, are you always this impatient?"

Gem drew her thumb and forefinger across her lips, turned an imaginary key, and tossed it over her shoulder.

"Ah, but you are right. She fell in love. She didn't want to, and she certainly hadn't sought out a lover, but she was helpless against the yearnings of her heart. Still, she had been strictly raised and was bound by the rigid conventions of duty and honour, so she did nothing to pursue her love."

Gem frowned. *I thought this was going to be a romantic story.* "Nothing?"

Cleo shook her head, her gaze distant. "Nothing. She only admired her beloved silently, never daring to speak her heart or make her love known. Until one day, her husband, who had remained totally oblivious, decided he was bored with his wife and sought to install one of his mistresses in her place. His first wife, having become an inconvenience, was disposed of."

"Divorce, huh? That sucks. I hope she took him for all he was worth and left nothing for the little floozy taking her place."

"Divorce? Yes, I suppose it was, in a sense. In any case, the first wife was cast out and lost all: her beloved children, her home, and the only person she'd ever given her heart to."

"Wait a minute? He cheated on her, *and* he got to keep the kids? Boy, did she have a lousy lawyer."

"There were no lawyers involved, Gem, only the precepts of an unequal society. But do not fret. She kept watch over her children from afar, protected and cherished them all their lives. They mourned her and honoured her and carried her line forward."

"Mourned her? Didn't she at least have visitation rights?"

"She was not in a position to see them regularly, and they were given to understand that their mother had passed on. Their father hoped that they would thus come to accept their stepmother."

"No way! He got away with that?"

Cleo gave a low laugh that sent shivers up Gem's spine. "Not really, no. The children despised and resented their new stepmother. And as each gained majority, their mother came to them and told them the whole story. Once all were of age and able to care for themselves, their father finally paid for his sins."

"Good. But, back up a minute. What happened to the one the woman fell in love with? Did she ever confess her feelings or do anything about them? After all, once her husband dumped her, she must've been free to declare her love."

"She was…indisposed for too long, and when she finally returned, it was too late. Her beloved had been claimed by another, so she withdrew and never spoke her heart."

"Bummer."

They sat silently; the customary sounds of the night were deadened by the thick fog.

"I guess I know what you're trying to tell me."

"Tell you? I merely sought to pass a pleasant interval with a new friend by relating a small tale. I would never presume to offer you advice." The amused half smile belied Cleo's dismissal as she gazed off into the fog.

"Yeah, right. Seriously, though, I do understand what you mean, but the circumstances are way different."

"Why?"

Gem jumped down from the marble monument and stood directly in front of Cleo, pushing her glasses back up her nose. The staples in her right pant leg had come out, and a wad of bedraggled material was bunched around her ankle. With a snort, she pointed at it. "That's why."

"Because your pants are ill-fitting?"

"Jesus, look at me. Kate can have any woman she wants. She's not going to look at a myopic, maladjusted misanthrope like me. Hell, I can't even carry off this ridiculous costume." Gem gazed enviously at Cleo. "If I looked like you..."

Cleo's gaze was warm and her smile affectionate. "If you looked like me?"

"Yeah, I mean if I looked like I just stepped off of the cover of *Vogue*—well, the Halloween edition, anyway—I could maybe march right up to Kate and ask her out."

Cleo slipped gracefully off the crypt and leaned back against it. Her hands were thrust in her pockets, and one ankle crossed over the other. She was the picture of insouciant elegance; Gem shook her head in despair.

"I'm not sure I think much of this Kate if she is as shallow as you say."

"Hey! I didn't say she was shallow."

"You tell me that she will bed some woman tonight based solely on her conquest's appearance. You tell me that she would never consider you because you are not graced with a similar beauty. This bespeaks a shallow soul to me. I don't believe she is worthy of the thought and devotion you bestow upon her. Surely there is another who could claim your heart if you would but allow it."

"Now wait a minute. You're getting the wrong idea about Kate. She's not like that at all. She's warm and friendly and funny and smart—"

"Then you do her an injustice by not allowing her the opportunity to know who you really are."

Gem opened her mouth to protest, then shut it abruptly. She was sure there was some flaw in Cleo's logic, but for the life of her, she couldn't put her finger on it.

Cleo pressed her advantage. "Surely if your Kate is as admirable as you claim, she would neither mock nor reject you."

"But—"

"If you never give her a chance, if you never speak your heart, you will never know what might have been."

Gem hung her head. "But what if she laughs at me again?"

A cool hand reached out and cupped her chin, gently compelling her to meet Cleo's gaze. Gem was struck by the urgency in her eyes.

"Believe me when I tell you, Gem, that laughter and finality are profoundly better than never knowing what might have been. If she does indeed reject you, then you have no further excuse to spend your life dreaming about her. Promise me you'll take the chance. Tonight. Don't waste another moment."

Mesmerized, Gem stared into those hypnotic eyes, until suddenly Cleo's head snapped up. She listened intently as she peered back down the path. Then with a smile, she stepped back.

"Tell me. What costume did your Kate wear tonight?"

Still dazed, Gem fumbled for an answer. "Uh, she was wearing a pirate outfit, I think. Yeah, that's right. She even had a sword."

"Then I believe she seeks you out. Go to her, little one."

Stunned, Gem spun around and saw Kate stride out of the mist.

Gem took a few halting steps back towards the path. As Kate drew closer, Gem cast a nervous glance over her shoulder, seeking reassurance from her counselor, but Cleo had disappeared.

Gem waited uneasily. She had no idea why Kate had come after her, if indeed that was what she was doing, nor did she know if she would be able to summon the nerve to take Cleo's advice. But she sensed that the next few moments would be life-altering.

Kate came to a stop and scowled. "Where the hell did you get to? I looked all over the house for you, for God's sake."

Gem blinked in surprise.

Kate poked her shoulder. "You left without answering my question. I think it's way past time. You owe me an answer."

"Um, question?" Whatever words had been spoken in Toni and Becca's kitchen had been wiped from Gem's mind by the memory of the woman fondling Kate's breast.

Kate's voice softened, but there was still a steely edge to it. "Uh-huh. Why aren't we friends? Why do you keep avoiding me? Why have you been avoiding me since we were in high school?"

Promise me you will take the chance. Tonight. Don't waste another moment. Cleo's words rang in her head, and for the first time in her life, Gem threw shyness and caution to the winds.

"I think it would be obvious: We don't live in the same world. You sure as hell didn't need any more friends in school, and from the look of things tonight, you're not exactly suffering from a lack of company now, either." Her words were sharper than she'd intended, and Gem was surprised to see Kate flinch. "Aw, look, I like you. A lot. I think you're a really good person. But women like you don't hang with women like me. That's just the way of the world."

"Says who? And what the hell do you mean by 'women like me' and 'women like you'? We're both just women."

Gem stared at Kate and shook her head. "You can't be serious. Did you even notice who was hanging all over you back there?"

Kate sucked in a deep breath. "Candice. She isn't exactly the subtle sort, especially when she's had a few, and she's definitely had more than a few. I was trying to... Look, do you know why I went to that party tonight? Why I traded four weekend shifts to get tonight off?"

"Because it's the biggest event of the year on the lesbian social calendar?"

"God. Are you really that dense? No, you idiot. I went to that party because Liz promised me that you'd be there."

Liz? What the...? Oh man, I'm going to kill her! Even as Gem fumed, a part of her brain began to process what Kate had said. "You...you went to see me?"

"I went because no matter how often I 'accidentally' run into you in the corridors at Riverside, you never stop to talk. You're driving me crazy. What does it take? Do you want me to chisel it in granite?" Kate looked around. "Guess I'm in the right place for that, actually. Well?"

She came to see me? Gem was having a great deal of difficulty believing she'd heard Kate correctly. "Um, well what?"

Kate rolled her eyes, took one step forward, wrapped her hands in the lapels of the old tux, and pulled Gem into a kiss.

The small vampire had nothing to compare it with, but she was sure that as first kisses went, this one was over the top. Heart-stopping, earth-shattering, knee-buckling... Gem was embarrassed when she realized that the moan she heard came from her own lips.

Kate's breathing was ragged as she brushed a hand gently over Gem's face.

Gem could have sworn delighted laughter echoed in the fog, but everything else was forgotten as she wrapped her arms around Kate and pulled the willing pirate tight against her body.

Cleo watched the couple as they stumbled off, barely able to stop kissing long enough to take a few steps. She smiled. Gem appeared to be a quick study.

"I wonder if they'll even make it out of the cemetery before Kate's shirt comes off." She looked at the marble mausoleum, and her smile faded. "We don't mind, do we? They're welcome to share the night with us."

She stepped out of the darkness. As she trailed her fingers lightly over the engraving that had become indistinct with time, her thoughts returned to a different century—a time when her husband's niece had first come to live with them.

"Veronice." Cleo recalled her first sight of the young woman as she'd descended from the carriage. A brave smile had concealed her fears at being sent to live with an uncle she barely knew, to help the mistress of the house care for her children.

William, Joshua, and Abigail had fallen in love with their sweet-natured cousin. As had Cleo.

For two glorious years she'd reveled in Veronice's companionship, never crossing the boundaries of propriety, but rejoicing in their ever-increasing intimacy and affection. She would never forget the night that Veronice had taken the first step and had said goodnight to her uncle's wife with a decidedly unchaste kiss.

Stunned, Cleo had watched a laughing Veronice disappear into her own bedroom. She would've followed, had it not been for Henry's imperious summons.

Cleo had always wondered where that first kiss might have led, but she was never given the chance to find out. Within two days, Henry had begun the process of installing his concubine as mistress of Shelton Manor—he'd had his wife abducted and her servant killed as they returned from an evening social call.

Cleo rubbed her throat, still feeling the leather that had tightened around her neck as she had been dragged deep into the forest that terrifying night an eternity ago. She'd fought desperately for her life, but had been overpowered by two men she recognized as being in Henry's employ. They had discarded her apparently lifeless body in a deep ravine, and thereby unwittingly bestowed immortality upon her.

For she had been found. A night creature had come upon her and taken her for his own. The vampire had borne her away and, helpless to resist, she had gone. When he had finally tired of her, she'd returned, unalterably changed, but unable to resist the need to see her children…and Veronice.

Things had changed in her absence. Henry had waited all of four weeks before having her declared dead, leaving him free to marry the new mistress of the manor.

Veronice was married off to a wealthy and titled visitor and returned to England.

Her grieving children were the only reason that Cleo did not immediately take retribution on her treacherous husband. But the very night that her youngest, Abigail, made a good marriage and left the family home, Cleo had found her spouse and his wife and had exacted revenge.

It was said that the servants who found their shattered and torn bodies the following morning were haunted for the rest of their lives by the horror of what they had seen in the blood-drenched bedroom. For years thereafter, lurid tales of their fate became fodder for delicious paroxysms of terror whenever men met to share whiskey, or women gathered to gossip.

William became custodian of Shelton Manor. It was he and his brother, Joshua, who had arranged the grandiose marble shrine to their mother's memory, despite the fact that there was no body to entomb. And it was they, by that time aware of what had truly transpired, who had ensured that their faithless father and stepmother were buried in unconsecrated ground on the outskirts of the estate.

It never failed to amuse Cleo that Henry's final resting place was now beneath a poultry packing plant.

In the years since, her children's many descendants had multiplied and scattered, though some could still be found living in the old port city.

Gem had never been in any danger from her. It was always a delight to encounter a descendent, and Gem reminded Cleo acutely of her middle child. Joshua too had been diminutive, near-sighted, and painfully shy, but with the sweetest nature a mother could have asked for. Of all her descendants, his line was the most cherished.

Veronice.

It wasn't until the advent of the Internet that Cleo was finally able to learn her beloved's fate. The young woman with the laughing green eyes had died of a fever on the voyage to England. She had been swiftly replaced once her highborn husband had reached land, becoming a mere footnote in his illustrious family history.

Cleo straightened. "You become maudlin in your old age. Time moves on, as must you."

She stroked the marble and stretched lazily. She'd fed early in the night, on a particularly repulsive cretin who had accosted her while she strolled through a dark downtown alley. The night was long, though, and she could move freely amongst the revelers, perhaps feeding again, or perhaps not. Though never absent, the urge had dimmed in recent decades, and she wondered if a time might come when she could just...stop.

For now, though, she would continue the night's lark. Cleo enjoyed donning the traditional, albeit theatrical costume on Halloween. There was little enough joy in unending life, so once a year, she allowed herself this small pleasure. Wherever she wandered in the next twelve-month, she would return on this night, to this place. And as she turned to leave, she cast one final glance at the faded engravings. There were many names listed—it had been a large and esteemed family—but it had all begun with one name...

"I know, Mommy, I know! It was Lady Cleodine Abigail St. Claire. Born November 29, 1793; died October 31, 1821. And I was named after her."

Joshua glared at his sister. "Let Mommy tell it, Cleo!"

Gem smiled at their children. From the time she had learned to talk, Cleo had never been able to resist yelling out her namesake's identity. It annoyed her little brother to no end, but it had become part of the annual family ritual.

"Okay, kids. Mama is waiting to take you out trick-or-treating. One last trip to the bathroom and you can go."

The children jumped to their feet and ran from the room, the excitement of the night making them fairly vibrate.

"I always love the way you tell that story."

Gem glanced up at Kate, who sat on the arm of the couch next to her. "Well, I do give them the expurgated version. They don't need to know everything about the night their mothers finally got together."

Kate toyed with a lock of Gem's hair. "I wonder if they'll ever realize it's not a family fairy tale."

"Maybe when they're older."

"Do you think she'll come by tonight?"

Gem nodded. "Doesn't she always?"

"I think she just likes to take credit for her matchmaking prowess."

"I think she just needs to know that love and family endure."

Kate leaned over and wrapped her arms around Gem.

Gem snuggled closer, but further intimacies had to be put on hold as Cleo and Josh ran back into the room. Gem and Kate parted with a kiss as the tiny wizard and the slightly larger fairy princess clamoured to start collecting their booty.

The doorbell rang and a holler could be heard at the front door, signaling the arrival of more trick-or-treaters.

Gem passed out candy and winked at Kate, who led their two children out into the night to begin their own rounds.

She got a wide grin in response, and knew that they would have their own celebration later, long after the candy had been sorted and two overly excited children were tucked into their beds.

And as her wife disappeared down the street, Gem noticed a shadow near the trees by the corner of the garage.

She smiled. "Come in. We've been expecting you..."

Moon Dance

Bridget Essex

"You know you're crazy to camp on Halloween, right?"

I stared at the park ranger, my eyebrows raised. He scribbled something on his clipboard and lifted a key off the back wall.

"I mean, the park's dead. It's boring as hell," he said, handing over the key while stifling a yawn. "It's too cold for most campers. Hell, I spend more time here, all cozy with my coffee and my TV, than I do out on the roads." His eyes traveled over my body. "So, if you get bored at any point, I make for great company—"

"I'll never be that bored." I snatched the key from his hand. Any other day I'd have dealt with him in a more eloquent manner. But I was already in a bad mood.

The skies were dark and heavy, rumbling with an advancing storm, rimming the edges of the hills as if they meant serious, rainy business. A gusty wind tipped with frost blew straight through my coat. But I've camped at this park, on Halloween, for the last five years. I knew what to expect—I'd brought my heavy-duty sleeping bag.

My bad mood didn't have anything to do with the weather or the park ranger.

It was a year ago that my girlfriend broke up with me.

And we'd broken up here. At the park. While camping.

Maybe it was a little crazy for me to commemorate one year single and miserable while doing the exact thing that had made me single and miserable. And it's not as if Allegany State Park were a ten-minute car ride from Boston. It's practically two states away, resulting in a ten-hour car ride. I had thought this out, planned it. Why did I go to the trouble of a ten-hour drive from Boston to camp where the pain is deepest?

I sighed and stared at the pines that ringed the ranger station. They loomed above me, curving toward the parking lot, as if they were trying to shield it from the oncoming storm.

I came because, honestly, I'm a sentimental idiot.

And I miss Alex.

She was perfect. She really was. I know that love blinds people, but I saw Alex clearly, because she was my best friend for five years before we decided to take the dating plunge, but I'd been in love with her since we first met. I'd never had the guts to tell her.

She had long, curly red hair that she always wrestled into a ponytail. The red came out of a box, so her skin was tan, and her brown eyes could pin a person to the spot. She always smelled of strawberries and hay—the strawberries from her shampoo, and the hay from her work at the stable. Sometimes I'd close my eyes and kiss the top of her head, inhaling deeply. She smelled like a perfect moment in summer, all sunshine and warmth and bright, rolling fields. She was warmth and all things good.

When she looked at me, she saw me. She saw who I was, who I wanted to be, all my faults as well as the best parts of me—and loved every bit of me. When she looked at me, sometimes I felt breathless because I'd realize that a woman I could never have imagined so perfectly was mine.

And then it all fell apart last year, when we were camping here. A drop of rain hit my cheek as I stared at the dark and terrible sky. I brushed it angrily aside—along with a white-hot tear that spilled down my cheek—as I walked to my car.

The ranger had assigned me to Horseshoe Trail. If it were summer, I would have asked for a different campground to avoid the families. But the park was just as deserted as the ranger had said it was.

Usually, a few brave souls camp over Halloween, so I hoped that I might have a neighbor. Otherwise, this was going to be a mighty lonely weekend. Just me and my thoughts and memories—and they were painful company.

A year later, I'm still wondering why Alex and I broke up. It was so strange, so unlike her. That night, a year ago, she came back to the cabin after an early-morning hike that took all day, her face as white as a skull. She was breathing heavily and sighing a lot, which wasn't normal—she was in tip-top shape.

When I asked her what was wrong, she just shook her head. I watched as she gathered her stuff and shoved it into her suitcase. If I tried to touch her, she would shrug me off. I followed her out to the car begging her to tell me what was wrong. I stood with my mouth hanging open. I couldn't believe she could throw away what we had, especially without telling me what was wrong. I took her home. The ten-hour drive was more like ten thousand and all of it in silence.

She lost no time packing her things and leaving. She left behind an empty apartment and an empty me. I sat on the kitchen floor and sobbed.

I tried to call her, but she wouldn't answer. She cut all her ties in Boston, including quitting her job at the stables. She was gone, completely gone, and I didn't know why. I blamed myself. I told myself that maybe I had done something, several somethings, for her to hate me so much. How could something so wonderful dissolve so quickly, so terribly? For no reason?

I pulled up to the cabin and stared at it.

I knew it was a bad idea to come back here. The park couldn't give me the answers I was looking for. Only Alex could do that. And she was gone. But I was here, feeling the pain that an entire year had done nothing to erase or ease.

I walked numbly up the cabin steps and unlocked the door. The cold, musty scent of the cabin spilled over me. Inside were the dual twin cots, each with a thin, stained mattress and the potbelly stove. There had been a time when I would have been excited about the trip and about how rustic it was. I wouldn't have been able to wait to build a fire in the stove and put some hot dogs on to cook.

But now, staring at those stained mattresses, at the empty cabin, I realized I shouldn't have come.

For a moment, I thought about going home. I could get a motel and drive the rest of the way tomorrow. Coming here had been a terrible idea. Why had I come?

I pressed my hand against the doorjamb for so long the rough wood left an imprint on my palm. I stared at my hand and decided to stay. I would decide if I wanted to cut the trip short tomorrow morning. It was peaceful here. Quiet. And I was so, so tired.

I scooted the two twin bed frames together, then carried my queen-size air mattress out of the car and up the cabin steps before setting it onto the frames. I got a little fire going in the small wood stove, and soon the room was warm. I unpacked the orange and black garland my preschool class made for me by gluing strips of construction paper together, handing it to me with hopeful expressions. "It's because of how much you love Halloween," Eric, my assistant, said with a strained frown.

Though the sentiment wasn't exactly true anymore, it was a sweet gesture, and I'd promised them I'd bring the garland with me when I went camping. Now I hung it up on the pegs around the room and lit a candle in my old-fashioned, antique lantern, hanging it from the biggest peg by the door.

The cabin was warm and cozy once I finished. Thankfully, it looked nothing like the one Alex and I shared last year, the one where my world fell apart. Where Alex left me.

I looked at the cooler I had placed near the foot of the bed. I was too exhausted to be hungry. Too tired and too sad.

I fell onto the air mattress, not yet made up, and decided to close my eyes for just a moment.

But I fell asleep.

I jolted awake. It was pitch black outside and the fire in the stove was out. The cabin sat cold and silent.

But something had woken me up. A sound.

There it was again.

The porch floor was creaking.

Someone or something was out there.

Allegany is famous for its overly friendly bears that start to salivate the minute they spy a camper's food supply and trash. So it was probably a bear. For a minute, though, I wondered if it was that skeevy park ranger. That simple thought made me reach for my barbecuing fork.

I stood for a long moment, breathing slowly and carefully in the dark, wielding the barbecuing fork. I thought about peeking out the window to see what was on my porch.

But before I could, there was a knock at the door.

I stood very still, barely breathing.

"Who is it?" I yelled, relieved that my voice sounded steady and angry, not uncertain and a little bit afraid. Which is how I felt.

There was a long pause before a low, rich voice answered, "It's Alex."

The sound of the barbecue fork hitting the floor made me jump, the metal tines clanging against the wooden planks. I stared, open-mouthed, at the door, but only for a heartbeat. I threw myself at the door and hurled it open.

Alex stood in a small patch of moonlight, barefoot with one hand on her hip, wearing jeans and a tattered t-shirt

Before I could take in much more, Alex was across the porch and pulling me to her. Her mouth crashed against mine. I was pinned against the doorframe, my hands instantly in her curly, tangled hair, my hands under the back hem of her shirt.

This had to be a dream. It had to be. It was too perfect, too impossible. I had wanted her for so long, and here she was.

I needed her. Before I woke up, I needed her.

I stepped back so that I could take in every inch of her. Alex stood in front of me, her brown eyes wide and ferocious as they roamed my body. I picked some twigs out of her hair, wondering why they were there, but I didn't have a chance to ask before we were kissing again. This was the most realistic dream I'd ever had. She turned her face, pressed her mouth against my wrist, against my palm as she reached for me, dragging me toward her so that my arms were wrapped tightly around her neck, my hips digging into hers.

"I've missed you," she said, her voice breaking, a single tear winding its way down her cheek. I stared at her, my heart pounding. She felt so real. I wrapped my arms around her neck and pulled her to me. She smelled of strawberries and bright, rolling meadows. She tasted like coffee and bonfire smoke.

Her lips met mine, and then her mouth was at my neck. Her tongue traced a hot line down to my chest and into my shirt that she was deftly unbuttoning with one hand, the other still tightly and possessively around my waist.

Alex shoved my shirt off my shoulders until it fell at our feet. She undid my bra with an expert flick of her fingers. She took one breast in her mouth as though she was starving. Her hot mouth captured my right nipple and bit it sharply. I arched closer to her. She'd never been this…desperate.

Her fingers were shoving the zipper of my jeans down and then shoving the jeans themselves down to join my shirt. She didn't wait until they hit the ground before her fingers were in my panties, curling up and into me.

I cried out, already wet and aching to feel her. The moonlight spilling onto the porch illuminated everything as brightly as daylight. I could see her flashing brown eyes devour me as she stared into my eyes, holding my gaze as if she was never going to let me go. I was naked against her, her fingers already inside of me.

"Alex," I whispered, wrapping my arms around her because it all felt too good, too much, and I couldn't hold myself up anymore. She bit the skin behind my ear, tracing her tongue over my earlobe as she growled gently into my throat.

"Alex, please," I whispered again, my knees quaking. "Please...the bed..."

We moved across the floor of the cabin to the bed, slamming the door as we went. I pulled her t-shirt over her head and undid the button of her jeans just as she pushed me onto the air mattress.

She climbed over me and pressed my wrists to the bed above my head, sliding in between my legs in a practiced, graceful motion that sent a thrill through me so strongly that I cried out when her jean-clad hips met my naked ones. She pressed herself against my center, pressed down with a savage growl that made me arch against her, crying her name out to the darkness.

"Alex, baby..." I whimpered as she kissed my neck, my throat, my breasts, winding her kisses lower. I tangled my fingers in her wild hair pulled her back up so that she lay on top of me, pulled her back to my mouth. I kissed her fiercely, pressing into her mouth as she pressed into mine. I wanted to taste every square inch of her, wanted to trace the curves I'd memorized so long ago with fingers that had ached so deeply to touch her. All this time without her... My heart, so full in that moment, was too full. It was close to breaking all over again.

Alex stopped rocking her pelvis against mine, stopped moving for an agonizing moment where every inch of my skin thrummed with life beneath her.

"I love you," she whispered, growling the words against my neck as she pressed my legs open farther, her fingers dancing down my thigh to trace softly against my aching center again. I hissed and moaned, rocking forward, begging her with my body to touch me. And she did. She curled her fingers through my folds and into me, curling upward and inward in a gesture so profoundly gentle that I almost wept. I pushed myself against her hand, wrapped my arms around her shoulders and my legs around her hips as if I would never let go of her again.

When I came, pressing myself against her hand, it was if my whole body had fractured into a million pieces, bright as silver from the moonlight coming through the window.

Alex held me close as I moved through the waves of pleasure. She kissed my mouth and drank me in, and I knew, in that moment, I was happier than I'd ever been.

When I stopped quivering, I opened my eyes and exhaled. Alex remained crouched over me, staring into my eyes, her brown eyes so alive and fiery that my heart caught in my throat.

"Where have you been?" I whispered, wrapping my arms around. I held her to me. I was afraid that if I didn't, this moment would dissolve. I'd wake up, and it'd all be over.

She searched my eyes, her breathing steady, her warm body covering mine as if it had never left. "You wouldn't believe me," she said softly, her voice almost like a growl, "even if I told you."

"Try me."

"I was bitten. By a wolf. And I've become one of them."

I searched her face for a sign of a joke. But how could she joke about something like this? Her expression remained utterly impassive, resolute and fierce.

She got up slowly, rising with a dignified grace that I ached to watch. She walked to the open door of the cabin and out into the moonlight.

I was shivering from the cold. But it didn't matter. I got up and walked, shaking, to the open door.

Beneath the moonlight, Alex, naked. It didn't seem strange. It seemed perfectly natural as she lifted her face to the moon. Her perfect curves reflected and were awash in the light, silver pouring from the skies to anoint her body. I stared in awe.

How could this be a dream?

There were a million stars overhead, spilling over the sky as though it was made of light. I couldn't stop staring at her. At my beautiful Alex, Alex who had left me, who had disappeared, the Alex who stood in the clearing, who turned me, her eyes shining.

"Baby," she murmured as she held her out her arms. Tears streamed down her face. "I've missed you so much"

I was speechless as I gingerly walked down the steps toward her. I crossed my arms over my chest, as much to warm myself as cover my breasts. I didn't want this moment to end.

She wrapped her arms around me so tight that it felt as if we were bound together. Our bodies swayed to the music of our pulses mingling together beneath the moonlight.

"Where have you been?" I whispered. And then the tears came, washing over both of us.

"I'm so sorry," she murmured over and over again. "I'm not who I once was. I needed time to understand it. I'm changed, baby."

I stepped away from her. "Changed?"

"Dance with me," she said, her voice catching. "There's not much time."

We danced together, merged together, there beneath the moonlight. There was no music other than the thrum of life, the whisper of the wind in the pines, the murmuring of the brook beside us. But it was all we needed. We moved together effortlessly, moved in a dance that was ours alone.

When the moon sank behind the trees, Alex pressed a kiss against my forehead, against the tip of my nose, and then, long and lingering, a kiss.

"Don't go," I whispered. I wrapped my arms around her, holding her to me so tight that the warmth of her body was my own. "Stay with me."

She stared deeply into my eyes.

"I can't. I have to go."

"Take me with you?"

She lingered a moment, her hands on the small of my back, her fingers wide and spread against my skin, hot against me. She shook her head.

"You don't know what you're saying."

"I would do anything to be with you."

She shook her head again and stepped back with a choking laugh. "You don't know what you're saying. You won't love me when you see I what I become."

In the last lingering beams of moonlight, I hugged myself. "Show me."

In an instant, where my lover had stood, was a wolf staring up at me.

She was gray and large and ferocious-looking, with tangled fur with pointed ears her hackled raised as she shook her head at me.

I crumpled to the ground as I stared at her. Everything in me told me to run. But I couldn't.

"Please," I whispered again, swallowing my fear as I held my arms out to her. I closed my eyes. "Please."

I heard the wolf's paws s they padded against the ground as she walked toward me. Then there was fur against me, against my breasts, my hands—the wolf pressed itself into my arms. I embraced her, sobbing into her fur.

"I love you, Alex," I said. "I love you no matter what you are."

There was an instant of pain in my shoulder that unfurled as the wolf's teeth bit me.

The Halloween moon slipped away, but the light no longer mattered as I changed, as the world erupted in a symphony of senses so clear and perfect that I could see the deer that stood on the edge of the clearing.

Alex and I ran into the night, joyfully alive and changed for good.

Together.

THE ROAD HOME

MAY DAWNEY

REBECCA LINDER STARED DOWN AT the hand clasped around her wrist and sighed, nervously licking her lips. Telling the story herself did not make it better.

"It's a local ghost story," she finally answered, meeting four pairs of watchful eyes in a sea of drunken college students. The serving tray in her hand wobbled precariously as an angel in a loincloth bumped into her. She stepped to the side as much as the hand on her wrist allowed—farther into the darkest corner of Tito's Bar. "He drowned, out in the river that runs along the road from here to Peton. Some asshole chased him down and he wrapped his truck around a tree. The guy who ran him off the road drove on, but Joe Wenton was stuck in his truck. Every Halloween since, he's come back to get his revenge: he picks one car and chases it down the road. Sometimes the crash kills them, other times they are lucky and get to walk away from the wreck, but it happens every year." She had to raise her voice to be heard over the noise of the overcrowded bar, but the four inebriated youths seemed sufficiently spooked, regardless.

"Bullshit." The guy who still had her arm in a deadlock squinted up at her.

"Nope, look it up. Every year, on Halloween. So, avoid the back roads tonight, guys." Rebecca tried to bring some amusement back into her voice, but she shivered, regardless. Every time she told the story, she wondered if she was drawing Wenton's attention somehow—as ridiculous as that sounded. Rebecca didn't *really* believe in ghost stories, but it never hurt to keep an open mind and be a little cautious—especially if the road home was the one you were describing.

"Arm?" she requested, and shook the appendage in question.

Shaken from his thoughts, the drunk space pirate let go, sending her a toothy grin, curiosity sated.

She smirked in reply. "Enjoy your drinks, boys."

Rebecca moved through the small, dark area carefully, avoiding flying arms and wobbly bodies, expertly holding up her tray. As she circled back to the bar, she caught Tito's eye, and he beamed at her, obviously excited to have so many people in his little hole-in-the-wall. Usually the Irish bar catered solely to the regular pensioners looking for a pint, so tonight's mayhem was a very welcome change. It would pay for rent two times over, Rebecca wagered.

Three hours later, she huddled under the bar's overhang while Tito locked the door behind him. Both were bone tired, but she hadn't seen her aging, wiry, far-too-gentle employer this happy in months. Rebecca suspected that tonight's success had been caused by the sudden deluge that had caused every partygoer and trick-or-treater to seek shelter at the nearest possible location. For a large group of Rebecca's peers, that location had been Tito's Bar.

"Be mindful of Joe, now." Tito grinned, giving her one of his famous winks.

She rolled her eyes, peeling herself away from the door. He'd been the one to tell her the story of Joe Wenton years ago, and he swore up and down that he had known Wenton back in the seventies.

"I'm sure he'll be good to me another year," she replied good-naturedly. "If not, it was good working with you, old man."

"Careful, kid." Tito shot her a badly hidden smile, and she grinned. "Don't forget who pays your wage."

"That money you still owe me for last week? Uh-huh. You just take care not to get pneumonia or something before you can pay me that 'wage'." Rebecca instructed, and he glared at her. At sixty-three, her boss really wasn't that old—and at twenty-five, she really wasn't that young—but they took any excuse to bicker.

"You just get home safe. I'll throw a little something extra in your check for tonight." Tito wrestled his umbrella open.

"You better—this shirt is done for." Rebecca peeled the beer-stained garment away from her skin with disdain.

Tito agreed immediately, and with one last look at the heavens, Rebecca rushed out from her shelter and to her car, soaking through instantly. She cursed under her breath as she slid inside and threw the door shut, taking a moment to shake herself out and run her hands through her short hair, slicking it back. The engine roared to life, and Rebecca pulled out of the parking lot, watching protectively through the side mirror as Tito rounded the corner, huddled in his jacket, umbrella over his head. At least *he* wasn't facing Joe tonight.

Flicking the windshield wipers to their highest setting, Rebecca turned onto the main road. She consciously forced herself to slow down. Even without Joe, these roads were treacherous: there were no streetlights, and guardrails were intermittent at best. The road led from a small town to an even tinier town and was obviously not a priority. On top of that, Rebecca had to rely on the one headlight that was still functioning on her beat-up Dodge Dynasty.

Trees flashed by, almost entirely obscured by sheets of rain blown by a heavy wind. Every now and again, a gust bashed into the side of the car, causing her to swerve a little. With every sharp turn into sharper bends in the road, Rebecca was reminded of the river below. She pictured Wenton's struggle for air as the cabin of his truck filled up with water, legs trapped, and no one around for miles to help him. It was a very fucked-up way to go, she determined with a shudder. Her hands fastened around the steering wheel just a little tighter at the realization that one false move could have her in exactly that predicament.

Ten minutes in, Rebecca was so preoccupied by the weather—peering out into the darkness, trying to visualize the road beyond the rain—that she missed the car coming up behind her until it was practically attached to the rear of her own. Suddenly aware of more light falling on the road before her, Rebecca's eyes shot to the rearview mirror. She squinted against the glare, blinded instantly. Fear spread through her system like wildfire as the engine of the pushy SUV—or was it a truck?—roared loudly enough to top the sound of the heavy rain beating down.

She shouldn't have told those guys at the bar the story—she should have ordered the space pirate to let go of her arm and find someone else to tell him about the name that was jokingly on everyone's lips. Joe Wenton wasn't exactly Voldemort, but you just didn't tempt fate like that—not if you knew you had to go through his hunting grounds on the way home. She cursed out-of-towners and her own stupidity as she sped up a little and found her pace matched instantly by her pursuer.

With her panic rising, Rebecca tried to find a way out. Dark eyes frantically searched the flooded road before her for an exit. It was a useless endeavor: a sturdy rock wall locked her in on the left, and on the right was the drop-off to the river Joe Wenton had so famously drowned in. The road did not have exits until it bled into the tiny town of Peton, West Virginia. The rain beating down on the hood of her car made her feel even more locked in—trapped. With a shaky hand, she turned down the volume of the car radio so she could focus better on getting out alive.

The windshield wipers groaned as the rain intensified. Rebecca's heart was pounding in her throat. She was caught; she had nowhere to go. *Ghosts don't exist, and this is just some asshole with an attitude problem*, Rebecca told herself, but as the seconds ticked away, this sage advice became harder and harder to remember. She couldn't get the image of a pale farmhand with spiky brown hair and overalls out of her mind.

She hit the brakes repeatedly, and the SUV backed off a little. But it was still behind her, chasing her down the road. Tense and flushed, breathing laboured, she glanced anxiously between the road ahead and the rearview mirror. Her heart was still in her throat. With every inch of ground the SUV gained on her, her heart pounded a little faster. She knew she needed to slow down, and yet she hit the gas pedal a little harder. Over and over, Rebecca's mind flashed forward to the inevitable crash, to being confronted with a ghost she knew did not exist but feared, regardless. Every horror movie she had ever seen flashed before her mind's eye and she tried to strategize. *You can't fight a ghost.*

Just as suddenly as it had come up, the SUV fell back, staying close but no longer forcing her to pick up speed to put distance between them. Rebecca watched it happen through the rearview mirror, and her heart settled a bit more securely in her chest. A manic sort of laugh welled up in her throat, born of relief. It died away instantly as she returned her eyes to the road ahead and saw the guardrail come up. *Fuck!* She tried to steer to the side to avoid the metal, but it was useless. The rain and mud that had pooled on the road caused the car to slip as she hit the brakes. Right before she crashed, Rebecca realized Joe had claimed another victim this Halloween night—that she had played right into his trap.

The side of her Dodge smashed into the guardrail with bone-crushing intensity. She groaned as she was flung sideways, first into the door, then towards the passenger side. Rebecca prayed the guardrail would hold. Long seconds passed, then the car screeched to a halt and the engine died. She was alive and unharmed. It took a few moments for the reality of her situation to settle in—moments roughly disturbed by a large car shooting past hers, narrowly avoiding a collision as it swerved and the brakes screeched. Rebecca watched in shock as the car came to a halt in front of hers, on the other side of the road, hugging the rock. The sound of its engine cut off abruptly.

Besides her frantic heartbeat and the rain beating down on the hood of her car, everything was finally silent. Experimentally, she tried her legs and hands, cracked her neck, and found all to be in working order. She was trembling, out of breath. She tried to keep her eyes on the SUV, but the rain obscured the windows. With trembling hands, she undid the clasp of her seatbelt. She could barely get her fingers to cooperate because of the adrenaline flooding through her system. Her usual tough-girl demeanour had vanished. The story of Joe Wenton's death ran through her head over and over again, mingling with countless other ghost stories.

Rebecca yelped audibly when something hit the driver's side window and proceeded to try the door handle. With a speed born of fearful desperation, Rebecca hit the knob that locked the door and backed away from the window until she was pressed against the passenger side door, legs pulled up, ready to kick. She didn't know if she could kick a ghost, but he could touch the door, so she sure as hell was going to try. *You won't get me that easily, asshole,* she promised. She was not dying without a fight.

Her jaw set as the door handle clicked, then clicked again. Behind the obscured glass, something shifted. Seconds ticked by, then someone wiped down the window. Skeletal features with hollow eye-sockets peered inside. Joe Wenton had found her on the road—*she* was his victim tonight, and because she hadn't died in the crash, he was going to finish the job by hand. Every muscle in Rebecca's body tensed, ready to fight for her life.

"Are you okay?"

The words were shouted into the rain, against the slowly fogging glass.

It took long seconds for them to register in Rebecca's adrenaline-flooded brain. She had been waiting for the glass to shatter or for a ghostly hand to push through the door. She realized that the figure out in the rain was not a ghost but a person, and they were not going to kill her; they were trying to help. The relief that flooded her system was so strong that Rebecca was suddenly fighting tears.

For long seconds, she couldn't get herself to move. She was still struggling with her fight-or-flight reflexes, and they were winning. She felt dazed, unable to wrap her mind around what was happening. *In and out...in and out,* she told herself, breathing deeply. She ran a hand through her hair and finally reached out to unlock the door. The head that dipped down to look in did not belong to a ghost at all but to someone in zombie makeup—well, what was left of it. The heavy rain had washed most of it off to reveal a distinctly Asian-looking woman around Rebecca's age with big, dark, very worried eyes.

"Hey, are you okay? Are you hurt? I'm *so* sorry. I never meant for this to happen—you just seemed to know your way around and I'm so lost. Oh God, you're hurt, aren't you? Okay, let me call an ambulance. I'm so sorry, I—" The strange girl was babbling now, a slightly foreign accent in her voice. Her eyes frantically searched Rebecca's body—probably for blood or injuries. Her hand hovered over Rebecca's sneaker but didn't connect. Obviously, she was afraid of getting kicked.

How fucked up do I look? Finally—finally—Rebecca's brain kicked in, and she realized she was making a complete fool of herself by huddling in the passenger seat, looking at a perfectly ordinary, very attractive, very terrible car driver as if she was going to maul her to death. She forced her muscles to relax and sat up more firmly.

"I'm okay. Don't call an ambulance, seriously. I'm okay, no thanks to you. What were you thinking?" Rebecca's voice was sharp and dark enough to make the other woman wince.

Zombie girl stepped back to allow Rebecca to slide out of the car. Immediately, the rain streaked down over her face, staining her clothes. The sensation was immensely steadying to her shaking legs. Now that her shock was wearing off, Rebecca realized that her ruling emotions were embarrassment and anger—and rightfully so, even if the latter was an outlet for her relief over not being dead. She was still trying to wrap her mind around that.

"Really, I'm so sorry. Please, I'll pay for the damage to your car, okay? Just tell me you're okay—you look okay. Are you okay?" The Asian woman was still babbling into the minimal space between them, obviously also in shock.

She talked with her hands a lot, Rebecca noted, and she was shorter than Rebecca—who was five foot six—had first thought. In the blinking alarm lights of the woman's oversized car, Rebecca could see how she completely disregarded the rain, how focused she was on Rebecca and her well-being, and how *truly* upset she looked. To offer up the money to fix her car right away was also a balm to Rebecca's spooked heart; she really didn't have the funds for that herself.

With gusto, she threw the driver's side door shut behind her, protecting the interior from the deluge. She sighed, running both hands through her already soaked hair, peeling it away from her face and slicking it back. Whatever natural curl it had to it had now disappeared under the weight of the water. *Deep, steady, breaths*, Rebecca reminded herself. Her heart was still racing and the last thing she needed now was a heart attack.

She wasn't sure if it was her embarrassment over falling for a ghost story or the other woman's nerves, but Rebecca slid into what her friends lovingly referred to as her 'butch-mode': to cover her emotions, she went for casual nonchalance and light flirtation, no matter the circumstance. There was no way to deny the state in which the woman before her had found her, so she had better just laugh it off and then never refer to it ever again, lest she die of embarrassment. This whole thing was bad for her reputation, and her friends would probably have laughed their asses off if they could have seen her just now.

"I told you, I'm fine. Promise. Thanks for offering to pay for the damages, though. I'm too broke not to take you up on that." She answered the question with the barest hint of mirth in her voice, sort of afraid to check on said damage. "Just...

stop apologizing. I'm Rebecca, and you are not Joe Wenton, so who are you?"

The hand that gripped hers lightly but surely was cold and wet, and shaking even harder than her own. When Rebecca forced her bar smile onto her face, the woman before her mirrored it right away—a crooked affair that was pretty cute, Rebecca mused. The relief in her full brown eyes was plain to read, although it was mixed with confusion and guilt. *She is probably wondering why she isn't being yelled at*, Rebecca figured, and bit back a smirk.

"Jenny—Jen. Hi. Who is Joe Wenton…?" Rebecca found the confusion in her voice endearing.

"You must be new in town. He's the local ghost; runs travellers off of the road on Hallow's Eve. I figured you were him," Rebecca commented dryly, owning her panicked reaction and feeling a cheeky smirk settle on her lips despite herself as she slowly released the hand in hers. Jen seemed a little shaken by Rebecca's demeanor, searching her eyes and face for a social cue to hang her reaction on and finding nothing solid to work with. Rebecca watched in amusement as Jen bit her lip; a nervous habit, it seemed.

Rebecca took a moment to take in the woman before her. Jen was dressed in a bright yellow summer dress that had fake blood drizzled all over it—fake blood that also stubbornly clung to her chin and lips even though the rest of her makeup had mostly washed away. There was still just a bit of blackness around her almond-shaped eyes, and the corners of her mouth were stained white—as were the insides of her ears. The rest of her was wet and clean, and she was shivering terribly. Rebecca didn't blame her—she was insanely underdressed and the rain was cold, even though they were mostly shielded from the wind by the surrounding trees.

"You thought I was a ghost? Oh God, is that why you ran off of the road?" Jen's voice was a mixture of shock and panic as she made a sign with her hand that reminded Rebecca of the way her nan crossed herself whenever she heard something she thought the good Lord would disagree with. At least Jen didn't make fun of her—another balm to her wounded ego.

"That, and the rain and the mud. Don't worry about it, zombie girl. Next time, though, back off of the rust bucket in front of you, okay?" She leaned back against the car a moment and patted it lovingly as she mentioned the words 'rust' and 'bucket'. "Ghost story or not, that was some crappy driving." Rebecca chastised her without malice.

"Again, I am so sorry. I think I took six wrong turns somewhere and ended up here. I just...you seemed to know the road, and I was hoping you would lead me back to town. I didn't want to lose you, so I stayed close—too close—and I'm sorry." Jen mumbled just loud enough for Rebecca to hear her over the pounding rain.

Rebecca shrugged. She glanced up at the nervous wreck before her with a confidence and airiness she didn't quite feel but wanted to project, regardless. Better that than show the last remnants of her nerves over the crash and the scare before that. She still couldn't believe she was alive; she had been sure this was going to be the end. Elation flooded her system: she had gotten a new lease on life.

"I told you, water under the bridge—I'm sure there is a bridge here somewhere, and we have water enough. Speaking of which, why don't we get out of that? I'm freezing my ass off and I could use a hot drink and a change of clothing. I live maybe five minutes from here, so maybe we can exchange details there for the insurance company? Perhaps we can also find out where you went wrong and get you on your way?"

Rebecca ran her hands up and down her arms to get some warmth back into them.

Jen regarded her. "Uh...yeah, that sounds really good, actually. Are you sure you don't mind...?"

"Nope, all good. I'm gonna inspect the damage for a bit and then we'll see if the car will start. That will make the drive a lot easier."

Jen grinned at the joke before she seemed to remember she was still feeling ashamed of her behavior. The grin disappeared.

Rebecca smirked but decided not to comment; secretly she had liked seeing that smile again. Facing the inevitable, she finally rounded the hood. It was dark, but even in this crappy weather, she was able to see huge scrapes and a big dent on the front of her moss green Dynasty. The headlight was busted, but it was the one that had already been out, so Rebecca didn't worry about that too much. Running her hand over the scrapes, Rebecca's heart bled for her poor car.

"Is it okay...?" Jen asked, leaning over the hood to observe her as she inspected the damage.

"I think so. Let's just give this a go," Rebecca answered after another moment, hoping she was correct. She kicked the shattered plastic pieces of the headlight cover under the guardrail—which had undoubtedly been her life saver. Without it, Rebecca would be half way down a hill right now and in far worse condition. She couldn't help but shudder at the thought.

Jen stepped back to allow her passage, smiling curiously as Rebecca brushed past her a little closer than strictly necessary.

Rebecca bit back a smirk. Flirting always made her feel better, and while she doubted Jen's sexuality was anything other than arrow-straight, Rebecca didn't let that stop her from some harmless interaction. Who knew what could happen, right?

After a night like this, she wanted to celebrate every joyful aspect of life, and what was better than a little romance?

It took two tries, but then the engine roared to life, sputtering and groaning, but staying on. She shifted into reverse, and as she backed up, the only scraping she heard was the sound of the car dragging past the guardrail. Once she had cleared that, the car seemed alright; even her remaining front light worked.

"Okay, let's go for it." Jen's broad smile was just as much relief over the car being in one piece as Rebecca's light tone of voice, Rebecca assumed.

"I'll be right behind you." Jen backed off towards her car, drawing Rebecca's attention.

She laughed as Jen caught herself a second too late. If it had been a little less dark, Rebecca just knew she would be seeing a deep blush creep up on well-defined features. It was a perfect slip of the tongue, after all. "Oh, I bet," Rebecca answered, amusement in her voice to soften the blow of her words. "Just get in the car, Joe."

Jen searched her eyes, then smiled, nodding as she hurried off to slide into the SUV and soak through her front seat like Rebecca was doing to hers.

Rebecca watched the car pull onto the road behind her, keeping a very leisurely distance. This time, she met her own eyes in the rearview mirror.

"Some night, huh?" she questioned out loud. Yet, as she regarded the SUV behind her, she couldn't help but smile. Near-death was about as rock-bottom as you could hit. It could only get better from here on out.

Although nothing went wrong and there weren't any odd sounds or smells coming from the car, Rebecca was still very happy to pull into the parking lot of the housing complex and shut off the engine. In a useless attempt to retain what little body heat had returned during the short drive, they hurried through the abandoned parking lot and rushed up the steps to the housing complex with a laugh on their lips. Rebecca held open the door for her guest and guided her inside with a hand on the small of Jen's back.

Jenny brushed closely past her, breaking eye contact only when she really had to.

Despite being frozen to the bone, Rebecca felt warmth flow through her body, ignited by dark eyes that had drawn her in and a hand that burned from the contact of skin on thin fabric. She shivered and let the door fall shut behind her. Maybe she had overestimated Jenny's straightness after all.

Rebecca's building was an old one, made mostly of brick, and their footsteps echoed through abandoned hallways as they moved past mailboxes and up the well-worn, carpeted stairs to the third floor where Rebecca had her small dorm room. That hallway was deserted as well. The primary university Halloween party was being held at rich kid Robert Camron's place, and almost everyone attended it.

Jen followed happily to Rebecca's room, looking about her as if she had never seen a student housing complex in her life.

Rebecca wasn't surprised to find her dorm room drenched in darkness. Her roommate Paige was undoubtedly out partying and wouldn't be back until midday tomorrow at the earliest. Flicking the overhead light on, Rebecca stepped aside to let Jen enter and smiled as her guest curiously scanned the room. Honestly, it wasn't much, but Rebecca's Spartan style of decorating kept the room quiet, and Paige's obsession with her university's white and blue brought a sense of homeliness to it.

"So, it's kinda basic but you can have the desk chair while I clean off the bed? We have a shower down the hallway, by the way, if you want to use it? You look a little miserable and I sure could use one so...?" Rebecca commented with amusement.

Jen was still shivering badly, arms wrapped around herself for warmth.

For the first time, Rebecca could actually distinguish details about her guest, and she realized she had underestimated Jenny's appeal; she had cheekbones even more pronounced than the norm and was a tad more muscular than Rebecca had first given her credit for. Nothing major, but Jen looked healthy and into sports—or at least working out. Rebecca—who was on the track, basketball, and soccer teams—appreciated that. Although she wasn't an expert, she was pretty confident that Jenny was of Chinese decent.

"I...don't have a spare set of clothes, so I don't think a shower would help. You go ahead, though," Jen answered regrettably, shivering in the dress that—Rebecca now noted—had a certain see-though quality to it when wet.

Rebecca swallowed heavily as she diverted her eyes from the dark contours of a bra that only partially managed to hide the fact that Jen was, indeed, chilled to the bone. *Straight as an arrow*, she reminded herself, *and a terrible driver.* That said, Jen was taking a lot of care *not* to look at the way Rebecca's clothes clung to her body, keeping her eyes level with Rebecca's no matter what. *Well then...* Rebecca mused, biting her lip as she turned to clear her bed. She fished her oversized sleep shirt, laptop, and anatomy books from her blankets and disposed of the latter two on the desk. The shirt she threw into her laundry hamper.

"You're not that much shorter than I am, so I should have something that will fit you? By the time we figure out how to get you home and fill in the paperwork, you'll be absolutely miserable if you don't." Rebecca continued tidying her half of the small space as Jen looked on, dripping water onto the standard sky blue carpeting. "...not to mention how soaked my chair will be if you don't. Seriously, there is no one here, and I'll be happy to lend you something, okay? The laundry room downstairs has a dryer so it would only be for a while. You could head home warm and dry which, you have to admit, sounds a lot better than cold and wet."

It took Jen a few moments before she sighed and uncrossed her arms from her midriff. She threw her hands up in surrender, a glint in her eyes.

"Okay, yes. Please. I'm freezing."

Rebecca nodded with a genuine smile, moving from the center of the room to her built-in wardrobe to fish out a black and electric blue tracksuit, as well as a tank top for Jen. She collected a fresh pair of jeans and a white top for herself.

She handed the first pile of clothes off to her guest with a smirk and a light brushing of fingers that Jen's eyes flickered to. When Rebecca winked, Jen smiled, searching her eyes. There was tension between them, Rebecca noted happily—tension that settled hotly in her gut as Jen licked her lips. There was no way Rebecca was going to act on that tension, though; she might be a little butch, but she wasn't that brave. Tearing herself away so she wouldn't crowd her guest, she handed Jen a fresh towel and added one to her own pile as well. Running a now steady hand through her wet hair, Rebecca inclined her head to the door with a smile that was mirrored instantly.

"Shall we? Warmth awaits," she joked lightly, attempting to break the lingering tension, and Jen nodded, baring even, white, teeth. Rebecca liked it when she smiled—maybe a little too much. To distract herself, she grabbed her toilet bag from one of the shelves over her bed, mulling over the eternal lesbian worry: how to discover if the girl you liked was into women as well. *At least the signs are promising*, Rebecca had to admit, and she held on to that hope as she led Jenny out.

"So have you lived here long?" Jen's eyes scanned brick walls, which were cluttered with Halloween party announcements and corkboards full of notes and ads.

Rebecca tore her mind away from the memory of lips being licked by a soft tongue and dark eyes observing her curiously from a minimal distance. "Almost three years, although I switched rooms in August. My previous roommate was pretty horrible, and Paige is a good friend. She's also almost never home, so that's even better."

Jen grinned at the suggestive note.

"How about you? Where were you trying to get to?"

"Carlton Airbase?" Jen answered, obviously wondering if Rebecca was familiar with it.

Rebecca did know it, although she had never been there. The military base was a good forty minutes away, in the opposite direction of where Jen had caught up with her. "Wow, you did get turned around. It's not too hard to get there from here, so you should be fine once we Google-map it. Don't you have navigation?" Rebecca held the door to the women's bathroom open.

Jenny slipped past, not meeting Rebecca's eyes as she brushed against her.

Rebecca wondered if that had been strictly necessary but didn't complain. They had become good at these stolen touches, and she hoped Jen's were as intentional as hers.

"I don't have one in the car; I usually just use my phone, but the party I went to tonight was pretty awful and some drunk guy broke it. I thought I'd remember the way back, but it seems I was wrong." Jen bit her lip adorably as she waited for Rebecca to direct her to one of the five shower stalls lining the left wall.

Rebecca nodded towards the first of the stalls, and Jen carefully set her pile of clothes on the bench in the unit, keeping the door open and peeking out once Rebecca spoke again.

"Shit, some guy broke your phone? I hope you got his info?"

Jen looked away a little, shrugging noncommittally, and Rebecca was fairly certain the woman's answer was a resounding 'no'.

"He was very drunk," Jen offered as an excuse. "Besides, I shouldn't have gone to the party in the first place. I don't even like parties; my mother was just stationed at Carlton, so my family moved here a few weeks ago."

"You couldn't get a dorm room?"

"You obviously don't know my father." Annoyance crept into Jen's voice, and Rebecca decided not to pry.

"Anyway." Jen sighed. "My father thought it would be a good idea for me to, you know, go out and meet people while we wait for the college transfer to go through. He'd seen posters around town of a Halloween-themed party, thought it would be some nice, supervised gathering, and encouraged me to go. Big mistake."

"Wait—you went to the *Night of the Living Dead* bash?"

Jen nodded, eyeing Rebecca curiously as she watched her set down the pile of clothes in the second cubicle.

"I know the guys who organize that party. I'll see if I can get you some pictures, and maybe you can pick out the guy who wrecked your phone?"

"Oh, that would be great. Thank you!"

Jen sounded enthusiastic, but Rebecca had a pretty good read on the slightly awkward woman already, and she figured the excitement was at least partially faked. She couldn't really blame Jen: showing up at some guy's doorstep and asking him to pay for the damages to a phone he probably didn't even remember wrecking didn't sound appealing to her either.

"At least you'd know his name. You can always decide later if you want to do something with the info?"

Jen smiled a slightly sad smile, nodding once. "Yeah, you're right. I'd love to see the pictures."

Rebecca decided to leave it at that and began to instruct Jen on how the shower and the stall worked, apologizing for having to share the bath products. Rebecca only had the one set. Jen didn't seem to mind sharing, nor the way Rebecca had to move past her in the small space of the stall to show her around. Rebecca was happily smirking by the time they disappeared into adjacent stalls.

She was momentarily distracted from her attraction to a complete stranger by the blissful act of peeling her soaked clothes off of her body, although she was soon even colder than before as a slight draft hit her skin. Next, she fumbled out of her underwear, dumped it on the bench, and stepped behind the half screen separating the changing room from the shower stall. Then she turned on the water, adjusted it, and stepped under the stream as she listened to Jen going through similar motions in the other stall.

"So...your mom's in the army?" Rebecca asked, mostly to break the silence left behind after light touches and a shared smile—although Rebecca's had been a lot more overtly flirtatious than Jen's. Jen had just done that head tilt that made her look up at Rebecca through her hair, which made Rebecca want to tuck the strands behind Jen's ear.

"Yeah, both my parents are. My mother is a flight instructor and my father is an aircraft mechanic. My mother got the opportunity to teach here and my father managed to transfer here as well. We live on base." Jen answered her over the sound of running water, and Rebecca listened as she blissfully soaked the cold out of her skin.

"Wow, so you're an army kid. Are you in the army as well?"

Jen chuckled. "No, I'm studying to be a veterinarian. Not much use for those in the US Army anymore."

As Rebecca picked up her shampoo bottle, she pondered that. "That's probably true. What do you wanna specialize in? Like, farm animals or pets?"

Rebecca slid the bottle under the divider and heard it get picked up moments later. She tried not to think about Jen's bare form just a few feet away, nor about running her hands through straight hair which she imagined to be very soft. It had been quite a while since Anne, her last girlfriend, and while Rebecca was usually fine on her own, the adorable Chinese beauty made her equally want to wrap her up in a blanket and feed her chocolate, and eat said chocolate off of her firm body. With force, she slid her head under the water, hoping the gesture would clear her head. It didn't; all that happened was that she missed Jen's reply.

"Sorry? I didn't catch that." She apologized quickly as she stepped back again, running her hands through her hair to rinse it.

"Pets, preferably, although I like all animals."

Rebecca hummed. She was fine with animals—as long as they belonged to someone else. Same with babies.

"What are you studying?" Jen continued, sliding the shampoo bottle back.

"Medicine."

"Sorry?"

"Medicine!" Rebecca repeated, rolling her eyes at the conversation. "You know, I've always kind of liked these dividers, but I'm not a big fan now."

She hadn't meant for it to sound like such an *invitation*— she had merely wanted to comment on the difficulties in communication—but she was pleasantly surprised that Jen didn't fall silent; instead, she heard laughter coming from the other stall.

"They are quite inconvenient, yes," Jen agreed amicably.

Rebecca had to beat her libido down with a proverbial stick at the images that played through her mind at that. She imagined herself shutting off the water, slipping out, and knocking softly on the stall door next to her. She imagined eyes wide with surprise as Jenny opened up, foam in her hair and a towel wrapped precariously around her. She imagined how she would step in, capture Jen's head in her hands, and kiss her; imagined smirking as Jen's hands came up to wrap around her and the towel fell away between them, forgotten on the ground as Rebecca backed the woman up against the cold wall, feeling her shiver. Damn it, she hadn't meant to get this invested; nothing in Jen's voice had made the words sound like an invitation, and she had no right to even think about the woman like this. *Down, girl. Down!*

"I uh…yeah." She answered lamely, completely unable to formulate a decent response. She wondered if she had imagined the light chuckle she thought she had caught over the rushing water, but still groaned with embarrassment.

"Are you done with the conditioner?" Jen asked.

Rebecca fumbled to thrust the bottle under the divider. "Yeah, here. Sorry," she said, even though she hadn't used the conditioner at all—instead she had been daydreaming about Jen, who now brushed *her* fingers as she accepted the bottle.

Rebecca shivered and bit her lip. She rushed to stand and use the soap before Jen had to ask for that as well, hoping the familiar motions of washing up would steady her.

Time for a reality check: Rebecca'd had a few one night stands, but those had developed out of bar visits or an online meet, and none of them had rattled her in the way her obvious attraction to Jen did. With her previous one night stands, both parties had been clear on the deal; now she was just helping out the woman who had run her off the road—sex was not part of that basic arrangement. She would be lying if she said she would stop it from happening, though. She liked Jen—her inherent mix of excitable awkwardness and coy shyness was alluring, and she was beautiful. Without the tension between them, Rebecca could easily see them becoming friends. With the tension between them, however, Rebecca couldn't help but wish for more than that. Almost dying had a way of making you feel alive and hungry to seize every opportunity.

"Here, soap," she offered, kneeling down again.

After a second, Jen's hand again found hers, and this time there was no denying the way Jen lingered. After a moment, a soft finger ran over her index finger and Rebecca heard a soft "thanks" before the hand retracted, taking the soap with it. It seemed Jenny had started to outshine her in the flirtation department, which made Rebecca equal parts excited and nervous. She liked to be the one in control, and that control was slipping from her with every touch of fingers and every husked word. Jen had seemed shy at first, but her actions as of late hinted at a far stronger personality than Rebecca had given her credit for at first glance. It was exciting.

Rushing through the rest of her shower, Rebecca hurried to dry off and slip into her clothing. She cursed herself for not remembering to bring dry underwear with her. Well, commando it was; at least that way she matched Jen. By the time Rebecca stepped out of the foggy cubicle, Jen was stepping out as well, smiling at her through one of the many mirrors that lined the far wall. She dipped her head before Rebecca could return the gesture.

Jenny had opted not to put on the jacket that had come with the tracksuit, drawing Rebecca's eyes to the tank top that fitted her frame very snuggly. She had obviously decided not to go with a wet bra either and the sight of firm breasts under a single layer of clothing brought back every bit of need in Rebecca. She had to force herself to look away, focusing on her hair instead as she tried to comb through it with her hands, getting the frizz under control a little.

"Much better," Jen commented, meeting Rebecca's eyes in one of the mirrors when she looked up again.

Rebecca nodded, wondering if Jen was talking about her looks or her own condition. *Where are you, butch mode? I kinda need you*, she chastised herself.

"Much," she managed to force out, clearing her throat as she ducked back into the cubicle to gather her clothes, towel, bath products, and self-control. When she emerged again, Jen was waiting for her, hanging somewhat coyly against one of the sinks under the mirrors, soap in her outstretched hand. *So tempting*, Rebecca mused, but she lacked the guts to just go for it. Rebecca took the bar from her guest a tad awkwardly and was awarded another crooked smile that sent shivers down her spine. Looking for an excuse to change the subject until she had herself under control, she noted that Jen had her wet clothes already set out on the edge of one of the sinks.

"We should get those into the dryer. You can wait in my room, if you want?"

Jen met her eyes, searching them a long moment before shaking her head. "I'll come with you," she decided.

Rebecca nodded with a smile as she took in damp and slightly messy hair that came down to just below small ears, soft and slightly flushed skin, and full lips she *really* wanted to kiss. She refused to allow her eyes to linger as they flitted down, finding bunched-up pant legs that fell over small feet. "Suit yourself," she answered with an amused shrug. "Sorry those are a little long. They don't fall off or anything, though, right?" She inclined her head towards Jen's pants.

Jenny looked down at her own body and shook her head, hands hoisting up the pant legs so she wasn't standing on them anymore. "No, they stay up pretty well. It's only for a while, anyway. Thank you for letting me use them."

Rebecca shrugged, finally finding her equilibrium again. "No problem. Couldn't have you walk around naked, now could we?" She added a wink to bring some lightness into the comment and Jen dipped her head, although her hair didn't cover her smile.

"That might have been a little awkward around the hallways, yes." Jen looked up at her through a curtain of damp hair as she bit her lip.

The gesture sent a flash of arousal down Rebecca's spine and threw her off balance again. *Damn it.* Jen was flirting with her. She had to be—right?

"I think you could have handled it, though," Jen spoke softly, a touch of depth to her voice that hadn't been there before.

Right away, Rebecca's mouth went dry and she was still staring at the door when it fell shut behind Jenny, who had taken off with her clothes in hand. *That was a come-on, right? That had to be a come-on,* Rebecca questioned herself. No matter what, she had to move and catch up before her poor ego took its second—or maybe third—hit of the night.

Jenny was waiting for her in the hallway, the picture of patient innocence. Rebecca felt like a flushed—and very horny—teenager, and judging by the glint in Jen's eyes, the other woman was well aware of her predicament. *Time to bite the bullet*, Rebecca decided. She needed to at least find out if Jen had any interest in women at all, or if this was just her own mind playing tricks on her.

"This way," she instructed gruffly and moved towards the stairs, followed by Jen, who was smiling nearly continually by now. She headed down the staircase to the first floor, all the while casually mining for information.

"So...where did you move from...?"

Jen sighed. "Arkansas, Oklahoma, North Dakota, South Dakota, then Arkansas again, and we moved here from Montana."

Rebecca looked up to find Jenny gloomily lost in memories. "That's...a lot of moving. Sorry..."

Jen shrugged. "It's the army life."

Rebecca nodded. What could she say to that? Jenny was right; if her parents hadn't been in the army, she wouldn't have moved around so much.

"Did you have to leave behind anyone special?" She asked, hoping to finally clear up at least roadblock number one.

Jen smirked a little as she regarded her from beneath a curtain of tangled hair.

Rebecca just hoped she would have mercy on her; this conversation would get mighty awkward if Jen chose to go for coy.

"No, no one special—not like that anyway. I left some really good friends behind but I ended things with my ex-girlfriend months ago so...no, no one special left behind in Montana."

Rebecca had to clamp down on a sigh of relief even as her heart sped up to a gallop. Jenny was gay, or at least bisexual, and Rebecca suddenly found herself with dilemma number two: finding out if Jen was also a little gay *for her*.

"Sorry about your ex. It's been a while since Anne, my ex, as well. Sucks, huh?"

Jen nodded. "It does. I mean, I am not actively looking, but...yeah...I'm open to meeting someone new." Jen smiled as Rebecca pulled open the door to the laundry room and moved past her, heading in.

"Good to know." Rebecca answered, going for nonchalance while taking a big bite out of that proverbial bullet. She closed the door behind her, happy the overhead lights were always on on this floor; the entire building seemed deserted and she wasn't exactly over the Halloween jitters. One brush with death was enough for tonight and a half-lit laundry room seemed a perfect serial killer hunting ground. It only took one look at Jen to wipe the horror stories entirely from her mind.

"Why? Are you offering?" Jen set her clothes on the island of dryers in the middle of the room and turned around as Rebecca stepped forward slowly.

Rebecca regarded the woman before her, tried to get a read on her voice, on the way she leaned back against one of the dryers, on the way dark eyes first drilled into her own and then flicked down her body and back up. She swallowed as she stepped closer. It was the sink situation all over again, but this time she knew Jen was into women...and she had just pretty much offered herself up to Rebecca on a silver platter. *Do or die*, Rebecca decided.

"Yeah," she answered. "I guess I am...so..." She trailed off, searching Jenny's eyes as she stepped closer, finally moving into the other woman's space.

This time it was Jen who swallowed as eyes flitted to lips, then back up. "So..." Jen whispered, staying still, arms to her side.

Rebecca aligned their bodies, reaching out to dump her clothes and bag on top of the ugly white appliance at Jen's back before setting her hands on the edge of it. They were close enough now for their bodies to press together and their breath to mingle. Her butch mode finally kicked in as she smiled, moving a single hand from the dryer to Jen's cheek. Quietly she ran her thumb over it, savoring the moment. Dipping her eyes down to soft lips, she pulled Jen's head forward just a little, feeling hands settle on her hips and pull her in by the loops on her jeans. A beat passed between them, another, and then Rebecca went in for the kiss, watching Jen's eyes sink shut just before hers did.

With her heart in her throat and her eyes closed as she inhaled deeply, she pressed her lips to Jen's and waited for a reaction—any reaction. Jen whimpered and pulled Rebecca harder against her, mashing their hips together. Rebecca leaned forward on the arm still resting on the dryer, instantly lost in sensation now that her advances were officially welcomed. Jen's lips were soft and full, still warm from the hot shower. They parted under hers easily as Rebecca slid her tongue over them gently, savoring this moment, this first kiss. Heat streaked up and down her spine.

Rebecca slid her tongue over the parted lips, teasing Jen until she pressed forward with both her body and her tongue, connecting them fully as their tongues slid easily together. Now it was Rebecca's turn to moan as she pulled Jen closer with the hand on her cheek. Jen slid her hand over Rebecca's back, up and down, scratching the skin as she pushed up her shirt. Rebecca shivered, moaning as she deepened the kiss, keeping them together a few more moments before pulling back with another peck on Jen's lips. She needed to breathe, needed to check in, needed a moment to come down from cloud nine.

She pressed their foreheads together and slid her hand down over Jen's arm to her waist. They were panting into the minimal space between them. Rebecca couldn't quite contain the smile that threatened to split her face in two, and when Jen started laughing—slightly nervously—she did as well.

"Just to check...are you okay with all of this?" Rebecca whispered softly as she leaned away a little, giving Jen room—room she was very unwilling to claim as she looped her fingers once more into the straps of Rebecca's jeans and pulled her closer.

"Very okay. I mean...I don't usually do this...but, you know, we're here and it feels good—*you* feel good. So yeah, I'm very okay." Jen blushed adorably, and Rebecca kissed her again— more softly, affirmingly. She liked this slightly awkward side to Jenny—especially now she'd gotten a hint of what lay beneath.

"Good, very good...so...how about we get our clothes into the dryer and go back to my room? We don't have to, you know, do anything, but—"

Jen surged forward, kissing her hard and passionately as she pressed her body against hers. Instantly Rebecca wrapped her arms around Jen, drowning in a kiss that she had zero control over, surprised to find she didn't mind the loss.

"Be quiet." Jenny husked against her lips in between kisses, and Rebecca grinned.

"I can do that." She went in for another round of kisses that quickly became familiar territory. This time she allowed her own hands to wander, sliding over the soft skin of Jen's sides and feeling goosebumps rise up under her fingertips. When Jen wrapped her arms around Rebecca's neck, she responded by pulling the other woman tighter against her, moaning into Jen's open mouth as their tongues met.

She still couldn't quite believe this was happening, that one of the scariest events of her life had led to *this*—and was about to lead to so much more. She wanted it to happen, though. She might not know Jen very well, but she was attracted to her. Anything else...well...they could figure that out later. Right now, heart fluttering, she pulled back. She kissed Jen once more—firmly, getting a bit of control back—and then untangled herself reluctantly.

As Jen watched, she wordlessly grabbed their wet clothes, threw them into the dryer, and turned the knob to a twenty-minute cycle. It should be enough, although she doubted they'd be there to collect the items once the cycle ended. With a full smile, she reached out her hand and Jen took it silently, following Rebecca up the stairs as they stayed close together, tension sparking and lips curved into excited smiles.

Jen lingered in the middle of the room as Rebecca shut the door. She locked it from the inside and turned on the standing lamp near the door as she flicked off the overhead lights, creating a bit more of a romantic atmosphere. A few seconds passed as they regarded each other, making sure they were both on the same page—that they both wanted this. They did, Rebecca decided, and any doubt was wiped away when Jen reached down to the hem of her tank top and pulled up the material, sliding it over her head and dropping it on the desk.

Rebecca was spellbound, taking in soft contours, firm breasts, shallow breathing, and a teasing smile that still held a touch of shyness. Even now, Jen skirted the line between adorable and drop dead gorgeous, and Rebecca had never been more grateful to be gay in her life. How any woman was not into girls was beyond her comprehension as she rushed forward to close the gap between them. Jen met her, wrapping her arms around Rebecca's neck and allowing her to trail her hands down Jen's bare back—something she did with abandon.

"Gorgeous," Rebecca complimented between kisses. Jen whimpered against her lips, wrapping hands in Rebecca's hair and pulling her closer. Where downstairs their kisses had been exploratory, need now caused them to become harder, sloppier. Rebecca was soon out of breath. She pulled at the hem of Jen's sweatpants and slid her hands inside to cup a small ass and press Jen closer. Jen groaned in reply, breaking the kiss.

"I was thinking of you in the shower," she confessed.

Rebecca's eyes flew open, and she pulled back just enough to meet Jen's darkened eyes. She smirked at the mischief she found there.

"You were...?" Rebecca's voice was a little gravelly. She allowed her hands to travel up impossibly soft skin, causing Jen to shiver and push closer to her so the next words to brushed over Rebecca's lips.

"I was thinking of your hands...your mouth...warming me up."

Rebecca bit back a needy groan and leaned forward, into a kiss that was met instantly. Hands wrapped into her hair, pulling her in tighter, and Rebecca dipped down a little to cup a firm ass. She guided Jenny's body against her, arranging her leg to provide a bit of stimulation even as her mouth found Jen's neck. She bit down lightly before easing the sting with her tongue.

Jenny threw her head back, moaning deliciously as she pushed her closer. "Bed...?" she gasped out.

Rebecca nodded, moving herself and Jen backwards until she could ease them down. Jen slid on top of her, settling against her as she hurried to connect their mouths again. Rebecca's hands were everywhere, exploring pronounced muscles under supple skin and gasping when Jen's leg pressed between hers.

"Fuck..." Rebecca cursed.

Jen chuckled as she dipped down to lick Rebecca's neck, then suckled the skin lightly.

Rebecca usually enjoyed the slow exploration, enjoyed taking her time, but right now she couldn't care less. Slow and steady would come later, after their first needs had been sated and the tension lessened. All she cared about right now was the feeling of Jen's breasts pressing into her chest, about the way heat surged up from any part of her body Jen touched, and about the way they were still wearing far too much clothing.

Tilting her head to the side, Rebecca allowed Jen access to her throat. She shivered as lips explored. Fumbling a little, Rebecca managed to press her leg up as well, feeling the other woman bear down onto her thigh willingly—deliciously—as she moaned. Jen's hips were grinding into Rebecca, who slid her hands to Jen's ass again to pull her closer. Urgently, she slid one hand up to tangle into drying hair as she pushed Jenny harder against her, making her bite down and making Rebecca's arousal skyrocket.

"I won't lie, I thought about taking you right there and then," Rebecca confessed breathlessly, pulling Jen up so she could chase the moan down her throat as the woman pressed harder into her in response. With an expert move, she rolled them over on the small bed, capturing Jen's wrists with her hand and pushing them up over her head as she dropped her mouth down to Jen's neck.

"Time to make up for lost opportunities," she husked against Jen's ear. Carefully, she captured a soft earlobe between her teeth and bit down lightly, causing Jenny to buck up. Now it was Rebecca's turn to set a steady rhythm with her hips as she trailed her lips down over Jen's chest until she was hovering over an already-hard nipple. She glanced up mischievously, relishing the way Jenny kept enough tension on her arms for Rebecca to have to struggle to hold them down but never enough to break the hold. Rebecca couldn't contain a smirk at the barely veiled need she found in the cloudy eyes that met hers. Gone were the awkwardness and innocence; Jen was a woman reborn.

"Please..." Jen gasped.

Rebecca swiped the flat of her tongue over the hard bud below, savoring the moan the motion produced in her new lover, and the way Jen arched up into her mouth.

"More."

Rebecca quickly fastened her mouth over Jen's nipple, sucking lightly as she swirled her tongue over and around, teasing until Jen truly tried to break the hold Rebecca still had on her arms. She tightened her grip.

Jen wrapped her legs around Rebecca's waist, pushing up into her with every tug of her lips, every bite, and every swirl of her tongue. Rebecca alternated between Jen's breasts, keeping a careful eye on Jen's face to see which of her actions had the greatest effect, just so she could replicate that.

"Tease...Terrible tease," Jen said in a haze.

Her words were cut off as Rebecca surged up, releasing hands that instantly wrapped around her to tug at her top even as she kissed Jen deeply, sloppily. Rebecca was overcome with desire now that she had seen how deliciously responsive Jen was to her ministrations. This wasn't going to last long, Rebecca could tell, but it was going to be delicious—and if it was up to her, the start of much more.

"It's only teasing...if I don't...make good on it...in the end." Rebecca answered in between kisses and soft bites to Jen's tongue and lower lip. "...and I plan to make good on it."

Jen pulled harder on her shirt in response. Rebecca peeled herself away for a moment, allowing Jen to tug the top fully off to expose small but firm breasts. Dark eyes fell on them right away, and Jen licked her lips before pulling Rebecca to her. Rebecca rushed to hold her own weight on her arms as Jen took one of her nipples in her mouth, sucking roughly. Jen wasn't teasing, Rebecca noted, and she almost sagged through her arms at the pleasure the hard stimulation produced.

"Fuck, Jen!" she groaned out, forcing Jen's head harder against her chest with one hand, balancing herself on the other. "Ohhh...fuck...perfect."

Jen took to the task with abandon, alternating between sucks and bites that soon had Rebecca right on the edge. Panting heavily, she pulled Jen away by her hair, forcing her to lie down as she settled against her side. Rebecca kissed her deeply, even as her hand travelled down Jen's firm body. She tweaked a nipple still at attention before dipping down over Jen's stomach and into the waistband of her oversized sweatpants. She wanted to show Jen what she was causing in her, show how much she wanted her, and find herself wanted in return. Jen didn't play coy, didn't stop her. Instead, she wrapped two hands in Rebecca's hair, parted her legs wider, and allowed Rebecca to slip sure fingers between already-damp folds. Rebecca was burning with need, spurred on by Jen's obvious desire.

It took a bit of searching but before long, Rebecca had Jen bucking into her hand, jumping with every rub over her clit. Jen was gasping in between kisses that had gotten even less controlled than before. As Rebecca slid her hand lower between lips she desperately wanted to taste, Jen broke the kiss, forced Rebecca's head down to her chest, and encouraged her to suckle, even as she parted her legs wider. Jen wanted this as much as she did, and Rebecca was burning up. She fought the hold on her hair to watch Jen's reaction as she slid a single finger through warm wetness and then slipped easily— so easily—inside her lover. Rebecca relished the gasp that fell from parting lips, relished the way Jen threw her head back and arched into her. Once she started moving her hand, Jen followed the motions with her hips, surging up with abandon as she forced Rebecca's head down again.

"Harder," Jen instructed.

Rebecca didn't fight her this time. She bit down on a dark nipple as she picked up the pace, pausing only a moment to add another finger before putting the muscles of her arm to work. Sharp nails dug into the skin of her back, and Rebecca was shocked at how easy this was, at how right it felt. She'd had one-night-stands where it was all awkward and tense, but Jen was open and beautiful, clear in her desires and generous with her responses. Bringing her pleasure was addictive.

"Harder..."

Rebecca drank the remnants of Jen's plea from her lips even as she complied, setting a faster pace, pressing harder, rubbing the pad of her thumb against Rebecca's clit as she fucked her. It was beautiful, thrilling, and well worth the cramping in her arm. She wrapped her other arm supportively under Jen's neck and held her tightly as she studied closed eyes, parted lips, and a chest that rose and fell rapidly. Next time, she would see all of her, Rebecca swore, next time she would taste her. For now, it was enough to feel strong walls clench around her fingers and watch Jen strain up off the bed.

She left kisses on Jen's nose, on her lips, on her cheeks, on the cheekbones Rebecca was so attracted to. She kissed her eyes and chin and captured her lips just as Jen's orgasm overtook her. Rebecca felt better than she had in a long time, observing as Jen's breath got stuck in her throat. Jenny stilled entirely for a few glorious seconds before collapsing back onto the bed in a sweaty, gasping, heap. Jen untangled her hands from the bed sheets and moved them into Rebecca's hair, pulling her down for a round of wet and uncoordinated kisses that Rebecca met with as much passion as Jen gave.

"Jesus, you are so hot," she whispered against Jen's lips.

Jen moaned, kissing her hard and deep, again and again, as she rode out the waves of pleasure still radiating from Rebecca's fingers inside of her—even though they had slowed considerably.

"You are..." Jen mirrored the compliment, devolving from hard presses to quick pecks until she finally realized how hard she had been gripping Rebecca's hair. She released her quickly, and Rebecca grinned, placing butterfly kisses on the puffy lips below. Jen was still adorably out of it, and even as Rebecca slowly pulled out her fingers—cupping Jen's sex instead—she didn't come to her senses entirely.

"I need to borrow your phone—call my parents."

Rebecca pulled back and arched a questioning eyebrow. "Huh?" she asked lamely. Jen's parents were about the furthest thing from her mind as she rode the high of having caused such obvious pleasure in her partner.

Jenny finally blinked her eyes open, and the level of need and desire Rebecca found in them sent a shock of arousal through her system. "I need to tell them I'm not coming home tonight..." Jen promised.

Rebecca grinned—an expression quickly wiped from her features by hungry lips as Jen rolled the two of them over, draping herself over Rebecca. They watched each other a moment, trailing hands over skin, savoring this instant connection and the way they fitted together so well. Later, they would lay together in the dark, talk...there would be dates, and they would get to know all about each other. Right now, they were forging their connection through an entirely different medium, one they could already tell was going to be a lot more effective.

"Happy Halloween," Rebecca finally whispered as the tension between them shifted momentarily from sexual to emotional.

"Happy Halloween," she replied, a soft smile on her features that Rebecca mirrored. They kissed languidly until passion overtook them again, ignited by greedy hands and wanting mouths.

In spite of her pleasure-soaked brain, Rebecca realized that Halloween had forever changed for her. From this point on, she would associate Halloween with Jenny and every promise that this night held for the both of them. She thought of Joe Wenton one last time, but it was no longer in fear. Without Joe, she wouldn't be here, making love to a beautiful woman on a cold, rainy Halloween. She owed him a debt of gratitude. As Jen moved down her body, Rebecca grinned and bit her lip, wrapping hands in hair that was, indeed, silky soft. In the light of day, she would find a way to pay her respects to Joe. For tonight, she was going to focus solely on Jen and the pleasure they could bring to each other. It wasn't safe outside anyway, on Halloween.

Hit and Run

Q. Kelly

Maxie

I FEEL SORRY FOR MY hero. Or heroine. I wish he or she would reach out to me. Somehow. I'd say, "Don't beat yourself up. Zachary had it coming. As a matter of fact, I'm extremely grateful. How about dinner? My treat."

I prefer a heroine over a hero. Of course I do. More fitting that way—a woman taking down the mean, abusive son of a bitch who was my husband. On the other hand, women are more prone to guilt. Yeah, I deal in stereotypes. Sue me. A man, a certain kind of man, I can see moving on from mowing Zachary down. A woman could not, not deep down in her core. She'd fret and fret and never forgive herself. Guilt and anxiety would drive her to an early death. The fear of being caught would accompany her every action.

In any case, I don't need to know much about my hero or heroine. I just want a quick meeting, a handshake, exchanged smiles. I would whisper comfort: *It's all right, it's all right, don't feel bad, he was horrible, just horrible, you did the world a favor.* Lots of encouraging smiles from me, lots of encouraging words to soothe the hero or heroine's guilt.

To look at me, to hear me talk, you'd never know I feel this way. My public face is appropriate—the grieving widow, Maxie J. Douglas, porcelain-doll blonde. I helped the police investigate. I appealed on TV for information leading to the apprehension of the driver.

Abuse is an ugly creature, and Zachary shamed me on several levels. Most importantly, how had I gotten into such a situation? How could I have let my husband do these things to me, no matter how gradually? How did my family and Zachary's not see it?

After Zachary died, my bruises took a month to go away. Some of my fractures and breaks will never heal one hundred percent, but I retain hope for my emotional scars.

Meeting my hero or heroine will bring tremendous closure, but five years have passed. I hold out little hope of this person coming forward, although I fantasize about encountering him or her. In these daydreams, I know the person immediately. How can I not? We are bonded. Forever.

This wicked person took my husband's life on Halloween night and slunk away like a coward. A terrible secret to keep.

My own appalling secret: I am thankful. Very.

In many of my fantasies, I meet this person on a Halloween night. It's appropriate, considering Halloween is when Zachary died. Maybe the person knocks on my door and is wearing a Jason mask from *Friday the 13th*. He or she merely intends to glimpse me, to make sure I am all right, perhaps to fleetingly touch my hand as I transfer a Snickers bar to him or her.

It's a cold night, and I wear an orange sweater. Tiredness nips at me, but then I see the eyes behind the mask. Will something inside me go *clickety click whoosh bang gosh darn THIS IS IT!* and I'll know? Might the excited chattering of little goblins and princesses fade into the background? Will the trees around us sigh in approval and rustle their branches in applause? Will the moon sprinkle a handful of fairy dust onto us, two sad and doomed creatures?

Might we not even need to exchange words? Might my eyes murmur: "Thank you, dearie," and will shock, and then some sort of confused understanding, appear in the person's gaze? I might need to pat his or her hand and say soothingly, "You are forgiven. Go forth. Live. You gave me my life back, and now I give yours back. This is my treat to you. Go on. Go on now! Live!"

PENNY

I used to be semi-famous. I still am, I suppose, in the way that people who used to be semi-famous remain semi-famous. The wonder of newspapers and magazines looking to fill anniversary issues and their "whatever happened to…" quotas. The miracles of Internet searches. Type "plane crash survivors," for example. Or "plane crash sole survivors."

When I was seven years old, my father won car salesman of the year at his dealership. The prize: a weeklong trip to Disney World. The run-up to the trip stretched painfully long, and I remember the colors more than anything.

Purple and blue: the two sand pails and shovels my mother bought at the dollar store before we left.

Yellow: my father's scowl and the curl of his lips as he said, "Disney World ain't nowhere near the beach."

Pink: my mother's cheeks. "Oh."

"It's an hour away," Dad continued.

Mom brightened. White. Gaily. "That's close."

"No," Dad said. "It's not. Why do we want to rent a car on vacation? Besides, pails and that crap, we can buy down there. Why haul them on the plane? You think we got space galore?"

Mom turned a sad violet. "I got excited, that's all. The pails were cheap."

Dad noticed me lurking and listening. He smiled and hugged Mom. Beckoned me over to share in their embrace. "You excited, baby girl? You and your momma get to experience your first-ever plane rides together."

The plane took off from Dulles in Northern Virginia and crashed on landing in Orlando. Number of people on the plane: one hundred fifty. Nice round figure. Number of dead: one hundred and forty-nine. Bit of a jagged figure, eh?

Here's an interesting fact from Wikipedia: Since 1970, two-thirds of plane crash sole survivors have either been children or members of the flight crew. Why? Well, it's not exactly the kind of thing a person can experiment with. Some people have theories, conjectures. For instance, children are more flexible, their bones more spongy. Children are smaller, so that means more objects can break their fall and bear their weight. As for flight crew members, they're sometimes strapped in and are closer to windows so they can escape.

I don't much remember my parents, so I fill in the blanks. I pretend to remember my mother giggling and prepping for weeks: sunblock, shovels, pails, swimsuits, diets to fit into her swimsuit. She frowned only when my dad was around. The memory of him scolding her for buying pails, I'm ninety percent sure that's a true memory.

I escaped the crash relatively unscathed. Fractured skull, broken arm, broken collarbone. Second-degree burns. My father's parents raised me.

Dylan, my son, is six years old. For the record, I am a six too—forty-six. Dylan was a surprise—the result of a fling with a much-married man, the father of one of my third-grade students.

Uh-oh. Yes.

Anyway, Dylan is all I have. In other words, I am all he has. He has no father, and my sole surviving grandparent, Pa-Pa Joe, is a wrinkled, shriveled, ninety-seven-year-old. Second cousins or cousins twice removed, whatever the difference is, round out my family.

Dylan is beautiful—blond hair, blue eyes, fair skin. He's the type of person who gets an eleven on scales of one to ten. Me, I'm plain. Brown hair, brown eyes. People look at my son, and their eyes go wide. I can tell what they're thinking: *What an exquisite child! Beautiful!* Then they look at me, the woman holding the hand of the gorgeous boy, and disappointment flickers across their faces. How can such an enchanting child belong to plain me? Ah! I must be the nanny or maid. Stepmother? Nope. I'm Dylan's mother, and too bad if people don't like it. He's mine. All mine. For now and maybe forever? I can hope.

This first day of August dawns humid and oppressive. Even the birds and their songs seek respite in shady and hidden spaces. Dylan takes no notice of the heat as he abandons himself under the backyard water sprinkler.

October 31 is a date in the distance, but it has become part of me. Zachary Douglas died almost five years ago on

Halloween night. I won't say he "passed away" or "moved to a better place" or "went to be with God." The plain truth is that Zachary Douglas died.

I killed him.

Five years ago, I promised that I would turn myself in on this particular Halloween if I hadn't already. I told myself that five years was more than enough time to flit among my second cousins or cousins twice removed to find someone marginally suitable to raise Dylan. I tried. I did. I even looked up the difference between second cousin and cousin twice removed—and promptly forgot it. My cousins live so far away. How could Dylan visit me if I were in prison? He would forget me. As for my friends...they are wonderful, but none of them are exactly right for my son.

I need to stop. I'm excusing. Justifying. That's wrong.

How does an airline rationalize the deaths of one hundred forty-nine people? How do you rationalize not turning yourself in for killing a man? The answer is simple. You don't rationalize. You can't rationalize. The best you can do is pretend—pretend you're doing the right thing for your baby boy. You pretend it's because you grew up without parents, and you want better for your son. You find yourself wishing your child was disabled in some way. Brittle bone disease, Down syndrome, cerebral palsy—any disability will do. Handicaps are something to be whispered about, tiptoed around, something skulking, something hidden. People hate imperfections, and they wouldn't question my motives too deeply, this mother of a child with disabilities. No one could fault me for not immediately going to the police. Who else can take care of this child? No one but his mother.

Alas, Dylan is perfectly healthy.

You pretend so much, you pretend so damn hard, you believe. Rather, you pretend to believe. You hope that the moment when your life turned upside down for the second time magically dissipates, goes away. It never does, and the guilt eats and eats at you. More and more. It swallows you whole.

An airline is soulless. I am not.

MAXIE

Three months after Zachary died, I told my parents the truth—that he'd been a wife beater. They looked at me funny.

My mother said, "Oh, now there. I'm sure it wasn't that bad."

I said, "Yes, it was."

Panic crawled across her face. "I see."

I have yet to tell Zachary's parents or his sister, but surely somewhere inside them, the truth whispers. It must.

Zachary's sister is named Alice, and she was twenty when her brother died. I often wonder if she is my heroine. There's something unsettling and undefinable about her. My husband was full of energy. Electric. Crackling. Alice, on the other hand, reminds me of a bomb—coldly metallic and sexy. You don't know what the bomb is thinking, which color wire to cut, and when it might go off. If it's even live. You know nil, and it frightens and thrills you at the same time.

At the funeral, her eyes, Zachary's blue eyes, flickered a faint and sad smile in my direction. It was the most emotion I'd seen from her.

My husband and his sister were born ten years apart, and they were never close. Nor were Alice and I close. But, yes, with the passage of time, I have begun to wonder if she is the person I am so thankful for. Did she plot? For how long? Did she procure a Ford Taurus, pay cash, leave it unregistered, and extinguish life from her brother? Did she suspect what he did to me? Did he do things to her too?

Families. A stew of secrets.

Alice and I have never discussed Zachary's death, nor do I imagine we will. For her sake, I hope she didn't do it. What a terrible burden. Killing someone accidentally is one thing, but plotting it…your own brother…

PENNY

I didn't mean to kill Zachary, and it is vanishingly possible I did not.

That Halloween night, it was raining on and off, pounding at times. About half the usual number of trick-or-treaters knocked on my door that night.

Ghosts. Ogres. Witches. Demons. In the past few years, I have become one of them; only, my ugliness lives on the inside.

I felt generous that night and gave the children full-sized candy bars.

"Aw!" said one tiny ogre. "Thanks, Ms. Powell!"

I beamed. "You're welcome."

Despite the rain, police recovered paint samples from Zachary's body. They were matched to a 1996 pacific green metallic Ford Taurus. There are lots of them, especially in the DC area. In a way, the commonness of my car has paved my freedom these past few years.

What are the chances that two of these Tauruses happened along the same road in the same time frame, and one struck a deer while the other struck a person?

Not high. But I do know odds. I'm a sole survivor, remember? It *is* possible I am not Zachary Douglas's killer. Ha! Talk about astounding denial. Of course I killed him.

Dylan was teething, crying through the night a lot. He enjoyed car rides, and I got to know the back roads of Northern Virginia pretty well. Many of those nights, I drove half-asleep. Or two-thirds asleep. I had not realized how out of it I was. It's like being drunk—your judgment is clouded, but you think you're fine.

So, that Halloween, close to midnight, my brain was fuzzy, overwrought. Dylan howled and screeched in the backseat, but the rain had died down.

Then: THUNK.

I swerved. Fishtailed, performed the driving stunts you see in movies. Adrenaline jackrabbited through me, and, miracle of miracles, Dylan stopped crying. The car came to rest on the side of the road, and my immediate thought was that I'd hit a deer. Country road. No houses around—people hit deer all the time.

I got out of the car, and a light mist drizzled my nose. Ghostly fog floated in the distance, and an owl hooted. The road was long and winding. That made me afraid someone would careen by and make mashed potatoes of me and Dylan. Determined to be quick, I retrieved a flashlight from my glove compartment, kissed Dylan, and shone the beam across the road.

Nothing except the ghostly fog creeping closer.

Absolutely nothing.

No sounds, either.

I looked along both sides of the road to no avail.

So the deer had gone on its merry way. It must not be badly hurt. I couldn't say the same for my car. The front bumper of my Taurus was dented like you wouldn't believe, the passenger side especially. I hoped my insurance gremlins wouldn't put up much fuss.

I climbed back into the car. Dylan gave a little sleepy baby smile, which I returned. We turned around and drove home.

Me back then, five years ago: Penelope Mary Powell, forty-one-year-old teacher of third-grade kids. Adorable, wee, wuvely third-grade kids. The only grandchild of paternal grandparents who raised me and who thoughtfully left me their house with its attached two-car garage. At the time, I used half of the garage for my car, the other half for storage.

I parked my Taurus there, hauled my son out, and we passed out in our respective beds.

Deer deer deer deer deer

I never watched the news, not the five o'clock, six o'clock, or the eleven o'clock. Nope. I'm not that kind of person. The next morning, however, I clicked on the TV and sought out a broadcast. The lead story concerned a hit-and-run. Same approximate place I had been, same time frame. Zachary Douglas hadn't been able to sleep—happened often for him—so he went for a jog. He loved the rain, so that was not a problem. A car hit him, and he died.

How extraordinary. What a coincidence, I thought, my brain clinging to denial. I'd shone the flashlight. I'd listened. I would've seen the body. I would've heard mewled whimpers for help.

Apparently not.

The next year crept by. I never again took my son for a nighttime drive. The Taurus sat unused in the garage, and I bought a Toyota Camry to get by. I kept expecting police to ram down my door and arrest me, or storm into my classroom at school. Guilt carved up my insides. Three times, I went to a police station to free my conscience. I sat in my Camry and tried to will myself inside. Each time, I told myself that the punishment I was already suffering sufficed—the lifelong guilt, the burden, the haunting, oppressive dreams. Why punish Dylan too? I needed to find someone suitable to raise him before I could turn myself in.

And now Zachary has been dead nearly five years.

His widow, Maxie Douglas, has cautious eyes. Don't think I know this because I've gone up to her. No, I know from TV, from newspaper photos. The closest I've physically gotten to Maxie has been across the room in a coffee shop. The shop was down the street from Maxie's house, and I needed to do something, anything. So I went twice a week in the months after Zachary's death, and sometimes Maxie was there. On those occasions, I turned and left immediately.

Maxie fascinates me. So does Alice, Zachary's sister. I wish I knew if she had any association with a Ford Taurus. Surely, the police checked her out. She must have an alibi. Free and clear. It's just...her eyes, there's something in her eyes. They draw me to her. I wish I could tell Alice what I did, but she scares me too much for that. If I am not Zachary's killer, she is.

I will tell Maxie. One day. Soon. She'll understand. She will grant me the forgiveness I desperately need. Please. Please.

MAXIE

I run into Alice today at the mall. Victoria's Secret. Lingerie. No, I am not dating anyone. I have not since Zachary died, although I have been thinking it is time. I am at Victoria's Secret for myself. I've always enjoyed the smooth, decadent feel of a good piece of lingerie. Now I can wear a teddy or garter or what have you—and see absolutely no bruises at all.

My husband's sister is examining bras, and I debate approaching her. I could turn away, and no one would be the wiser. *Don't be stupid*, I tell myself. I nail a smile to my face and go over to Alice.

"Hi!" I exclaim.

She looks up, surprise lacing her smile. "Maxie. Hello." I can't tell if she is pleased to see me.

"Been a while."

She plays along. The game of social niceties. "Gosh, yes," she says. "Three years?"

"You look great." Alice, like Zachary, has always been stunning.

Alice flutters a hand in feigned embarrassment. She's somehow grown softer. "Oh, thanks. So do you."

"I guess you're done with college?"

"Mmm. For now. Might get a master's in a few years."

"Are you working?"

"Here and there," Alice says.

My associate's degree is in communications, but Zachary forbade me to work while we were married. "I answer phones at Tyler's Auto Repair," I say. "Across from the mall."

"I know the place."

Why auto repair? Maybe so I can keep an eye out for Ford Tauruses with damaged front bumpers.

I gesture at the lacy pink bra Alice holds. "Pretty."

She smiles, and I wonder if she is seeing anyone. What keeps me from asking? A dark wave of loneliness hits me. Zachary has been dead five years, and when we were married, he isolated me through his abuse. There's been no excuse for my isolation since his death. I suddenly want to know his sister—at least to suss out if she is my heroine.

"Do you miss him?" she asks. She has moved closer, and her breath blows hot onto my face.

Pleasure and arousal spread through me. I never expected Alice to take an interest in little ol' moi. But now a vexing dilemma—lie or tell the truth? What is the truth anyway? Many moments, I do miss Zachary. His deep breaths in bed. His lips on mine. His arms around me. The fullness of him inside me. What would the fullness of Alice's fingers inside me be like? Being alone is...well, let's not get into that.

"Do you miss him?" I answer.

Alice sets the pink bra down. "I should go."

My heart falls. Go? Why? We've just started our conversation. I reach for her and put my hand on her arm. "I would like to have lunch or dinner sometime this week."

Her eyes search my face, reaching into my thoughts. "Are you sure you want lunch or dinner, Maxie?" Her voice is low and shrewd. Interested.

Yes. Oh yes. One hundred percent sure.

"I don't do relationships," Alice tells me over spaghetti thirty minutes later.

"Oh," I say, a bit of chain-restaurant breadstick lodging in my throat. Alice's forthrightness is admirable—also scary. The statement itself...she doesn't do relationships. Does she assume I want one? Do I reek of desperation? "Why, uh..." I wash down the breadstick with water. "Why not?"

She answers with a question. "Did you know I'm gay?"

"Can't say I did."

"Are you surprised?"

My fork hasn't been properly cleaned. Unidentifiable orange goop sticks to its backside. "Nothing about you would surprise me."

Alice evaluates the statement. She holds it in her hand like it is a crystal ball and surveys it from all sides. "Why is that," she says at last. Not in a questioning way but rather in a genuine and happy way.

I wave for the waiter and show him my fork. He blushes and whisks it off. A gleaming fork takes its place.

"Don't bother," Alice says. "Please."

Don't bother with what? I'm confused.

Alice drops my fresh utensil on the floor, extracts her fork from a mound of spaghetti, licks it clean with her darting, pink tongue, and hands it to me.

"Use mine," she says. "Please."

Oh boy. Do I ever wish she did relationships.

PENNY

I could not keep Dylan out of the garage forever. I knew this. So I never made a show of keeping it off limits. One day when he was three, I casually mentioned, "See how messed up this car is? Yeah, Mommy hit a deer one night. Silly Mommy. But the deer was okay. It wasn't hurt."

He made a face. "Big mess!"

Of course, he will never know particulars, such as date, time, and location. And a day will come when he asks questions. Even if the car is gone by then, he might ask: "Mom, you know that car you used to have? A Ford Taurus? Really damaged front bumper? Why didn't you ever take it in to be fixed?"

What will I say? Probably some nonsense about how it hadn't been running well anyway, and I never got around to calling a tow truck.

Or I could get rid of it soon. Like now. ASAP. I've planned it plenty of times in my mind—a drive to a lake, pushing the car in.

Fears stop me. The car being recovered, tied back to me, an investigator asking how it ended up in this body of water, running a search on accidents involving such cars...

Plus, I always planned to turn myself in after I found a new home for Dylan. Well, that is not happening. My new idea is to go on vacation several states over. Me and Dylan in the Taurus. I start the car every few weeks, and it runs fine. Whichever state we go to, I'll take the car to a junkyard and have it crushed into rubble. I'll rent another vehicle for the drive home. Simple. Dylan is young enough that any memories he has of the Taurus can be manipulated.

Memory. A marvel.

I must decide where to go on vacation and when. Winter break? Or Thanksgiving break, which is sooner? Or even a long Labor Day weekend a month from now?

I decide on Missouri, around St. Louis. Not too close, not too far. Perfect. Dylan and I will leave on a Thursday. It's not as fitting as getting rid of the car on Halloween, but it will do.

MAXIE

After the spaghetti dinner, I follow Alice to a hotel. Most of my life, I've been a proper lady—listened to my parents, crossed my legs, did every piece of homework and extra credit. I even waited until marriage to have sex. Look where that got me.

Why did Zachary marry me? I like to think that at some point, he sincerely loved me. However, when I look back, I see no reason why anyone should have truly loved me. I was young. Still am. Didn't know who I was. I only knew to follow rules and obey orders to please others. Zachary intuited this, I am sure. Swooped in and grabbed me for himself. He found a punching bag who only wanted to please him.

Alice. Wild Alice. My heroine?

I kept her fork from dinner. Snuck it into my purse as Alice and I left the table at dinner. She paid. And she paid for the room, too.

I am in the bathroom now. On the toilet. Willing a tiny drop of urine to fall. Anything to delay our consummation, because it will be the first and last time. How can it not be? Alice Douglas does not do relationships. I want our only time together to last as long as possible. If that means starting later, that is fine.

The drop of urine eventually falls, and I wash my hands. My face in the mirror appears terrified, as pale as the kiddie ghosts who roamed the streets hours before Zachary died. He'd been in good spirits that night—joked around with me and the trick-or-treaters. He talked about us going to Disney World someday.

Alice is naked when I return to the room. She stands in front of the window, its curtains closed. She is a goddess—beauty beyond imagination—but disappointment tickles me. I would have preferred slow, teasing disrobing.

Alice tilts her head. "What's wrong, Maxie?"

My gaze wades into her lush breasts, the cursive curls of her hips, the bold, light hair between her legs. I shake my head. "Nothing."

She turns to display her back. "I have a tattoo."

She does. It's a hockey mask like Jason Voorhees wears in the *Friday the 13th* movies. I bet you're imagining a gleaming white mask with unblemished red paint. Wrong. This mask is after Jason has been on several killing sprees. It is worn and filthy. It's a weary, exhausted mask. It's a mask tired of life.

I recognize the blue eyes peering out at me from behind the mask, but whether they are Alice's or Zachary's, I cannot tell. The mask gives them a reptilian glint.

The tattoo scares me.

"I felt I needed to show you," Alice says, her back still to me. "In case you happened to see it later."

"That's..." I swallow. "That's good thinking." Questions race through my mind: *Why Jason? What does this tattoo mean? Are you crazy? How scared should I be?*

Alice turns again and holds her arms out. "Come here."

I set my questions aside—as if I've been on a picnic and have decided it's time to wrap up and box the leftover food, put everything back in the picnic basket. I'm too scared to leave the room. What might Alice do to me? So I go into the embrace of my dead husband's sister. It is the most daring act of my life.

Alice takes my clothes off. Her eyes are gentle, nothing like those behind the mask. She spreads me on the bed and kisses my stomach, then my breasts. Her touch, sweet and tender, awakens sleeping desires within me. The tattoo gradually disappears from my mind. I like being with Alice. With a woman.

"Will you kiss me on the lips?" I ask.

Her lips tug up. "I would love to."

Her expression gives me hope that the unthinkable will happen. Maybe she will stay the night.

While Alice kisses me, I see Zachary's face. Not as it was five years ago, but as it must be now—rotting, decaying, worms squelching out of his eye sockets.

"What's wrong?"

Even the voice has ceased to be Alice's and is Zachary's rumbling baritone. A leer, and any trace of Alice disappears.

"Hi, baby," Zachary says. "Miss me?"

I blink furiously, and Alice returns. So does the memory of her tattoo.

PENNY

I am stuck. Labor Day weekend has arrived, and I cannot get rid of the Taurus. Let me explain. Everything I have done up until now has been passive. By way of example: hiding myself, stowing the car, doing nothing. I did go to the coffee shop after Zachary died, but that doesn't count, because I ran whenever I saw Maxie.

Pulling the car out of the garage and exposing it to sunlight—melting it under the harsh rays of truth—and driving it thirteen hours to St. Louis is rather active. So is taking it to a junkyard. I can't do it. I can't actively conspire to conceal a killing, not even with myself.

I did try. Dylan and I packed our bags. We got into the car five minutes ago, he in his back-seat booster chair.

"Mommy!" he cried. "Turn the key, and let's go!" Excited little fella. I'd shown him photos of St. Louis, of the Mississippi River. The old-timey riverboat we'd go on.

"Mommy is not feeling well," I whispered to my son. "I'm sorry. Really sorry. Let's get in the other car and go to the park."

An opportunity presents itself at the beginning of October—nothing to do with the car and everything to do with the widow Maxie J. Douglas.

Filled with shame and self-loathing, I venture back to the coffee shop near Maxie's place. The coffee shop has spared no expense for Halloween. It's been turned into a veritable haunted house. Bats hang from every nook and cranny, as do spiders. Ghosts open their mouths in frozen howls, and devils smirk everywhere. I hate it, but at least there aren't any Jason masks from *Friday the 13th*. I can tolerate anything but him.

I ignore the less-than-savory decorations, order a doughnut, and settle into an armchair by the window. Maxie shows up less than ten minutes later. Not alone. No, she is with Zachary's sister, the mysterious Alice Douglas. Double the trouble. My pulse thuds. My skin itches. I watch these two women, both blond and blue-eyed like my son. I soak in every detail: the closeness of their poses, their easy but awkward smiles, their little touches and lingering gazes. They remind me of... Could it be? Are they a pair? Together? Yes. The urge to crack their newly-in-love perfection seizes me.

They sit. They laugh. I strain to hear their conversation. The gist goes like this:

Maxie: "Are you sure you won't consider dinner this week?"
Alice: "It would lead to more. We shouldn't go there."
Maxie: "We're adults. What's wrong with this?"
Alice: "I don't do relationships. I don't."
Maxie: "But why?"
Alice: "I just don't."

Guilt assails me for eavesdropping on their conversation, so I distance myself. Plus, I'm happy. These women aren't in love.

Nothing like that. A few moments later, Alice leaves. After fifteen minutes, she has not returned. It has come down to this. Years of hiding, and it's come down to this moment. I know what I must do. I feel right, at peace. I close my paperback novel and approach the widow, Maxie J. Douglas. She needs me. My life will change dramatically. I will either become much happier or much less happier, nothing in between. I sit next to the wife of the man I killed, the woman who has been screwing her own sister-in-law, but my presence passes unnoticed. A book—*Purple Haze* by Raymond Mondale—has captured her attention.

I clear my throat. Still no reaction.

And then she looks up with light cornflower blue eyes. She really is beautiful.

"Hi," I say. "Um, hey."

"Yes?" she says cautiously.

I've no idea how to continue. "My name is, uh, ah…" Should I give my real name? Yes. All or nothing. "Penelope Powell."

"Penelope Powell."

"Call me Penny, like the coin."

A half smile. "All right, Penny."

"I apologize, but I couldn't help hearing part of your conversation with the woman who left a while ago. I wanted to make sure you were okay."

Gratitude settles into her eyes. "Thank you." She sticks out her hand. "I'm Maxie."

We shake. "Nice to meet you."

Electricity passes between us, just as much as between her and Alice. Or maybe that is wishful thinking.

MAXIE

I fall in love with Penelope Powell. I do not deny that it might be because I am on the rebound from Alice's dismissal, but the feelings are true. In less than a month, we are inseparable. She introduces me to her son. Tells me about being the sole survivor of a plane crash. Tells me about the colors of the experience—the orange smell of burned flesh, the loud blue of tears, the green hue of blood. One night, I drink too much wine and tell her that Zachary abused me. I tell her I'm glad he is dead.

For some time, Penny becomes a different person, like a statue who has heard too many secrets and can't bear any more. I see cracks pulling her apart.

"You're happy he's dead?" she says in a relieved croak.

"Yes." I tell her my fantasy about my hero or heroine. When she gets a *look* in her eyes, I realize she's the one and that I knew it all along.

She breaks into tears, waterfalls of tears. I hold her, and she tells me about that night, shows me the Taurus with the Zachary-sized dent. Her guilt is heavy, palpable.

I told you, didn't I? That a woman couldn't move on from something like this.

I need a purpose, something to do. I agree that Penny needs to take care of the car.

"I'll make the drive," I volunteer. "To St. Louis. I'll get rid of it for you. Give me your driver's license, the car title, and whatever else is necessary. If I dye my hair, I could pass for you. Salvage yards probably don't look too closely at paperwork."

She nods gratefully, and, a week later, on Halloween night, I pick up the Taurus from her house. Trick-or-treaters are long gone, and it feels appropriate to begin the process of dumping the car exactly five years after Zachary died. I have spent the past few hours handing out Tootsie Rolls to children in my neighborhood. Zachary always insisted on selecting the candy we would distribute. I've never told anyone this, but I will tell

Penny someday: I used to be afraid Zachary would poison the candy, that he'd buy a thin needle and inject the stuff. My husband was that crazy and mean.

I kiss Penny good-bye. "Be careful, love," she whispers. "I'm a coward to make you do this."

"You make me do nothing. I'm happy to help. Seriously."

A feeling of utmost power emboldens me as I take the first turn out of Penny's neighborhood. Here I am, a formerly battered wife who cowered at the sight of her husband, driving the weapon used to kill him. Who's the boss? Who's in charge now, Zachary, huh? Up yours!

It is stupid, I know, but I drive the car home, to the house I used to share with my husband. Because it is night and my neighborhood is dark, I don't worry about my neighbors making any connections. Besides, I love the thrills running up my spine, the risks, the anticipation. I am more alive than ever, and Zachary is more dead than ever.

I've decked the house out for Halloween. A giant spider glares from queenly webbing on the roof. A zombie head growls from near the front step. Sheet ghosts drift among the trees.

Inside the house, I find the boxes of Zachary's photos and odds and ends I packed a long while ago. I load them into the car. Somewhere on the way to St. Louis, I'll trash them.

I grab the last box and lock the front door behind me. Ten minutes later, the police pull me over. Busted taillight. I never noticed. Of course. My luck.

ALICE

Guard, I will be honest with you, but you have to try to believe me, okay? I don't belong here. I didn't do it. Will you sit and listen a moment? Great. Thanks. I really do appreciate it. An open mind, that's all I ask. Are you ready? Great, okay.

My brother always reckoned himself a stud and a genius. Truth is, he came out of our mother's vagina a no-good boy and stayed that way. Oh, Zachary had his nice moments. He helped puppies sometimes, burned them other times. Made tomato soup for our grandma but "accidentally" spilled it on her. She went to the hospital and was never the same after that.

With some people, it's hard to tell they're evil. I could always tell with Zachary. The hardness and flatness in his eyes, but I was his sister. I knew him. Other people didn't and were blind to what I saw. He liked women, weak women. Maxie certainly was one, and when she came up to me that day at Victoria's Secret, I hoped she would go away. No such luck.

I tried to make nice. "Do you miss him?" I asked.

Pleasure flushed her cheeks. "Do *you* miss him?" Her voice was timid.

I had no use for echolocation loops. "I should go," I said.

Her face fell, and she laid her hand on my arm. "I would like to have lunch or dinner sometime this week."

I saw something in her gaze. A flicker of... I didn't know—otherness? Evil? Similar to Zachary and yet different. I won't lie. It scared me. Especially with what I knew. Shortly before my brother died, he told me that his wife was crazy. Like certifiably crazy, as in hallucinations, multiple personality disorder, schizophrenia. One day, he was tossing back beer after beer at a cookout. He shot me a lopsided grin and said: "Her other personality is named Penny. Can you believe it? Penelope Powell. She's a teacher and has an illegitimate son named Dylan."

"Has she sought help?"

Zachary tossed empty beer cans to the grass and crushed them under his feet. "Nah. I kind of like Penny." He winked. "Almost as much as I like you."

I waited, but he didn't elaborate. Later, after Zachary died, I considered telling you police guys what my brother had shared but decided not to. What point would it serve? Maxie seemed fine. We were around each other a lot for days—talking with TV reporters, appealing for help on TV, that kind of stuff. I never got a flash of this Penelope Powell. Zachary had been pulling my leg. He loved to lie.

Lunch or dinner with Maxie was a bad idea. I knew it, but I couldn't abandon her. I figured I'd investigate a little, see if she was still possibly mentally ill. Get her help if she needed it.

"Are you sure you want lunch or dinner, Maxie?" I asked.

She beamed. "I'm sure."

We went to a cheap spaghetti place. Food was decent. Afterward, we kissed each other on the cheek and parted ways. She seemed fine—odd but not insane.

She showed up on my doorstep at the beginning of October and said she was sorry, but she couldn't stop thinking about me since that night we slept together.

Slept together! Whoa. I tried to reason with her. Told her no such thing happened. She insisted it did and proffered a hotel credit card receipt in my name. Well, that sure explained the card I thought I'd misplaced. I found it in my purse one day later.

Guard, she was mad at me. You see? I wasn't interested in her romantically, so she framed me. I didn't do it! I swear. What kind of sister kills her brother? Help me. Please.

Hey, you know what? You're awfully pretty, and I get lonesome. How about it? You have kind eyes, I can tell. Look into my face. That's right. Come on. You know I'm telling the truth. I didn't kill my brother. That wife of his and her lover, Penny, did it. I can't be found guilty. I can't.

Dr. Elisabetta Vogel

Alice Penelope DOUGLAS has been a patient at Meadowbrook Sands Center, a mental institution, for the past ten (10) years. She was admitted after being found not guilty due to insanity in the death of her brother, Zachary Douglas. She received several psychiatric diagnoses, including multiple personality disorder and schizophrenia. Her three main personalities were herself, a woman named Maxie, who was Zachary's wife, and a woman named Penelope Powell, who was blamed for killing Zachary.

From the beginning, Alice Douglas implicated Maxie Douglas and Penelope Powell for killing her brother and covering it up, but it was Alice the police pulled over five years after the fact, driving the Ford Taurus used to kill Zachary Douglas. Alice Douglas identified herself to the police officer as Maxie Douglas and tried to flee. She was quickly apprehended.

It appears that the Penelope Powell personality has been with Alice since childhood, but the Maxie Douglas personality did not emerge until a couple of years after Zachary died. This personality allowed Alice to bridge the chasm between Penny and Alice.

Thanks to a combination of intensive therapy and medications, much progress has been made on returning Alice Douglas to such a state that she can be released into the general population.

As a child, she most likely suffered heavy abuse by her brother. Alice recounts one Halloween night in particular. She was seven years old and trick-or-treating with a couple of friends and one set of parents (not her own). She dressed as if she was going to the beach (it was unseasonably warm for the end of October). She wore swim goggles and a swimsuit. Instead of a plastic pumpkin container or another traditional

Halloween accessory for collecting candy, she toted a purple sand pail. The sweet, beachy smell of sunblock filled her nostrils. About halfway through her trick-or-treating, she noticed that a red Ford Taurus was following her group. The person behind the wheel wore a Friday the 13th Jason mask. Alice didn't recognize the car or the mask, but somehow she knew the driver was her brother. He liked to intimidate her, and it was only a matter of time before he crossed the line from intimidation into something worse.

It happened that night after she got home, after her parents retired to bed. Wearing the Jason mask, Zachary tied Alice's hands behind her back, duct taped her mouth shut, and used a lighter to burn the upper parts of her arms. In the following years, she sustained broken bones and more, which she attributed to being clumsy and a variety of other causes. At one point, child services investigated, but as far as I can tell, nothing was decided or done. In an effort to cope and survive, her psyche fragmented and Penelope Powell was born.

When Alice turned sixteen and got her driver's license, she decided that one day she would kill her brother. It remains uncertain whether she was consciously aware of this decision, but subconsciously, the matter had been resolved. The Penelope Powell personality bought a 1996 pacific green metallic Ford Taurus (red would have been too obvious, she says). She also got the Jason mask tattooed on her back. It covered up most of the scars Zachary inflicted on her. She was determined that her brother would no longer hold power over her. She knew he often couldn't sleep at night and would go running, so every Halloween night, she waited for him to go out. The Halloween when she was twenty, he finally did. She turned off her headlights and followed him until she (or "Penelope Powell") saw the opportunity to hit him. She slipped on a Jason mask she had bought and performed the deed. Afterward, she drove the car to a self-storage space, where she switched it with her usual car. At the time, Alice was a student at a college about an hour away from the accident site. She lived alone in her apartment, and because police ruled Zachary's death as a hit-and-run, Alice was never seriously questioned.

For a couple of years, the "Penelope Powell" personality was able to keep her guilt at bay, but enough finally broke through that Maxie Douglas had to be invented, complete with sets of new and refurbished memories. Maxie's purpose was to give both Alice and Penny outlets that the other personality could not. Maxie, like Alice, was abused. She allowed for an expression of happiness over Zachary's death. In Maxie dwelled the possibility that Alice would become aware of what she had done under the guise of another personality. Maxie's purpose was to link Alice and Penny.

Alice's parents admit they were aware of the abuse, and Alice has grown close to her second cousin, Philip Newell, during her time here. Philip is eager to have Alice home with him, and I have every confidence in his ability to support Alice.

My recommendation is for full release as soon as possible.

Sincerely,
Dr. Elisabetta Vogel

ALICE

Well, that was close. That's ten years of my life gone, wasted, but it is what it is. Better a mental institution than prison. I never thought it would work. I mean, multiple personalities *plus* schizophrenia? Who falls for that, right?

Turns out a lot of people want to believe. Never mind that I hadn't done any research. I did what I could—strained to recall snippets from movies such as *Fight Club* and *Sybil* and read a few books here and there. It was my only choice. I was caught driving the murder weapon five years after I mowed down my brother. You'd have done the same in my place, unless you're a coward who rolls over.

Funny thing happened, though. In the years I spent with Maxie and Penny...they became real. I hear them in my head all the time. I was sane when I entered Meadowbrook Sands, but maybe I'm coming out insane! Maxie and Penny have become demons possessing me.

Ha ha.

You don't believe the doctors, do you? Please say you don't. I'm sane. For real. I was sane all this time. Just faking.

Why did I kill my brother? Did he abuse me? Yeah, he did, but that's in the past. I did what I had to do, and life begins anew. I'm only thirty-five years old. I'll meet a fantastic woman, and we'll have kids. Maybe we'll name our firstborn Dylan.

Life is good. So good. World, here I come!

P.S. Yes, I said life begins anew. But my parents knew what Zachary was doing, and they did nothing. I'll get 'em sometime. Just you wait and see.

A Lesson in Magic

Cori Kane

"Halloween sucks," Erin said to the barkeeper as
he set a beer in front of her. She held his eyes for a moment,
and they seemed amused. He had probably heard too many
half-drunk patrons complaining about life to be impressed by
her comment.

He looked down at his attire. "At least you didn't have to
wear a stupid ass costume to work today. I'm pretty sure you're
not even wearing one now, are you?"

She gave him an easy smile. "I'm dressed as a person who
hates Halloween."

"So, mainly you're dressed as yourself?"

Her smile grew wider, and she showed him some teeth.

Chuckling, he turned away to serve another customer.

Erin picked up her beer and took a sip, swiveling on
her barstool to survey the bar. She knew most of the people
present—they were friends of her friend Melanie, who had
rented the bar for the evening. Melanie *loved* Halloween. In
Erin's opinion, she was obsessed with it. But her friend said it
was the only night of the year she felt free to celebrate something
other than roughly two thousand years of Christianity, and
Erin couldn't disagree with that assessment. She also didn't

disagree with free booze or humoring her best friend for one evening out of the year, and that was why she was at *Jinxed* on All Hallow's Eve instead of on her couch watching an assortment of more-ridiculously-funny-than-scary movies, which she would have vastly preferred.

"Hey, you made it."

Erin was drawn from her thoughts by a familiar voice close to her ear and a hand on her shoulder. She turned and looked at the Scarecrow from *The Wizard of Oz*, who was, in real life, Melanie's husband Charlie. He gave her a goofy grin.

"Hey, you look great," she told him as he hugged her.

"Thanks. And you look...like yourself. How did you get past Mel without her sending you home to change?"

"She hasn't seen me yet." Erin tried a smile, but only managed to contort her face into a mask of embarrassment.

Charlie rolled his eyes at her. "Do you know where she is?" He looked around, but it was crowded at the bar and he was not very tall.

"I think I heard her belting 'Monster Mash' in the other room earlier."

"There's karaoke?" Charlie's eyes lit up in obvious anticipation of whatever epic hymn his mind conjured himself crushing—or possibly killing—later.

"I didn't say that," Erin deadpanned.

He frowned. "You shouldn't tease about something as serious as karaoke, Erin. Not when you're in desperate need of being protected from the wrath of the Wicked Witch of the West."

"The Wicked Witch? I thought—Well, I guess if I had given any thought at all to her costume, I wouldn't have thought she was going as Dorothy, not her style. Still..."

Erin shook her head. In truth, The Wicked Witch of the West was very much in accord with what her best friend would choose as a Halloween costume, convention be damned.

"Aw, you know Mel. She loves screwing with people's expectations. She actually wanted me to wear the Cowardly Lion so she could put a leash on me. You know, all BDSM-like. But I refused. I'm not that submissive." He grinned at her.

Erin returned a forced smile. "And that's really none of my business."

"All right, I'll see that I find my mistress and talk her into letting you stay sans costume. But you owe me your firstborn and a plate of those delicious muffins you're always making. Oh, and a brain, of course." He tapped his head and then pulled some straw from under his hat.

"Deal," she said, laughing.

Charlie waved at her as he went his merry way into the deeper reaches of the bar.

Erin took another sip of her beer, smiling at some of the people who greeted her, admiring their costumes or frowning at some strange costume choices.

She wasn't close friends with any of these people. They were Mel's friends from work and her city-wide social circle. Erin and Mel knew each other from college, and that was possibly why Erin was there, the only readily recognizable lesbian in the place. In her case, readily recognizable meant that all of Mel's friends knew that she was a lesbian rather than having to discern that fact from the plaid tank top combo she was wearing.

"Good evening."

The deep voice came from her left, and Erin steeled herself to deflect any flirting from one of the few people there who apparently didn't know how she swung. She turned, already answering, "Good—"

Her mood changed from slight bemusement to blinking perplexity. The man sitting next to her was attractive. Not necessarily in the general sense of the word, but to her. That was new—or old. Erin couldn't even remember when she'd last found a man attractive. Or, more truthfully, she could remember, but she preferred not to. The life of a teenager could be confusing at times.

"Did I say something wrong?" the man asked with an easy smile as she continued to stare at him.

"No. I...erm... I just thought...I knew all of Mel's friends. You don't look familiar." She saved what small shred of dignity she wanted to go home with tonight and tried not to smile at him too encouragingly.

"I'm not. I came with..." He looked around as if looking for someone, "...a friend of hers." He didn't point anyone out, so Erin still had no actual idea who that friend might be.

"I see. And you came as Jack the Ripper. That's...well, not nice, obviously."

"And the costume comes fully equipped with his favorite tool." He opened his coat. A long, old-fashioned looking knife handle was just visible, sticking out of a hidden compartment in the lining.

Erin's eyes widened. "Is that—"

"A knife," he confirmed before she could finish the question. "It's..." He let his coat fall closed. "This must look bad. I...I'm a bit of a nerd when it comes to Halloween, and I like my costumes to be as authentic as I can make them. I'm sorry if I scared you."

"I'm not—Well, I do think it's...a little creepy, to be honest. A real knife?"

He nodded, seemingly embarrassed.

"I take it your friend came as Mary Kelly, then?"

"Oh no. He would look ridiculous in a corset. He doesn't really have the equipment for it," he answered with a slight grin.

"They're not for everyone," Erin agreed with a laugh, secretly delighted that he actually knew some details about the figure he was dressed as. Too often people just chose their costumes oblivious to history or literary implication. Another reason Erin hated Halloween.

"Certainly not, though I'm sure you could pull it off." He winked at her.

Erin raised an eyebrow. "I'm not gonna say thank you."

They looked at each other, and then they both started to laugh.

Jack—as she thought of him since he hadn't yet introduced himself—looked down the bar and waved his hand at the barkeeper to get his attention. It gave Erin a moment to assess him. There was something in his face that made him beautiful, not handsome. He had warm brown eyes the color of caramel, a nose that suited his face, and a strong jaw. The planes of his face were generous and tan, half-hidden by a closely trimmed beard which was a shade lighter than the hair on his head. At first Erin thought that the attraction she felt for him could have stemmed from there being a quite well-disguised female body underneath the costume, but the beard was the genuine item, and the body—while not overly tall—showed no signs of hidden curves. Jack was a man, all right, and Erin could only wonder at the reason for her close perusal.

The barkeeper came over in response to Jack's wave. "What'll ya have?"

"I'll have a scotch and..." he turned to Erin, "...another beer?"

She nodded automatically, but her eyes were glued to her companion. It was so very strange to feel this pull toward him, this tingling anticipation of what he might say or do next. Erin cleared her throat, at the same time trying to still the fluttering of the butterflies in the pit of her stomach.

"The name's Raymond, by the way."

"Erin. Nice to meet you."

When they shook hands, his grip was firm but not overwhelmingly tight or strong. He wasn't trying to prove anything.

"I should probably tell you now that I'm a lesbian, 'cause I wouldn't want you to think that we'll get drunk and comfy together." The words tumbled from her lips without conscious thought.

He didn't look surprised, he simply nodded. "That's good to know. I'm rather partial to women myself, exclusively so," he said as if their sexualities were just another topic they would discuss.

Erin found that she liked his attitude, and that she wanted to continue their conversation.

Their drinks came, and they clinked glasses.

"So, who are you dressed as, or is it a secret?"

Erin shook her head. "I'm not in costume. And when Mel finds me, she'll probably tell me to go home and change, but I'm not into the whole concept of...Halloween, I guess."

"That's a pity. Halloween is for play, to have one evening when you don't have to be yourself but can...let loose and play at being someone else."

"And you chose to be a serial killer," she deadpanned.

He grinned rakishly, and she smiled in return.

"It's Halloween, the scare factor is a must," he replied.

"At least Jack the Ripper is more original than another Dracula, Lestat, or Edward. I don't really get the fascination with vampires."

"Then I'm lucky we didn't meet two years ago."

"I'm not even gonna ask." Her head jerked around at the song that began to play. It was '*Jeepers Creepers*,' and it was one of her favorites. She was smiling when she turned back to Raymond.

"Would you like to dance?" he asked before she could even say that she loved the song.

Erin hesitated. She was not in the habit of dancing with men. She didn't detest it, but she'd turned them down more often than not—even some guys she knew and liked, because she didn't feel like giving in to conventions that didn't coincide with her preference for dancing with a woman. Still, she hesitated over saying "no."

"It's just dancing," he said with a soft smile, his low, throaty voice becoming even deeper.

It seemed to vibrate in Erin's spinal column. "All right," she said as if challenging herself.

He held his hand out as she slid from her stool, and she took it as they made their way through the crowd to the dance floor.

Raymond was a good dancer. He wasn't like so many guys, who put on airs or shuffled around because they didn't have any moves. He seemed to enjoy music and moving to it, and he looked good.

Now if only he had boobs, he'd be perfect, Erin mused, though she was well aware that boobs weren't the only requirement to being a woman. She couldn't explain why she enjoyed this man's company, how she trusted his smile and didn't second-guess him like she usually did with men who claimed to want to be friends with her. He had an aura, a sphere of trustworthiness—or something less ridiculous sounding that would still have the same meaning. And yes, the possibility that she had been drugged did occur to her for a moment, because she wasn't one to trust easily, no matter the gender of her companion. Still, from what she had heard, roofies worked a little differently, and that was seemingly the most common date rape drug used to make women willing and mute.

"You've got moves, man," she called out to him over the loud music.

He grinned toothily. "Helps to be part Latino," he shot back. "And I'm not the only one with moves," he added as he watched her with obvious pleasure.

"Which part of you is Latino?"

"My feet and my hips mostly." He took her hand and pulled her to him, only to push her away and twirl her expertly.

She gave a surprised laugh.

One song ended and another began, and still they were dancing. As the second song glided smoothly into the tune of a third, a slow dance, he opened his arms with a questioning look. She raised an eyebrow at him, or maybe at herself, but then stepped close. She was surprised to find that Raymond was slightly smaller than she was. He had seemed taller to her, but so close, the truth was revealed. He put an arm around her waist and took her right hand into his left.

She leaned casually on his shoulder, but it felt awkward. She frowned as she contemplated that she was usually the one leading when she danced with a woman.

"Is this okay?"

"Yeah, I guess. As long as you don't..." She looked pointedly at the space where their hips were not touching.

"I won't. I respect that you know who you are and who you want."

"But?"

"No but."

They were so close, she could smell his cologne, feel the heat of his body and the strength of his embrace. It was somehow enticing, even as her brain tried frantically to answer some questions. Was this how straight women felt? Was this what she should have felt all along?

But that wasn't how she saw the world, or herself. Thanks to understanding parents and a liberal upbringing, she had never felt an obligation to be anyone but herself. But how had she come to suddenly feel attracted to a man? Was that part of her now? Or had it something to do with him? Or was it all just confusion and she would go back to being her own normal self again in the morning?

Maybe I've been enchanted, she mused, and grinned at the thought. *All Hallow's Eve strikes again.* "You're one of those woman-whisperers, aren't you?" she said aloud.

He laughed, and it was a delightful sound. There was mirth and no malice in it, or in his person, it seemed to her. "Is seducing lesbians a challenge you set yourself for Halloween every year?"

"Not at all. I'm not saying I'm not good with women, though I have had my fair share of experience. I'm not, however, a player or someone who's keeping score. I leave that to a younger generation. But Halloween does have a special significance in my life—a kind of prophecy, you could say. I'm supposed to meet my soulmate on All Hallow's Eve." A slight frown creased the skin between his eyes.

Erin swallowed hard. "Your soulmate? I hope you're not thinking...that I'm that soulmate."

He looked at her intently. "I don't know."

Erin wanted to pull back then, but his eyes held her, and it was clear to her that she had indeed been enchanted. But how to break the spell? She felt she couldn't.

And then there was a hand on her back and a voice at her ear asked, "What are you doing?"

Erin turned. "Mel! Hey, listen, I'm sorry about the whole costume thing." She noticed that her friend wasn't looking at her, but at the man she'd been dancing with.

"Who's your...date?" Mel lifted a challenging eyebrow.

"Oh, Raymond's not my date, Mel. I mean...we met here."

Mel crossed her arms over her chest. "Really? Well, then I'm even more curious, because I know all the people I invited and I don't know you." She raised her voice to make sure that Raymond could hear her over the music.

"The name's Raymond Muñoz. I came with a friend, a colleague, really." Raymond gave her his easy smile.

Mel smiled back, but it barely reached her teeth let alone her eyes. "And what is that colleague's name?"

"Grant," Raymond provided quickly. When the woman in the witch costume merely stared at him, he elaborated. "Grant Phillips."

Mel nodded and looked around before turning back to Erin. "You know, you could at least have made an effort," she scolded, looking at Erin's clothes.

"I thought of doing it like Oz from *Buffy* and pinning a name tag on my shirt that said 'God.' But I didn't want to engage in discussions about blasphemy all night." Erin grinned.

"You could've put a stake in your pocket and come as Buffy," Mel suggested.

"Because I have so many stakes lying around my place," the blonde deadpanned.

"'Kay, you're off the hook, but just for coming without a costume, not for..." Mel looked over at Raymond with a frown. She grabbed Erin's shirt and pulled her toward the bar.

Erin didn't protest. She knew her friend too well to resist. Mel could be a tough nut if she thought she had to be, but she had also been Erin's best friend since their sophomore year of college, and Erin knew that Mel never did anything just for the sake of making her life miserable. She usually had a good reason when she put Erin on the spot and, of course, this time she didn't even have to give a reason. Erin knew that she was acting a little beside herself, somehow off. At the same time, she felt that she had a right to. And why not? It was Halloween, the perfect night to act unlike yourself.

"Out with it, what's wrong?" Mel asked when she finally released Erin. They were standing near the bar, but Mel was looking back to where Raymond still stood on the dance floor, looking a little forlorn to be alone among couples. Some of those looking at him suspiciously had probably overheard Mel talking to him. Or, knowing Erin's preferences, they might even have been surprised to see him with her.

Erin pitied him, but he regained his equilibrium. Putting on a soft smile, he made his way back to where they had left their drinks, making a wide berth around Mel and Erin.

"Nothing's wrong, Mel. It's not...what it looks like. God, why do I have to explain why I'm dancing with a guy?"

"Because you're a lesbian. Also because I know that dancing with guys makes you uncomfortable. You didn't even dance with Charlie at our wedding. And, you were making bedroom eyes at this guy." Mel gestured in Raymond's direction.

"I was what!" Erin shook her head impatiently. "I'm pretty sure you couldn't even have seen that, and you're wrong."

"No, I'm not. What's going on?"

"I don't know what... I...I..." Erin tilted her head back as she took a deep breath, then let it out in a dramatic huff. "I find him attractive," she finally admitted.

Mel looked at her thoughtfully for a long moment. "It's Halloween, dear, not April Fools."

"Ha ha," Erin said without the slightest hint of humor. "I'm serious."

"No you're not. You're trying to get back at me for making you come to this party. This is some kind of...weird passive-aggressive commentary that links Halloween to heterosexuality, which would mean that although you're not wearing a costume, you've come as 'Straight Girl.' Next time, you might wanna consider ditching the plaid, though," Mel lectured.

Erin rolled her eyes and drew another deep breath. She didn't say anything, just looked at her friend with what she hoped was a sincere expression.

"You're not serious," Mel said. When she received no answer, she added, "How is that even possible?"

"I wish I knew. Believe me, it's throwing me for a loop, too," Erin admitted. "I mean, he's...he is attractive, isn't he? I mean as a guy...and he is a guy. Do you think he's attractive?"

"He's not really my type. I mean, he's not tall, not... handsome. He's got nice bone structure, though."

"You don't like him at all?" Surprised, Erin looked over to where Raymond was sitting at the bar. He wasn't looking at her, but she knew that he was waiting for her. She also knew she was going to rejoin him when her conversation with Mel was over. She felt almost eager to do so.

"No. I...I don't know. I get a weird vibe from him. I don't like his looks, Erin. And who goes to a costume party dressed as Jack the Ripper?"

"It's Halloween," Erin defended.

"It's fucking creepy, is what it is."

Erin shoved her hands into the pockets of her jeans. "I think he's... sexy. God, that sounds weird, but...there's something in his eyes and in the way he expresses himself, the way he holds himself."

"Meaning you don't want his dick."

"Mel! Urgh. Do you have to—" Erin stopped herself, as she knew her friend did indeed have to be so crass, if only to drive home a point—the fact that Erin was gay. "You're right. And I told him I'm gay, so—"

"So he doesn't think you'll do him later. That would be perfect, if he went on to another 'available' woman, but he didn't, Erin. What does he want from you?" It was a question, but it sounded like a warning.

Erin knew she should leave Raymond alone, should just tell him to find someone who would actually want him, but she felt disinclined to do it. Because she liked him. She more than liked him. "Do you think that maybe... I mean, I'm pretty sure the beard is legit but..."

"A transguy? Hm. I mean... I don't know, Grant has many friends in the community, but I don't know, Erin. Maybe you should ask him. Or maybe you should just let it go."

"Maybe." Erin could tell by Mel's expression that she wasn't buying the tentative consent.

"But you're not going to."

Erin shrugged.

Mel sighed. "Okay, do whatever you want, just...stick around. Don't go anywhere with him, okay?"

"Where would we go?"

"I don't know, just don't," Mel insisted.

"You know I can take care of myself."

"Yeah? I bet all the women the Ripper killed said that at some point in their lives. Probably not too long before their lives ended."

"He's not... Okay, whatever. I'm gonna stay at the bar, have another beer or two, and then I'll find you and we're gonna dance. And then I'll go home. Alone!"

Mel rolled her eyes. "And they say that married people are boring."

"People who say that have obviously never met you and Charlie. Great costumes, by the way." Erin gave her friend the once-over, not shy about stopping at Mel's generous green cleavage.

"I wanted Charlie to come as the Cowardly Lion—"

"Yeah, he already told me. Thanks for the visual."

Mel laughed. "So sensitive," she teased.

"You know it."

"You wanna go and talk to the creep now, don't you?" Mel looked over Erin's shoulder to where Raymond was sitting at the bar.

Following Mel's gaze, Erin turned and saw Raymond talking to the bartender.

"Maybe."

"All right, go. Just don't get yourself murdered."

"What better day to die on than Halloween?"

"Maybe, but not on my watch. Are we clear?" All the teasing was gone from Mel's voice.

"He's harmless."

"He's a stranger in a creepy costume," Mel disagreed.

"I'll be careful, I promise. I always am, you know that." Erin took Mel's hand and leaned over to her, but stopped before her lips touched the green cheek. "Does this stuff rub off?"

"Only one way to find out," Mel said.

Erin kissed her. "Are my lips green?"

"Who cares? You're not planning on kissing anyone else with them, are you?"

"Bye, Mel. See you later, Mel. Don't do anything I wouldn't do, Mel," Erin answered playfully, waving her hand in the air dismissively as she walked away from her best friend.

Erin picked up her jacket from the stool where she'd left it and sat down. She looked over at Raymond, observing him closely for a long moment until he turned his head, meeting her eyes. Erin almost gasped at the intensity in the dark, chocolate-brown pools, her pulse beating rapidly. *What the hell is wrong with me?*

"I take it your friend is very protective of you."

She heard something in his voice, a hint at an inside joke that only he could understand. It made her frown. "She is."

"Good for you." He took a sip of his drink.

"You're a strange kind of guy, you know that?"

He raised his eyebrows. "How so?"

"The things you say, the way you say them—they're not at all what one would expect a man to say."

"And do you have a theory about that?"

Erin smirked. "You could be a feminist."

"I'm not gonna deny that."

She breathed a surprised laugh. "Really?"

"Why not? Feminism advocates equality between the sexes—all sexes. I think that's a worthy goal."

"All sexes? That's an interesting side note. Are you trying to tell me something regarding your own sex?"

Raymond smiled. "Is that another theory you have about me? That I'm not a 'real' man? I'm sorry to disappoint, Erin. I'm very much a man—all parts." He raised a challenging eyebrow.

Erin looked at him for a long moment. She reached for her beer, which had been standing on the bar the whole time—unattended. She pushed it away and hailed the barkeeper, ordered a fresh drink, and then turned back to Raymond. "I'm not interested in your parts."

"I know, but you enjoy talking to me and I enjoy talking to you. Does it have to be complicated?"

"It is complicated." Erin took a sip of her cold beer.

"Because you're attracted to me." It wasn't a question, it was a statement.

She looked at him, not so much surprised as irritated. Because he had said it. She didn't respond. They sat in silence and drank from their respective glasses. Erin watched Raymond closely in the mirror above the bar, wondering for the nth time that night what it was about him that so completely captured her attention. He was just a guy, not even a really good-looking guy, if Mel was to be believed. He certainly was not conventionally handsome. There was a presence to him, though. It wasn't like that of a movie star entering a room and turning every head, it was more understated. Maybe that of a teacher entering his classroom and pupils settling down because they respect him, because they value the knowledge he's about to share with them.

Not good-looking, not in a conventional sense, Erin thought. But there were those captivating chocolate-brown eyes looking back at her. A strong face, with a pointy, little chin, even though his beard strove to obscure it. His lips—

"What do you say we go for a walk?" His voice sounded close to her ear.

Had he actually moved his head to whisper to her? How could she have missed it while she was staring at him? Erin blinked her eyes rapidly and turned her head. Their faces were close, and Erin's senses filled with everything Raymond, as if she were drowning in him.

"I shouldn't," she breathed.

"Because I'm dressed as a serial killer?"

She nodded dumbly.

Raymond flashed her a beautiful toothy smile. "I've never killed a woman in my life and I'm not going to start tonight." He held out his hand. "Trust me."

Erin took a deep breath to clear her head. She looked around. This party was so normal, like all the parties she'd ever been to, all the parties Mel had ever dragged her to. People were talking and dancing and laughing and shooting pool and drinking. Everything was normal—except what was going on between her and Raymond. That was not normal; that was confusing.

Erin slid from her stool and took Raymond's hand. He smiled at her, and she accompanied him outside.

The cool night air reminded them that November was mere hours away. *At least it isn't raining*, Erin thought, even as she detected a hint of moisture in the air. She slipped into her jacket.

Raymond suggested a direction, and they set out at a leisurely pace.

There were people about—some in costume, some in normal attire. She and Raymond hardly stood out, but they weren't alone either. Erin felt that this was okay, even though Mel's words of warning were still echoing in the back of her mind.

"You said something earlier about a prophecy," she reminded him. "What was that about?"

Her companion sighed. "You will think it weird, but...well, my grandma was a witch."

"A witch?"

He nodded, and they looked at each other.

"I wouldn't say that's weird. Different, maybe," Erin said after a while.

"Ah, Generation Political Correctness."

"Is that a bad thing?"

"No. Just...most people think witches weird, not different or interesting."

Erin acknowledged that with a nod that also encouraged him to continue his story.

"When I was twelve, Granny told me that she'd had a vision of me meeting my 'forever' on All Hallow's Eve. She wasn't clear on when or where, only that I was gonna be an adult and in disguise." Raymond pushed his hands into the pockets of his coat.

"How mystifyingly vague."

"Yes, but I never doubted her power, though I have grown a little weary of the prophecy in the last twenty years. Imagine something you really want to happen, but that you are only able to go looking for one day every year," he mused.

"At least you know that it will happen. That's more than the rest of us have."

He laughed, and the sound made Erin smile without her even being aware of it.

"Doesn't everybody, in our culture at least, believe they will meet The One? Don't you believe that?"

"The One," Erin echoed with a sigh. "I don't know if I even believe in that concept. Why not just be with people you like and respect and feel attracted to, and not expect or offer a magical connection that might well be a myth?"

"I've seen too many mythical and magical things happen to not believe in that kind of love," Raymond answered in a dreamy voice that was little more than a whisper. Erin looked up in surprise, swallowing at the light flutter constricting her chest. His voice was almost like a tender caress on her skin, and it gave her goosebumps. A strangled noise escaped her mouth, like the singular tone of a yearning she never even knew she had.

Raymond stopped and turned to her. He touched the sleeve of her jacket and let his hand slide down to her hand, slipping his fingers between hers.

They were standing at the mouth of an alley which loomed darkly behind him. His silhouette was that of a Victorian Joe Average against the streets he'd inhabited all his life, the smelly, cruel streets of his poor upbringing.

He tugged at her hand. "Come with me."

"Into a dark alley where no one can see us? I don't think so." Her denial was determinedly nonchalant, but panic crept up into her throat and strangled the last word.

"I want to kiss you, but not here in the open."

Her muscles tensed, and she took an instinctual step back.

He held onto her fingers, but not tightly. Erin had the feeling that she could slip them out of his hand and run if she wanted to.

She simply didn't want to. "I told you—"

"You're a lesbian. And yet, I know you want to kiss me, too."

Her knees weakened at the simple truth of his statement, but she was afraid. She was afraid of the dark alley, she was afraid of what was going to happen between them, and she was afraid of her whole life changing, of her own desire. "Have you drugged me?" she asked him breathlessly.

"No," he answered without hesitation and without the smile that might have belittled her fear. "And I haven't lied to you, either, not once. Do you trust me?"

She nodded, but said, "I don't know. Have you put a spell on me?"

The question was unexpected to both of them, and for just a second, Raymond's countenance faltered as he stiffened. He let go of her hand and took a step backward, into the alley. "No, I haven't put a spell on *you*," he said, emphasizing the last word.

She blinked in confusion. "What does that mean?"

He turned and slipped into the alley. "Only one way to find out," he called over his shoulder as he walked away from her.

It was a siren's song to Erin's ears. She took a step forward, then hesitated.

Strangely, the further Raymond went into the darkness, the more he seemed to fade into it. Soon he would disappear altogether. Her chest constricted with the fear of losing him, Erin took a step, then another. She was following him. "Raymond," she whispered to his retreating back.

He turned and smiled.

She stepped closer to him, relieved that she was able to see his face again, his attire, his complete figure. She stepped close to him, as if she wanted to dance with him again, standing right before him but not touching him. Her senses were once again engulfed by him—his smell, his visage, his voice.

"You're beautiful, Erin."

"What did you mean when you said you haven't put a spell on *me*? Who did you put a spell on?"

He smiled confidently, ignoring her question.

Erin swallowed down another rising panic, wondering whether it was too late to turn and run from this...from him, and at the same time, not wanting to leave him at all.

He took her hand and laid it inside his cloak where his heart was beating beneath his shirt. "Do you feel that?"

She nodded.

"Nice and steady. If I were going to kill you, don't you think it would be erratic and excited?"

"Not if you're a psychopath who thinks killing women is just part of your daily routine."

"Do you think I'm a psychopath?"

She shook her head without hesitation. "But I've been known to be wrong about people."

"Kiss me, Erin." There was no urgency in his voice, just his earnest desire to feel her lips against his.

Her eyes flickered to his lips—assessing their distance, their position, their degree of temptation. Erin pressed forward and claimed them passionately.

She'd imagined it differently. She thought the beard would obstruct and distract, that his lips would be harder, his demeanor more demanding. But it felt like it should—soft, tender, sexy, with a promise of more. And Erin let herself fall into the kiss, giving and taking. Her hand cupped the soft subtle flesh of Raymond's—Erin gasped and broke the kiss, stepping back and staring at her hand, which rested on...a breast...of the female kind, held in by the formidable bodice of a...dress.

Erin's eyes whipped up and encountered...a woman. She had Raymond's eyes, his wide smile, his lovely face, but there was no beard, no manly set to this face, and no Ripper's costume. This woman was wearing a fabulous witch's dress and a pointy hat. Erin pulled her hand from the woman's bosom.

"What? Where? Who?" Erin stuttered, blinking her eyes rapidly. "What?" she finally settled on, and it came out harsh and demanding.

Her companion flinched at her tone, but attempted a smile.

"I'm sorry. I... My name is Reyna. I'm a witch." Her voice even sounded like Raymond's—higher pitched, yes, but still with a subtle throatiness and the same cadence.

"I...I can see that," Erin said dumbly, pointing at the woman's attire.

"Oh, this is just a costume. I'm not usually... I'm... I didn't mean to...startle you," Reyna apologized.

"You did quite a bit more than startle me! What kind of trick is this? Where's Raymond?" That last question came out with less vehemence than Erin had intended, and she wondered if it didn't indicate that she already knew where Raymond was. Because he was still standing in front of her, only he was different.

A light blush coloring her cheeks, the woman looked at Erin earnestly. "There's no trick. Raymond is...well, I guess you could say he was my costume for tonight. This is what I usually look like."

Erin shook her head, not because she didn't believe but because her whole life experience had taught her that this was impossible. This kind of...trickery just didn't exist in this world.

"That's not true. What... Did you two do this on purpose? Did you...just do this to confuse me? Or possibly cure me of my evil ways?"

The familiar stranger shook her head. "No, no, of course not. You know who you are, Erin, and I...I know who I am, too. I just—"

"You just what!"

"I didn't want this Halloween to be the disappointment all the others have been. I didn't want to become a slave to my grandmother's prophecy again this year, and I thought dressing as a man would ensure that." Her voice was low, pleading for Erin to understand.

Erin's gaze locked on the soft chocolate-colored eyes that had looked back at her the whole evening, and a deep sense of calm settled over her. It was disconcerting, and she would have liked to be angry still, but those eyes were enchanting. *Enchanting.* The word echoed in Erin's mind. "You did put a spell on me."

Reyna took a step closer. "No, I only put a spell on myself. Everything else, even I don't know how to explain. But it is real, Erin."

Erin shook her head. "It...can't be. How... How?"

Reyna's smile lit her face with sheer beauty.

Erin felt a stab in her chest. Reyna took her breath away.

"Magic?" the witch suggested, blinking her eyes as if she was confused herself.

"There is no magic," Erin retorted automatically, then frowned, because she wasn't sure that she still believed that.

"Look." Reyna lifted her right hand in the air and whirled it. Raymond once again stood before Erin. He smiled. Then he turned his hand back, his lips moving in silent incantation—and Reyna was back, as glorious and beautiful as before.

Erin stared. "That did not just happen," she murmured without conviction.

"It did," Reyna insisted.

Erin knew that arguing against what her eyes had actually seen for themselves didn't seem sound for some reason. But his deceit was true, and she could argue with that. "You lied to me. You said you were a man."

"I was a man, at least in outward appearance. Everything you saw, and felt, was real. But it was also temporary."

"And you chose to change your appearance again when you kissed me? That was a lousy moment to break the news, you know."

"First, *you* kissed me. Second, I didn't choose anything. You broke my spell. Your kiss made me reveal myself."

Her mouth agape, Erin stared at Reyna. "What if it hadn't?"

"But it was supposed to."

"So you knew that would happen?"

"I wasn't sure," the witch admitted, her chin jutting forward with indignation.

Erin took a deep breath and blew it out explosively. She threw her hands in the air and turned away from this... positively enchanting creature. She couldn't think while looking at Reyna; the mere sight of her confounded Erin's senses. "What the actual fuck!" she ground out through clenched teeth. She put her hands on her hips and shook her head. Not looking at the witch made this more believable, somehow explainable, or easier to ignore. It was all nonsense. It had to be.

"Erin," the deep voice called to her. "This is real. Don't deny it. Please. Don't turn into a rational disbeliever who only accepts those things that her mind can explain. You know this is real."

Erin whirled around to face Reyna. "What I know is that you made me believe I was falling in love with a man. Do you know how confusing that was!"

"I had every confidence that you knew who you are. You do know who you are. You looked beyond my disguise and you saw me, and that was..." Reyna floundered, seeming only now to register what Erin had said, and then repeating it. "I was who you were falling in love with."

"But you planned it. You came into the bar, and you...you came over to me, knowing—"

"I didn't know anything, Erin. I saw you crossing the street to the bar and felt that I wanted to meet you. I didn't know you were gay. Maybe I guessed, but...I didn't know you would...be..."

"What? Your...your soulmate?" Erin had wanted to make it sound scoffing, disbelieving, uncaring. But she couldn't. The word vibrated down to her stomach, where it unhinged a great mystical fluttering of winged anticipation, excitement, anxiety, and fear. Could this be? How could this be?

"I think you might be her, yes. I feel...completely enamored of you. Like..." Reyna breathed and stepped carefully closer until she was standing right in front of Erin. The blonde didn't step back, and the dark-haired woman continued. "Like I'm drowning in a...fog or...a cloud of you. You're all I sense."

Erin's pulse quickened. A tingle emanated from Reyna's touch on her hand as she took it and drew her closer. And she greeted Reyna's lips as if they were old new friends that she had longed for all her life, that she had missed for an eternity.

As they walked back to the bar, hand in hand, Erin's heart felt lighter than she ever could remember. "So, what does a witch do?"

"What everybody does—go to work, come home, prepare dinner, sacrifice a goat to the moon goddess," Reyna answered casually.

"What?"

"Just joking...about the goat," Reyna said with an easy laugh.

Erin joined in, shaking her head at the same time. "Is that witch humor?"

"I guess, but maybe it is just humor. Or maybe it's lesbian humor. I'm not just a witch, you know." There was a twinkle in the soft, brown eyes.

"Sorry." Erin kept shaking her head, not quite sure she should believe in witches, even while knowing that Reyna was one. It was a leap of faith she felt she wasn't ready to take just yet.

"It's quite all right," Reyna said. "I know it's...challenging to find your way back to those kinds of beliefs, beliefs we're taught only children should have."

Erin nodded. She looked at *Jinxed* with beckoning awareness that it was the real world, a world in which Mel would be furious and demanding an explanation. "What am I supposed to tell Mel?" she asked herself more than her companion.

"The truth?" Reyna suggested.

"Isn't there some ancient edict that demands that your identity remain a secret?"

"I don't know, I'm not that old. I was born in the 80s, just like you."

Erin looked at Reyna and started to laugh like that was the wildest thing she had heard all night. Reyna joined in, and they had to hold on to each other to stay upright. In the end, they just held each other.

Erin brushed a lock of hair from Reyna's eyes, letting her hand linger on the other woman's face. Her smile couldn't be contained, neither could the tingles and flashes beneath her skin. This was it; nothing had ever felt so right, so utterly amazing.

"I'm gonna tell Mel that you're a witch and that you were Raymond...for the sake of Halloween. She'll appreciate it in the morning. And then I'll tell her that we played a trick on her—you, me, and your twin, Raymond. I don't think Mel is ready to know that there are witches in this world, or that I could have fallen for a man."

Reyna grinned. "Or that there are fairies," she added.

"Fairies? Really?"

Reyna nodded as she pulled open the door to the bar.

"What about vampires? Werewolves?" Erin asked eagerly as they re-entered the ruckus of one of thousands of Halloween parties in the city.

STREGA

R·G· EMANUELLE

DARKNESS HAD ENVELOPED THE FOREST when Raffaella awoke, propped against a pine tree. She didn't know how long she'd been there, but the full moon, high and bright, told her that it had been several hours.

She struggled to her feet, holding onto the tree for support, and looked around. The forest was dense, and the moonlight broke through the weave of branches in patches. How had she gotten this deep into the woods? Icy fear went down her spine.

As she stood clutching the tree, ready to either jump behind it or climb it if anyone or anything approached, a familiar smell filled her nose. A woody, sweet, acrid smell. Fire. And it was near. It wasn't the choking, consuming smoke of a forest fire, but the warming, welcoming smoke of a pyre. Maybe it was a fireplace in someone's home. Or maybe a campfire of thieves or marauders. She'd have to be careful.

Raffaella sniffed and turned, trying to find the direction of the fire, but the smell filled the air all around her and she couldn't determine its origin. The black of the forest ahead of her began to lighten. Still murky, but there was definitely a glow up ahead, and she started in that direction. Now she could make out trees, fallen limbs, and rocks, and before long, the forest opened into a clearing. Somewhere near, water gently lapped against an embankment.

A bonfire, stacked high with wood, burned brightly near the banks of a river. In the shadows cast by the flames, numerous people—maybe ten or twelve—were on their knees, heads bowed, by a large tree. Raffaella stood back to observe. One person, cloaked so that Raffaella couldn't see the face, knelt in front of the tree. The figure bowed down low, forehead to the ground, then stood, picked something up off the ground, and raised it high. The object looked like…a rope? A long tree branch?

The object wriggled in the figure's hands, and to Raffaella's horror, she realized it was a snake. She shrank back behind the tree, her hands and knees trembling.

The one with the snake began to speak, and Raffaella knew then from the soft cadences of her voice that the figure was a woman. She listened.

Dea delle foreste e della Luna,
Diana della mezzaluna d'argento,
Io canto le mie lodi a voi.
Alzo le braccia al Crescente celeste.
I miei ringraziamenti a voi per la protezione delle foreste e del bosco.
Me e la mia tutela, perché noi siamo i vostri figli spirituali.
Bella Diana, io canto le tue lodi.

These were not prayers of the Catholic Church. These were the prayers of devil worshipers.

The woman was a *strega*. Witch. And this was probably her coven. Raffaella had stumbled upon a witches' Sabbath.

Raffaella's parents, devout Christians, had warned her about *le streghe*. Her chest tightened and her stomach constricted as fear turned to bile. She needed to leave, and without anyone seeing her. But if she managed to get back where she'd been before, where would she be? All she saw around her were trees, and she didn't think that running through the woods in the dark was a good idea. But she had to find a way back home.

She stopped. No, not home. She no longer had a home.

The only logical thing to do, she decided, was to walk along the edge of the clearing until she could quietly retreat. She took a step, and then a voice made her jump nearly off the ground. Her limbs shook uncontrollably, and her heart slammed against her breastbone, but she turned calmly.

Standing before her was a cloaked woman, hood down so that Raffaella could see her face clearly in the light emanating from the fire. Not a hag or monster, as Raffaella had expected. No hooked nose, warts, or blackened teeth. Then again, witches had the power to change their appearance, or so she'd heard.

Long, black, wavy hair, worn loose, framed a diamond-shaped face and thin, pink lips. Raffaella couldn't see the color of her eyes but she could tell that they were dark and deep.

"What are you doing here?" the witch asked.

She hesitated, because speaking to a witch could bring *mala fortuna*. "I was lost," she managed.

"You must be, to be alone in the woods after nightfall." Her voice was low and melodious.

Raffaella stared at her, unable to move, as if the leaves beneath her feet had turned to quicksand. "Please, I'd like to go home. If you could just show me the way out of the forest, I'll leave you in peace."

The witch took Raffaella by her elbow and encouraged her to walk. Her hand was firm but gentle.

Oh, God, she's going to kill me and bury my body in the woods. Or she'll chop me up into pieces to use in her wicked magic. Panic and desperation roiled in her stomach, and she tried to pull free of the woman's clutch. "Please, don't bother yourself. I'll find my way." She freed her elbow and walked away as quickly as she could in the bouncing light of the bonfire.

"*Signorina*," the witch called out. Raffaella stopped and turned halfway. "Follow the banks of the river and you'll find a road. It will take you into Benevento." The woman turned around and headed back to the congregation and to her Sabbath.

Raffaella, breathing hard and trembling, watched the witch's retreating back. Chanting rose in the quiet of the night, and Raffaella ran. There could only be evil in that clearing.

Yet she followed the witch's directions. For some reason, Raffaella believed her.

Dawn was breaking. As Raffaella walked through the town of Benevento, the outlines and corners of the structures solidified, and the houses dotting the hillside brightened, no longer dark and forbidding. She almost cried when she saw a cross puncturing the sky.

The ochre walls of the church quietly displayed the Moorish design. An obelisk stood sentry in the front courtyard as the centerpiece of a fountain. She sat on the narrow steps encircling the fountain, hugging herself, but she couldn't stop shivering. She looked around. Benevento. She'd heard of it and its legacy of witchcraft. Was the whole town filled with witches, then?

The spray from the fountain hit her back as it gushed into life for the day, and she wanted to move. But where would she go? She knew no one here. A clank and screech came from the church door. Someone was unbolting it. Maybe she could ask for sanctuary. Yet Raffaella sat silently, waiting for a sign.

"Are you all right, *signorina*?"

Raffaella jumped up and turned. Water now surged full force from four lion heads surrounding the obelisk, and through the falling water, she saw her.

"*Strega*," Raffaella whispered.

"Yes, you are correct, *signorina*."

Raffaella flushed at the realization that she'd said it aloud. No matter who this was, she didn't wish to be rude.

"It's not like you think," the witch continued. She moved closer. Raffaella wondered if the moonlight played tricks on her the night before, but even in the light of day, the woman was not a hag at all. She was an attractive smooth-skinned woman, who Raffaella would never have taken for a witch had she not seen the ritual.

She looked at the door of the church. She could run inside, but would a witch enter hallowed ground?

The witch's gaze shifted to the church door and back to her. Raffaella thought she saw a hint of a smile at the corners of her lips.

"I am guessing you're in some sort of trouble. Why don't you let me help you?"

"I don't need your help," Raffaella snapped. Her mother would have slapped her for that. Then again, this was one of the devil's minions.

The witch approached, her hand outstretched. Raffaella recoiled and took a few steps back.

The witch stopped and put her hand down. "I'm not going to hurt you. I want to help."

Raffaella turned and ran to the church door. She threw herself on its iron handle and began to pull when the witch called out, "Raffaella."

She turned from the smooth wood of the door, her heart pounding. "How do you know my name?" she asked through labored breaths.

The woman smiled and splayed her hands out. "I am a *strega*."

Raffaella stood frozen with her hand clutching the door handle. "Leave me alone."

"I'm a healer. I can help."

"Why do you want to help me?"

The witch inched closer. "Because I understand your pain. I know what it's like to be an outsider." She held her hand out again. The sleeve of her cloak hung down, and Raffaella had an inexplicable desire to crawl into the dark woolen cavern. It exuded warmth and safety, even though it belonged to a witch. "Please, Raffaella, let me help you." Her eyes were indeed dark, like a bowl of blackberries.

Raffaella didn't move for several moments, but finally let go of the door. Her options were few, and as much as she fought the old stories about the evil of witchcraft, nothing about this woman suggested anything like that. She tentatively reached out to take the witch's hand. She shivered, but it wasn't entirely unpleasant.

The witch gently pulled her forward until they were only inches apart. "I am Serafina." She turned and began walking, their hands entwined, and a strange sense of both security and something else engulfed Raffaella, who looked up at the lions of the fountain as they passed. She searched their carved stone features for reassurance.

"The lions of the Church of Santa Sofia. They would tell you to come with me," Serafina said with a soft smile, and Raffaella knew she was right.

In the rays of the morning sun, and with a light mist settling on her face, Raffaella followed quietly, her breathing settling into a calm, even rhythm.

They walked through Benevento, nestled in the hills at the foot of a mountain range. Serafina led Raffaella through the Arch of Trajan, back to the outskirts of town and back into the hills. She sometimes held Raffaella's hand, and when she did, Raffaella hoped she'd hold it longer than the last time.

Their journey ended at a small stone house. Serafina beckoned Raffaella to follow her inside. The first room was a small kitchen, and from the window, she could see Benevento sprawled out below.

"Our Apennine Mountains are beautiful, no?"

Raffaella nodded and thought that Serafina was beautiful too, no matter what the old tales said of witches.

"Come and sit," Serafina said. "You must be hungry."

Raffaella had the strange feeling of being home and safe. There was something familiar about the emerging life of the town below, and Serafina's kitchen bore no sign of evil magic. Besides, she was hungry, and she quickly turned her attention to the small rough-hewn wooden table in the center of the room. She sat down, more eager than she would have liked to have shown. A loaf of bread and a wedge of cheese sat on the table. Serafina broke off a piece of bread and set it onto Raffaella's plate. Cheese followed and Raffaella ate, all thoughts pushed aside.

Serafina watched her for a moment before she began to eat. She had removed her cloak and revealed a simple brown dress covered by an apron. Serafina, like her home, was simple and unadorned, clean and neat, but quietly noble.

Serafina's cheeks were pink, and Raffaella felt her own cheeks flush. Serafina's eyes on her made her quiver, so she looked down at her plate. Was Serafina bewitching her? She stole a look at Serafina, who was tearing a piece of bread from the loaf, her features a study in concentration. She glanced up from the bread and caught Raffaella staring at her. She smiled and her eyes lit up, warm and dark. Raffaella forgot to swallow.

"Another?" Serafina handed her the piece of bread she'd just torn off.

Mutely, Raffaella accepted.

After Raffaella finished her cheese, and then two more pieces, Serafina said, "Tell me what happened."

Raffaella wiped her mouth with the back of her hand. "If you're a witch, don't you know?"

Serafina smiled. "Not everything." She got up and began clearing the table. Raffaella wanted to help, but her limbs felt like logs. She stared at the table's surface.

"I—I..."

"What?" Serafina asked, looking up from her chore. "You can trust me."

"Can I?" she asked, even though she knew, deep down, that she could. "You worship the devil." She felt strangely ashamed to say that.

Serafina's face grew dark and she turned away. She put the dishes in a bucket of water, throwing them so hard they clanked together. Raffaella flinched.

Serafina wiped her hands on her apron and sat back down. With her hands splayed on the table and her back straight, she said in an even tone, "We don't worship the devil. We worship Diana, Goddess of the Hunt."

Raffaella waited for more, but Serafina's silence told her the subject was closed, at least for now. She decided that she had nothing more to lose. "I ran away," she said.

"Why?"

"My husband."

Serafina's eyes narrowed. Raffaella felt almost a physical penetration, as if Serafina was probing into her very soul. "Did he beat you?"

"No. But he treats me no better than a stray dog. He took everything from my family and then took me far away from them. I didn't want him as a husband. I never wanted any husband."

"Where were you before the forest?"

"Campobasso, where my husband took me."

Serafina blinked a couple of times. "You walked all the way from Campobasso? That's where you were coming from last night?"

"Yes. I had to."

Serafina's expression held such compassion that Raffaella's chest tightened. She wanted to cry.

"Then you need to rest." Serafina rose, took Raffaella's arm, and coaxed her up. Her fingers on Raffaella's skin sent warmth through her, both exciting and confusing her, but she was too tired to ponder it.

Serafina led her to a bedroom at the back of the house. A looking glass hung on the wall, and Raffaella was shocked at her reflection. Her usually lustrous chestnut hair was limp and greasy and had a leaf sticking out on one side, which she plucked out. Her eyes, normally bright, were dull and underscored by circles. She looked up at Serafina and brought her hand to her cheek, suddenly ashamed of her appearance. But Serafina seemed not to notice.

Gently, she brought Raffaella to the bed and motioned for her to lie down. Raffaella sank into the mattress with a sigh and the comforting smell of fresh straw to soothe her. Serafina took some blankets from an oak chest and arranged them on the floor, where she made herself comfortable.

Through encroaching slumber, Raffaella heard her say, "Don't worry, you're safe here."

Once again, she believed.

It was dark when Raffaella awoke, long past twilight, and Serafina was gone, her blankets neatly folded on the chest. From across the narrow hall, she heard something like clinking bottles and rustling that she couldn't identify. Following the sounds, she tiptoed through a small room that seemed to be a wash and sewing room and found an archway, closed off by an old woolen blanket tacked to the wall. The noises were coming from behind it. Carefully, she moved the blanket with one finger and peeked in. Serafina stood behind a table, her back to the entrance. She had tied her dark hair back with a cloth strip, and Raffaella wanted to touch the tresses, let them wind around her fingers. Heart pounding, she let the blanket go and quietly went back to the kitchen.

"You must be wondering what I'm doing." Serafina's voice made Raffaella stop, but she didn't turn. "I'll show you when you're ready." Serafina walked past her toward the kitchen. Raffaella followed, and it was only then that she smelled the stew. Her stomach rumbled, and she forgot to ask, "Ready for what?"

"Sit. You slept a long time. I hope you feel rested." Serafina picked up a long spoon and stirred a big pot suspended above the hearth on an iron stand.

"I do. Thank you."

Serafina pulled the spoon out and sampled the contents of the pot. She turned to the dish cabinet and took two bowls off a shelf. After she poured Raffaella a portion, she served herself some as well. A loaf of bread awaited them on the table.

Raffaella ate about half her stew, and her stomach stopped rumbling before she said, "I'm sorry. I'm taking advantage of your hospitality."

Serafina peered over her spoon. "No one takes advantage of me. I give only what I want to give."

She wondered why then, this woman, this *strega*, wanted to feed and shelter her.

"I suppose you're wondering why I'm helping you."

Raffaella stopped chewing. The hair on her arms stood up, fear mixed with curiosity about Serafina's obvious power. She wished she had some power. Any power.

"My sense is, you're a lost soul," Serafina said. "You're searching for something. I am drawn to lost, searching souls. And to you personally." She smiled, a warm, pretty smile. Not what Raffaella expected from a witch, and her comment made her feel like kindling that had just been sparked.

"Have you been a witch a long time?"

Serafina swallowed a mouthful of stew and answered with a cautious tone. "All my life. My family were all witches."

"Where are they now?"

Serafina hesitated. "They died."

Raffaella decided not to pursue the subject. "So you are here alone?"

"Yes."

"No husband? Children?"

Serafina gulped. "No." She furrowed her brows. "Like you, I am perhaps not the type for a husband."

Raffaella started to say something, but Serafina spoke first. "You can stay as long as you wish. I ask only one thing."

"I promise, I won't tell anyone you're a witch."

One side of Serafina's lips quirked up, as if she wanted to laugh. "That's not it. I want you to take this." She pulled something out of her apron pocket and held it out on her flattened palm.

"A walnut?" Raffaella frowned.

"It's a special walnut. From a special tree. It will help you understand."

"Understand what?"

"Whatever it is you need to understand."

Raffaella took the walnut. She was puzzled but sure that she probably shouldn't refuse a gift from a witch. Especially one as beautiful as Serafina, who made her feel strangely intoxicated.

Serafina smiled again, and Raffaella reached for another piece of bread, wondering what sort of magic a walnut might have.

Raffaella kept the walnut in her pocket constantly. Every now and then, she would reach in, feel its hard ridges. Slowly, over the course of the passing month, her thoughts began to turn from a dark, bleak, passionless abyss to a warm, vital circle of energy. An awakening, a new awareness and sense of independence. She didn't know where this awakening would take her, but she did know that she was changing, and at the same time, drawing closer to Serafina, in ways she had not expected. Serafina had not asked her to stay on, but Raffaella knew that she could.

Serafina spoke the truth when she said she was a healer. Occasionally, someone would show up on her doorstep. She would speak to them a moment and then go to her medicine room and return with a package, which she gave to the visitor. Sometimes she'd let them in. Those she did were usually people who were sick and needed help. Raffaella would watch Serafina administer a potion, then send them on their way.

Meanwhile, Raffaella helped Serafina all she could with the housework. She wanted to repay her for her kindness, but she also wanted to spend as much time as possible with her. Somehow, Raffaella knew that Serafina was part of her awakening. And, little by little, Serafina began to teach her some of her formulas.

At first, it scared her to concoct the formulas, for she feared poisoning someone. But Serafina was patient. It didn't take long for Raffaella to master the basic formulas, in spite of her initial reservations. She had shown a natural aptitude for it. For the first time in her life, Raffaella felt as if she had a purpose.

The work that Serafina did seemed benevolent enough—people asking for a tonic to be healed, a talisman for good luck, a spell to ensure love or fruitful crops. But one day, a customer came and requested a death spell on his business rival. He was ready to pay handsomely for it. Serafina was not home and

Raffaella, uncertain what to do with such a request, instructed him to call again later that evening, when she would be home.

Raffaella's stomach lurched as she repeated the man's request to Serafina. The dark side of witchcraft, the one everyone feared and her parents had warned her about, reminded her of what Serafina could be. Raffaella felt sick, but when she looked into Serafina's dark eyes, she knew that she was a healer, and hers was not a den of black magic.

Serafina watched her, as if listening to her thoughts. Then she spoke. "There is much evil in the world, perpetrated by all manner of people. We all make decisions about what we do. We are all responsible for our actions." She took Raffaella's hand. "Think twice before agreeing to any dark requests. Whatever you do will come back to you threefold." She pursed her lips. "We will turn his request around and convince him that, rather than cause death to his rival, he should take instead a talisman for business success. That way, the deed will be for good rather than for bad."

She beckoned Raffaella to follow her. In the back room, she taught her how to cast a spell on a talisman for business success. Raffaella wondered how it was that people believed that all witches were bad.

When the moon was full, Serafina readied her cloak. Raffaella watched her lay the cloak on the bed, which they had begun sharing since that first night. Perhaps the walnut had the kind of magic she had needed to reveal this part of herself, the part that loved Serafina. She watched the movements of

Serafina's fingers, the way her hair fell around her face, and how she prepared a cloak for Raffaella.

"Are you sure I should go with you?" Raffaella asked.

"Yes, *cara*, you should. I think you'll enjoy it."

She loved it when Serafina's called her *cara*. Serafina's voice wrapped itself around Raffaella like a blanket, and the word was the key to her safety. Serafina made her feel whole in many different ways.

Raffaella thought back to that night when she had watched the coven perform their rite by the great tree. Had it been a walnut tree? Was that where her walnut came from? It hadn't occurred to her until that moment. She fondled the ridges of her walnut. Without another word, she followed Serafina's lead and put on the cloak.

Serafina went into her medicine parlor and returned with a burlap bag in her hand. In silence, they went to the front door, where they both picked up lanterns.

By the light of the moon, they walked along the edge of town to the opposite side of the city, back into the hills. There, among the pines, was the clearing Raffaella had encountered a month before, and the tree. Around the base of the tree, fallen walnuts were scattered, their thick green skins forming a fuzzy blanket on the ground. Several people waited for them.

As they approached, the members of the coven all bowed to Serafina. One young woman neared Raffaella and whispered, "You're very lucky to have befriended Serafina."

The group formed a circle, Raffaella included, with Serafina in the center. Serafina welcomed everyone, with a special mention for Raffaella. She asked the goddess Diana for blessings and said a prayer for health and safety.

It was then that Raffaella realized that Serafina was the high priestess of the coven.

The witches opened the circle and faced the massive tree, Serafina in front of them. They kneeled and bowed low, as they had when Raffaella had first seen them.

The witches straightened their backs but remained on their knees. Serafina stood up and went to the tree, bag in hand. She reached in and removed an object from the bag, but Raffaella couldn't see what it was. She thought she heard a hiss and saw a flick of a tongue, but she couldn't be sure in the moonlight.

No, it was alive. It writhed in Serafina's hands, but something didn't seem right. The snake seemed weakened, and Raffaella surmised that Serafina had drugged it. She held it with both hands high above her head and recited,

Goddess of the forests and the Moon,
Diana of the Silver Crescent,
I chant my praises to you.
I lift my arms to your heavenly Crescent.
I thank you for protecting the forests and groves.
Protect me and mine, for we are your spiritual children.
Beautiful Diana, I sing your praises.

When she was done, she placed the snake on the ground and put her foot on its head. Raffaella watched, enthralled, as Serafina brought her dagger down and cut the snake's head off.

Rather than feel revulsion or fear, Raffaella felt something inside her break free. It was as if she were a sunken boat that had been tethered to the ocean bottom by seaweed and weighed down by rocks and barnacles, and then set free. She floated on the surface of a sparkling sea, sailing to new shores.

Serafina stood up with the snake's head in one hand and body in the other, and moved closer to the tree. She placed the snake in a hole and pushed dirt into it. With her hands raised, palms up, she incanted,

We bring the serpent unto you,
Oh, powerful Diana
So that you will grant us
Strength, prosperity, and peace.

When Serafina completed the burial, she stood up and walked to Raffaella. She took her hand and led her to the tree. "This is *Il Noce*, the sacred walnut tree. This tree has for centuries held the power to bless or curse anyone who goes near it." She plucked a walnut from the branches and held it up. "It has been known to infect the mind of those who have slept under it, rendering them mad. But it has also protected those who ask of it from evil spells and spirits."

She held out her left hand, and Raffaella held out her left hand. Serafina took it, turned it palm up, and covered it with her other hand.

"Raffaella, I welcome you to our coven, *nostra covo di streghe*. Here, in this sacred *boschetto*, we worship Diana, Goddess of the Hunt. I ask you now if you wish to join us."

Raffaella stood a long time with Serafina holding her hand between hers, but for how long, she didn't know. Everything seemed to stop—time, movement, the very air around her were all suspended.

The voices of her parents blew through her head, cautions and condemnations, in the name of the Roman Catholic Church, to avoid and denounce the evil sorcery that plagued humanity. But looking at Serafina's face and seeing the compassion, love, and devoutness there, Raffaella knew that her parents were wrong. There was no evil here.

Her hand warmed, and as she stared into Serafina's eyes, a sparking, almost burning sensation spread up her arm and down into her chest. Her torso vibrated as if she was being infused with knowledge and familiarity. She nodded. "Yes."

Her mind, answering a call that her ears did not hear, shut out everything around her. She closed her eyes and turned her head upward. The lightness she felt was terrifying only for a second, then it was freeing, and then joyful.

And then she knew. She knew that this was where she was supposed to be. In Benevento. Honoring *Il Noce*. With Serafina.

When she opened her eyes, Serafina was facing her, dark eyes holding fast to hers. Raffaella lifted her hands to Serafina's face and held it gently. She leaned in and softly kissed her lips. At last, she was sailing freely.

Raffaella raised her hand to the tree and touched it. A gripping energy seeped out from the bark and entered her skin, and she knew that it was welcoming her. The energy reached her chest, and she took a deep breath, allowing it to enter her lungs. She was renewed, and she was happy.

Raffaella reached under her cloak and into the pocket of her skirt. She took out the walnut and placed it in Serafina's hand, closing her fingers around it.

Serafina put her hand on Raffaella's arm, gently turning her. "You will stay with me?"

Raffaella smiled. "Yes, I will stay with you."

Serafina smiled as well. "It's fitting that you ended up at the Church of Santa Sofia that first day we met. *Sofia*, in Greek, means wisdom, and all you needed was the wisdom to see who you really are, to open your eyes to your destiny."

"And you knew, didn't you?"

Serafina nodded.

Raffaella put her hands on Serafina's face and kissed her again, pressing firmly this time. Serafina led her away from the walnut tree, through the worshippers, and onto the road home.

Object Permanence

Steph Gottschalk

I TRIED TO MAKE MY wife coffee this morning.

Simple things like that have been hard for her since the accident. Hard for me, too. It takes three tries for me to push the button to start the coffeemaker her sister gave us for a wedding present. Clear boiling water drips into the jug below. I search for the coffee grounds, and find them on the floor. The can must have slipped from my grasp after I opened it, spilling all over the kitchen floor. I don't remember that happening.

I open the closet and take out a broom. I drag it to the kitchen, but it falls with a clatter that wakes my wife. She stumbles sleepily out of the bedroom in her favorite tattered fuzzy bathrobe as I fumble to pick up the broom. She stops, and stares at the scene before her. I stare back. She does not say anything.

She does not see me.

Slowly, she walks to the kitchen. She turns off the coffeemaker, and then leans forward against the kitchen counter, resting her head on her right arm. Her shoulders shake as she sobs. I want to hold her, comfort her, tell her everything will be all right, that I am here, but I can't.

Not since the accident.

It had been a friend's Halloween party—her friend, not mine. She always had more friends than me. More friends she introduced me as her wife to, anyway. I never talked to my friends about my personal life. I don't talk to them at all anymore.

My wife's friends are strange. They're either hippies, vegans, communists, or some combination of the three. I never fit in. I liked hamburgers and sports too much.

We stayed at the party later than I would have liked, and maybe I lied a little about how much I had been drinking because I wanted to be out of there. In any case, my wife was in no shape to drive, and perhaps it would not have made a difference. It was raining that night, raining hard. Lightning flashed as bright as day, and the house shook as thunder crashed right on top of us. My wife's friend offered to let us stay the night, as most of the party guests had elected to do, but I said I wanted to leave before things got worse. I did not say I wanted to leave before I got hungry enough to try the tofu.

We plowed down the street with water spraying in our wake, dodging fallen branches and downed power lines. Finally, we made it onto the highway.

I don't know what happened. I don't know if I lost control of the car or if someone else hit us or if the hand of a vengeful god reached down from the sky to push us off the road. All I remember is the windshield shattering, and a blast of icy air, and everything was cold, cold, cold...

My wife slowly cleans up the mess on the floor. It is a painstaking process as she only uses her right hand. Bits of coffee stick to her pink flannel pajamas, and she brushes them off one-handed when she is done, while waiting for her coffee to brew. This time with coffee actually in the coffee maker.

I think my wife is the most beautiful woman in the world, even first thing in the morning with her black curls all tangled from sleep and sticking up on the left side. She always falls asleep on that side, facing the window. She hasn't put on makeup yet, and there are more lines and bags than I usually see, along with the mole under her right eye and the angry red scars from the accident. Her dark eyes are haunted, her naturally golden-brown skin taking on a grayish pallor.

She is my wife. She is beautiful.

My wife reaches into the cupboard and takes out the mug I gave her last Christmas, the tacky one with the kittens wearing Santa hats. She loves things like that. She stares at it for a long moment before setting it on the counter and pouring coffee into it. I wonder if she is going to cry again, but she does not.

She stands in the kitchen, sipping her coffee slowly. Very slowly. At this rate, she will be late for work. I try to pick up her keys, the ones attached to the Mickey Mouse key ring that I bought her on our trip to Disneyland. Normally my keys are on the ring next to her, with a similar Donald Duck ring, but they were in my car when we had the accident.

The keys resist me, and stay on the hook, jingling uselessly.

My wife flinches at the sound, slopping coffee over her hand. "Shit," she says, and sets the mug back on the counter. She turns on the cold water in the kitchen sink, and runs her hand under it. That same hand turns the water off. She does not reach for a paper towel or a dishcloth, choosing instead to wipe her hand on her robe. She does not look at the keys.

I try to pull the coffee mug away from her, to tell her it is time to go, but the mug only slides across the counter, dangerously close to the edge. When my wife turns to pick it up, she misjudges its location and knocks it to the floor. The mug breaks into two large pieces and several smaller ones, and a puddle of hot coffee spreads across the floor. My wife steps back but not before getting her toes scalded.

"Shit," she says again and sits down on the floor, hugging her knees to her chest. She stares at the broken mug and the spilled coffee. Then she begins to cry.

She does not go to work today.

After the accident, I was cold, so cold.

I was alone in the house. My wife was gone. I lay in our bed alone and I was so cold.

Then she came back, and I was still cold, but she was warm. She was the only warm thing in the house, the only warm thing in my world. I stayed close to her at first, but she shivered every time I touched her, so I stopped.

I am still cold.

That afternoon, my wife sits quietly watching TV. Or perhaps it was a different afternoon. Time moves strangely since the accident. Sometimes I find myself slipping out of it entirely, only to return and find things not as I left them. Sometimes I try to move them back, but it upsets my wife when I do. Besides, I cannot quite recall where things go anymore.

My wife is sitting on the couch watching one of those quiz shows she likes. She usually tries to guess the answers ahead of the contestants, and she is usually right. I told her more than once that she should try out for one of those shows, but she always laughed me off. Today, however, she is silent, and I am silent as well.

Her eyelids droop and her head nods against the back of the couch. It is the same ugly couch from the college apartment where I met her for the first time. It is the same couch we sat on when we kissed for the first time. It was old then, and older now, a faded purplish color with innumerable stains and covered in cat hair. My wife keeps saying that she wants a new one, but we never find the time to go shopping for one.

She is almost completely asleep now, her head thrown back against the couch, snoring softly. Her legs are tucked up next to her, and her hands drop limply to the couch cushions. I take her hand in mine. The left one. It is the only thing that feels real to me anymore. I feel the soft heat of it, and the solid outline of her wedding ring. Time goes by, and leaves me behind.

My wife mumbles, half awake. It is dark out, the television showing the evening news. "Kayla?" my wife mutters and then comes fully awake. She stares at my side of the couch and shivers, rubbing her left elbow until I can no longer feel her hand.

After the accident, my wife's mother took care of our cat. This morning she brings the cat carrier to our house, and lets Galileo out. Galileo, a fluffy brown tabby just out of kittenhood, is busy exploring the house, making sure everything is in its place. She can tell something is not right.

My wife starts to pour the water for tea. She has two mugs, both from state parks I don't remember visiting.

"Let me get that," her mother says.

"It's fine, I got it."

"But it would be easier if I—"

"I said I got it. Okay, Mom?"

I've always liked my mother-in-law, though my wife finds her overbearing and wishes they lived farther away from each other. My wife and her mother both have forceful personalities, and they often clash. My own parents stopped talking to me after I came out. They did not even come to our wedding, though my wife insisted on sending them an invitation.

Galileo finishes her rounds and comes into the kitchen for food and water. She stops and stares at me standing next to her purple plastic water bowl.

"Is kitty all right?" my wife's mother asks, blowing on her tea. "She's not eating."

My wife turns to look at the cat. Her mother takes out her tea bag. She likes her tea weak. My wife leaves her tea bag in until she is finished drinking. "She probably just needs some time to adjust to being back. Or maybe she hears a mouse in the wall. My friend's cat used to stare into space like that all the time, and eventually they figured out that they had squirrels in their walls. We used to joke that the cat was seeing ghosts."

I had told her that they were probably ghost squirrels, but my wife does not repeat the joke to my mother.

I reach down and stroke Galileo. She flinches, and bolts out of the room.

My wife shakes her head. "Cats," she says.

In the morning, my wife is brushing her teeth when she sees my reflection in the foggy mirror. She gasps, and chokes, dropping her toothbrush to the bathmat. She leans over the sink, spitting and coughing hard. While she is catching her breath, I reach over her head and trace a heart in the fog on the mirror. I always liked tracing things on foggy or frosty glass. I would leave pictures for her on her car in the winter. Usually simple things, like a smile or a cat, or a smiling cat. And hearts, of course.

I try to add words, but as she looks up, my fingers fade, leaving only incoherent smudges. It's just as well. What words can be enough, at this point?

My wife stares at the glass. She can no longer see me, but she can see the heart, and she looks at it for a long time.

"Kayla?" she whispers.

I am silent.

Then time lurches past me again, and she is leaving for work, but I know she will be late.

I do not think my wife should be working yet. She comes home more exhausted than I have ever seen her, even when she was training for a marathon. Even then, she still had the energy to cuddle with me on the ugly couch and listen to me complain about my day. Now, she simply throws a frozen dinner in the microwave, changes into her pink flannel pajamas, and eats in front of the TV. We never ate with the TV on unless something important was going on, like the Packers playing the Vikings. She is from Wisconsin originally, but I am Minnesota born and raised, so the household always gets a bit strained during those times. I think we both pretended to be more upset than we really were, though, just so we could make up. I know I did.

Ever since the accident, she doesn't care what she watches. It could be the sort of game show or reality show that she used to sneer at for being inane (yet for some reason could not stop watching), a food show that used to have her taking notes and googling recipes, television dramas or comedies that make offensive jokes that used to send her into a raging tirade...she doesn't seem to notice what's on anymore.

Sometimes, she does not even bother to eat and just sits down, staring blankly at the TV until she drifts off to sleep, not moving until she wakes up the next morning to go to work. If I can, I turn off the TV and the lights, and sit with her, holding her hand. Sometimes Galileo joins us, sitting in my wife's lap. My wife never forgets to feed Gal.

Sometimes, however, her hand is not there, and I cannot reach the lights.

My wife's friend Terry comes over for a visit.

I like Terry. They're perhaps the only one of my wife's friends I would consider my friend as well, rather than a secondhand friend. Terry likes cats and comic books and is quiet around people they don't know too well, but quite animated around close friends. Or so my wife tells me. Terry and I were not quite at the close stage before the accident, and I have not seen them since.

One of Terry's many eccentricities that I had not known about is that they own a Ouija board. It is currently sitting on my kitchen table, still in its box, while my wife and Terry sip tea and stare at it silently. I do not know how long they have been sitting like that, but Terry's tea is nearly gone.

My wife is the first to speak. "I feel kind of silly now," she says, with a laugh that sounds forced. "I mean, look at it. It's a toy. We used to play with this in middle school. We may as well expect answers from Twister or Monopoly."

"Don't judge it by its looks," Terry says, drinking down the last of their Earl Grey. "I once held a séance using a piece of notebook paper with the alphabet scribbled on it for a board, and a shot glass for the planchette. That was my most successful attempt, too. If something's there, it'll make itself known, no matter what we use."

My wife shakes her head. "It isn't 'something' we're looking for. It's Kayla."

"Well, that's what we're hoping to find out," Terry says. For a believer, they're quite the skeptic. They shove their mug aside and open the box.

My wife's hand grips her mug tightly. It is still half full of soothing chamomile. She hates chamomile, and only drinks it when she needs to relax or fall asleep. Better than pills, she claims. "It is Kayla," she insists. "I'm not imagining things."

EDITED BY JAE AND ASTRID OHLETZ

"I never said you were." Terry lays out the board with the letters facing my wife and places the planchette in the center. "But there are a lot of things on the astral planes, and they're not all benevolent. Or honest."

My wife shakes her head resolutely. "It's her," she says. "Sometimes I feel like she's just in the next room, and she's going to jump out and surprise me like she used to." My wife sets her mug of cold tea down with a nervous clatter. It is a new mug, patterned with birds or leaves or something. I can't quite make it out. I have never seen it before in my life.

She places her right hand on the planchette, and Terry adds both of theirs. "What now?" my wife asks. "Do we just... talk? Like we did in middle school?"

Terry shrugs. "I don't see why not." They look around the kitchen, their gaze passing right through me. "Spirits and beings of the astral plane," Terry intones in a rather melodramatic voice. "We seek the soul of the one known as Kayla. Kayla, if you are here, move the planchette to YES."

I look at the board. ABCDEFGHIJKLMNOPQRSTU-VWXYZ YES NO HELLO GOODBYE. I give the planchette an experimental push, but it is slippery and does not budge.

"My hand is cold," my wife says quietly.

"Mine too," Terry replies just as softly, as if they might blow me away with a strong breath. Perhaps they could. "Does this happen a lot?"

"Sometimes," my wife says. "Usually just before I fall asleep, so I'm not sure if I'm dreaming it or not. But sometimes I'll feel a cold touch, and if I close my eyes, I'll get the feeling that she's right there next to me. And sometimes..." My wife hesitates, then says the next part all in a rush, stammering a little. "Sometimes...you know that phrase phantom limb pain? Sometimes I feel her holding my hand. My left hand."

Terry's eyes widen slightly, and they start to speak, but I manage to get a good grip on the planchette and get it to slide a little ways across the board, where it lands more or less on 'B.'

There is a shocked silence in the room.

"Did you do that?" my wife whispers, barely more than a breath.

"No," Terry says, in a voice that is only a little stronger. "I take it you didn't?"

"Of course not."

Both of them stare at the board.

"B?" my wife says. "What could that mean?"

"It's...sort of towards the YES, I suppose?" Terry says dubiously. "Maybe that's what K—what the ghost was going for? The only time I got this to almost work, we only got nonsense letters."

"It's Kayla," my wife whispers. She is trembling.

Terry has never been good at dealing with other people's emotions. "It could be," they say, still wary. "What do you want to ask?"

"I—I don't know," my wife says, in the sort of whisper that means she is holding back tears. "I think about it all the time. I imagine she's sitting right next to me, and think about what I would say and what she would say. And it's always the strange, goofy, random things, like...like, how would a werewolf survive the apocalypse, or what if dragons were real but they were the size of pigeons? It never really mattered what we said to each other, it was the being together that was important. And this..." My wife stands up abruptly, jerking her hand away from the board. "I can't do this. I can't pretend..." Her voice catches in a sob.

Terry looks quite alarmed, but after a few seconds, they stand up and move to gingerly pat my wife on the shoulder. I add my own embrace, and my wife shivers, pressing her face into Terry's shoulder. I can tell Terry is not happy with the gesture, but they stretch their arms out to hug her, pushing me away.

There are boxes in the living room. They are full of my books, my comics, my video games, my music. My guitar leans against them, still in its case. There are more boxes in our bedroom. My wife fills them with my clothes. The ugly Christmas sweater her niece made for me that I wore faithfully every year. The t-shirt I spilled ice cream on the last time we went to the beach. My favorite pair of jeans that fit just right and had pockets that held my phone and wallet comfortably. The paint-stained flannel I wore while redoing the outside of the house (blue, my wife's favorite shade of periwinkle, to replace the original dingy gray).

She lingers over the flannel, pressing it to her face and inhaling deeply. Does it still smell of me? Or just dust and old paint?

Eventually, she adds it to the box, closes the lid, and drags it out to the living room with the rest.

She sits on the couch with a mug of tea. Galileo jumps into her lap, demanding to be petted, and my wife complies. The cat stares at me, wondering why I don't pet her anymore, and meows loudly in complaint.

"What the matter, Gal?" my wife says. "Seeing ghosts again?"

I try to sit on the couch next to her, but it is insubstantial and I move right through it. She bought a new one, a classy white sofa in cat-proof vinyl. I don't remember how long she has had it, though I vaguely remember that I have tried and failed to sit on it many times. I vaguely realize that I am the one who is insubstantial and not the couch.

I am very vague these days.

When the boxes are gone, the house seems much emptier. I know the hallways and the photographs, the cat and my wife, but almost everything else is gone.

I wander the halls, knowing they will not be here much longer.

"Galileo! What have you got there?"

The cat has batted her new catnip toy under the fridge, and in attempting to retrieve it has unearthed two dusty pens, a superball, three old receipts, four bobby pins, and a guitar pick.

The woman picks up the guitar pick. "Oh," she says, after staring at it with a puzzled frown for several seconds. "This must have been Kayla's."

A flicker of sadness crosses her face, but it is the ghost of grief from long ago. She hesitates, glancing toward the trash, then drops the guitar pick into the broken teacup that holds her loose change, next to the sleek new coffeemaker. She scowls at Galileo in mock severity. The fat old cat waddles creakily into the living room, the short-lived urge to play forgotten in favor of the urge to nap. "I'll deal with you later. You are *not* going to make me late to the board meeting." The cat ignores her, as cats are wont to do, curling up instead on the well-worn couch.

The woman sighs, picks up a ring of keys with a cat-shaped charm, and heads out the door.

The door closes behind her, and the house is still. Not a soul stirs.

TAYLOR-MADE

CATHERINE LANE

TAYLOR SAW THE JACKET OUT of the corner of her eye as she left the Italian restaurant. Its bright blue color—fashion magazines would probably call it a thalo or a cyan blue—grabbed her attention, and the way the jacket sat casually and forgotten on the back of a chair invited her over. She couldn't help herself. She veered out of her way to take a closer look.

As she passed the empty table, she nonchalantly reached over half-eaten pasta and grabbed the jacket. *Did I just take that jacket?* She had never even taken a pen home from the office at the end of the day, so when she looked down at her hand clutched around the jacket, she gasped. *I should put it back.*

But she didn't. She didn't even turn around to check if anyone had noticed. She just rushed out of the restaurant, like the criminal she was, as fast as she could. Were they coming after her? She listened for rushing footsteps or accusatory shouts.

Nothing.

It wasn't until she was safe in her Prius that she truly started to calm down. Her breathing settled. She even managed to steal a few looks at the jacket sitting calmly on the passenger side seat without feeling as if she were going to have a heart attack. Up close, the jacket was gorgeous. She couldn't quite place the material. It looked like silk and felt like cashmere, but the shimmer coming off the jacket was unlike either of those materials. *Oh God. What a rush.*

She took one last look at the restaurant just to make sure. All was silent. But she could never go back there again—a big loss. *Pasta Primavera* was close to her office, and their signature dish, handmade pasta with cream and vegetables, was out of this world. More important, no one there ever made her feel self-conscious when she asked for a table for one.

What the hell happened back there? She had stolen that jacket. Taylor hadn't thought herself capable of such an act. She was a paralegal for Christ's sake—on the side of law and order and all that stuff. Maybe it was the mind-numbing boredom at work lately that had made her take it. She'd spent the last month hidden away in her cubicle, going through forty-three banker boxes and pulling any document that had to do with travertine tile. An hour ago, she had put the lid on the last box—freedom! The lunch special at *Pasta Primavera* was the treat she'd promised herself for meeting the October 1st deadline.

Normally, Taylor would have felt at a loss without a new project at work, but the jacket, just a foot away from her, was all she could think about. She reached out to touch it again. It felt warm, almost alive. *I have to try it on. Now.* No way would she be able to wait until she finished work tonight.

Jane in the cubicle next to hers at work picked up at the first ring.

"Hey, it's me, Taylor. I...I need the afternoon off." She forced the words out in a rush. Her voice sounded small, thin, and unsure.

"Oh, I'm glad you called. Mike has some questions. When are you coming back?" Jane prattled on, not stopping to listen.

Taylor pulled at the jacket's cuff and balled it tightly in her hand. A strange force rose up in her. "I'm not. I'm going home. Tell Mike I'll talk to him tomorrow."

"You want me to tell Mike, your boss and the lead attorney on this case, to wait until tomorrow?"

"Yes."

"Seriously?"

"Forget it. I'll call HR myself." Taylor hung up and realized that she had practically crushed the jacket's cuff in her hand. She smoothed it out. It didn't seem any worse for wear. At the next light, she easily turned right towards home rather than left towards the office.

Taylor stood in front of her bedroom closet and regarded herself in the mirror. Before this moment, she had always thought that these sliding doors were the worst feature about her dingy apartment. They screamed cheap and angled out in ways that showed Taylor her every physical flaw. The same ones her last girlfriend had pointed out at their all-too-public breakup. Taylor didn't want to be with anyone so shallow to judge an entire relationship on looks, but even she had to admit that she had let herself go since, rather than deal with the hurt of that statement.

Today, though, she was actually thankful for the mirrors. They allowed her to see all of her body, and when she slipped the jacket on, she would be able to see it from all sides. No going back. She'd be a thief if she tried it on. She could still take it back to the restaurant. No harm, no foul, right?

Her answer was to slip one arm through the jacket's sleeve. *Ooh. So soft.* But it wasn't enough. She had to feel it on her skin. She slipped out of the jacket and quickly tore off her rayon blouse, one of many identical ones that she wore to work. The cream color looked dull and almost grey against the bright blue of the jacket. *Ugh.* She dropped the blouse to the floor and once again slid her arm through the jacket.

Much better. The material, whatever it was, caressed her skin, and as the jacket covered her shoulders, she relaxed into it. A steady warmth flowed down her back and downward into her legs. Years of tension simply melted away.

The jacket fit perfectly, as if it had been tailor-made for her. Beyond that, it was flattering in ways that no other jacket had ever been, making her seem taller and thinner. She pulled the mirror out a bit so she could admire the back panel, which made her bottom pleasingly full rather than just plain flabby. Then she stepped back and took in her whole image.

Strange. Even her hair looked good today, less frizzy and maybe even a little blonder.

A second glance told her it was true. Her hair, normally a flat dishwater brown, now had golden highlights running through it, and her usual frizz was beginning to kink up into smooth ringlets. *That crazy extract shampoo was worth what I paid for it.*

Taylor kept the jacket on for the rest of the day. She puttered around her apartment, doing nothing really, but the whole time she felt completely at ease. Ordinarily, she didn't spend more time in the cramped apartment than absolutely necessary. This afternoon was different. She hung two vacation photos in the dark hallway and pulled the heavy curtains off the living room windows. They desperately needed a wash, but when she saw how the dappled sunlight flooded into the room, she dropped the curtains into the trash bin outside without a second thought.

That night, she took off the jacket and hung it carefully in the closet. She opened the sliding door so she could see it from the bed. It was the last thing she looked at before she fell into the best night's sleep she'd had in years.

The next morning, Taylor dressed with only one thought. She would wear the jacket to work. She grabbed a bright white T-shirt, wanting something plain to highlight the lovely blue of the jacket, and tried on her favorite pair of tan pants. When she went to button them, though, they were way too big, almost sliding-down-her-legs big. *That's strange. They fit last week. The diet must be working. Finally!*

She rummaged around in the closet for a smaller skirt that belonged to a time two girlfriends ago. It fit perfectly. A soft smile spread across Taylor's face as she studied her reflection. Usually, she did only a quick check to make sure she hadn't spattered toothpaste all over her rayon blouse. Today, she lingered, turning first one way and then the other. The skirt flared out, revealing a surprisingly shapely calf. Taylor's smile deepened into a grin.

She still wore the grin as she got into her Prius. She hit three green lights in a row and zipped through the line at the drive-in Starbucks.

"Double, venti, sweet, non-fat caramel macchiato." Her cheeks heated with the ridiculous order. What could she say? She liked her coffee sweet, not creamy. Taylor hunkered down in the car's seat, getting ready for the barista's snarky eye roll or his asking her to repeat her order. She would beat him to the punch today. "Double, venti…"

"Gotcha. Name please?"

"Taylor."

With a nod, the young man vanished back into the store. The nutty aroma of freshly ground coffee drifted out the window.

While she waited, she cleaned out the side pocket on her car's door. First she balled up old napkins from fast-food restaurants and then a map from a trip she'd planned but never taken.

"My sister's name is Taylor." The barista interrupted her task as he leaned out of the window with her coffee. "So I gave you something special."

Taylor took the cup to see an ornate caramel "T" scripted on the foam.

"Don't forget the lid."

Delighted with this simple gesture, she shared her earlier grin with the young man behind the window. He smiled back. She carried his smile with her on the rest of the drive to work. She didn't hurry; she even switched the channels on the car radio from NPR to an oldies station. The up-tempo beat filled the car. She hummed with it at first and then found herself singing out loud.

Her good mood lasted only until she got into the elevator. Jammed with the 8:58 a.m. crowd, the elevator looked like a tin of packed sardines, but she managed to squeeze in. The man next to her breathed heavily, and the one on the other side drummed his fingers on the wall during the short ride. The tension of yet another workday closed in on her, reminding her that the situation upstairs was probably going to explode in her face.

She snuck out of the elevator behind a tall man so that Jenna, the buxom blonde at the receptionist's desk, couldn't alert anyone of her arrival. Ringing phones, earnest conversation, and the general clatter of a thriving business greeted Taylor as soon as she entered the cubicle farm. She kept her head down so she wouldn't be noticed, but her palms began sweat the moment she slunk into her own cubicle by the back. How long could she avoid Mike?

"Mike wants to see you." Jane popped up like a malevolent jack-in-the-box from the cubicle next to Taylor's. Her voice was full of glee. "You should go find him before he gets too mad. Ooh, never mind. Here he comes."

Taylor looked down the hall.

Sure enough, Mike marched right towards her. Other paralegals and secretaries immediately put their heads down to avoid meeting his roving gaze.

"Taylor?" He looked around; clearly, she was not important enough for him to remember which cubicle was hers.

Taylor took a deep breath. *What, is no one ever supposed to take personal time around here? How bad can it be?* "Can I help you, Mike?"

"You can't even help yourself. HR said you took some personal time. You can't skip out after lunch like you own the place. I've informed HR that you're now on probation." Mike wasn't even looking at her. He was making eye contact with everyone else in the area.

It was bad. Even so, she found herself standing up a little straighter.

"Now if you had a doctor's note dated yesterday and a parking receipt..." He finally looked up from the large pile of work he was carrying. He tilted his head. "...that would be the only way you could contest..." His gaze drifted down her front and stopped at her chest. The jacket was open in just the right way to flatter her breasts, which had always been her best feature, even in her worst times.

Mike's gaze lingered there and then flicked back up to her eyes. His brows creased. "Never mind. Will you step into my office to discuss this case further?"

What the hell? Did he just check me out? "Of course." She pulled the jacket more tightly around her and followed him down the hall to his big corner office, smirking at Jane as she passed. Jane's mouth hung open.

Even though Taylor had worked at the firm for over ten years, she had never been in Mike's office before. Not many of the paralegals had. It was common knowledge that Mike would rather have any talk with a subordinate out in the cubicle farm because he liked publicly humiliating the paralegals. Only one woman had ever defied him by saying no to one of his outrageous requests. Martha, a woman old enough to be his mother, had refused to work every day over a long weekend. When the rest of the paralegal team came back on that next Tuesday, Martha's cubicle was completely empty, all traces of her wiped clean—like a horror film. No one had heard from her again.

Taylor looked around at his office as she entered. The large bank of windows overlooked the San Fernando Valley. It was an uncharacteristically smogless day, so she could see all the way to the San Gabriel Mountains. *So this is how the other half lives.*

Mike crossed to his desk but didn't invite her to sit in one of the leather-and-chrome visitor's chairs. His gaze drifted down to her breasts again and then to the pile of papers he still held in his hands. "Look, Taylor. I'm really sorry."

Taylor's eyebrows rose. An apology from Mike? Had hell frozen over?

"I know it took you a long time to go through all those documents, but I need you to do it again. The hotel has widened the suit, and this time you're looking for Aztec Madrid tile as well."

The warmth of the jacket seeped through her T-shirt. Her body began to tingle. Sighing, she prepared to nod and agree to whatever he wanted, but instead she heard herself ask, "In all forty-three boxes?"

"Yeah, in all forty-three boxes."

"But, Mike, um..."

At her mild objection, his eyes narrowed.

Her heart pounded as she waited for his response. Would he yell or, worse, fire her? She had no earthly idea what was coming next. The jacket snuggled into her, making this uncertainly seem not so bad.

Mike dropped the pile of papers on his desk. "You know what? Screw it. You're right. I'll ask Jane to do it. It's too much to ask you again."

Taylor nearly toppled over. What was going on here?

"Besides, I have another case I want you on right now."

Twenty minutes later, Taylor found herself in Mike's convertible Mercedes driving over Topanga Canyon to Malibu and the beach. She relaxed into the supple leather seat and warm sun of the beautiful October day, not even worrying about what the wind was doing to her hair. *Who would have guessed this is where I'd be when the day started?*

Mike chose this exact moment to slide his hand up her leg.

Somewhere, Taylor found a strength that she hadn't known she possessed. She didn't scream or panic or just grit her teeth and bear it. Instead, she simply took his hand and returned it to his side of the car. "I'm gay, you know?" *What the hell? I just rejected my boss and came out to him in one fell swoop. I must be completely insane.*

To her utter surprise, Mike just laughed. "You don't have to pretend. I can take rejection." And he immediately put his hand back on her leg.

"No, seriously. I'm gay. I think it's even in my personnel file. Part of your diversity hiring."

This time, Mike removed his hand himself. "Damn, you're a protected class."

Power flowed through Taylor. How easy it had been to put Mike into his place. She should have done it years ago.

Mike took a sharp turn onto PCH and the land of multi-million-dollar beach homes.

Somehow, she felt different today, as if something was buffering her from how hurtful the world could be. She wanted to laugh out loud and swing her arms about the car. She felt as if she could make anything work. "Protected like Fort Knox." She tried out the new feeling.

"No worries."

Taylor raised an eyebrow. Her statement hadn't been an apology.

"There's other fish in our firm. What do you think of Jenny down in reception?" His tone implied that they now were buddies on the hunt for girls together. "Cute, huh?"

"She's a little too blonde for my taste. And, for the record, her name's Jenna."

"You're on the job here, Taylor. So no flirting with our client." Mike chuckled as if it were a joke, but he also rose up on his toes as he spoke, putting his full height behind his statement.

"Okay. Who's the client?" Taylor shrugged off the obvious insult. Watching Mike in action for the past hour had taught her a few things. She had known that he was an A-class jerk, but she hadn't pegged him for an insecure little boy. She almost felt sorry for him.

"A big shot," Mike said. His chest puffed as led the way to the front door.

The house, as most residences on PCH did, looked like nothing special from the street side. A white, wooden box containing far too many garage doors. But once they went through the security gate set in a tall wall, Taylor saw the truth. *I was wrong. This is how the other half really lives.*

The house celebrated modern architecture in the best sense of the word—clean, simple lines that married form to function. Large glass panels rose up from the ground, all on different planes, but each highlighting the house's best feature—the stunning view of the Pacific Ocean. Blue water stretched out for as far as the eye could see. It took Taylor's breath away. Then the door opened, and her breath really left her body.

The stunning woman in front of her made the sea, the view, the whole house pale by comparison. She was tall, even taller than Mike. She stood at the door, leaning casually on one of the jambs, and welcomed them with a simple "hi" and a dazzling smile.

No way! That's Maggie Benton! Taylor had drooled over her at the last Academy Awards show. Maggie had won an Oscar for Best Original Screenplay. *Dirigo* was about two sisters solving a sinister family mystery in a small town in Maine.

Some critics whined her win had been purely political since one sister was gay. Surely, she had just capitalized on how trendy lesbian characters were in Hollywood at the moment. Those who had seen even a page of one of Maggie's scripts paid no heed to her detractors. All Taylor had noticed was how stunning Maggie looked in her vintage Vera Wang dress and Tiffany jewels. Maggie had seemed a part of a completely different world then, and now, unbelievably, she stood in front of Taylor in the flesh.

Mike introduced them, his chest puffed to maximum capacity.

Maggie stepped in front of him to take Taylor's outstretched hand.

Taylor intended the handshake to be firm, but the softness of Maggie's hand threw her. Their touch became more of a caress than a professional introduction.

Meanwhile, Maggie's scrutiny wandered down Taylor's body.

Holy shit! Did Maggie Benton just check me out? Taylor blushed, but she forced herself to meet Maggie's gaze as it drifted back up. Her eyes were a light green, the exact color of the dress that she had worn on the red carpet last winter. Maggie gave Taylor's hand an extra little squeeze before releasing it. A hundred butterflies fluttered in her stomach. *So this is love at first sight.*

"Excuse the mess." Maggie brought them into a living room cluttered with boxes. "I'm just starting to decorate for my Halloween party. You do it once, and then suddenly it's a tradition. It's kind of fun, though, to see everyone compete for the best costume. I have prizes." Shrugging, she pointed to a dozen cheesy T-shirts on the couch that had Best Costume in big orange and black letters.

Oh my God, she's adorable. Out of my league, for sure. But I'm going to savor every moment of this.

"We won't take too much of your time," Mike said. "Can I see the windows?"

Maggie led them to a large bank of windows on the north wall. They were sliders that opened up to a huge, well-appointed outdoor patio, the kind that Taylor had previously only seen on HGTV.

"See, the condensation just won't go away." Maggie pointed to the water vapor inside the double-paned windows.

What followed was a long, tedious conversation about the windows, receipts, and broken promises that the window company had made. Taylor spent the whole time openly admiring Maggie. The way she spoke, moved, and tilted her head when she laughed—all of it was perfect. Occasionally, Maggie directed a comment to Taylor, who, now that the business part of the day had started, had no idea why she was actually there. Maggie's gaze lingered sometimes too, but unlike Mike, she kept it on Taylor's face.

I've got to be making this up. She can't be flirting with me.

"I'll sue them if I have to, but all I want are new windows. Before the party." Maggie got up from the sofa and slammed her hand for show against the offending windows.

"You can rest assured. Horowitz and Kane will get those windows replaced. Before the thirty-first." He punctuated his statement with a small bow.

Wow, what a kiss-ass.

The meeting was over. Everyone moved to the front door when Maggie's phone rang. "I'm sorry, but I have to take this." She lifted a version of the iPhone that wasn't even in stores yet to her ear. The person on the other end did all of the talking.

Taylor took advantage of Maggie's distraction to study her features more thoroughly—full lips, high cheekbones, a narrow jaw. Strangely, she didn't feel the least bit self-conscious staring point blank at someone who was less than two feet away.

Maggie's look soured. "You're kidding. Okay, Billy. Good luck with that." She ended the call. "Shit. My researcher just quit. He sold a pilot. A drama. I didn't even know he was writing one." She tapped the iPhone against her other hand. "Let me show you out."

Even before the door shut behind them, Taylor's heart raced along with her thoughts. *This can't be it.* Unexpectedly, the tingling started again and the warmth too. She found herself clutching the cuff of the jacket and praying to some higher power. *Please get me back inside that house. Please.*

"Crap. I forgot that stack of invoices," Mike said, leafing through the papers in his hand. "Taylor, do you mind? I'll get the car."

Thank you. Thank you.

When she rang the doorbell, Maggie opened the door, but instead of giving her an appreciative glance, she looked right through Taylor. Her whole demeanor had changed with the phone call.

"Sorry. Mike forgot some papers."

Maggie stepped back without a word and led her to where Mike had carelessly left the bills.

Taylor bent down to pick them up and then froze. *What if... No. It is completely crazy. I can't do it.* She opened her mouth once, but nothing came out. Then from somewhere deep inside, a place that had been sealed only yesterday opened wide. Long-held dreams, half-baked ideas, notions that she didn't even know that she harbored flooded through her. All of these things had been buried so deeply inside they might as well not have existed until she'd taken the jacket. *The jacket! It's the jacket.*

"I can do research." The casual tone suggested that Taylor was only offering to do a simple favor for Maggie. Her shoulders relaxed. She had never said something so important so well before.

Maggie did not reply.

Ordinarily, this would have undone all of Taylor's resolve. However, it wasn't her resolve that was fueling this moment; it was the jacket. She would have to consider how later. For the moment, she gave the jacket a thankful hug. The familiar warmth rose up in her.

"I did research in college. For this crazy English professor who was writing a book on Christian demons. Terrible book, but the reviewers said it was exquisitely researched. Now I review documents at Horowitz and Kane. I can do it." She marveled at the fact that she actually believed she could.

Maggie studied her. "I don't normally hire pretty women. It can get way too complicated."

Too late. Maggie had just called her pretty. "I'm just offering my skills as a researcher." *But we both know I'm offering more. Much more, if you want it.*

Maggie's pause was so long Taylor was afraid all was lost. The jacket wasn't magic after all. Maybe she'd just had a bit of good luck that had now run its course. *Come on. Come on.* She pulled the jacket tight around her. *Work your magic.*

"Okay. I'll take a chance."

Taylor barely resisted the urge to pump her fist.

"When can you start?"

"Right now. My first duty will be to get rid of Mike."

Pop music blasted from speakers. Trendy cocktails circulated on platters. Beautiful, important people mingled with slightly less beautiful, less important people. Maggie's Halloween party was the only place to be on October 31st in Los Angeles. Stars, producers, and directors had been calling Hector, Maggie's assistant, for weeks, begging to be on the guest list. Gift baskets had come every day as bribes, and now well-muscled security was on PCH, turning away the gate crashers.

Taylor stood by the bar, sipping a Moscow Mule when someone tugged on her jacket.

"Who are you supposed to be? You just look normal."

Taylor turned and looked down at Darla Hobbs. The preteen starlet was currently the toast of the town, starring in a hit network show about an innocent country girl. Apparently, Darla's innocence was only an act, though, because now she was dressed up as a sexy vampire, wearing too much makeup and showing too much cleavage. "Me?"

"Yeah. You're not wearing anything. I thought everyone had to wear a costume. It said so on the invitation, you know?" The girl's entitled tone suggested that adults always told her that she was right.

"You're wrong, sweetie." Taylor resisted the urge to wave a finger at her. "I'm wearing the best costume anyone has ever seen. You wouldn't believe me if I told you."

Darla looked at the jacket and rolled her eyes. "Whatever." She dismissed Taylor with a shake of her head and moved into the crowd.

Taylor took a pull at the cocktail. She rolled the freshly squeezed lime and ginger beer mixture over her tongue, savoring the exotic taste. She had never had a Moscow Mule before and had certainly never rubbed elbows with so many stars. *Guess I'm not in Kansas anymore.*

In fact, she wasn't even in the same universe. Her life had changed so much in the four weeks since that fateful lunch in *Pasta Primavera*. She knew without even looking in a mirror that her hair was soft and curly and shone in the tea-lights hanging above the deck. Her face, which had been nothing special before the jacket, had settled into a lovely symmetry. Everyone now took a second look. Most took a third and a forth. But these changes weren't even the half of it.

The real changes had occurred inside. She now had a new confidence that seemed to create its own luck. Within a week of signing on with Maggie, she had stumbled on the story of Stikla, a female Viking warrior who sailed the seas to avoid marriage in Norway during the 800s. Maggie had run with the idea and now was in pitch meetings from dawn to dusk. It looked as if there would be a bidding war for the script. Maggie had even started calling Taylor her good-luck charm.

"Okay. So who are you supposed to be?"

Taylor turned to see Mike, of all people, sidling up to her with a bright red drink in his hand and "cute", buxom Jenna on his arm. He was dressed as an English lord and Jenna, a French maid. He had scored an invitation only by getting the windows replaced before the party. He had cut it close; the last caulking had gone in yesterday.

"Enough already. Why does everyone keep asking me that?"

"Because you're not wearing a costume."

"It doesn't look like it, but this is a mask." Taylor touched her face. "Underneath, I'm the ugly duckling."

"More like the beautiful swan." Mike released Jenna to give her an awkward side hug. His arm lingered around her shoulders. Now that she was someone to know thanks to Maggie, Mike's demeanor had completely changed.

Taylor tried to take a step away, but the crush of the party pushed her back towards him.

"Look at us," he said, wrapping the other arm around Jenna. The red cocktail sloshed onto the deck. "Here at the party of the year." His words slurred together. How many of those red drinks hadn't hit the deck?

Taylor threw Jenna a cautionary and questioning look, but her former colleague just shrugged.

"Excuse me, Mike. Can I borrow our girl?" Maggie pulled Taylor from his arm. "It's almost midnight. The bonfire is about to start." At the last moment, she had changed her costume from a woodland fairy to Stikla, the Viking warrior queen. The costumer on her last film had dropped everything to design it. A tight dress split up the sides, high boots, and a low bodice showed off her lithe figure. A rose-gold choker, the same shade as Maggie's auburn hair, shimmered on her neck, and she wore a prop knife strapped to her arm. Encrusted in fake jewels, it lent an air of danger and excitement to Maggie as she moved about the party. The result was breathtaking, not to mention great native advertising for the new script.

Every time Taylor looked at her, her heart skipped a beat.

"Come over here. We can see the bonfire better."

"Thanks for the rescue."

Maggie smiled and led her to the highest step on the deck, which overlooked the "set". Each of Maggie's parties had a theme. This year, it was Samhain, the Celtic roots of Halloween, where the community gathered to make offerings to the gods. Maggie's guests stood in an ancient Irish countryside. Unbelievably, in the heart of Malibu, a dirt path now cut through green, mossy hills. None of it was real. Workmen had started at eight sharp for the past week to build the hills on either side of the deck out of chicken wire and plaster. A set decorator arrived only that morning with literally a truckload of fresh moss, which the men had painstakingly applied to the bare hills. The moss now gave off a wonderful, woodsy smell, and partygoers constantly drifted to the hills to run their fingers through the green plants. In the "valley" between the hills, fake boulders and rocks acted as tables, and servers circulated in period costume offering delectable tidbits with deep Irish brogues. The bonfire pit at the very center of the deck, too, had chicken wire at its center, but the fake crops and animal bones on top gave it a real sense of authenticity. If Taylor hadn't known better, she would have been completely fooled.

"Ladies and Gentlemen, may I have your attention, please?" Maggie's voice boomed out from speakers over the deck. "It's almost midnight, and to celebrate Samhain as the Celts would've, we now need to sacrifice to the gods."

A deep rumbling sound came from the center of the fire pit.

"Please, everyone, gather in. Hector is handing out your offerings."

Hector, dressed as a Druid high priest, passed out little burlaps bags tied with black ribbons. People grabbed them with glee and crowded in close to the bonfire. Over the deck, a recording of an ancient wooden flute blew the first note of midnight. At the same time, the red glow of flames from the bonfire lit up the dark sky.

It was a movie fire full of special effects, and, like the movies, it was better than the real thing. The audience oohed and awed as the fire grew in intensity and richness. The flute finished its last strike of midnight and transitioned into an eerie, ancient melody. The fire danced to the notes and rhythm of the song.

"Now, if you will, open your offerings."

Everyone did with squeals of excitement.

Taylor tugged at her string. Inside the bag were tiny, bone-shaped pieces. Not like a dog bone, but exquisitely created pieces of art that looked as if they could have been real if they were ten times the size.

"In the olden days the Celts would come together on this night and throw bones into the fire." Maggie's voice sounded almost otherworldly. "Yes, that's where we get the word *bonfire.* They thought it would keep the spirits on their side of the portal. Let's see if they're right. Ladies and Gentlemen, to your task."

The guests moved to the fire, took their bones, and threw them in. As soon as the bones hit the fire, all sorts of colors sparked through it. Amazed oohs and aahs rose like tiny soap bubbles popping all around the crowd in the night air. Then, just as the mood settled into playful and fun, Maggie, the master of suspense in her screenplays, hit the button in her hand.

Ghoulish faces, demons in all their dark glory, and evil witches appeared in the fire. They zoomed around, interacting with the flames, and then rocketed out into the audience in phenomenal 3-D effects.

An actor who hadn't had a job in years shrieked theatrically. Darla buried her face against the shoulder of the woman next to her. Krista Kane, whose face and dissolving marriage were currently splashed over all the gossip magazines, took a step closer, stretching out her hand in an attempt to touch the phantoms. "It looks so real," she whispered into the night.

Taylor thought so too, even though she knew how Maggie had done it. She stole a look to the projectors on the roofs that were sending out the images to mingle with the fire. And then she peeked at the woman at her side.

Maggie immediately met her eyes and gave that little shrug that melted Taylor's heart.

She likes all this. Who wouldn't? But she's embarrassed by all the extravagance as well. It makes me love her even more.

"Throw your bones in." Maggie gave her a gentle push to the fire.

Taylor wove her way through the crowd until she was at the fire's edge. She hesitated for several seconds with the tiny bones in her hand. The moment was here. The one she had been careening to since the instant her fingers had first touched the jacket. She wasn't sure how she knew this fact with such certainty, but it was just like all the other things she now understood with the help of the jacket. If she stepped over the next threshold, would she still be herself?

Maggie drifted her hand down Taylor's back and let it rest intimately in the hollow.

A shiver crisscrossed her body. *Oh God. Is that an invitation or a promise?* The answer didn't matter; she threw the bones into the fire with confidence in the magic and the future it offered.

As soon as the bones hit the fake flames, a bright blue spark radiated from the fire. Instantly, the jacket came alive with heat and something more. For a moment, it seemed to bond to her body—through her blouse and skirt and into her very soul, pouring all of its power into her, and Taylor realized that everything she had felt up to now had just been a tease. The whole world opened up to her, and she drank in every single one of the possibilities.

"You're hot." Maggie quickly withdrew her hand.

"You don't know the half of it." Taylor didn't think twice. She didn't even think once. She just turned to Maggie and, in front of all of those strangers, took the beautiful woman at her side into her arms. When she leaned up for the kiss, Maggie's lips were already there.

"What're you going to do today?" Maggie rolled over on top of Taylor, sliding her hands down her naked body.

"Nothing. I have a couple errands to run." Taylor pulled her closer and kissed her deeply.

"You're not going to tell me?"

"No. The costume is a surprise. I told you." Taylor wriggled out from under her and got out of bed. She smiled down at Maggie, who was tangled up in the sheets on a bed that had seen some serious lovemaking the night before.

"Well, for future reference, what you're wearing right now is my favorite costume."

"Mine too." It didn't even feel like a costume anymore. "You're going to be late for the meeting at the studio unless you get up." Taylor waited until Maggie was safely in the shower before she went to her closet. It was a beautiful walk-in closet, all her own, complete with an island and enough shoe racks for a small nation. She'd come a long way.

It had been almost a year since the Halloween party and the moment the jacket gave her its power and the courage to kiss Maggie in front of all of Hollywood. Since then, her life had been a dream. The stuff fantasies were made of, literally. She had happily, wonderfully moved into Maggie's beach house and into her life. It turned out that the same talents that had made her a great document reviewer were also making her a great producer. Preproduction of *Daughter of the Sea*, the movie about Stikla, was in high gear, and casting would start in early November. Every A-List movie star was campaigning for the part, and Taylor was actually someone to court in Hollywood.

"Did you call Brant about the skeletons?" Maggie voice drifted in from the bathroom that was in between her closet and Maggie's.

"Yes."

Maggie had chosen an old-fashioned haunted house for the theme of this year's Halloween party. Even though it was only October 1st, Taylor had already cleared the bottom level of the house of its furniture. Brant was coming over to install scary skeletons in all the closets downstairs. They would be just one of the many things waiting to pop out and scare the guests.

"When will he be here? I want to make sure I'm home."

"Two." That would give her plenty of time. Taylor riffled through her vast wardrobe. At the back of one compartment, behind a striped Armani pantsuit and an Alice + Olivia floral tank dress, the jacket hung limply on a hanger. The material, which had once been so full of life, now looked like cheap rayon and was cold to the touch. What's more, the bright, electric blue had faded to a dull grey. Taylor hadn't worn it since the party last year, but she had looked at it a lot, at least in the beginning. She knew with every fiber of her being that something magical had occurred, although she couldn't explain a lick of it. She had hoped that the jacket at some point would give up at least one answer, but it didn't. Then she had worried that the magic would run out, but it hadn't. Finally, she was concerned that the jacket had changed her true self. But, eventually, she poo-pooed that as well. In the end, she decided it was better to stop worrying and be grateful—to the jacket, to fate, to whatever power had given her this amazing, life-transforming gift.

She slipped on the jacket over a pair of designer jeans and a silk T-shirt and looked at herself in the mirror. The jacket was still flattering, but she wore everything well now. The designer who was making her costume for this year's Halloween party had told her that she should be a model. She would certainly stand out as sexy Lofn, the Norse goddess of forbidden love and Stikla's lover in *Daughter of the Sea*. But before she could put on that costume, there was something she had to do.

The bell on the door jingled as she entered *Pasta Primavera* exactly as it had a year ago to the day. The business lunch crowd hadn't yet arrived, so most tables were empty.

Karla, the hostess, looked at her but didn't seem to recognize her. Taylor was used to getting blank stares from people who'd known her before the jacket. She was also used to the appreciative second glance that Karla gave her. *It never gets old.*

Karla came at her with a smile. "Hi. Table for one?"

When Taylor nodded, Karla started to guide her to a back table.

"I'm sorry. Can I have this one?" Taylor pointed to the small table right by the door.

"There are nicer tables in the back. Bigger. You can spread out."

"I'd really like this one, if you don't mind."

"Sure." Karla sat her at the table in front and handed her a menu. "Your waitress will be out to take your order in a minute."

Taylor listened to all the specials out of courtesy and then ordered the pasta primavera.

The usual lunch crowd, support staff from the surrounding buildings, started to pour in, arriving either alone with a digital device or in pairs talking quietly about work with the same beaten-down tone of voice that Taylor used to have. Perfect timing. Within minutes, the restaurant was completely full.

Taylor scanned the restaurant.

A woman with a pinched face sat at the corner table and tapped away on a cracked iPad, pausing only to bite off a fingernail. Across the room, a bald, unsmiling man slashed through a legal brief with a red felt pen.

When the pasta came out, Taylor arranged the plate on the woven mat the way she recalled. Had the fork been in the pasta or not? She decided that it had been and slid the fork into the cream and noodles. She then placed two one-hundred dollar bills under the plate and got up.

After slipping out of the jacket, she hung it casually over the back of her chair. It looked grey and dull. For a moment, panic swept through her. Was the magic in the jacket or in her now? She didn't know. But she had to find out. She took a deep breath and gave the jacket a final, nervous pat. *Thank you. For everything. I can do it myself now.*

Second thoughts and severe doubts crashed in on her as she wound her way through the small gathering at the door waiting for tables. She barely fought the impulse to run back and grab the jacket. Leaving the restaurant without it might be a death sentence for her new life. Could she go to Mike to beg for her old job back? She didn't think so.

As she opened the front door, the fall sunlight enveloped her. The familiar warmth that she had associated with the jacket spread through her. She hadn't felt it in a while, but she would never forget it. The truth hit her hard, like a wallop. *It's not the jacket. The magic is everywhere. You just have to know where to look.* She glowed with this sudden knowledge as she strode out into her future.

Laurie sighed deeply. She could afford to have the iPad fixed if she told her landlord that the check had gotten lost in the mail. *No, it's wrong. I can't do that.* Where was her food? She glanced around, looking for the waitress. Her gaze fell on an abandoned plate of pasta and then shifted to the chair. *Wow! That jacket is really blue...*

GHOST LIGHTS

ERZABET BISHOP

MELANIE SCOWLED. "I CAN'T BELIEVE you brought me out here for this."

The row of shops with spooky sounding names ranged alongside a cobblestone street, an appropriate setting for the ghost tour for which this part of the city was famous. As the starting point of this tour, the street was cordoned off. The stage dressing didn't change the way Melanie felt about ghost tours—tourist traps and shysters, the lot of them. Their sole intention was obviously to rake in the tourist dollars. So what if the woods and cemetery were reported to be haunted, with ghost lights that appeared out of nowhere? If any of it was real, Melanie was prepared to eat her left shoe.

Rachel batted her eyelashes and gave Melanie an award winning smile. "Don't be such a whiner, Mel. You know I couldn't come out here all by myself. I need someone to scare off the ghosts. They won't stand a chance with you around, little Miss Skeptic. Besides, once I hook up with Jessica, you can go shopping or head home."

"Whatever."

Eyeing the motley group waiting for the ghost walk to start, Melanie had to resist the urge to bolt. A group of teenage boys was laughing loudly as they gave hell to a retirement community group that had arrived on some kind of mega bus. Melanie sighed. The sky was darkening, and there was a storm brewing in the distance. It was going to be a very long night. The tour mistress of the Ghost Light Tours, the illustrious Jessica, had not yet put in an appearance, and Mel was fervently wishing she had done the same.

"Oh! Look. Here she comes!" Rachel trilled.

Sure enough, the buxom Jessica approached. Wearing a tight-fitting corset and a short leather skirt that looked as if it was painted on, she made her way up the walk, thigh high boots clicking on the boardwalk with every step.

Melanie rolled her eyes. Rachel would have eyes only for Jessica the rest of the night. Relieved that she could leave Rachel to her own devices, she looked down the dimly lit street and hoped there was someplace she could grab some tea and something to eat.

"Rachel, I'll see you tomorrow."

Waving distractedly, Rachel followed the ghost tour as it traipsed down the street into the "haunted" part of town. She had already been on the tour once, and wasn't up to seeing the haunted One Upsman Deli or the Old Peterborough Cemetery again. It had been boring enough the first time. There hadn't been a ghost in sight, let alone the famous glowing orbs.

Sighing, Melanie trudged along the cobblestone street in search of a place where she could relax. Twilight had darkened into night while they'd been waiting for the tour guide, and many of the touristy shops had already rolled up their sidewalks. Her stomach rumbled as she looked longingly at the row of closed shops. Not only was she hungry, but she could feel the beginnings of a chill in the air through her summery frock.

Her sandals thumped along the old fashioned wooden boardwalk, and Mel patted her stomach, trying to squelch its growling, all the while becoming more and more irritated at Rachel for dragging her out to the edge of nowhere. She would have to grab something from the drive-through burger place on the way home.

Suddenly, out of the corner of her eye, she caught a glimpse of light. A moment earlier, everything had been dark.

Weird. The Ghost Light Tea Room. Figures. Everyone tried to capitalize on the tour, she supposed. Her stomach emitted another pathetic growl, and that settled it. She would just pop over and see if they were open. If not, it was back to plan A, the burger joint.

The window was fogged with condensation, but she could make out a lighted pastry case. Hopeful, she went to the door and pulled it open. A bell tinkled, announcing her presence.

"Hello?" She stepped inside and closed the door behind her. "Are you open?"

The tea room showed its age, like most of the shops in the area. Classical music played faintly in the background, giving the place a calming atmosphere. The aroma of baking scones wove trails of cinnamon bliss to Mel's nose, and her stomach gave another growl of hunger.

Wooden tables with doilies pressed under glass were placed strategically around the room. China tea sets and pots of ivy and ornamental trees gave the place a homey charm. The pastry case against the wall was the crowning glory. Even looking at it from near the door, Melanie could see confections piled high with tempting mountains of whipped cream and chocolate wonderment.

"Why have I not been in here before?" Melanie whispered, walking over to the front counter where a chalkboard displayed the tea and soup flavors of the day.

Soup of the day:
Chicken Tortilla
Cream of Mushroom with Aged Cheddar Croutons

Iced Tea:
Ginger Peach
Raspberry

"Hello."

The voice came out of nowhere, and Melanie started as a leggy brunette with a pixie haircut and a warm smile emerged from the kitchen.

"Hi." Mel swallowed, suddenly nervous. "I hope I'm not intruding, but your door was open and the lights were on..."

"And you were hoping for some dinner?" The young woman grinned and snapped up a menu from the stand next to the chalkboard. "No worries. We are closed, but I think I can fit you in."

The pixyish woman led her to a table next to the pastry case, and Mel struggled not to stare at the pies and cakes calling her name.

"Thanks." Melanie pulled out a chair, setting her purse on the floor as she sat. "You didn't have to let me stay."

The woman smiled. "My name is Vykky, and yes I did. Can't send you home starving to death. Starvation is not a nice way to go. Trust me."

A shadow crossed her features, but she snapped back to impish merriment so quickly, Mel thought she must have imagined the melancholy look.

"We still have the mushroom soup with the homemade croutons. Those are really good." Vykky thought a moment. "I can bring you some of the crusty bread that we usually serve with it, if you want."

"That sounds great." Mel felt herself relaxing, content in the warm tea room and lulled by Vykky's friendly banter.

"Do you want to try some of the Ginger Peach tea? It seriously rocks." Vykky went to the front door and locked it, flipping the Open sign to Closed.

Mel bit her lip, noticing for the first time how lithe Vykky's form was as she bent over to close the blinds on the front windows. Her jeans molded to her body like a second skin, and her tee shirt was tight against her breasts, showing every jiggle of her voluptuous cleavage as she moved. Mel fidgeted in her seat, more than a little aware of the moisture beginning to gather between her legs. She swallowed hard.

"Are you sure you don't want me to just take it to go? It's sweet of you to even serve me, I don't want to keep you."

"No. I insist." Vykky swung around and started toward the kitchen, stopping to look back at Mel for a moment. "You want that iced tea?"

Mel looked down at the table and the bits of napkin she'd shredded between her nervous fingers. She knew she should leave, but her mouth said, "Um. Sure."

Vykky's eyes narrowed thoughtfully as she entered the kitchen, returning moments later with a tall glass of iced tea and a straw.

"Here you go. If you want to sweeten it up, there's sugar on the table."

"Thanks." Mel met Vykky's gaze, and she felt her mouth go dry. She couldn't look away.

"I should go get your soup."

"I suppose." Mel found she was holding her breath, suddenly not hungry. At least not for food.

"You picked a good night to come by," Vykky whispered. She stepped closer, until her breasts were at Mel's eye level.

"I agree." Mel licked her lips at the tantalizing orbs that were inches away from her mouth. Her pussy spasmed, and she shuddered.

Vykky moved around behind Mel and wove her hands into her hair, drew it away from her cheek, and kissed the side of her face.

Melanie gasped as Vykky's hands wandered to her breasts, and, startled, Vykky pulled away.

"I'm sorry. I shouldn't have done that."

"What?" Mel's head was spinning, but the one thing she was certain of was that she didn't want Vykky to stop.

"You're probably straight. I'm sorry. You looked so beautiful sitting there, I just had to kiss you and feel my fingers in your hair."

Melanie stood on shaking legs and reached for the zip on the side of her dress, letting it fall from her curves in a puddle of fabric. She unclasped her bra and kicked off her shoes, then slipped out of her panties, leaving her naked in the middle of the tea room.

It had been such a long time since Mel had met a woman she had even considered dating, let alone sleeping with, that she couldn't see past the haze of lust fogging her vision. "Just to be clear," Mel approached her, "I couldn't take my eyes off you when you were pulling the shades. Come here."

Mel eased Vykky against her, and the sensation of their nipples rubbing against one another made her folds moisten to an uncomfortable level. The sticky wetness was beginning to coat the insides of her thighs.

Vykky stepped back, kicked off her shoes and shimmied out of her jeans in seconds. She grabbed the tee and pulled it over her head, and the bra was unclasped and on the floor before Melanie realized what had happened. She laughed, easing her nerves.

"That was fast."

"Well, we have always been known for our fast service here." Vykky winked and took her hand. "Would you like to be seated, ma'am?" Vykky purred, leading her to a large booth at the back of the tea room.

"This looks just perfect."

"Oh, it is. Now, if you would be so kind as to sit right there." Vykky pointed to the top of the wooden table in the booth.

"Um. Okay." Mel winced as the cool wood hit her warm ass.

"Now, what would you like to order?" Vykky's eyes glowed with mischievous intent.

"Hmmm. What would you suggest?"

"Why don't we start off with the house special?"

Vykky crawled onto one of the padded seats and wrapped her lips around Mel's nipple. Licking and sucking, she moved from one to the other, leaving them pebbled in desire. Vykky hands traced the lines of Melanie's body, homing in on the juncture of her thighs.

"Ohhh," Mel moaned, her heart racing in her chest.

"Now for the next course." Vykky slid off the bench and settled between Melanie's legs.

She nuzzled along Melanie's inner thighs and pressed her legs open wide.

The rush of cool air against her wet pussy lips made Mel shudder, and as Vykky's mouth got closer, she began to squirm.

"Oh my God. Are you sure about this?" Mel breathed. It had been so long since anyone had touched her there, she felt a moment of panic.

Vykky raised her head just long enough to wink, and dove back in, heading right for Mel's moist folds. Her tongue licked from the top of her folds to the bottom of her slit. Vykky nibbled along the outer lips, then drew her clit into her mouth and sucked.

Thrashing as the feelings became unbearably intense, Mel screamed as the orgasm blew through her. "Oh my God!" Her pulse pounded erratically. When the tremors had subsided, she closed her eyes in exhaustion.

"No you don't. I'm not done with you yet." Vykky jumped up and grabbed a bottle of chocolate sauce from the table beside the pastry case, then hurried back to the booth, her beautiful breasts jiggling with each step.

"I want seconds." Vykky poured a generous helping of chocolate sauce over Mel's breasts and mound.

"But—"

"Nope. Mine."

Vykky began to lick and suck her way across Mel's breasts. When the artful tongue reached the apex of her thighs, Melanie bucked up to meet her, electricity threading through her body as another wave of orgasms lifted her into oblivion.

Awakened by the sound of a key clinking into a lock, Mel struggled to sit up. *Where am I?* Looking down at her body, she found she was naked and sticky and lying across a table. *I'm in the tea room. Oh my God. Where is Vykky?*

Mel scooted off the wooden table and crouched low, hunting for her dress and underthings. *Please don't let them see me.*

The key turned in the lock, the door opened, and she heard voices.

"I don't know. Apparently a girl went missing last night. Was supposed to have gone home, but her roommate says she never got there. Her car is still in the lot out back."

The man's voice had a country twang. He was probably the owner of the building.

An older woman came into Mel's restricted view. Her face was lined with age, but there was a kindness about her that reminded her of someone. She stared at her a moment more and her Aunt Marlene came to mind. She'd always felt at home in her aunt's kitchen.

"Jed, look at this. There's a glass of tea on the table again, and there's a dress on the floor."

Footsteps came closer to where Melanie was hiding. Her heart beating like a jackhammer in her chest, Melanie waved her hand in the air. "Down here," she said.

A gasp echoed in the room, and to Melanie's shock and horror, the old couple began to laugh.

The woman sputtered, and then Melanie winced as her dress was handed down to her.

"This must be yours, dear."

Melanie's embarrassment crept up the back of her neck.

"Now, Jed, turn around. I swear, you have no manners at all." The woman clicked her tongue on the roof of her mouth. "Would you like your unmentionables?"

"Um. Yes. Thanks." Melanie pulled up the zip on the side of her dress and then balled up the panties and bra and hid them behind her back, her face burning. "I'm so sorry. I just...I..."

"Hon, you don't have to explain at all." Jed peeked out of the corner of his eye to be sure that the coast was clear, then turned around. "Martha, why don't you get this girl a cup of coffee. I have a feeling she's going to need something a little stronger than tea"

Martha smiled as she handed Melanie her purse and shoes. "Here you go, dear."

"Thanks," Mel mumbled. Her phone was vibrating, and she pulled it out of her purse and found several text messages from Rachel.

Where are you?
I know you are not ignoring me.
Not funny Mel. Where the hell are you?
Mel!!!!

Shaking her head, Mel texted back that she was in the tea room and was just fine.

"I'm so sorry I scared everyone. I came in last night to have something to eat, and Vykky let me stay a while..." Mel looked away, ashamed to meet the man's penetrating gaze.

Martha came back in carrying a tray with a blueberry muffin and a cup of steaming coffee. "Here you go. Best put something into your stomach."

"Thanks." Mel took a bite of the muffin and gulped the coffee down in a few scalding swallows.

"So you saw our Vykky." Martha wiped at the ring of water the iced tea glass had left on the table top.

Mel smiled. "Yes. She was here last night, closing up the shop." She took another bite of muffin.

The door to the tea room burst open, and Jessica and Rachel appeared in a flurry of activity.

"Where the hell were you last night?" Rachel demanded. "You scared everyone half to death."

Melanie sputtered as she tried to choke down the bite of muffin and talk at the same time. Fortunately, Martha interrupted.

"Good morning, Jessica. Pretty active tour last night?"

"No, ma'am." Jessica nodded at Rachel, and they sat down at a table next to Mel's. "It was pretty dead, actually."

Martha looked up from cleaning the iced tea ring on the table and exchanged glances with Jed. "Your friend here saw Vykky."

Jessica started, her eyes widening. "What?"

"Where is Vykky? I wanted to thank her for letting me in when she'd already closed for the evening." Mel's eyes fell to the paper napkin rolled on the table, and she had to consciously resist shredding it into bits like she had the one the night before.

Martha smiled at her sadly. "Honey, Vykky's a ghost."

Startled, Mel looked up. "What do you mean? I just saw her." More than saw her, actually. Her face burned with heat as she recalled the tender touch of Vykky's tongue on the moist folds of her slit.

Rachel gasped. "What's going on?"

Jessica laughed and took Rachel's hand. "Your friend here got jumped by our resident ghost. Found her naked? Right?"

Martha and Jed nodded in unison. "As a jaybird."

Mel bristled with indignation. "Hey! I'm right here."

Her hand covering her mouth in feigned horror, Rachel sat down next to Mel. "You scored with a ghost?"

Jessica grinned from ear to ear. "Why do you think I started this tour line? Vykky was my inspiration."

"But who was she? I can't believe..." Mel stared down at the crumbs on her plate.

"Vykky worked as a hostess at the tea room about twenty-five years ago. No one knows how she died, but we do know that once in a while, if a lonely tourist finds herself in front of the tea room, Vykky has been known to make an appearance and offer her own personal brand of hospitality." Jessica smiled.

"But I don't believe in..."

Mel stopped, suddenly realizing the truth. She had just been a leading character in a ghost story of her very own. Out of the corner of her eye, she caught a flicker of ghost lights moving through the shadows in the back of the room, and Melanie smiled.

Well I'll be damned, she thought. *Ghost lights.*

A WINTER STORY

S. M. HARDING

THE TURNING HAD BEGUN FIRST in the hollows by the creek, then climbed its way up the mountain side. Lighter green, flaming gold, muted orange, marking the time until the cold winds came from the north and stripped the aspens naked.

Epifania Gordy lifted her head to watch the single raven wheel into the wind. The damn bird had been dogging her movements for the past four days. If it was a spirit messenger, it had better spit out its communication soon or she'd shoot it. She stood, balancing for a moment on the boulder known as the Listening Stone before she headed for home. Her worn, winter moccasins made no sound to compete with the rattling leaves scudding across the ground. Only the wind and the leaves. The critters were already hunkered down. Snow was coming sooner that she thought.

Epi unlatched the front door and stepped into her family's homestead. She shrugged off her down vest and hung it on the peg driven into the log wall. Sturdy, solid walls, two feet thick in some places. Hand hewn timbers, the old adze marks now another texture of the walls. Made by her great-grandfather's hand saws, adze, ax. As a kid, every time she had closed her eyes and touched the walls, she had seen him. Sweat pouring down his bronze face, forming rivulets on his lean torso. A smile as big as the sky and she wished she'd known him, hadn't lost him.

She'd lost the sight when she'd left the land because New York City had no patience with visions, except for those drug-induced. The same was true of art; she'd learned that quickly.

She opened the door of the wood stove, poked the two pinon logs that were left, and added a cedar one to the fire. These days, she was always cold. She sank into the one piece of furniture she'd brought with her, an Eames chair, and swung her stockinged feet onto the ottoman. She stared at the ceiling and the yellow pine flooring of the second story. A feathery touch of cold air brushed her cheek.

This was the time of year to begin the winter stories, and Epi remembered sitting on her grandfather's lap, entranced by the story of the seven Gordy brothers and their arrival in America. Somewhere in the Appalachian Mountains, they had decided to stop wandering and ask their father for direction. The father who'd died in a battle with the English, the reason they had left the highlands and traveled over the sea.

Her grandfather's voice echoed in her memory: "Sure, betwixt Samhain and All Soul's, that's when the veil is thinnest. The time, it is, when the spirits of our beloved can travel back."

The language bespoke the auld country, the soft burr in his words seemed exotic coming from her grandfather, who took after his Ute heritage. A winter story.

Then he chanted the incantation, and Epi almost saw the spirits hovering and felt the presence of all the ancestors. Kilts, broad swords, battles, clashes, wars. Her grandmother had hushed him saying, "You will conjure every *chindi* in the Four Corners. Hush, Husband. Now."

No wonder I'm weird—coming from Scots and Navajo ancestors who always argued about the state of the dead. Would it be dangerous? Or comforting? Whatever the outcome, whatever the cost, she had to try. Those last years with Sadie had been so barren, lost in an unending moonscape. The sterility of drug-induced nightmares. They hadn't talked and neither had she listened to the silence.

Epi removed her feet from the ottoman, sat forward, and addressed the ceiling. "Grandmother, I need to talk to her. To beg for her forgiveness. I would give anything to hold her in my arms. Anything."

She shook her head, knowing time was too short to ramble through the past. Epi had to expand the past and push into the future. Tonight.

And if she failed? If Sadie wouldn't come to her, she would go to Sadie. The Colt .45 was cleaned and loaded.

A half-hour before the "witching time," she gathered the objects she'd use tonight. Her father's old hunting knife, the silver goblet come over the seas with the brothers, a piece of willow branch with a crystal at the end, a small clay brazier. The black Santa Clara bowl, filled with water. She lit the black candles.

Scots didn't smudge, at least not her clan. She took a broom, began to stroke the air with it in a wide arcs. "Any spirit not of the Light, be gone!" she commanded. She continued around the room, swiping at each corner, the ceiling, the floor.

Opened the front door to a blast of cold air and snow. "Leave this place now!"

Epi slammed the door shut, slid the bolt into place, and placed the broom across it.

She sat before the altar, tucked her legs in tightly, and placed both palms on the black fabric covering the table. She closed her eyes, slowed her breathing until all she heard was the ticking of the mantle clock and the pinging of the stovepipe. Snow pellets peppered the windows, a scattered sound in the silence.

The words. Epi remembered only fragments of the chants for calling those who had passed over. Her family had lost them, generation by generation, until only threadbare remnants were left. They'd have to do.

"Spirits of the Four Corners, heavenly beings of Light, I call you here tonight. Stand at the corners of this altar, listen to my request. Bring it forward. So mote it be!"

Epi picked up the goblet, heavy in her hands, and offered it to the cardinal directions, sprinkling a few drops of water at each. She repeated the chant with the brazier, blowing smoke from finely cut pieces of oak with a raven's feather. Repeated it again, with the wand, inscribing the Circle held together by the four points.

She picked up the knife. "Spirits of the Four Corners, I ask that you cut the veil that separates worlds." She slashed air with each word. Syllable. "Cleave the veil, cleanly cut the cloth that keeps me from my lover. So mote it be!"

Epi made the final cut and released her breath in a low keening. Listening, she heard only the stovepipe. Ping, ditty-ditty-do. The snow rattling the windowpanes.

Epi looked into the bowl, onto the surface of the water so dark infinity was possible. "Sadie, beloved woman, come to me. Come, come, come!"

She thought she began to see strands of blonde hair, and below them, eyes as blue as an Eastern sky. A violent gust slammed down the stovepipe, extinguished the fire, blew out the candles. The room howled in the blackness.

Epi couldn't breathe. Sense. Anything.

Epi awoke to a warm breeze on her face, rhythmic and slow as the tick of the clock on the mantlepiece. She opened her eyes to see a fan, the intricate, delicate kind wielded by ancient Spanish crones. She glimpsed a woman's white hand moving it back and forth, slower and slower.

"Who are you? How the hell did you get in here?" Epi asked, feeling far too vulnerable to force out more words. This woman was not Sadie. What had she called into her home?

"Ah, you recover," the woman said in a soft voice. "Can you sit up? Just a little?"

Epi looked at the woman's ragged clothing, all black, including an old woolen shawl with tassels. Her black hair was a wild mane, though her dark eyes were kind.

"Who are you?" Epi asked again, not moving an iota.

"I was lost in the blizzard. The door was open. I saw the light, and it guided me to you." Her voice was slightly accented and gave her a gentility her hair belied.

Epi struggled to sit up and looked at the room. The fire was burning steadily in the stove, candles glowed on the altar.

She was sure she'd closed the door, bolted it. She looked for the broom. It was propped by the door. "I don't understand how you got in here. The door was closed and bolted, and there was no light in here. Everything went dark."

The woman shrugged. "I never would have found you if there were no light."

"What are you doing out on a night like this?"

"I seek sanctuary."

"This isn't a church."

"Sometimes the church provides no sanctuary. Force enters too easily," the woman said, staring. She stood and extended a hand to Epi. "I need to provide for myself, so I offer my services in exchange for a room. I will clean and cook for you."

"I don't need a housekeeper," Epi said, struggling to her feet by herself.

The woman reached out and steadied her. "Would you turn away someone who asks for your help? Your family never refused a stranger."

"What the hell do you know about my family?"

"My name is Caritas Ortiz," she said.

Epi stared at the dark eyes, like peat pools encased in alabaster. Instead of calling her lover, she had brought this scarecrow of a woman into her home. She shook her head in an effort to clear it and listened to the icy pellets that pounded the window in a rising crescendo. "Stay tonight, but you'll have to find another place tomorrow."

"Would you like to eat a light dinner now?" Caritas asked.

Epi shook her head, food the last thought in her mind. Although, she felt light-headed.

"Go, sit in your beautiful chair and rest, Epifania. I think you are quite shaken."

Epi collapsed into her chair, confused and aching. She would have sold her soul to tell Sadie how sorry she was.

Epi awoke smelling coffee and bacon. Sun glared through the window, sparkled on the wall. The storm must have passed.

Coffee? She sat up, discovering she'd been covered with a Hudson's Bay blanket from upstairs. She didn't remember going upstairs, didn't remember much of last night. She sat up straight, dislodging the blanket. Caritas!

She wanted to flee this strange creature, but the promise of coffee overwhelmed and she crept into the kitchen. "Storm's over, you should be on your way before another comes."

Caritas smiled and motioned to a chair at the table. When Epi sat down, suddenly disoriented as if this was no longer the home she'd grown up in, Caritas placed a mug in front of her. "Breakfast is almost ready."

A moment later, a plate of scrambled eggs, seasoned with bits of chorizo and chiles, was set before her, along with thick strips of bacon. Epi had no memory of having bacon in the house. She ate without conversation and kept her eyes on the plate. As soon as she was finished, she fled outdoors.

Epi's muscles complained, so she stopped climbing. She spotted a cardinal on the branch of a spruce, its winter red brilliant against the dark green. He turned his head toward her and fussed.

She quietly turned her back to him, then completed her reversal by carefully lifting each snowshoed foot and placing it in the opposite direction. This was one of her favorite views, high enough to see the valley and distant mesas. She soaked in the view, the peace of it, the certainty of it. She felt as if she were standing on the rim of an overturned bowl, possibilities pouring from the exultant blue sky to the waiting land. Father Sky, Mother Earth. Elemental wisdom, circular transfer of transformed energies flowing through the conduit of their union. Nowhere else was this complementary bond so apparent as here, this delicate perch on the side of a mountain in the middle of a precipitous land called New Mexico.

Epi felt clean up here, new, as if she could approach redemption. She took a deep breath, closed her eyes and watched the zig-zag of light dance on her lids. Everything danced here.

She squatted down, let her gaze roam over the horizon. A few puffy clouds floated over the Jemez Mountains far to the south. No snow today. She looked at the ground, fresh animal tracks with their edges still sharp, older ones blurred by sun and wind. A wing print in the snow where a rodent's tracks stopped, three small drops of blood glistening red on the white surface.

Just like the crimson petals on Sadie's arm.

Epi was never sure if Sadie had picked her or if she had chosen Sadie. The attraction had flamed from the very beginning, polar opposites attracting in a death grip. Sadie. Anglo in a long line of whites that began at Plymouth Rock. Educated in France. Wealthy, able to afford every whim, including Epi. She wondered if the relationship began to change when Sadie saw how her lover's rage-induced constructions had begun to sell, when Epi had become a name glittering in the Artworld. Usurped the momentary spotlight from Sadie.

She stood, took a deep breath of the pure mountain air, and made a prayer for this land, its beauty, its harshness, its light. She wanted to create a prayer that others could see and feel and propel them to join in the communion. She hadn't made an image since she'd been home, nothing, had lost all desire as she had let the drugs and alcohol leach from her body and soak into this holy land to be transmuted.

Somehow they settled into a non-companionable arrangement, Epi and Caritas and the ghosts they both fed. The old house had never been as clean and shining, and Epi hadn't eaten so well in years. She felt her stamina returning, and along with it, her unease. Who the hell was Caritas Ortiz? A woman who always dressed in old-fashioned high-necked and long-sleeved dresses, who deflected questions with a smile, who looked as if she were ready for flight at any moment. To where?

After breakfast on this day, Epi decided it was time to face her workshop, the place where she'd dumped all her paints and brushes and carving tools. She'd brought no canvas, no steel or torch, leaving them behind with disgust. How had she ever manufactured those monstrosities? Those constructions of rage and alien values? Those pieces that were only an homage to ugliness? The answer came: money. Easy money, as the Artworld fawned. So Epi had kept manufacturing the rage and the suckers had rushed to buy. She realized that she had been the sucker; she'd been swept up into the gallery scene and big money, without even a sense of playing a joke on a bunch of pompous asses. She'd been played by greed.

The truth was, as her star had risen, Sadie's had faltered, lost its course across the firmament. But Epi's drug-riddled brain hadn't noticed, hadn't really cared that Sadie's voice had stilled, that words no longer flowed. Death for an author. When Sadie had started doing heroin, Epi had only said, "Be careful, it's dangerous." Had stuck to the new varieties of acid that allowed her to wallow in anger, and capture the scenes of massacre and death for her monsters. She'd forgotten how to create and could only destroy.

Was the ability to create with beauty still alive in her soul?

She walked to her workshop and fit the key into the padlock. "Think of the land, Epi. Think of the land and make prayers."

The month had been a series of unrelenting storms and sub-zero temperatures. Caritas had seemed content with cooking and cleaning and reading in the evenings. It struck Epi as unusual that Caritas showed such a seductive smile when she read the old battered copy of *Curious Wine*. But perhaps Caritas had broader horizons than Epi thought. This silent woman drove Epi crazy, well, crazier. One afternoon, she decided she deserved some answers to the questions she hadn't asked.

She walked into the kitchen where Caritas tended a large pot of something that smelled delicious. She sat at the kitchen table and cleared her throat. "Who are you?"

"I am Caritas. The name was given to me by my father, who was something of a scholar. It is Latin and means care, concern, charity. The Spanish *caridad* has much the same meaning. But those old Romans gave it another twist. It also means the cost of living."

"You've told me your name."

"The price one pays, the sacrifice required to have people whom you love in your life is *caritas*," she said quietly. "The cost of living is more than my name, Epifania."

"Then, where are you from? Who's your family?"

Caritas turned, put the lid on, and took the other chair. "Why would it comfort you to know where I lived my life?"

"I don't know a damn thing about you and you're living in my house. I think you owe me an explanation about what brought you here."

"My service to you is not sufficient to repay your hospitality?"

"No, it's not that." At first, she'd watched every move the woman made, but all Caritas did was work. Each day, besides the cooking, she found a project that restored another part of the Gordy tradition. She allowed Epi the time to recover from the failure of Samhain and to think again about joining Sadie. She was quiet, and Epi felt a strange protective membrane wrapped around her. But she was beginning to think Caritas had been raised by wolves who knew Latin. "Don't you have family who are concerned about you?"

Caritas turned slightly, the warm light from the lamp caressing her cheekbones, kissing her full lips. The woman looked like a Madonna, an El Greco perhaps. A painting, waiting for the brush, the oils, the impassioned hand and unerring eye.

"No. They are long gone," she said. "I lived near Mogote."

"Colorado?" Strange little town, Epi thought. Not much more than a burned-out church and a scattering of old buildings settled on the valley floor, west of Antonito. Farms mostly, some ranching. "Your family ranches?"

"Not anymore."

Epi slapped her hand on the table, her frustration point reached. "You walk in here uninvited. You're still here. If you knew my family, why don't I remember any of them mentioning you? Mogote isn't that far from here, yet we never visited." This Madonna could be a lunatic, escaped from the asylum. Or maybe this was the asylum.

"When the time is right, I will share my story with you," Caritas said.

"And when will that be?"

"Soon, I think."

Epi sniffed the air, turned her head to meet the wind. Snow, and soon. People in most of the rest of the country never knew this smell. They lived with moisture, took it for granted.

The mountains around her had disappeared, shrouded by scudding clouds, masked where sky met earth. "A sacred moment between them," her mother often said, "so it should be private."

Epi turned toward the mesas. They were hidden, as well, by a white wall moving across the high desert. She'd better get her walk in before the wall encased her.

She started up the trail to the Circle, a place of prayer since the first Gordy. When she stood before it, she took out a cigarette, shredded the end, and scattered it before her. She found the matches, cupped her hand against the wind, and drew the smoke into her lungs. The action took her back to the loft she and Sadie had shared, filled with smoke when either one of them had been awake. She didn't smoke like that anymore, had maybe one or two a day. Didn't drink or do drugs at all. She'd fought through the withdrawal with the help of Grandfather Sola. Not her grandfather, though she thought he was somehow related. Tribal relationships were complicated. As the fog had lifted in her head, the pain in her heart had become more severe. She had holed up on the homestead, hiking the land during the days, trying to wear herself out so that she could sleep without dreams.

All she could remember of the ten years together with Sadie was the life that had swallowed them both. Sadie's parents hated Epi, what she had done to their beautiful daughter. Made her queer, gotten her hooked on drugs, ended her brilliant career. And life. Unrelenting hate from them, told her to get out of the loft. Go to hell. So much bitterness.

As much as Epi tried, she couldn't remember the early years when their love had been young and tender. She'd prayed in this circle day after day, to remember, to ease the pain with memory. And had met with nothingness. This day, Epi didn't enter the Circle, just stood and smoked and decided she couldn't live like this much longer.

When the cigarette was finished, tobacco scattered, Epi shouldered her .30-30 Winchester. Caritas wanted a turkey for Thanksgiving.

Thanksgiving. Epi knew she should feel grateful for each breath, but she didn't.

Epi rolled over on her side, pulling the down quilt around her. Pitched over on her back. Buried her head in the pillow, her arm flung outward. The raven, perched on the foot board of the bed, watched, her black eyes searching the images of the woman's dreams. Now was the time.

Epi heard rolling thunder that came closer and closer. Sought the hand of her lover. Thunder became pounding hooves. Rough voices, wild whoops. Gunshots. Bells from the church clanging madly. Running, running. Find sanctuary. Tripping, sprawling on the dusty ground. Rosa! In the swirl of dust and noise, where had she gone? A thousand shadows created by the flaming torches. Crawl into the shadows. Hide! Rosa! Rosa. Cool adobe walls of the church. Safety. Running down the dark aisle to the light in the sanctuary. To the Padre's arms. Black cassock protecting, smelling of soap and starch. "I lost Rosa, I cannot find her. Please help us."

Others huddled at the foot of the altar. Booming knocks at the barred door. Breaking, splintered wood shrieking in the tumult. Riders on horseback sweeping through the shattered door. Smoke. Unwashed bodies. Sweat. Chairs and kneelers breaking under horses' hooves. Terrified neighing. Jangling spurs. Footsteps. The offertory bell rolling down the stairs. The priest beginning to speak. Crack! The Padre, stumbling, falling. The men and the horses a swirling mass. A callused hand, whiskey breath. No. NO!

Epi sat up straight, threw off the covers. Her body was soaked with sweat, her heart pounding to the beat of galloping horses.

The terror squeezed her heart shut.

Epi watched the tiny, dry flakes dance down and around. The sun hadn't risen this morning. Or if it had, it was hidden by dense clouds and snow showers that marched across the high desert as moving columns. Until they overtook, surrounded, obliterated. She hunkered down beneath the ponderosa and took off her snowshoes.

She couldn't shake the feeling from the dream last night. The violence and brutality. Where the hell had it come from? Most strong was the memory of losing her lover's hand in the chaos. The failure to keep her safe weighed like a cross on her shoulders.

She'd never known a Rosa.

She shrugged the feeling away, switched her mind to the snow, a slowly falling grace. This year, Taos would have plenty of snow to reflect the soft glow of the *farolitos* for Christmas. She and Sadie, home for the Christmas visit. The last Christmas together. Sadie had always been welcomed into the celebration, the family. So unlike Sadie's family, who had banished her until she died. Swooped in and taken everything.

"Don't dip into that bitter dish," a voice said. "Go back to the times when beauty shone."

Epi looked around. Even sober, she hallucinated.

Epi had always played Lady Bountiful, bringing extravagant gifts to replace the bonds she no longer held tight. The last trip, she drank her way through the celebrations, through the family, through the land she avoided. The one stark memory was her mother, asking what was wrong in both their lives that she and Sadie were so absent.

She'd had no answer.

Still didn't. Somewhere in her heart, she knew she needed help, then and now. The dreams, the voices. They were interfering with her plan to join Sadie, distracting her, making her doubt. Having left the Spirits of her ancestors behind, could she really come home to them?

A snowflake caught on her eyelash, melted, moved down her cheek as liquid. She brushed it away. The others that followed.

The view through the window was a wall of slowly dancing diamonds against the black night. The snow fell like the old women danced, skirts swaying from waist to ground, dignified steps echoing a life of wisdom and constancy.

Epi sighed, leaned her forehead against the cold windowpane. A storm coming in from the Gulf, so that the sedate steps of the women would be replaced by the pounding feet of a young men's grass dance. A behemoth was coming.

Epi had piled firewood on the back porch, covered with an old blue tarp faded to the color of the horizon. Fueled the oil lamps and trimmed the wicks. Filled all the empty plastic milk gallons with water. Primed the old hand pump in the summer kitchen. A long day of preparation to survive the storm. Why this effort?

"Are you all right?" Caritas asked from the shadows at the foot of the stairs. She wrapped the shawl tighter around her shoulders.

"Storm's going to be a doozy." She crossed to her chair, picked up the novel she'd been reading.

"What is the matter, Epifania?" Caritas asked as she moved into the room. "The storm? Or your dream?"

Epi's head snapped up. She stared at the woman.

"Only it is not your dream. It is my life." She moved over to the box of wood, placed two logs carefully in the firebox of the stove. Closed the door with a little clang. Turned to face Epi. "Would you like to hear the rest?"

Epi's startled gaze hadn't left her. "You're going to tell me the rest of my dream?" She marked her place in the book. The expanding metal of the stovepipe and the ticking of the clock were the only sounds as the two women stared at one another. Ping-dit, ping-dit, tick, tick, tick.

"What makes you think I've had the same dream for the last four nights? Or that it has anything to do with you?" Epi asked, placing the book onto the table.

"I will tell you the dream, and you can judge." Caritas perched on the seat of an ancient chair that had made its way across the ocean. "Will you listen?"

"I can't leave, can I?"

"You always run away, that is your pattern. From your home. Your ancestry. From tragedy. From your feelings. You run, but it does you no good, nor will it."

"Who *are* you?"

"That is what I am about to tell you," Caritas said calmly. She then told Epi all of the scenes in the dream, the sounds, the smells. "But that is not the beginning, nor the end. I lived on a *ganaderia* near Mogote growing up. I loved the freedom, but Mama thought I was too wild. She had Papa send me to a school in Santa Fe. I met Rosa there and we fell in love. When I was eighteen, we returned to my home. My papa was enraged when he found out the nature of our relationship and banished me. My Tia lived in Mogote and welcomed both of us."

"You're lesbian? With a Catholic aunt who took you in?"

"Your dream begins with the attack, when the men working to make the railroad rode into town. Payday, and they were already drunk. Mean drunk and looking for trouble. They started rounding up the people, pushing them into the street. I do not know what they planned.

"It was late at night, the townspeople were not prepared for war. The gang shot anyone who tried to stop them. Rosa and I were wakened by the church bells, and we hid Tia Adelita in the root cellar. She wanted us to stay, but in my pride, I insisted we go to the church to defend the town."

"Can I ask questions?" Epi said. When Caritas nodded, she pulled her thoughts together. "What do you mean, making the railroad? Rode in on horseback? When was this?"

"My story will answer your questions, if I may continue."

Epi felt something shift in her heart and was sure she didn't want to hear the rest of the story.

"Rosa and I were separated by the crowd." Caritas wrapped the shawl closer around her. "She was killed that night. Someone said it was a run-away horse. I tried to find her in all that chaos, but I failed. I went to the church to Father Rodriguez, for sanctuary. Though I didn't believe in the dogma, I recognized it as a holy place. Those men set the roof on fire, rammed the door open. Shot Father. Took the women. Took me." She wrapped her arms around her thin body. "Does this not match your dream?"

Epi huddled in her chair, lit a cigarette, and watched the smoke drift toward the stove. "What I dreamed was so chaotic. Could match the dream with the horses, the shots. The priest. But this is an absurd conversation."

"Is it?"

Epi pushed herself from the chair, walked to the window. "How can you read my dreams? Or are you doing some mind-control thing?"

"I sent you the dream so that you might understand what followed. I thought if you could feel—"

"You sent me that nightmare? How could you? My head's fucked up enough without your nightmares."

Caritas watched the woman. "I did not mean to cause you pain. I have come to help. I thought the way was to share my story."

"This is supposed to help me? You're more screwed up than I am."

"May I tell you the rest?"

"Why not?" Epi rubbed her forehead, returned to her chair. "What's better than a ghost story in front of the fire with a blizzard outside? Jesus Christ!"

Caritas stood, began to pace in front of the stove. "I was in shock after. My brothers brought me home. I was terrified of everything, even my brothers. Can you understand?"

Epi looked away, rubbed the bridge of her nose. "Sure, if any of this is true."

"My father could not tolerate my behavior, or my grief. He decided to send me away to relatives in the southern part of the state." She moved back to the chair, barely sitting on the seat. "We stopped at Taos for the night. I was so restless, so unsettled, I slipped out and walked to the plaza. You see, my virtue was ruined—it made no difference that I walked alone in public."

The light in the kitchen went out, throwing Epi and Caritas into wavering shadows. Caritas stood and lit an oil lamp from the sideboard. The flickering flame made her long nightgown, tousled hair and old shawl seem long familiar in the rough-hewn house.

"In the plaza, I saw an old friend, a girl I had gone to school with, although she was several years older. Her name was Maria Vargas."

Epi looked sharply at her.

"Sí. A handsome young man was walking with her. She introduced me to her new husband." Caritas looked toward the wall of photographs. "To Charlie Gordy."

The icy wind swept into the room, turned Epi's hands cold. The stove pinged as if it were carrying on its own monologue. "You want me to believe you knew my great-grandfather? Sweet Jesus."

"What I want is irrelevant, because it is your choice." She returned to the chair and sat ramrod straight. "Maria and Charlie saved me. They brought me here and gave me shelter. Sanctuary."

"Seems to be a family habit," Epi said. "At least if you believe fairy tales."

"Though they were so kind, I could not rid myself of my guilt for Rosa's death, or for the agony she suffered before she died. If I hadn't wanted to flaunt our love, if I had never brought her home..."

The shadows danced on the walls, a fancy dance with thrust and swerves and revolutions. Epi didn't move a muscle and watched the gyrations of flame and phantom with her eyes only. "So, you killed yourself. I'm talking to a real ghost. Is there a purpose to this farce?"

"Rosa was the love of my life," Caritas said softly. "I buried myself in darkness and could feel no light, no warmth. Everything became too heavy, too much. I existed, sealed in a walking coffin of my own guilt. I let nothing touch me. All I thought and felt and dreamed was loss. My constant prayer was Rosa, come home."

Epi nodded. She knew the feeling well.

"Winter was coming and I could not endure the emptiness anymore. I found Charlie's Colt revolver and took it into the mountains. I said an act of contrition and pulled the trigger. In that very moment, I knew I had made the most dreadful mistake. One I could not change." Her black eyes blazed. The fire spit and popped.

Epi sank deep into the chair, brushed her hand over her eyes. "I'm supposed to believe this morality tale? Next you'll deliver a message from Mama. Or my brother. Or Great-Grandpa Gordy. Right?"

Epi turned to the window and saw that the slow, skipping skirts of the old women, dancing constancy and love to the heartbeat of Mother Earth, had changed. The flakes pounded the earth like the intricate steps of a male dancer, swirling, flattening everything that stood. A downdraft hit the chimney, scattered sparks with a whoosh.

"I have no messages from your beloved family. I only ask that you think about what I have said and understand my deepest regret. I allowed myself to feel alone, deprived. Empty. During all the time I wallowed, I forgot I was loved, not just by Rosa, but by Charlie and Maria. As you are loved by those in your life. I chose not to think of the grief I would leave behind.

"I must go now, Epi. The only message I carry I have delivered to you."

Caritas walked slowly to the shadows at the foot of the stairs, turned to glance at Epi before she began to climb into the pitch black above.

Epi woke up stiff and cold. She fed the embers bits of small kindling until flames licked their tongues on branches. She added a couple of small cedar logs, shut the door firmly. She felt a draft anyway and went in search of its source. The back door was open, snow drifting on the kitchen floor. Epi went to slam it shut when she saw the tracks. She followed the small footprints until they simply became snow disturbed in a drift. She took a few tentative steps forward, and saw where they just...ended.

She quickly returned inside, searched the whole house for Caritas. Nothing. She said she had to go, Epi thought. But why the hell couldn't she wait until the storm ended and we could dig out? She put on her winter mocs and parka, grabbed her snowshoes on the way out. She followed the tracks as far as they went and scanned the snow. Where the footprints stopped, two claw prints showed a bird had lifted off, and a little beyond, two wing prints, individual impressions of feathers in the crisp fresh snow.

Epi heard the "haw" of a raven, looked up. The bird looked down at her, pushed off the limb where it had perched, and flew upward out of sight.

THAT DAY

ORHEA THE DREAMER

IT WAS UNSEASONABLY CHILLY FOR Texas, or so the weatherman said. I wasn't too worried. I was confident that my ankle-length jean skirt and well-worn cowgirl boots would provide enough cover to keep my legs warm. On the way out of the house, I picked up my camera and threw a pale green shawl over my airy white peasant blouse. I climbed into my battered truck and headed into the ominously cloudy autumn day.

Seems like a day like any other, right? Seems like you are expecting me to say that I went out, took a few good photos, and went home, right?

Wrong.

I digress; excuse me. I am, or rather I was Angela White—amateur photographer, former teacher, lover of literature, crazy hippie, sad, lonely, thirtysomething lesbian. I am...or I was... all these things. Until the day I met *her*.

Now I am something else; I'm not quite sure what. For that matter, I suppose I never was sure. Let's start out by saying I'm from a rich ethnic background. To be specific, my father was of Scotch-Irish descent, and my mother was African American. I was born as pale as milk and, over the years, darkened to an olive complexion. I was never fully accepted by either side of my family, so it took me years to learn who I was and accept it. I suppose you could say I spent most of my life trying to figure out who and what I was…and then this.

Anyway, back to the day I met *her*.

It was Halloween. I remember specifically, because it is one of my favorite holidays. I love the whole idea of everyone dressing however they want and people being so accepting of that. Only on Halloween can you go out wearing a yellow leotard with a neon pink tutu and not have your sanity questioned. I love the legend and lore behind the holiday, and I love the change of seasons.

In Texas, October is when you finally start to get relief from the hot, humid summer. That day, I carved my jack-o'-lanterns early and lined them up on my porch in anticipation of Halloween eve, and then I headed out in my truck. There was a Halloween block party on Main Street, and I wanted to take pictures of the older buildings, as well as of any person who caught my interest along the way.

Winding through the curves of the dirt farm road, I came upon an uncommon sight—a handsome woman sitting on a trunk that appeared to be an antique. She was just sitting there, her legs sprawled out in front of her, encased in denim jeans tucked inside black boots that fitted snugly to mid-calf. Her shirt was a plain V-neck T-shirt—white, but already stained with sweat. It looked dingy, as if it had been washed a few times without bleach. Her cropped brown hair held golden highlights, and there was a mess of earrings in her left ear. She held a leather jacket thrown casually over her left shoulder. Her right elbow rested on her right thigh, hand held with the thumb jutting out. I thought to myself, *Who the hell hitchhikes these days?*

Still, I slowed down, and when my eyes caught hers, I stopped.

I knew it was a dumb move. Normally I wouldn't have done it, no matter how well those jeans fit that lean form of hers. And good Lord, when she stood up, I could see the soft curve of her breasts under the fitted white tee. Her skin was dusky, almost coppery, and if I'd had to hazard a guess, I would have said she was Latina, or perhaps an ethnic mix that included Native American. Her piercing brown eyes also had a golden glaze, and there was just a hint of smile lines around her lips, which quirked into a sardonic smirk as she slowly approached my side of the truck.

I released the breath I was holding and checked myself in the rearview mirror. Despite the light sprinkling of freckles around my nose that no amount of bleach cream could fade, my face looked fine. I checked my hair to see whether my pins had come out of the bun. Satisfied that I was as together as possible, I rolled down the window just as she came to a stop beside it.

She wasn't very tall. In fact, I am five two, and it looked as if we'd stand nose to nose. From my height advantage in the cab of the truck, I assessed her features. Her nose had a bump on the bridge, as if it had been broken a time or two. Her lips were a little on the thin side, and her jaw was almost square. There was a thin white scar just above her left eyebrow. The naturally confident way she carried herself gave the clear impression that she liked to take charge.

She was *so* my type.

"You look like you need a lift," I said, glancing over at the old brown trunk by the side of the road.

"Yes. Can you help me out?"

Her voice was deep, and slightly rough, like she'd swallowed a hot chili pepper that had burned the back of her throat. It was damned sexy.

"Did I miss your car? I didn't see anything coming from my direction."

I tried not to stare at her lips, or into her eyes, for that matter, for when I looked too long, it seemed like I was falling in...

"No. I left my car. It's a long story. If I get in, you're not going to shoot me, are you?"

I grinned. "You're not from around here." I pointed at the trunk. "You need help with that?"

She shook her head. "Nah, I got it."

As she doubled back to retrieve that heavy-looking trunk, I was treated to a good long look at the finest derriere this side of Texas. She bent and lifted the thing with ease, and I noted that when she put it in the back, the truck bed bounced a little under the weight. A moment later, she got into the truck, slamming the door shut as she sat down.

I hit the gas and returned to the road. "I'm Angie, by the way," I said, subtly inhaling the deep scent of sweat and Cool Water cologne.

Now that she was in such close proximity, I was starting to feel a little nervous. To be honest, there was a prickling up my spine, as if I were in danger. I pushed it away, silently praying that I was wrong. I was in danger, yeah...in danger of throwing myself on this perfect example of hard woman and begging her to... to...

"Sarah," she said. "Sarah Wheeler. You are from around here?"

"Yeah. I live a few miles back the way I came."

We lapsed into silence, and I could feel her gaze raking over me. I didn't have to look; I could literally feel that she was sizing me up. When I could stand it no longer, I finally asked, "Where are you headed?"

"Cemetery."

Surprised, I glanced over at her, momentarily taking my eyes off the road. Sarah was looking straight ahead, her lips pursed in a line, indicating that there was a story that went with the reason for her destination. I wasn't sure whether it was polite to ask what that was.

"Sorry for your loss."

"It was a long time ago," she said dismissively. "You've likely heard of the cemetery. It's called Mount Carmel."

I nodded. "Sure, it's right on the outskirts of town. Listen, do you need to call Triple A or something for your car? I'll get a signal once we cross the county line."

"Don't have it. Don't worry about it. You can just drop me off at the cemetery, if that's alright with you."

"Okay."

Watching her out of the corner of my eye, I adjusted my mirror, just for something to do. There was a tear in the fabric of her jeans, and it revealed a tantalizing patch of copper skin. I couldn't help noticing how shapely her leg was, almost muscular. I don't typically lust after people I've just met, but Sarah was, is, magnetic. The longer I sat in that truck with her, the more I felt drawn to her. The more questions I wanted to ask, the more silent I became. All too soon, I saw the weathered wrought iron sign for Mount Carmel Cemetery. A soft sigh escaped me as I turned into the gates.

"Thanks a lot. Maybe I'll get to pay it forward someday, Angie…?"

"White," I said. "Angie White. I hope you do get the chance." I offered a polite smile, mentally kicking myself, because I knew I wasn't going to ask for her number. This was yet another opportunity slipping away.

Sarah's thickly lashed eyes traveled to my lips for an instant, and she nodded, then slipped from the truck as agilely as a cat. I waited a moment as she let down the tailgate, lifted the trunk out and set it on the ground, then closed the tailgate. Without a backward glance, she picked the trunk up, and I watched her until she disappeared behind a tree.

For some reason, goose bumps raced along my arms and legs, the clouds overhead darkened, and a cool wind gusted against my truck. I shrugged, feeling at once lost and relieved as I drove out of the cemetery and into town.

For the next two hours, I strolled around the older part of town, taking pictures of kids in their costumes and random items of interest in the community gathering. Eventually, the ominous rolling of thunder sent most of the revelers running for the safety of their cars. I agreed it was a smart idea. Since there was nothing left to take pictures of in the square, I thought I would try my luck at getting more Halloween-themed photos at the cemetery.

Oh, come on. I know what you're thinking, and you're right. I wanted to go back to Mount Carmel for more than the pictures. I thought I might see a certain well-built woman lugging a mysterious trunk. I tried to tell myself that I was only trying to be chivalrous, though Sarah might easily have met up with someone at the cemetery, or even hoofed it into town to call someone about her car.

I stopped the truck in a designated area, retied my shawl, and proceeded to pick my way among the headstones, looking for Sarah. Cemeteries are sacred places, and I was careful not to step on anyone's grave as I snapped photos of hanging branches, shadowed headstones, and an occasional perching bird. The creepy, yellowish light preceding the storm produced an eerie feeling in me that I hoped I could capture in my pictures. Mount Carmel is a huge cemetery, as old as the town itself, the last resting place of some of the first settlers that squatted in Texas when it still belonged to Mexico. I wandered into the older section, where many stones were broken or in disrepair. That's when I heard it.

There was an odd, screeching sound followed by a shout, and then something that sounded a lot like gunfire. By the time I heard a wail, I was already crouched low, running back to my truck. I heard heavy footfalls behind me, and a scream tore its way out of my throat. I didn't look to see what direction the chasing sounds were coming from, or if someone or something was headed toward me, but to my surprise, I was able to increase my speed. It was the fastest I'd ever run in my life.

Everyone is familiar with those awful horror movies where some idiot teenager trips over her own shoes as the killer pursues her. Well, I have a new empathy for that idiot, because unfortunately for me, I slammed into something solid and hairy, and I fell...hard. Stunned, I couldn't even try to get up. Maybe I couldn't have stood anyway. Suddenly I was yanked upright by my arm, so violently that I heard a nasty popping sound. I was jerked up so high that my feet were dangling in the air.

Flailing and kicking as hard as I could, I realized the arm that was holding me was huge...and hairy. Eventually, I was exhausted with emotional and physical fatigue, and I went limp. When I looked behind me, shock and horror precipitated another scream. Faster than I can describe, I was jerked around to face the monster. A huge, fleshy hand wrapped around my throat, cutting off my air supply, effectively keeping me from screaming again.

My captor had the head of a wolf and the torso of a woman, a really tall, hairy woman with grey skin and hard, pebbled nipples. She was naked, and I could see the coarse hair on her pubis jutting between her thighs. And unlike a dog's tail, her long, bushy, black tail was erect. Her snout was large, lips peeled back to reveal a foaming mouth that dripped saliva from the largest canine teeth I'd ever seen. She grunted and pressed her nose to my neck, her ears perked and alert, moving around the side of her own head like a dog's ears...listening.

Since I couldn't speak, I begged with my eyes: 'Let me go. Please don't kill me!'

Her dark eyes glowing red in the darkness, she tilted her head back and delivered the creepiest, most evil grin I'd ever seen outside of a movie. And then she laughed, she actually laughed, but this laugh was not like any I had heard before. It was a serrated sound, like a broken circular saw. Rasping, tearing, it terrified me, and I began to shake uncontrollably. I felt the powerlessness, the weakness of my humanity. Her chuckles died as she applied pressure to my windpipe until I was grasping at her monstrously clawed hand in sheer desperation. Dots appeared in front of my eyes, I was going numb all over, and I knew that I was dying.

I started to feel faint. One minute I was staring into the terrible black eyes of the giant wolf monster, the next, my eyes were closing. I heard another gunshot go off, this one sounding like an echo in my ears because it was so close yet so far away. Then I was falling.

The wolf beast howled in pain, clutching at the liquid red blooming on her chest, dropping me as she started to sink to her knees. When I hit the ground, my entire body became alive again, with pain. As I struggled to my feet, my thick, dark curls escaped their pins and fell into my eyes. Half delirious with shock and fear, I failed to notice the odd angle and excruciating pain in my pinky finger and the scratches on my arms and knees.

When I looked at the wolf creature, she was reaching for me. Her sharp talons dug into my skirt, and I screamed as I kicked her away. Curiously, the wolf-like features started melting away, and in their place was a pale-skinned woman with lovely red hair and brilliant green eyes. She was slender, like an elf from some movie, and yet her face, which was angry—violently so—wore a horrible look that I will never be able to erase from my mind. I was looking into the eyes of a creature who truly wanted to kill me, and the knowledge chilled my soul. Then her mouth went slack, her eyes wide and aware of her impending death. She collapsed backward and lay still, and the blood that had been spurting from her wound slowed to a trickle. She was definitely dead.

"You okay?"

I whirled around at the familiar voice. "Sarah?"

She seemed to materialize from the shadows on a knoll between the trees. She was wearing her jacket now, and an impressive looking shotgun dangled from her shoulder. She dropped down, balancing lightly on the balls of her feet as her hands gently probed me.

"Why are you here?" she asked as her hands slid to my arms and finally to my hand.

That was the first I noticed the odd angle of my pinky. "Oh God!"

She gingerly felt around the dislocated finger, and before I could even summon a breath to protest, executed a quick yanking motion that popped my finger joint back into place.

I fainted.

When I came to, it was to the sounds of gusting wind and a steady thumping beneath me. I opened my eyes and saw Sarah behind the steering wheel of my truck. Her sharp profile was pretty much all I could see in the darkness. I sat there for a long few minutes, trying to figure out how I had ended up on the passenger side of my own truck and why Sarah was driving, and then the memories came flooding in, flash after flash, in chronological order. All the way until...

"Shit" I pushed myself upright. "What did you do to me?"

"I didn't do anything to you other than load you into your truck. And now I'm driving you home."

"You don't know where I live."

She glanced over at me, her expression serious. "I know more than you think"

I looked out the windshield and, sure enough, we were about to turn into my driveway. Several thoughts came to mind—she was taking me home so I could be her hostage or to murder me, or she had no idea where else to go. It concerned me that I didn't know which one it was.

She parked in front of my garage and cut the engine. "We need to talk about what you saw out there."

I thought about how readily she had fired the shotgun that now rested against her door, near her left hand. "I didn't see anything. As far as I'm concerned, I had an awful, awful dream. Don't shoot me, okay?"

I retreated to an inward dialogue where I chided myself for all the times I had jokingly said that I wanted to die. I ruefully thought about how many years it had been since I'd last had sex, all the gorgeous women I could have dated had I just had the courage to ask. I thought about all the things I still wanted to see...

"I don't kill innocent people, Angie. Angie?" Sarah snapped her fingers in my direction.

I jumped. Then I looked into her eyes. Those deep, dark pools that had me sinking...sinking... Her lips were moving, so I made an effort to tune in.

"What you saw was a werewolf. That's the closest I can describe it to you in a way you'd understand. It must have been hiding there for a while. Have you heard about any...bizarre murders lately? Maybe in the paper or on the news?"

My mind pushed through the murky jumble of my thoughts, trying to recall. "I did hear something about people being mauled by wild animals."

"Damn, a pack this close to the Mexican border is odd." Sarah's observation was made mostly to herself, but her attention turned back to me as she said, "Are you going to invite me in?"

My mouth went dry. I took the keys from her and nodded. I didn't know what else to say. What I had seen wasn't normal, and while I like to think I am a little quirky, I am not batshit crazy. Not yet anyway. And she had mentioned a pack, which meant more of those huge wolf monsters. I figured it was a good idea to have a woman with a gun near me.

My automatic porch light came on as soon as I climbed the first step. I found the warm glow comforting, and my hand shook less as I unlocked the door and went inside, Sarah close at my heels. My house is a one-story, with a bedroom in the rear and one to the side that I used for an office. The kitchen is in the heart of the floor plan, and there are a family room and a dining room which are separated by a half wall. I strode past the living room, straight for the kitchen for ice for my throbbing hand.

"I am a hunter," Sarah offered from behind me. "Werewolves, vampires who violate the rules—I hunt them all. What happened tonight has not happened for a very long time."

I felt her staring, so I held a dripping piece of ice on my hand as I turned around and gave her my full attention. Her tough-looking leather jacket and stern features seemed odd in my kitchen, which I now admit is very feminine. She happened to be standing in front of my collection of tea cups.

I reached for a towel to keep from dripping water all over my tile floor. "What's going to happen now?"

She shrugged. "Your town has an infestation. I'll need to kill them all, or no one will be safe. It would be one thing if natural weres were here, but these are werewolves-turned-monsters who are only thinking of food. They know I killed one of their own, and they'll be able to track the body of their fallen companion here eventually."

"You brought it here!"

"It's better to remove the evidence from such a public place. I couldn't leave it there. Don't worry, werewolf bodies decay quickly. Anyway, your major concern tonight should be your own safety."

"Oh God!"

"It will be a few hours before we have to worry. They primarily act on instinct, so they'll be looking for a snack, preferably stray dogs, squirrels, or cats, before they come looking for us," she murmured. "You should get cleaned up. You look like hell."

I shot her a spiteful look. "Look who's talking?"

She smirked.

Twenty minutes later, I was sitting on my couch, legs folded under me as I flipped through channels on the TV and tried not to think of the sexy hunter in my shower. Using my soap. Wearing my clothes. She was lucky I had found a pair of jeans that didn't bag around her narrow waist. It was one of those I-could-wear-it-once-I-lose-a-few-pounds pairs that I would never be able to wear. I also found a decent gender-neutral T-shirt from my college days in the bottom of one of my drawers.

Imagining her pulling my shirt over her hard body, I growled at myself and tossed my remote across the couch. From a kitchen cabinet, I pulled down the bottle of rum I keep for the few special occasions when I want to whip up a drink and relax. I had discovered werewolves existed, and was lusting after a crazy but sexy hunter lady, and having a nervous breakdown—all in one day. A stiff drink was definitely in order.

I don't really like the taste of hard liquor unless it's diluted with something else. However, this was an unusual situation. I poured a shot into my coffee mug and downed it, grimacing at the taste and the heat that ran down my throat. I poured another shot and downed that too, coughing a little. The heat filled my chest as the rum sent calming messages to my brain.

I set my mug down and went back to the couch, wrapped a crocheted throw around my shoulders, and waited for Sarah.

I felt the dip in the couch as Sarah sat down, and I looked at her. Her hair was spiked with dampness, and her nipples were standing erect underneath the shirt.

"Cold?" she asked.

"Mmhm."

"I always run kind of warm."

Fuck.

"You were sweating this morning," I said, trying to distract myself. "You're definitely not a native Texan."

She laughed as she leaned back, legs splayed in her trademark confident manner. She looked up at the ceiling a moment, then at me. "No, I'm not. I'm from up north, way up north."

"Where?"

"Wyoming." She sighed. "It was a long time ago."

Her gaze focused on me, and I felt the heat flush my cheeks and spread to my lower regions. "Why are you looking at me like that?" Heart pounding in my chest, I tried to tear my eyes away but found I couldn't.

"You are fucking gorgeous, you know that?"

The compliment was paid so unexpectedly, so vehemently, that I actually raised my hand and fanned myself nervously. My stomach was doing somersaults, and suddenly, I wasn't all that cold. "I'm alright," I said lamely. "Now you, you look like you came straight out of a movie."

Her hand slid over to mine and lightly grazed my injured hand. "That shouldn't have happened. What were you doing out at the cemetery?"

"T...taking pictures," I stuttered, unnerved by her touch. "It's more of a hobby. I'm currently between jobs. I'm not sure I want to teach anymore, so I took some time off."

"Teacher, huh?"

Her voice had dropped an octave, and her hand was slowly sliding up and down my arm. I didn't pull away.

"Yes."

Why couldn't I look away from her gaze? I tried to get my mouth to form the words to ask her why she was a hunter, but I couldn't. I was totally focused on wanting her to kiss me. The desire was so strong that, without her saying a word, I was leaning toward her. She met me halfway.

I thought her lips would be hard, but they were soft. Soft and open. The first kiss was a mere brushing, testing. The second, her tongue lightly traced my lips. I felt the tension leave my body. A warm flood of emotion I could not define spread from my chest, spilled into my stomach, and settled between my legs in the form of arousal. I groaned into her kiss. I'm sure it only lasted a few seconds, and yet it felt like hours. Her tongue, which tasted surprisingly sweet, danced with mine. Her hands gripped my shoulders, and I clung to my shirt she was wearing.

Suddenly her mouth tore from our kiss and trailed down the side of my jaw, down my neck, and over my collarbone. She undid the buttons on my shirt. I was not wearing a bra. I heard her growl, felt her mouth against my aching breasts. I wanted this, had wanted it from the first moment I saw her. I was helpless to stop it. I arched my nipple into her mouth, which prompted a gentle sucking. She drew back just long enough to push me down onto the couch; I went willingly. Her mouth, her wonderful mouth, explored the curves of my stomach. I was not a skinny person, I did have curves, yet I wasn't nervous.

I was totally caught up, totally enthralled by the whirlwind that was Sarah.

She hooked her fingers into my pajama bottoms and dragged them down over my thighs. It was sweet, aching torture as she settled between my legs, focusing on the flesh of my thighs, my lower belly. When her mouth finally wrapped around my aching clit, I thought I would die of ecstasy. She caressed me, coaxed me with her tongue and lips until I was gripping her hair in passion. I'm sure I must have torn out a few strands as I screamed my release.

My limp fingers fell from her hair. I could feel that I'd aggravated my injured finger, but I didn't care. She slid up my body and kissed me. I could taste myself on her tongue, but before I could deepen the kiss, she moved her head and kissed my neck.

"I shouldn't have done that," she murmured.

I ran my hand over her back, thinking to return the favor. "What?"

She sighed. Pushing up on her hands, she stared down at me. "You are too good for me, too clean for my life. There is nothing beyond this moment. When the werewolves are dead, I will move on."

The passion that I'd felt just moments before fizzled out like an extinguished match, and anger took its place.

"I didn't ask you to marry me. Shit!" I tried to push her off; she didn't move a single inch. Either I was extremely weak, or she was incredibly strong.

"Angie…" Her voice was tender, and then I felt her stiffen, and she looked up. "Get dressed!" she said.

"Damn right I'm getting dressed!" I snapped, lunging for my pajamas.

I was filled with righteous anger that this woman, who *clearly* had come on to me, could then reject me so quickly. I felt stupid, and I felt betrayed. I finished fastening the last button on my shirt, but when I looked up, prepared to give her a piece of my mind, she was standing near the window, shotgun in hand. Howls echoed just outside my door, and the icy chill of fear washed through me.

They were here.

Sarah shook her head. "Something is wrong. They tracked us here way too soon."

She ran to her trunk, which was now situated near my front door. I couldn't see all the contents when she opened it, however I did catch a brief glimpse of a faded black and white photograph taped inside the lid. She extracted a very large knife, which she strapped to her calf, and another smaller gun; I couldn't tell the make.

"Stay inside, lock your door, and go to your room. You can maybe get out the window there if things go wrong. Angie, if you do get out, you need to run, and don't stop running."

Her eyes were soft and held something I didn't understand. I opened my mouth to tell her to be careful, but she was already gone.

I ran to the window to watch the proceedings, but the night was so dark, I could only make out shapes—the great, horrifying shapes of three large werewolves and the lean, short figure that was Sarah. They were talking, but I couldn't hear a damn thing, and then suddenly, one of the hulking monsters lunged for her.

Sarah was quick, really quick, and I watched as she raised her smaller gun and fired three rounds into the creature. It faltered but didn't stop. She ran away from the house, and the shapes disappeared behind the barn. I heard a series of howls and shouts, then the sound of gunfire and wailing. Afraid for her, I pressed my face against the glass but still saw nothing.

I heard glass shatter somewhere in the vicinity of the back room, and I whirled around. In that brief quiet moment, I could hear my heart pounding in my chest. Should I run out into the night where the werewolves would surely find me and make me a snack? Or should I get a weapon and fight whatever was coming? If it was a fourth werewolf, I figured I was dead anyway. They were way too strong and way too fast, and as I have mentioned, I was never an athlete.

I glanced at Sarah's box. It was still open. The photograph I had glimpsed earlier showed a young woman who looked just like Sarah. Her hair was long and straight, she was wearing a traditional looking Native American dress, and her arms were wrapped around a small girl. Of course, the picture was entirely too old for the woman in it to be Sarah. There were only a few other small items still inside the box—a wallet, another knife, some crumpled letters. I dove for the knife. It was at least six inches long with a serrated edge, a hunting knife, and I held it to me as I edged toward the front door to take my chances outside.

My bedroom door opened with an eerily slow creak, and a great hulking shadow soon filled the hallway. My bedroom was dark, the hallway was dark, and so it seemed as if the blackness was growing fuller, until I could see the outline of the massive creature, so huge he actually had to hunch his neck to keep from slamming his head into the ceiling.

He sniffed the air and then snarled, his attention focusing on me. I wanted to run, but my legs felt like lead. Transfixed by the monster, I continued to inch toward the door. I had thought the female was huge, but this male must have been triple her size. His yellow teeth glinted in an evil, canine smile; his red eyes were large and dangerous. I glanced at his wide, muscular chest and his thick, hairy arms, then down to his waist, which was naked. There was a thick cropping of hair where his... It was swollen, and standing at full attention. He was aroused by the idea of ripping me from limb to limb, or worse.

"Oh my god!" I screamed.

This time I did turn; this time I did run. There was hope I could get outside, hope I could make it to my car and maybe drive out of harm's way. My hopes were dashed as I was, for the second time that night, lifted into the air, this time by the waist, and slammed into a wall. The impact sent a sharp pain through my arm, and I continued to scream, because I feared it was broken.

He didn't try to stop my screaming. Instead, he applied pressure against my shoulders so I could feel his strength, smell the musk of him as he breathed down into my face.

"Please, I didn't do it," I said pathetically. "Just don't kill me."

His laughter was ten times more horrifying than the female's, and I felt as if I might vomit. His thick, meaty tongue slid from between his teeth, and he dragged it slowly down my chin and neck, and then he dropped me and I plummeted to the ground. He barked a word, and when I didn't move, he said it again. This time I understood the rough, garbled language.

"Run."

I can honestly say that I can't remember the exact details of what happened next. I remember making a mad dash for the door, and I know I didn't make it. I remember getting tossed at a wall, feeling intense pain, hearing my own screams as rough talons dragged over my body. After that, things went black.

In the darkness it was warm; it was safe. It wasn't quiet. At first, there was crying, gut-wrenching crying that made my heart ache for whoever was making that sound. Then the chanting started, accompanied by the sound of rattles and drums; I didn't recognize the language. The chanting continued for what seemed like eternity. The longer it continued, the more I was wracked with emotions, ranging from confusion to simple acceptance that I might very well be dead and somehow stuck in some kind of limbo-like afterlife. Then the pain began, chasing away everything else.

The pain was unlike anything I can describe here. It was like a steady burn that started from the centermost part of me and spiraled out throughout my body. It got so intense, so continuous, that I found myself praying for the release of death.

"Hang in there."

They were the first words I heard in my eternal darkness.

"Angie, you need to hold on. I know it hurts. You shouldn't die like this. Angie? Please."

"Sarah? It's dark."

"Open your eyes."

"I'm so...so tired"

"I know, sweetheart. I promise you can rest later, just open your eyes."

Something in the tone of her voice, the way she called me sweetheart, gave me the strength to try. My eyes were so heavy that they almost felt glued shut. I had to will them to open.

"Angie?"

The first thing I saw was Sarah. She was gorgeous—those golden brown eyes, that sharp nose, high cheekbones, square jaw, and shapely lips. Her skin was glowing.

"You are so pretty." My voice sounded rough, even to my own ears.

She glanced over her shoulder, and then looked at me. "You need to take it easy. Here, sit up."

With Sarah's hands on my shoulders to help me, I sat up. I was becoming very aware of my body. Everything in me felt tight, like a rubber band stretched to its limits. I was also insanely hungry. But of all the things that came into my mind, I said, "Where are we, and where is my house?"

"The alpha destroyed your home. I felt something was wrong; I should have gone with my instincts." She sighed. "I hope someday you can forgive me."

"Forgive? You mean my house is gone, like actually gone?"

"The evidence needed to be destroyed. Angie, what do you remember?"

"Destroyed?" I echoed dumbly, looking around at my current surroundings. I was sitting on a blanket with bright designs, on a hard-packed dirt floor. When I looked up, there was a hole in the roof. I smelled fire, and found that the source was a small fire pit circled by stones, a foot or two away from me. The fire was low, mostly smoking coals.

"Where am I?"

"Someplace safe."

I felt Sarah's eyes concentrated on me, so I looked up at her. She did not look happy. "What?"

"You were hurt because I didn't follow my instincts. You were hurt because I didn't heed the warning signs. You see, most packs of weres do not have an alpha. An alpha is a special class. They are more cunning, less instinctive. The alpha must have been cautious about my presence, so he had his pack call me out while he stayed behind, watching. Either he could smell you, or he knew you were with me. I think he was thinking he could use you for leverage, or at least to get revenge on me, but he didn't count on me being a true hunter. His pack died quickly, and you had to pay for it. When I realized what had happened..."

For the first time since I'd met her, I heard Sarah's voice crack.

"I came as fast as I could, but he'd already torn at you. You were damn near dead. I thought you were dead." A shadow crossed her face, and there was an unexpected vulnerability in her eyes as she sat a short ways away from me. "After I killed him, I found you. I immediately realized the change had already started, so I called in reinforcements." She shook her head. "You might as well know."

She picked up something from behind me and set it in my lap. It was a crumpled newspaper

"Mount Carmel house fire." I read the headline aloud, hearing the disbelief in my own voice. "You burned down my house? My house!"

"We had no choice, Angie," she said gravely. "Made alphas are extremely contagious. Weres can be made or born. Those who are made are wild, feral creatures that prey on humans. Most alphas are born; this one in fact was made. He was very old, and he was unstable. I couldn't risk an investigative team coming in and cutting themselves on a piece of bloody glass, or worse. Everything had to be destroyed. Angie? Angie, listen, you have been infected."

That's my story.

Maybe you're wondering why Sarah didn't kill me if I was infected. Well, her people have a way of "domesticating" weres. It's a risky process, and it almost never works, but I guess I got lucky. I'm an omega, which means I am not infectious.

I'm not the same person, of course not. Had I not been changed, I would still have become different from when I drove down that dirt road that Halloween. Now before you go off thinking this story has a happy ending, there are some things you should know.

My collar doesn't make me any less a monster; I just happen to be a monster that is bound to a hunter. I really love her, even though she's never said the same to me. The sex is wonderful, and I help her trap or kill my own kind. But if I were to make one wrong step, I know Sarah would kill me. It's her job. I am glad, because I would prefer it that way. I love her so much that I think I'd rather she kill me than anyone else. I know that sounds a little weird. Fuck it. I'm a werewolf; what *isn't* weird about this whole story?

Sometimes I hear a little voice inside of my head telling me I need meat—meat that is red, raw, still quivering with life. Sometimes I wake up in the middle of the night and find that I am mauling a package of ground hamburger from the freezer, with no idea how I got there.

I'm telling my story for two reasons. First, I want to preserve the last vestiges of the me that was once human; I want to keep the essence of the Angie that I was, safe from the monster inside of me. Second, I want to warn others. Hunters are a dying breed, and you cannot rely on them for protection. We are stronger, we are faster, and we can survive multiple gunshot wounds, so your aim better be true.

Follow the signs: Have you heard about any strange animal attacks in your neighborhood lately? Or maybe you have noticed many domesticated animals have gone missing. Perhaps you've heard unidentifiable shuffling noises outside your window. One night, you might just turn off your lights and go to bed, unaware of the red, glowing eyes of a hungry, bloodthirsty beast watching its prey.

Someday...though I really hope not...that beast might be me.

FRESH BLOOD

EVE FRANCIS

ALLIE BOGGS HELD HER COFFEE cup close to her nose, smelling her drink before she took a sip. The mocha Frappuccino was sweet and salty, a rich caramel scent that offset the rain and gasoline odor of the Chicago streets. It reminded Allie of the perfume Violet wore at night. She smiled as she sniffed again.

"Now I understand," Chip McDonald said with a wry smile.

Allie didn't allow her fear—or even slight paranoia—to stop herself from rolling her eyes. "And what exactly did you just figure out, Chip? Have we cracked the case?"

Allie and her partner Chip were on their usual night shift. On a Friday night this close to the full moon, anything could happen. Allie didn't like to put too much stock in supernatural occurrences, but then again, she had to admit: strange stuff did happen on these nights. Violet, Allie's long-time girlfriend, had worked in the ER long enough to truly see that in its full capacity. If Chip had finally figured out that Allie herself *was* one of those supernatural beings he joked about on a regular basis, then she wanted to give the guy a medal. It was about time.

"Nothing that extreme," Chip said with a laugh. Currently, they were investigating a string of gunpoint robberies in the city. They had gotten a fairly good geographic profile from some of the desk cops and decided to stake out a location near the hot zone where the robbery duo was suspected of striking next. It was a long shot whether or not this particular store fell within the robbers' choices for tonight, but it was still a good position to be in. Their radios were also on, so they could attend to any call ins if needed. "But I know now how you stay so skinny even though you always get those sugar-filled drinks."

"And how's that?"

"You just smell them. I don't think I've ever see you drink a full coffee. It's usually me who throws out a cup in my car at the end of the night. So tell me, do you even like it?"

Allie smirked. She took another big sniff of the coffee before placing her lips on the edge. She swallowed some, but it always tasted the same. Trite and overdone. Human food was always so...*intense*. It had way too many flavours that competed for attention, which left Allie feeling wholly unsatisfied. She swallowed it like it was sludge and then shrugged her shoulders.

"You know, Chip, I think you caught me. I'm not a coffee person."

Chip laughed. He took a big gulp of his own drink. "Why bother buying it, then?"

"Well, first of all, I try to get other people to buy it for me whenever possible," Allie said with a wink. "But I suppose it makes me feel normal, most of the time."

"Here, here." Chip nodded. He clinked their coffee cups together in a muted toast before looking back out at the barren road. Rain had fallen earlier in the night, leaving the large potholes filled with rainwater which reflected back the lights of the city. Their black, unmarked police car was tucked inside a small alleyway, close to a liquor store and a convenience store, both of them broadcasting OPEN in large, neon-red letters.

The moon moved behind the clouds. Chip regarded it in the rearview mirror and then craned his head to really look at it. Chip was thirty-five and pure cop material. If his horribly stereotypical name and broad shoulders didn't allow him an easy entry into the police force, then Allie wasn't sure what would allow anyone inside.

She had gotten into the academy on a technicality. She was only promoted because she was a woman—check one for diversity—and a lesbian—check two for diversity. The fact that she was a vampire and preferred the night shift was another asset. Not the vampire part, since no one but Violet knew of her proclivity for blood and darkness. Chip was only dragged into doing the night shift because he had Allie as a partner. And though he was a better cop and should have been allowed more power, he liked Allie. He hung close to her and therefore, was always on nights too. At least Allie let him drive.

"You see that?" Chip asked after a moment.

"What?" Allie set her coffee into the cup holder. She looked behind at the empty road. The river was close by, as dark as the night sky. She gazed back at Chip and tried to follow his line of sight. He shivered suddenly.

"Oh, man. Though I saw a shadow circle around the trees over there. Or come up from the river."

"You watch too many horror films," Allie laughed. She looked back towards the river, the moon overhead, and decided to play along. She shivered. "Oh, man. I think I saw something too. You're getting to me."

Chip nudged her shoulder. "The full moon is out. You never know what could happen. What does your girl say about the full moons?"

"The crazies come out. But she's superstitious. She has to be—when you work in emergency and in the trauma department, I mean. Those cases are finicky, and half the time she just prays to get out on time and without too much blood loss."

"I hear that," Chip said again. He was about to lift his cup and clink their drinks together again, when the low rumble of a motor caught them both off guard. Chip glanced out his driver's side window at a green motorcycle that sped around the corner and came to a halt. Another bike followed afterwards. Both riders wore dark leather jackets. One, with long hair pinned back around his shoulders, was smaller than the first. The other one kept the brim of a baseball cap pulled down over his eyes.

Not that out of the ordinary, Allie thought to herself. Motorcycle riders really needed to bundle up or their bodies degloved if they hit the road. Violet had shared as much from her trauma ER experiences. She absolutely hated motorcycles for that reason alone. They made the body so fragile, so permeable, that it could suddenly break when in contact with the smallest resistance. It was like playing catch with a raw egg. If there was anyone else more superstitious than night shift ER workers, it was someone on a bike. They were playing with fire.

"Didn't the last robbery happen with motorcycles?" Chip asked.

"I thought that was a Vespa? And only one vehicle between them?"

"Aren't all bikes basically the same?" Chip asked. "The person could have been wrong. It happens all the time. Witnesses…"

Allie cut him off with a sudden hand motion before he could say "suck." She leaned closer to Chip, almost in his lap, as she peered out his window at the guys on bikes. She watched as the biker with long hair picked up a large duffle bag and tossed it over a shoulder. The bag seemed mostly empty, until the taller biker undid the zipper, and there was the flash of a metal object. *Objects*, Allie corrected herself. There were guns in the bag. Allie sniffed the air outside; the heavy pollution from the Chicago downtown area tickled her nostrils, followed by the smoke of the bikers' engines and the faint hint of gunpowder.

"That's them," she said.

"How do you know?"

"I just do. They have guns," Allie moved in her seat, undoing her belt and then working to grab her gun from her waist. "When have I been wrong before?"

Chip laughed. "You and your nose, always getting us into trouble."

There was no time to laugh or joke. The taller of the two bikers gestured to his partner before they both walked into the liquor store.

"Should we…go?" Chip asked.

"No. Wait. We have to catch them in the act."

Both Allie and Chip moved out of the unmarked car. Placing themselves behind the hood, they waited in a crouching position. Allie could already feel the excitement, the electricity in the air. It was a good thing she didn't really drink coffee, or else she would have been too overloaded. When you had Chicago at night, and criminals on the loose, there wasn't much else anyone needed for stimulation.

A gunshot went off.

"Motherfucker," Chip said. "They didn't shoot at the last robberies! Just used the gun as leverage."

"Well, times are changing…"

Allie stood up, holding her gun in the air. She watched through the large glass window as the two people on bikes turned around. She was close enough to see that both of their faces were young, rosy-cheeked with excitement. They ran out of the liquor store with their bag half-done- up, while the clerk lay in his own blood by the counter. Allie could smell the blood like alcohol; it invaded her system and made her toes curl. Blood, type AB, and healthy. *Fresh blood.* She sniffed, taking a deep breath in that didn't arouse too much suspicion. The clerk was not dead. The wound hadn't hit a major artery; he would most likely be fine.

Allie turned her attention towards the robbers. She fired once, hitting the back of one of their bikes. The shot pinged off metal. Their running did not slow down until they reached their bikes. *Damn*, she thought. She fired again, hoping to hit their wheel so they couldn't flee. She didn't want to kill them, even if they had already fired their weapons. It was always a lot easier if Allie didn't kill anyone; their blood was less tempting that way. Her gun fired into the black night, the bullet hitting nothing she could hear as it soared through the air. In retaliation, another bullet came towards their unmarked car and dinged the front fender.

"Shit," Chip said. He backed his body up under the door of the vehicle. "That's too close."

"Get in," Allie instructed. "On my side. I got this."

The chase began then. The kids pulled out on their bikes quickly, heading through the Chicago downtown area and towards the docks. Allie shot a few times from the window as she drove, one hand on the wheel. Chip shot too, but she could tell he wasn't really aiming. His human heart was too scared, the prospect of death too close. Allie knew that even if she was hit, she would bleed like a human and feel pain like a human, but it wouldn't really get her. She could waltz into the ER room, see Violet, and then have herself patched up. Violet wouldn't bat an eye at the odd test scores or the vast quantities of blood Allie would lose without getting light-headed. Violet would probably give Allie Band-Aid, a kiss on the cheek, and maybe even a sucker before sending her home.

Violet, Allie thought as she took a corner that launched the cop car onto two wheels. *Oh, I want to see you.*

Allie debated crashing the car into the men on motorcycles just so she could see Violet. But she didn't. A couple more minutes of chasing and all her predictions about motorcycles would come true. Those were the odds on bikes, and eventually, the kids were going to run out of luck. They would fumble, fall off onto the asphalt, their skin peeling—

"Watch out!" Chip stated. A bullet came at the front windshield. The glass cracked and rippled outwards like water in a pond. Allie turned the corner and came into a large alleyway in an abandoned construction site with nearly no light. She couldn't see, not even with all her senses heightened. She slammed on the brakes. The screeching of the tires felt deafening to her—which meant they were probably giving Chip a heart attack.

"You okay?" she asked. She turned to see Chip's head between his own legs, his gun resting in his hands but limp.

"Yes, I'm fine. I'm not hit," he muttered. He lifted his eyes, chancing a glance. "Just...fuck. Are they getting away?"

Allie stuck her head out of the vehicle just before she heard the crash. There was a sudden and earsplitting scream, and sparks flew as the metal carriage of the bike hit the asphalt. The kids' cries were worse than a baby being born. Allie could feel the leather wear away from the biker's sides, his bones and skin falling through and meeting the night air. The stinging, the pain, and the blood. Allie smelled the blood most of all. The fresh tang of dripping blood, the thick smell of plasma and cells. She swallowed hard.

"They're both down," she said. She sniffed the air with her eyes closed. She sensed the cells dying, the blood turning stale as it hit the air. "I think one's dead."

She *knew* one of them was dead. The other kid, the one with long hair, had crashed his bike into the wall of an abandoned building. He was on the ground, the sudden impact allowing his body to not come loose from his skin, like a skeleton trying to escape. He would probably live. Broken bones, physical therapy, and a life on the disability ward of the prison. But he would live.

Allie stepped out of the car and walked over to the dead body. His eyes were black. Body battered and bruised, where it wasn't exposed to the night air like a vivisection. She was glad he was dead. If the impact hadn't killed him, he would have already lost too much blood by then. She stared at his body. Chip got out of the car and called to her.

"Help is on its way. I radioed in."

"Okay," Allie said. "They're not going anywhere."

Chip nodded. He turned around and looked towards the river close by. He spoke into his walkie-talkie frantically. Allie chanced another glance at the bodies in front of her. While there was still time, with Chip distracted and praising God that he was still alive, Allie bit down on the carcass of the first boy. She had to get at him quickly, while the blood was still fresh.

Everything was cleared up rather quickly. From the prints gathered inside the store, the CSPU team was able to confirm that yes, these two were responsible for the string of robberies across Chicago in the past six weeks.

"It was actually a brother-and-sister team," Chip stated. He and Allie were just outside the emergency room, under the harsh lights of the walk-in area of the hospital. The store owner would be fine. He had a stomach wound and the doctors were working on getting the rest of the bullet fragments from his body and replacing the pints of blood that he had lost. He would definitely have a scar, a forced vacation, and a story to tell everyone later. But he wasn't dead, and that was the main point. Chip held a cup of cheap coffee from the hospital cafeteria in his hand as he talked, bringing her up to speed. Allie had nothing.

"It's not just the Chicago robberies that CSPU is talking about, either. There were some reports of similar crimes in Canada, around Alberta, but they're not sure yet. The Canadians have a different scanning system, so the fingerprints will take a while to match."

"Uh-huh? Neat. Glad we got there when we could," Allie said. "They try to kill anyone else in Canada?"

"No, this was the first person they shot. They're also not related, not technically. We have their names now and their records are being forwarded. The foster care system put them together in a home and they've been together ever since. Birthdays are the same, at least according to their IDs. Could be a lie, though."

"People don't lie about the day they're born. Just the year. It's probably true."

"Ah, okay. Well, they had the same birthday and were put in the same foster home. They probably aged out of the system the same day and then started their crimes. They're...young. Really. I didn't realize it until I saw the woman being pulled in on a stretcher. Sure makes you think, huh? Life is short—and precious. Too precious to waste."

Allie nodded along, not paying much attention. Their jobs were done, right? They had gotten their man—and woman. So it should have been time for them to leave, not wax poetic outside of the hospital as moths moved towards the hot lights. Allie felt full and sick to her stomach, like how Chip must feel after a steak dinner. The blood from her feeding was strong and thick, and it sloshed around inside of her. The sudden smells inside the emergency room didn't bother her as much as they normally did, since she was so full. The antiseptic and patina of illness that seemed to scum over the doors made her feel woozy, but there was nothing she could do.

Maybe some of this feeling was guilt, Allie wondered. She hadn't fed from a fresh body in over two years, not since she and Violet had moved in together. But she hadn't meant to feed tonight, not really, right? This couldn't be as bad as stalking her prey. The man was going to die. He was a criminal. The body was there. And Allie had taken what she believed to be rightfully hers.

"There was nothing you could have done," Chip said. He placed his free hand over Allie's shoulder, his brown eyes soft and sympathetic. "He crashed his bike. No helmet. Even if he had been wearing one, it would have been bad. And he was one of the bad guys. You did good, Allie. Don't beat yourself up because you lost one. There are still two alive, and the most important one, the storekeeper, will be thankful."

Allie nodded along with Chip's words. She mumbled something that sounded like a greeting card saying, as her mind wandered. The crash victim's body haunted her, but not because of her own duty as a police officer. She replayed the promise she had made to Violet in her mind.

"No more feeding," Violet had said, her dark bangs matted to her forehead. She had been angry, her voice shaky and full of tremors. Her small hand formed a pointed finger, which she shook at Allie as their argument progressed. "I mean it. No loopholes either. No feeding."

"I'm not going to get you," Allie said calmly. "I'd never get you. I can control myself, you know."

Violet rolled her eyes. "Oh, I'm sure. But I'm not worried about me."

"Then what are you worried about?"

"Other people. You don't need to take from them so harshly. I have access to blood. To people who have wilfully signed away their rights to it. Consenting parties."

"Right," Allie said. "So it's not the fact that I drink blood that grosses you out, it's the murder and lack of consent as I feed?"

Violet nodded. "You are who you are. I can't—and don't want—to change that. But you should have morals about what you do, even if it is for survival. So, no more feeding from unknowing victims."

"But it's not like those people who donate blood know it's going to be given to a vampire. That's still not perfect consent…"

"No, but they know it's going towards helping someone. They don't get to pick and choose who they help when they donate. For all they know, their blood could go into the arm of a gunshot victim who is really a mass murderer. You don't know when you're a nurse or a donor who you're really helping. But you help because it's the principle that matters. And this blood I give you will help save others who would have normally died. Don't look at it as for you, Allie. Look at it for your future victim's sake."

Allie had quieted then. She had let Violet win that discussion, because her girlfriend had clearly thought about this professional qualm long and hard. Violet knew what she was getting into with Allie, and instead of waltzing into it like Bella Swan or a romance heroine, she was going in with gusto—and a list of rules. She knew what Allie's past had been like, and she understood their future together. But to go against her oath as a nurse—to do no harm—was too much. She insisted on providing the blood to Allie. And hey, it had been good so far.

But fresh blood, Allie thought. She could feel it inside of her and how full it made her. The plasma that Violet gave her was good, but it was like those coffees full of sugar. While consuming it made her feel normal, as if she weren't a monster, it also made her realize that she would never really be fully satisfied.

"Is Violet around here?" Chip asked. His hand slipped away from Allie's shoulder and into his pocket awkwardly. "Maybe you should see her?"

"No, she works at a different hospital."

"Right," Chip said. He sighed. He knew where Violet worked—he remembered most things that Allie said about Violet, probably because he thought Violet was cute—but he was at a loss for things to say. His face revealed the discomfort of someone who wanted to comfort someone injured but had no idea how to sympathize with the pain. "Do you want some time to call her?"

Allie met his eyes and nodded, though she was definitely not going to call her girlfriend. Not now. "Thanks. That would be nice."

"Not at all. I'll be here, waiting around for our chief. We will have to do a lot of paperwork for tonight. I suspect that when he gets here, he'll allow us time for that rather than being on foot patrol. I'll let him know where you are, okay? But take your time."

Allie nodded. She glanced back into the hospital emergency room. The group of injured people and doctors were new now, their bodies in near constant motion as they tried to stop more bleeding from other patients. "Is someone guarding the door?"

"To the other motorcycle rider? Yeah. Don't worry."

"Okay. Thanks, Chip."

"Not at all."

Allie waited for another moment in the outside hospital lights. Like the moth that constantly bumped up against the hot surface, Allie lingered by the hospital doors. When it opened, as another stretcher was pushed inside, she followed the paramedics in.

Allie went to the roof first. She stood at the edge of the building, the rubber soles of her shoes making her feel solid on the ledge. She looked out at the blinding lights of Chicago's city, now three in the morning, and felt small amongst the night. It was a nice thought. Occasionally, the overwhelming feeling of being a supernatural being got to her. She was someone who could take a life if she really wanted to and someone who could slip out of the hands of the justice system. She had already restarted her life several times now in the wake of being found out. Someone like Violet, who had stayed after the revelation fell, was a rarity.

Allie sat down on the hospital's ledge, her feet kicked out at the side. She looked down at more bodies as they were filed in and out of the white ambulances. She thought of the brother-and-sister pair that she and Chip had stopped in their tracks. Not really brother and sister, she reminded herself. They were in foster care, which formed the worst kind of family, since it was made without blood attachments and during all kinds of crises. This made it one of the hardest bonds to break. It was no wonder to Allie that the two siblings had gone across the Albertan Badlands, robbing and committing crimes, until they had ended up in Chicago. It must have seemed like the only ending to their story. They had never harmed anyone before they shot the clerk. And that shot at the clerk, at least from Allie's point of view, seemed like a classic downward spiral and call for help. They had wanted something beyond themselves and the life that they had been given. No one could fault them for that, even if their actions lead to their own downfall.

And now there was only one of them left to pay for the crimes and keep the legacy alive. It didn't seem fair, even with Allie's twisted sense of justice. Allie thought of Violet, more and more, as she stirred over a new idea in her mind. Her mouth tasted bitter, like copper from pennies. She watched the skyline and replayed the crash. So easily. Everything could fall apart in the blink of an eye.

She walked down the backstairs and towards the sister's room. A guard was outside, like Chip had assured her.

"Hey, have you had a break yet?"

The young officer shook his head. His dark skin shone with sweat, as if the hallway were too hot.

"I can take over, then. Go to the bathroom. Get a cup of coffee." Allie produced her badge with her name, BOGGS, written on it and her serial number. The officer looked her up and down, his eyes widening as he realized who stood in front of him.

"Well done tonight."

"Thanks. Don't mention it. Just get me a coffee while you're gone."

The young officer nodded with a smile. "Sure, no problem. What kind do you want?"

"Surprise me," Allie said. "So long as it smells good."

He tipped his head to Allie as he left his post. She waited until he was in the stairwell before she glanced back at the woman in the bed. Her pale skin and freckles looked like blood spatter across her nose. She was bruised, black around her eyes. Her arms were in casts and one of her legs, too. Handcuffs were slotted around her wrist and cast and then attached to the bed. She looked pretty rough. Allie breathed in deeply the faint smell of antiseptic, blood, and of course, the lurking possibility of death. This woman could die. She was straddling the line, not really making a commitment either way.

I wonder, Allie thought, if she knew her brother was dead, if she'd really want to live.

Allie walked over to the woman's bedside and held the hand not inside a cuff. Her fingers stuck out of the plaster cast, white and unharmed. Allie could feel the woman's blood course through her skin. Her mouth watered. She looked back towards the morphine and shut it off for a single moment.

The woman coughed awake.

"Shhh," Allie said. "You're in a hospital. Are you okay?"

"Ap—ap—"

"Your brother?"

The woman paused before she nodded.

"I'm sorry. He's gone. He died before we could reach him."

The woman's eyes grew darker. Even through the bruised skin and scrapes on her face, Allie could see the pain etched there. The woman tried to sob, but the tubes in her body and the bruises around her jaw must have made it too difficult. She closed her eyes again and groaned.

"Do you want me to stop it?" Allie asked.

The woman paused. She opened one eye a crack. A questioning, fleeting glance.

"Stop it," Allie said. "I can make the pain go away."

The woman's eyes went wide. But she wasn't afraid.

Allie nodded, squeezing her hand, and understood. The woman's chin moved ever so slightly, nodding along. If there was no more family for her to go home to, then the woman really had nothing. What was best in this scenario? Give up her life to save her the pain of a trial and prison—and then to save another person from being Allie's victim? This was doing no harm, even in the face of death. Allie tried to convince herself a little more before she began to prepare her next meal.

Allie wanted to hook up the morphine again to give the woman a moment's peace, but she knew it would taint the blood. Make her a little woozy after her meal, like having too much wine with dinner. This blood was even fresher than before. Even more precarious and overwhelming. Allie wanted it. She wanted it so much, it frightened her. It had been so long since she had fed on a live body, still warm in her hands. Her fingers trembled as she moved. Just a little bit wouldn't hurt.

"Please," the woman said.

Allie nodded, a soft smile on her face. She felt her teeth spring forward. She leaned over and took the first bite, the woman's limp hand still in hers.

"What happened?"

"She slipped away. It's a bad scene in there," Allie explained to the officer once he had returned. A nurse ran into the room, her eyes wild and afraid. She muttered under her breath as the machines went haywire, the sudden code blue announced down the long hallway. Allie kept her back to the door even as the doctor pronounced. Allie waited, and in her extra-sensitive skin, she swore she could feel the cool chill of one life leaving and another walking in. She licked the back of her teeth, still tasting the woman's blood.

"She lost too much in the crash. It shocked her system," Allie added. "Nothing could have been done."

The officer sighed. He still held the cups of coffee in his hands as his face twisted with worry, and then relief. "I suppose it's for the better. I mean, we were only going to arrest her as soon as she came to."

Allie nodded. "Life has a way of balancing out, I suppose."

"Something like that," the officer said. "Here's your coffee, by the way."

"Thanks." Allie took her cup gratefully from his hand. She gave him a small smile and sniffed it before turning to walk down the hallway.

"I guess I'll see you around?" the officer asked.

Allie looked over her shoulder and nodded. "Sure. Why not?"

Inside the elevator, she chanced a real sip at the coffee. Even that tasted better after she had real blood inside of her. She nearly devoured the whole cup before she realized it was almost five in the morning. Even if their chief did get down here on time to give them paperwork, it was almost time to go home. Allie felt a small tremor of fear run through her. Violet, she thought softly. Oh, Violet. I'm so sorry. How do I explain?

She took another sip of her coffee before throwing the rest out.

"Where were you?"

Allie walked inside the apartment slowly. As soon as she placed her keys on the front table, she felt her headache begin, as a blinding pain that felt like a fracture of her skull. The clanging of keys against the wooden table made her bite her lip as it echoed inside her mind and split against her temple.

"Oh, God," Allie let out a loan moan.

"It's not like you to cry out for something you know isn't there."

Allie could hear the laugh in Violet's voice. Violet rustled around in their living room, but her movements were muffled inside Allie's mind. She clasped her temples and tried to respond.

"Haha, yes, very funny. Just because I'm a vampire doesn't mean…"

"Shhh," Violet said. She moved out of the living room and leaned against the hallway in the low light. Her small, heart-shaped face was tense with worry. "Shhh, the neighbours could hear."

"And who would believe them? I'm a cop," Allie said. She pulled out her badge, boasting slightly as she laid it down on the front table. The pain came back. A white light appeared around Violet, as if she were subsumed by the sun.

"Oh, God. Again, I know. But my head *aches*, Vi." Allie chanced another glance at Violet. The white light and blinding pain still remained. Allie sighed, knowing this only meant one thing. "Are you—"

"I was worried. I waited up for you," Violet said, crossing her hands over her chest. She store wore her purple scrubs from work. "I needed to know if you were okay. The sun is up, Allie. That's usually bad news for you."

Allie nodded, struggling to take off her jacket with her eyes closed. "You do know that I don't burn up in the sun, right? That was something a movie studio invented for vampires so their production didn't violate copyright infringement with *Nosferatu*. I don't burn up in the sun, just...get a little bit drowsy. Like being drunk. And only if I'm *in* the sun. The apartment is fine."

Violet sighed. "We've been together for a while now. I think I know what you do in the sun, or indoors during the morning hours. But there was no guarantee that you were safe in the morning—or that anyone else is. I just knew that you were gone. So...I was worried. You can't blame me for that."

Allie nodded. The pain was still bad in her head, but she was getting used to it. Her vision was back and not blinding so long as she squinted inside the apartment. She dipped into the front pocket of her jacket and took out a few pills. Iron pills, actually. They seemed to do the most against pain relief for Allie whenever her head started to swell like this. She swallowed the pills back without water.

Allie wondered vaguely if her sudden pain was from the blood. She had taken her meal from two separate people tonight. Maybe their blood types clashed with one another. Maybe they were sick in some way. Her system wasn't used to the rich qualities of fresh blood, so she could be falling from a high like a kid on sugar. When Allie raised her eyes to Violet again, she felt the cluster of pain at the front of her skull emerge. And she was reminded again of what was really going on.

"Good Lord, Violet. Are you wearing silver?"

Violet stuck out her tongue and displayed the stud at the center.

Allie rolled her eyes. "You know how much that *hurts*."

"And you know how much it hurts me that you stay away for so long and don't even bother texting."

Violet turned around and stomped over towards the couch. From her sudden frown and saddened movements, Allie knew what was really wrong. Violet only pouted like this whenever Allie was late—not because she worried about Allie's physical health, but the safety of others. In the same way a nervous lover wonders about their spouse cheating, Violet was always, at some level, worried that Allie would feed on a live person. Normally, when these accusations surfaced, Allie would spring in to defend herself right away. But now she remained quiet. In that pause, Violet seemed to already know the response. Allie *had* fed. She couldn't deny it—and to Violet that meant the silver was on and would stay on until Allie had rectified the situation.

This had happened a handful of times before in the beginning of their relationship, but not in the past year or so. Allie had always tried to fix the situation before by promising to be true to Violet—and the blood she supplied. Usually after a long, intense fight followed up make-up sex, things between them would go back to normal. But it was clear to Allie then that Violet still worried about Allie and the people she'd kill. Violet *had to* since she was a nurse and it was part of her job. Allie felt the guilt of her kill emerge again, because she had proven Violet's worries true. She sighed, unsure how to proceed.

With Violet on their couch, the pain in Allie's head was less. Silver was yet another thing that old monster movies and TV shows like *Supernatural* got only half-right. Silver was bad for *all* supernatural creatures, not just werewolves, and not just in bullet form. As long as someone wore silver on their body, it protected them from any creature getting too close without splitting headaches or white light blinding their vision. A creature could, in theory, power through the pain they got when they approached silver, but it took far too much willpower and most monsters were lazy. They always preferred the path of least resistance.

Most of the silver that civilians had was also not as strong as the good stuff. It was often cut with nickel or other metals, which severely limited its power—and its effect on the monsters who got near it. Violet had one of the purest silvers on the market, something which she had put a lot of time into finding and procuring. It was important to her, not only to have something she could use to annoy Allie with on occasion, but also for the night shifts on the ER (you could get some really fucked-up spirits there, not to mention psychopomps who wanted to usher people from one side to the next). She normally wore a silver cross underneath her nursing scrubs that she left in her locker to continue to ward off bad spirits. Her pure silver piercings were something she only broke out when she was really, really mad.

The iron pills began to work for Allie. Her vision became clearer and she wandered closer to Violet on the couch. Violet folded her arms across her chest, still pouting.

"You know I can't do anything unless you tell me how to fix what you're feeling," Allie stated. "And you know it's harder for me to get close to you when your wear silver. So tell me, what's up?"

Violet was quiet. She refused to meet Allie's eyes and instead stared out their sliding door. Allie felt the sudden crisp intervention of the sun through their blinds. They were on the top floor, their apartment looking out at Chicago. As she walked over to close the blinds, Allie thought back to the case earlier today.

"Well, if you're not going to tell me anything, I will begin with my day. Chip and I were on the nightshift."

"I don't like Chip."

"He's okay. But I think only his mom truly loves him. Anyway, he was fine tonight. We were supposed to stake out a place in case there was a robbery. Lo and behold, the people actually showed up. They shot the clerk—don't worry, he survived—and then took off on their bikes. Motorcycles, you know. Very fast and very dangerous."

This got Violet's attention. She turned to face Allie, her mouth twisted into a contemplative pose. "Marla. You remember her, right?"

"How could I forget? I go to all these hospital cocktail parties. She wears a lot of silver."

"Not the good stuff, though." Violet smirked. "Well, she calls motorcycles organ donations on wheels."

"I remember you telling me that. The reality isn't far off. At least, not tonight." Allie moved to sit down on the couch with Violet. Violet's gaze was still icy, but Allie felt as if she could warm her demeanor up. She clasped one of Violet's hands in hers, a thumb tracing around the outside of her skin.

"We had to chase him. It was pretty bad. Chip wasn't driving; it was just me and the road for a while. Everything passed in slow motion. They crashed, because that's what happens if you drive like that for long enough. I could tell, as soon as he hit the pavement, that he was gone. There was nothing we could do. Chip called for backup, and the ambulance came to take the other one on the bike away. But the other guy, the brother of the girl, I was alone with him and... he was...I..."

"You fed?" Violet said. Her sudden forgiving demeanor was no longer present. She pushed Allie's hand away. "I *knew* it. I thought I told you I would get you blood? There's some in the fridge for you right now! Isn't that how this little arrangement is supposed to work?"

Allie sighed. She had known that this was what would happen if she tried to confess. All confessions were useless in her world. But in Allie's world of humans, of light and dark and suffering, she thought it would have been better. She could make the gesture, at least. But Violet seemed to know that Allie was only going through the motions—it was probably half the reason why she was already wearing the silver as punishment.

"How could you tell me this? After everything..." Violet trailed off, running a hand through her dark brown hair.

"I know," Allie said. "But the blood you get me isn't fresh. It's good. It keeps me alive. But I miss the fresh stuff every so often."

"And I like having a job. You know how much I risk when I do that?"

"I know, and I want to thank you but..."

"You're so ungrateful." Violet got up from the couch. Her blue eyes turned purple, like her scrubs, in her sudden rage. "Just because you think you have forever to fuck around doesn't mean I do. Things never have any real meaning for you!"

"I don't have forever," Allie said. "I could still die, Vi."

"Yeah, with a stake and whatever else there is. These little silver migraines don't count."

"But I still could die. That's what I was trying to tell you before. That's what I realized when I saw the guy on the bike crash. Life is precious."

"And yet, you fed from him. Very precious. Very well done."

Allie watched mutely as Violet ran her hands through her hair again. She seemed to want to pout more, huff and get angry, but her eyes revealed a deep tiredness. Without another word, Violet walked out of the living room and down the hallway to the bedroom. Allie sighed and then followed her a few paces behind. Violet watched as Allie took out her earrings—white gold—and set them down on the vanity. She pulled out the stud in her tongue, but Allie knew not to get too excited right away. If Violet relinquished the tongue stud that quickly, it meant she had more silver elsewhere. Violet pulled her purple scrub shirt over her head, revealing a black tank top underneath. Green vines from a tattoo on her back poked out from under the fabric. The green vines, heavy with flat leaves and thorns, worked their way across Violet's back and down her spine, roses blooming against her pale skin.

Allie had met Violet when she got that tattoo done. Violet had many more scattered across her ankles and the backs of her legs, mostly flash pieces. But this back garden, wide and expansive, and very large, had been Violet's proudest moment. She had to return to the tattoo parlor for several sessions lasting hours at a time until it was done. All of Violet's tattoos were hidden under her clothing, none visible when she was in her full nursing attire. Like her piercing, Violet's secret side remained hidden.

Except to Allie. She had walked to the tattoo parlor on her way to the precinct. Sometimes, she skipped that side of the street, because the smell of blood from that place was too strong. Tattoo parlors were worse than hospitals for driving

Allie crazy. The blood there was fresh, youthful, and not full of sickness like it was in hospitals. The inks made Allie excited, crazy even, especially since each one had its own flavor to her. When Allie had walked by, and had seen the small woman with blue eyes and dark hair enter the tattoo parlor, she had been skeptical. No way someone like that was getting work done. But then she heard the slow buzz of the needle and smelled something sweet, and Allie knew it was her. Violet had always smelled like her name implied, delicate, beautiful—and oh, so sweet.

Allie had never wanted to harm her. She wanted to get close to Violet, to see what she was like beyond the marks and scars she kept hidden under layers of clothing. When Allie did get close, she wasn't disappointed as much as she was surprised. The rose garden on Violet's back was simple, sweet, and devastating. It was a constant reminder of death and love, since roses were flowers for lovers and flowers for funerals.

"Mary, Mary quite contrary. My, how your garden grows," Allie had said to Violet when they had first had sex, and dropped all their clothing to the ground. "Why do you have a tattoo of a garden on yourself?"

"Because I like it," Violet had replied coyly. That had been all she was willing to share about the tattoos at that time. Eventually, after they had been together for a while, Violet told Allie the secret of her tattoo's meaning. When she was a young girl, she had been digging in her parents' garden and found the bones of a corpse.

"It molded me," she had said. "I watched as the police came and tried to solve the crime. I became obsessed with the passage from one stage of life to the next and how good things could come from it. My parents' garden was full of life, even when there was something bad lurking beneath the surface. So nursing made sense, especially in the trauma unit."

"Not a cop?" Allie had joked.

"Why bother with cops, when I have you?"

Violet had fallen in love easily with Allie. When the secret of who she really was came out, Allie had expected her to leave. She had wanted her to leave. All Allie had ever known was a constant push-and-pull battle of secrecy and running, so she had set herself up to do that again. But when Violet had laughed and pulled Allie in for another kiss, Allie had not known her next step.

"No, I'm serious," Allie reiterated. "I'm a vampire."

"And I thought I was a psychopomp after I found that body. Maybe I still am."

Allie knew that Violet wasn't a psychopomp or anything else, not even close. She was a regular human being with a couple of quirks—like all good humans. But Allie had been won over by her kindness. As the news that Allie really was who she said she was sunk in, Violet had grown excited. She was no stranger to darkness, and having her own private window to the underworld she had longed to study and learn from seemed too good to be true.

Two years later, with lots of history and even more tattoos between them, Allie didn't want to let any of it go. She lingered by the doorway as Violet continued to change out of her nurses' gear, her movements jerky with anger.

"Don't just watch from the sidelines," Violet chided. "It's creepy."

Allie laughed. She stepped into the room and placed a careful hand on Violet's shoulder. The white light and rolling sound of thunder inside her mind came back. Allie groaned.

"What else are you wearing?"

"Lots. I was mad at you. And apparently I did have a reason to be."

"Was? Did?" Allie asked through closed eyes. "That's past tense. So you're no longer mad?"

"I'm ambivalent. Working it out." Violet turned around, her smile more of a devious smirk. Allie realized that Violet must have come home after her shift, changed out of one set of scrubs, put in her silver jewellery, and then gotten dressed in scrubs again. Quite mad, indeed.

"What can I do to make it up to you?"

"I don't know yet. I'm still thinking. Processing my feelings. You know how it goes." Violet took off her tank top in front of Allie. Beneath her bra, Allie spotted the notched of her nipple rings.

"You are the strangest nurse I have ever met," Allie said with a smile. "And I need you to be nice to me. I was trying to have a moment before on the couch, trying to tell you how much I appreciate you."

Violet rolled her eyes. "You're always having those moments, though. You're always standing atop a building in the middle of the night, breaking into churches, and apparently feeding off motorcycle men, and then claiming it as some large revelation in order to excuse your behavior. For someone who doesn't believe in God, you're having a lot of epiphanies."

Allie smiled, though Violet's tone was serious. "I can't help it."

"Yes, you can."

"Well, sure, but then life is boring. Life is so banal. Even the vampire stuff starts to get old after a while. Breaking into places and having epiphanies keeps things interesting for a while longer."

Violet suddenly laughed. Her tense face became rosy, her eyes brighter. She sat on the bed, her skin folding over and some of her tattoos making new designs. Allie stepped closer, hoping to take advantage of her sudden good mood.

"What's up?"

Violet brushed a hand over her bangs. "Nothing. I just thought that I was the one boring you."

"No," Allie said. She sat on the bed with Violet, taking her hand again. "No, you never bore me."

"Really?"

"Is that what you were worried about before? Why you were so mad? You thought I fed off someone because you were *boring*?"

"That's what I'm *always* worried about," Violet said in a rare honest moment. She usually tried to obfuscate—or hinder Allie's thinking process with silver stuck in all the best places of her body. But now, she turned towards Allie and looked up at her in awe. "Of course I'm worried about the people you kill. But that's…an afterthought, really. I just don't want to be the Bella to your Edward. The Mina or even Jonathan Harker to Dracula. I never want to be the boring narrator, longing for something she can't have. When you feed, it reminds me that I'm not like you—and I worry that you'll want to leave."

"I don't want to leave at all. Those are just stories, Vi. Some of them bad stories at that."

"But there is truth to them, you know? I don't want to be the mortal person wishing for a better life as a vampire."

"And I don't want to be the one who turns you. Never. I only eat to—"

"Kill. I know. That's the point of fresh blood, right?" Violet rolled her eyes then sighed. "I don't want to turn. You don't want to turn me. We're interspecies, and we make it work. Or something like that, whatever."

"Whatever."

"Don't tease me!" Violet said playfully, nudging her shoulder against Allie. "Even if we're both agreed on what we want out of this, I always worry that I'm still boring for you. That you'll want to find a vampire, so you can relate better. I always worry that this life won't always tolerate our differences instead of revelling in them."

Allie felt the deep pang of despair in Violet's voice. She leaned forward and took her face in her hands. "Never, Violet. Never." She kissed her once, softly on the lips. She wanted to embrace more, but the silver from the studs in Violet's nipples began to hurt when she got too close. Allie pulled away, but still kept her hands on her body.

"You know, I did live with a vampire," Allie mentioned.

"Yes, you told me. Hester."

"Yes. And that *was* boring."

"But why? I can't imagine…"

"Because the stuff that's exciting to you is boring to another vampire. And the stuff that you find boring, like your need for coffee in the morning or how you sleep after long shifts, is not boring to me. I love making you coffee, even if I don't have any myself."

"But nothing happens for me the way it does for you."

"*Everything* happens. Even now, when we're talking like this and I know you're mad at me, I'm happy, because I can see inside your mind for a bit. How your face gives away all of your feelings in small gestures."

Allie touched Violet's nose, and this time, Violet was calmer. Softer than before. Her anger melted away as soon as her insecurity was dealt with. Violet kissed her first and Allie lost herself in the embrace for a while. Then she remembered her first epiphany up on the roof and the second one as she fed from the second female motorcycle rider.

"I wanted to tell you I loved you tonight," Allie said as she pulled away, "because of that motorcycle guy and his partner in crime. They're mortal. Fragile. Their life can just disappear. And I know that you are just as precarious. We must take life seriously. I could very easily die. I could get found out, which is like dying, because it takes me away from you."

Violet smiled weakly. She looked down at their hands together. She pulled back suddenly, her eyes wide.

"Sorry," Violet stammered. "I was wearing a ring. Silver again. I think I may have burned your skin."

Allie looked down. A section of her palm was now pink. A small blister formed underneath the skin. She was shocked she hadn't felt it before.

"I'm sorry," Violet said. She tossed her ring onto the nightstand, folding it inside a silk cloth that she kept most of her jewellery in. The silk neutralized the silver's power. "You're right. I don't want to ever be without you."

"Good," Allie said. "Because from my calculation, if all goes well, we have at least another forty years together."

Violet smiled. Her lips lingered on Allie's mouth as they kissed again.

"And from there?"

"Let's not worry about that right now, okay? I have much better plans for us." Allie slipped down from the bed, placing her hands over Violet's legs. Her scrub pants were still on, and Allie worked on helping her take them off. Violet laughed, a low throaty giggle, before she lay down on the bed. She slipped her hands around to her back and slid the bra off her body.

"Before we go any further…" Allie trailed off. She tossed the scrub pants behind her as her eyes fixed on Violet's bejewelled nipples.

"Right." Violet ran her fingers along the underside of her breasts, cupping them slightly. When she laughed, they bounced even more. Allie wanted to enjoy the show, but all she felt was the slight circle of pain behind her eyes.

"Come on, now," she said, whimpering. Her hands went to Violet's knees and she held them there. Violet laughed a little more.

"Oh, sweetheart. I love you like this."

"What? In pain?" Allie laughed. She touched her temples. "I thought you took a vow to do no harm. Now you're laughing. Enjoying this, even."

"Because it's one of the few times that you're human, too."

Allie raised her eyes. Violet's blue ones stared back at her. Violet's face was so wide, expansive. Innocent. She knew all about the underside of life, the worlds in between sleeping and dreaming, and yet she kept this innocent demeanor. Not even her tattoos or personal history could change the way Violet looked right then.

"I love you," Allie said.

"I love you too," Violet reciprocated. She smirked. This time, after waiting only another few seconds, she went to remove her piercings from her breasts. She tossed the silver piercings down onto the silk cloth before grabbing another plastic set of piercings to slip in instead. Her nipples tightened as she worked, her mouth forming a small *O*. Allie's head felt better, immediately. Her mind focused on other tasks, like removing the rest of Allie's dark underwear from her body.

"Is that it?" Allie asked. "No more hidden studs left in to trip me up?"

Violet rubbed her hands over her nipples, tense between her two fingers. "That's it."

"How do I know...?"

Allie kissed her knee. Her fingers slid down between Violet's thighs and pushed them open. Violet also had another piercing, Allie knew. She was devious with her piercings and tattoos, keeping them under wraps at all time. The first time that Allie undressed her, she had been surprised every step of the way. Through the sheer black fabric of her underwear, Allie could see the slight bulge of a clitoral hood piercing.

"You don't know," Violet said. She lay down on the bed, topless and breathing heavily. She propped herself up on her elbows, her smile wide again. "You just have to trust me."

Allie sighed. She moved her body over Violet's, still wearing her old jeans and T-shirt from her locker at the precinct. Their lips met, and this time, there was no white light. The tension in her body was removed. For a moment, Allie thought of the woman in the bed at the hospital, thought of taking her life and watching as it left her body. The woman's eyes had been happy when she died, knowing that she would be with her surrogate brother. She had succumbed to Allie. And now, Allie longed to make Violet succumb to her own desires.

Violet's hands moved towards Allie's pants. She ran her fingers around the belt buckle and pulled it back. Violet always knew what she wanted, too.

Allie's lips moved to her ear. "I trust you."

"Good," Violet said. She pulled the belt completely away from Allie's body. She looked up at Allie, her grin wide. "You're wearing far too much. How do I know you don't have anything hidden?"

"I have nothing. Nothing that would work on you—nothing to disarm you."

"I don't know about that," Violet said. She lay back down on the bed and stuck her fingers in her underwear. She didn't remove it, but toyed with it instead. "You should help me. Disarm me this way."

"What do you want, you covetous creature? For me to undress or for me to undress you?"

"Both," Violet said. "I always want more from you, I know. I'm testing you...I'm—"

Allie dropped down to her knees, her face between Violet's legs again. She took her own shirt off while retaining eye contact for as long as she could. She dropped the fabric behind her, shedding it like old skin. Like an old way of thinking. Her pants were loose without the belt. She could practically shimmy them off. As she carefully stepped out of them, she felt the carpet press into her skin, now supersensitive since she had touched silver. Allie hissed, just barely, as she stepped forward

"You okay?" Violet said. She moved to sit up in bed. Allie grabbed Violet's wrists and pinned her down, looming over Violet's body.

"I'm fine," Allie said.

"You're burned still. You should be careful with that hand."

"You were the one that burned me."

Violet didn't say anything. She struggled, just slightly, under Allie's arms. Violet struggled so she could feel the tension between them, Allie knew. She did it to see what Allie would do.

Allie pressed their lips pressed together, hard and fast. Violet moaned into Allie's mouth. Allie was so close to her that she could hear Violet's heartbeat, the swell of blood beneath her body. Sex was always such a cerebral and desirous experience between them. Allie could feel her influence under Violet's skin as their bodies and instincts blended together.

Violet was a fiend in bed. She wanted to be dominated, she wanted to be pinned and taken care of. She liked pain—that much was obvious from the tattoos and piercing. Not always the case for people, but for Violet it was. She liked to be pricked and watch her blood flow. And more than anything, she liked to watch Allie squirm as their bodies got closer and closer together to their final ending.

"Take me," Violet said, whispering into Allie's ear. "Take my pants off. And go down…"

Allie breathed heavily. She felt her own heart, slightly different and restless, beat and undulate against Violet's. Together, this close, they were almost the same creature. Allie didn't know if that meant she was more human or Violet was more monster and beast.

"Take me," Violet demanded again. "Didn't you hear me?"

"I did," Allie said. She kissed Violet again, tongues in each other's mouths. Violet's saliva tasted better than before. Better than coffee and sugar, better than food, and even better than blood. Allie would devour Violet if she could, only metaphorically, only if Violet could still stay alive. She wrapped her hands around Violet's breasts, freeing her girlfriend's wrists, and moving her fingertips over the hard nipples. Letting out a moan, Allie shifted so that she could press Violet into her own chest and demand pleasure.

"Suck," Allie whispered. "Please, baby. Suck me."

With a quick flick from behind her back, Allie's bra fell down. Violet's tongue wasted no time following orders. Her teeth grazed Allie's nipple before her tongue coolly ran over her skin. She felt herself grow harder in Violet's mouth.

"You taste like gunpowder," Violet said. Her breath made Allie's skin cool. She let out a moan.

"I was in a fight."

Violet looked up for only a moment before she sucked on Allie's other nipple. Her free hand went to the small of Allie's back and pulled Allie against her waist. Violet struggled to remove Allie's panties as her mouth and tongue continued to perform. For a moment, Allie thought Violet would tear them off of her in sudden sexual frustration.

"Why am I doing all the work?" Violet asked playfully. She squeezed Allie's breasts in her hands before letting them go. "Take me."

Allie nodded, her jaw slackened and her body almost paralyzed by desire. She felt how wet she had grown, how hard her clitoris was. She could smell her wetness on herself now, feel her body pulsate and crave more. Allie got back down on the carpet, in between Violet's legs. She took the small strap of the underwear and tugged it forward with her teeth.

Violet let out a low groan. "Not those teeth."

"What?"

"Not *those* teeth. Cut it off me with your fangs."

Allie stared at Violet with solemn, serious eyes. "You know how dangerous that is."

"I do," Allie said. "So you better be careful."

Violet ran a hand through Allie's blonde hair. Allie swallowed hard. She felt her jaw shift, the teeth coming forward. It was likes supressing a yawn. The idea was put into her mind, and then, all of a sudden, the teeth were there.

Violet smiled, biting her lip as they emerged. "Kiss me."

"I—I..."

"Kiss me," Violet demanded. Allie leaned forward, no longer of her own free will. The real blood from before gave her the strength to control her civilized mind while her teeth etched out a more bestial desire.

Violet pressed their mouths together, and her tongue came forward towards Allie. Allie tried to work slowly so she didn't hurt Violet. But Violet wanted to play a dangerous game. She kissed Allie, more and more, until she finally sliced her own lips with Allie's fangs.

"Fuck," Allie said, pulling away. She could taste the coppery tang of Violet's blood inside of her. Her heart palpitated, her skin rose in gooseflesh. Allie struggled to put away the urges and to move forward.

Violet tongued her wound, a pleased smile on her face as blood streaked her teeth.

"You said you didn't want to change."

"I don't," Violet said. "This won't change me. But I like to have fun every so often."

Violet grabbed Allie's shoulder and opened her legs more. "Take it off me. Be careful."

Allie looked at Violet's underwear, dark—but even darker now that her wetness had grown. She could smell and taste the arousal in Violet's blood. Allie's teeth were still present and sharp inside her mouth, but she breathed in a little easier. She could control herself, she knew it. She had done so many times before. She could....she could get so close to Violet, rip away her panties, and then go back to sex the way humans did it.

But would they ever really be human? Allie asked herself. That answer was always going to be no. And even if Violet didn't want to be changed, she wanted to play dangerously. She wanted to play with fire. She was always going to be a beast in Allie's eyes, just for a few moments, just to reinforce her humanity.

That was it, Allie realized. Violet wanted to play, because she wanted to remember she was human. That she *could* die—but didn't, for the night. Like the man and woman on the motorcycles, Allie and Violet had stayed together in spite of blood, because it made them feel as if they belonged. They had all broken the rules and committed crimes, because it meant that there was still some order in the world. Even death meant that the scales evened out. Moreover, Allie had taken the bikers' lives, had drunk their blood, because it made her feel like who she was. Everybody had their limits, both humans and monsters, Allie knew. Playing dangerously was the best way to push them.

Allie leaned down over Violet's body and slid her teeth across the fabric. One bite and one drag of her sharp incisors was all that it took. The fabric fell away, exposing Violet's most sacred bits, the parts that made her the most human, and they waited. Both of them, blood pumping, waited and watched.

Allie's teeth sunk back into her mouth. She shifted, her more controlled brain coming back. She smelled Violet's arousal and then felt Violet's hands on her own shoulders.

"See? You're fine." Violet smiled. "I knew you could do it."

Allie looked up at her with a grin. She pressed their lips together in a kiss and then slid her hands in between Violet's legs. She ran a finger along Violet's exposed pussy, touching it softly, before she moved faster. Violet breathed heavily inside Allie's mouth before she broke their kiss. With their foreheads pressed together, Allie's hand continued to explore.

"Yes," Allie said. "The night may be over, but I have only just begun with you."

Violet let out another long luxurious laugh before Allie dropped down between her legs. Allie breathed in a deep sigh of Violet's body, before she placed her mouth against her and began to work again.

About The Authors

Erzabet Bishop

Erzabet Bishop is the author of *Sigil Fire*, "Written on Skin" (a *Sigil Fire* series short), *Fetish Fair*, *Temptation Resorts: Marnie's Tale* (upcoming), *Temptation Resorts: Jess's Adventures* (upcoming), *Pomegranate* (upcoming) and multiple books in the *Erotic Pagan Series*. She is a contributing author to *Club Rook*, *Hungry for More*, *A Christmas to Remember*, *Forbidden Fruit*, *Sci Spanks*, *Sweat*, *When the Clock Strikes Thirteen*, *Bossy*, *Can't Get Enough*, *Slave Girls*, *The Big Book of Submission*, *Gratis II*, *Anything She Wants*, *Coming Together: Girl on Girl and more*. She was a dual finalist for the GCLS awards in 2014.

Erzabet lives in Texas with her husband, furry children and can often be found lurking in local bookstores.

Website: erzabetbishop.wordpress.com
Facebook: facebook.com/erzabetbishopauthor

Elaine Burnes

Elaine Burnes grew up and lives in Massachusetts. After earning a B.S. in biology, and learning it qualified her for pretty much nothing, she worked first at a pet store, then at a bookstore, and finally broke out of retail by attending secretarial school. She spent the next 20 years working and writing for a variety of environmental nonprofits. Finally wearying of reality, she turned to writing fiction in her spare time, publishing her first short story, 'A Perfect Life', in *Skulls and Crossbones* in 2010.

Since then, she has had several more stories published: 'Lily Gets a Flu Shot', in *Venus Magazine*; 'The Stranger' in *Read These Lips Take 5*; 'The Gift, Forget-Me-Not', and 'Tracy Arm' in *Khimairal Ink*, and 'The Game' in *Best Lesbian Romance 2011*.

Facebook: facebook.com/elanie.burnes

MAY DAWNEY

May is a twenty-nine year old fiction writer. As a lesbian, almost all her work focuses on portraying lesbian relationships. She has been writing for as long as she can remember, making comic books with her mom as a child, finding her voice through on-line role-play, and honing her skills through fan fiction. She is relatively new to original fiction, but is quickly growing addicted to the freedom it offers.

May lives with her long-term partner, and their eighteen year old cat, in The Netherlands where she balances far too many projects for her own good—and she loves every single one of them.

Website: maydawney.blogspot.com

R·G· EMANUELLE

R.G. Emanuelle is from New York City and spent more than 20 years in publishing. She is co-editor of *Skulls and Crossbones: Tales of Women Pirates*, as well as *All You Can Eat: A Buffet of Lesbian Erotica and Romance* and *Unwrap These Presents*, both from Ylva Publishing. Her short stories can be found in numerous anthologies, including the 2014 Goldie nominee *When the Clock Strikes Thirteen*.

When she was a child, a neighbor called her a vampire because she only came out after dark, so it's fitting that her first novel, *Twice Bitten*, is about creatures of the night. Her 2013 romantic novella, *Add Spice to Taste,* stars a love-burned chef, but she is always summoned back by the things that go bump in the night.

Blog: rgemanuelle.com
Facebook: facebook.com/RGEmanuelle
Twitter: @Rgemanuelle

Bridget Essex

Bridget Essex was supposed to be a violin teacher, but her heart wasn't in it. A life-long writer, Bridget wanted to tell the stories that she wished existed in the world. With the urging of her extremely supportive wife, Bridget began to share her heartfelt lesbian paranormal romances with the world, and she hasn't looked back.

Website: bridgetessex.wordpress.com

Eve Francis

Eve Francis's short stories have appeared in *Wilde Magazine, The Fieldstone Review, Iris New Fiction, MicroHorror,* and *The Human Echoes Podcast.* Romance and horror are her favourite genres to write in because everyone has felt love or fear in some form or another. She lives in Canada, where she often sleeps late, spends too much time online, and repeatedly watches old horror movies and *Orange Is The New Black*.

Website: evefrancis.wordpress.com
Tumblr: paintitback.tumblr.com

STEPH GOTTSCHALK

Steph Gottschalk earned a B.A. in German and Linguistics from the University of Wisconsin—Eau Claire, but currently lives and writes in Minnesota. Besides writing, Steph enjoys reading, crocheting, and becoming proficient at various types of weaponry. As a teenager, Steph once helped a friend try to contact a ghost via a Ouija board; the result was rather anticlimactic, but the experience came in handy as part of the inspiration for *Object Permanence*.

S. M. HARDING

S. M. Harding has had two dozen short stories published in various crime fiction publications, both on-line magazines and in print anthologies and magazines. Two of the most recent include *A Snake in the Grass* in *Spinetingler* and *Scarecrow Field* in *Indiana Crime Review*. *Spirit of Christmas Past, Christmas Future* is forthcoming from Ylva Publishing. The novel *I Will Meet You There* will be published by Bella Books in Spring of 2015. She teaches classes at the Writers' Center of Indiana and participated in panels for their annual Gathering of Writers, also at Indy Author's Fair, Magna Cum Murder and various local libraries. She edited and contributed an essay to *Writing Murder*, a collection of essays by Midwestern authors about writing crime fiction.

Blog: storytellersfire.wordpress.com
Facebook: facebook.com/profile.php?id=100004961079442

LOIS CLOAREC HART

Born and raised in British Columbia, Canada, Lois Cloarec Hart grew up as an avid reader but didn't begin writing until much later in life. Several years after joining the Canadian Armed Forces, she received a degree from Royal Military College and on graduation switched occupations from air traffic control to military intelligence. Lois married a CAF fighter pilot while in college, and went on to spend another five years as an Intelligence Officer before leaving the military to care for her husband, who was ill with chronic progressive Multiple Sclerosis and passed away in 2001. She began writing while caring for her husband in his final years and had her first book, Coming Home, published in 2001. It was through that initial publishing process that Lois met her wife-to-be. She now commutes annually between her northern home in Calgary and her wife's southern home in Atlanta.

Website: www.loiscloarechart.com

CORI KANE

Cori Kane has an addiction: stories. Whether they come as books, movies, tv shows or even song lyrics, she wants them—and uses them as inspiration for her own work. She started writing at 14 when her first crush inspired her to write some "seriously lovely, seriously naive poetry."

Many years later, Cori Kane still hasn't given up on entertaining herself and others with her less lovely and—hopefully—less naive fiction. When not writing she indulges in all the other ways to feed her addiction and loves to take strolls in her hometown by the sea.

Blog: kanebookworm.wordpress.com
Facebook: facebook.com/pages/Cori-Kane/268830173306877
Twitter: @corikane

Q. KELLY

Q. Kelly is weird. She likes being weird almost as much as she loves corny jokes. Send any good ones her way! Her favorite color is purple, but her writing is gray. Life is not black and white, and she often writes about issues and characters where there is no "right" answer. She is a Lammy and Golden Crown Literary Society finalist. She also penned the incredibly popular and bestselling novel Reality Lesbian. She's currently working on In Need of Resolution, a lesbian romance serial.

Website: www.qkellybooks.com
Facebook: facebook.com/yllekq

CATHERINE LANE

Catherine Lane started to write fiction on a dare from her wife. She's thrilled to be a published author, even though she had to admit her wife was right. They live happily in Southern California with their son and a very mischievous pound puppy.

Catherine spends most of her time these days working, mothering, or writing. But when she finds herself at loose ends, she enjoys experimenting with recipes in the kitchen, paddling on long stretches of flat water, and browsing the stacks at libraries and bookstores. Oh, and trying unsuccessfully to outwit her dog.

She has published several short stories and is currently working on a novella.

ANDI MARQUETTE

Andi Marquette is an editor and award-winning author of mysteries, science fiction, and romance. Her latest novels are *Day of the Dead*, the Goldie finalist *The Edge of Rebellion*, and

From the Hat Down. She is also the co-editor of the anthology *All You Can Eat: A Buffet of Lesbian Romance and Erotica*.

Website: www.andimarquette.com

ORHEA THE DREAMER

Orhea the dreamer resides in East Texas. In her spare time she gardens, raises chickens, and takes pictures of everything under the wide open sun. A self-professed eclectic, she studies the human experience through various outlets, whether it's jewelry making, painting, writing, or simply observing. She also prides herself on her multicultural background boasting Native American, African American, German, and Scotch/Irish ethnic heritage. She started writing as a child, but started writing lesbian fiction when she expressed her desire to a favored author to see more characters with multicultural backgrounds and was told to write what she wanted to see. Now she dedicates her time to doing just that. Orhea has a love for humanity in all its goodness and some of its awfulness and hopes her work expresses that to each reader.

OTHER BOOKS FROM YLVA PUBLISHING

www.ylva-publishing.com

When the Clock Strikes Thirteen

ISBN: 978-3-95533-155-9
Length: 175 pages

Midnight Messages
by Lois Cloarec Hart

Luce Sheppard can't ignore it any longer. She has to make a decision and time grows short. But refusing to make a decision is a decision, and she retires to bed, prepared to accept the results of her non-decision. That night an unexpected midnight visitor lands on her doorstep. Keira Keller, a distraught teenager, has lost her way home after a disastrous party. Luce steps in to help and in doing so receives answers to questions she didn't know she'd asked.

Batteries Not Included
by L.T. Smith

Alex Stevens is a workaholic and a loner. Nothing and nobody can get past the cool exterior and solitary walls she has painstakingly created.

Until one night in October. One night that makes her step back and reassess what it means to be alive.

LOST AND FOUND
BY EMMA WEIMANN

Laura Sullivan flees to her grandparents' old cottage to escape the haunting memories of finding her brother in bed with her girlfriend. But even in rural Ireland, tranquility is easier to find than peace—especially when she meets an otherworldly being that leaves her a reminder she didn't count on.

CHRYSALIS
BY JOAN ARLING

Tara is a nice little girl. Her friends, on the other hand, are... peculiar... A breeze of a story. Or the other way 'round.

SISTERS OF THE MOON
BY DIANE MARINA

The week before Halloween, Nicole joins her friends on a local ghost tour. In addition to visiting spooky sights and haunted grounds, she meets an enticing woman who makes her spine tingle. Who is the mysterious stranger? And how will the encounter end?

WOLF MOON
BY ERZABET BISHOP

Seeking diversion from her job as a bookstore manager, Lindsay goes to a Halloween party at a convention center—and finds much more than she bargained for.

Werewolf Detective Taggert responds to a bomb threat at the convention center. An explosive situation, especially when raw chemistry hits them full force.

Can Lindsay open her heart and accept the fierce love of a red-hot shifter, or will they go their separate ways?

LOVE BITES
BY R.G. EMANUELLE

New Orleans. Vampires. Jodi goes to the former and finds the latter. She feels a mysterious pull that leads her to The Big Easy and to freedom, passion, and the startling revelation of what having too many daiquiris can make her do.

BEYOND AND BEGONE

Lois Cloarec Hart

ISBN: 978-3-95533-177-1 (epub),
978-3-95533-176-4 (mobi)
Length: 15,000 words

Erin has retreated from the world after the loss of her wife, Gwen, in a hit-and-run accident. Her best friend, Mariel, who is also her late wife's sister, is the only person she's interacted with for years. Finally, Erin dips her toes back into the dating pool, only to find that very odd things begin to happen. Mariel's medium, Zahra, insists that Gwen is trying to reach her with a warning. Erin has no use for psychics, but as the incidents mount, she reluctantly turns to Zahra for help and finds herself swept into a maelstrom of danger and intrigue. Can the love of her life save her? Or will she join Gwen, beyond and begone?

SIGIL FIRE

Erzabet Bishop

ISBN: 978-3-95533-206-8
Length: 131 pages

Sonia is a succubus with one goal: stay off Hell's radar. But when succubi start to die, including her sometimes lover, Jeannie, she's drawn into the battle between good and evil.

Fae is a blood witch turned vampire, running a tattoo parlor and trading her craft for blood. She notices that something isn't right on the streets of her city. The denizens of Hell are restless. With the aid of her nest mate Perry and his partner Charley, she races against time before the next victim falls. The killer has a target in his sights, and Sonia might not live to see the dawn.

SECOND NATURE
(2nd revised edition)

Jae

ISBN: 978-3-95533-030-9
Length: 496 pages

Novelist Jorie Price doesn't believe in the existence of shape-shifting creatures or true love. She leads a solitary life, and the paranormal romances she writes are pure fiction for her.

Griffin Westmore knows better—at least about one of these two things. She doesn't believe in love either, but she's one of the not-so-fictional shape-shifters. She's also a Saru, an elite soldier with the mission to protect the shape-shifters' secret existence at any cost.

When Jorie gets too close to the truth in her latest shape-shifter romance, Griffin is sent to investigate—and if necessary to destroy the manuscript before it's published and to kill the writer.

COMING FROM YLVA PUBLISHING

www.ylva-publishing.com

GOOD ENOUGH TO EAT

Jae & Alison Grey

Robin's New Year's resolution to change her eating habits is as unusual as she is. Unlike millions of other women, she isn't tempted by chocolate or junk food. She's a vampire, determined to fight her craving for a pint of O negative.

When she goes to an AA meeting, hoping for advice on fighting her addiction, she meets Alana, a woman who battles her own demons.

Despite their determination not to get involved, the attraction is undeniable.

Is it just bloodlust that makes Robin think Alana looks good enough to eat, or is it something more? Will it even matter once Alana finds out who Robin really is?

DRIVING ME MAD

L.T. Smith

For Rebecca Gibson, her journey to a work convention will be one she'll never forget. After driving around for four hours, Rebecca stops to ask for directions at an isolated house on the outskirts of Kirk Langley, Derbyshire.

Her initial meeting with the house's attractive owner, Annabel Howell, seems strange and unsettling, but at her hostess's insistence, Rebecca spends the night.

Plagued by nightmares, Rebecca senses that her dream world has blended with what she believes is reality. When she leaves the next day, her life has changed.

Can Rebecca solve a mystery that has been haunting a family for over sixty years? Will she find love along the way?

Or will the events drive her mad?

Banshee's Honor

Shaylynn Rose

Warleader. This is what the people of Y'Dan used to call the proud warrior Azhani Rhu'len.

Banshee. Oath breaker. Murderer. These are words that slip off their tongues now.

Azhani Rhu'len, once one of the greatest of Y'Dan's warriors, is now just a common criminal, escaping the justice of the kingdom she swore to serve.

Kyrian Stardancer. Goddess' Own. A healer and priestess, she is inviolate until one day, when her world is turned upside down and tossed over the back of a horse—literally.

Torn from all she knows, Kyrian finds her fate now rests squarely on the shoulders of the oath breaker, Azhani Rhu'len.

When signs of ancient evil appear, Azhani and Kyrian must choose whether to ignore the warnings or stand and face the terrifying menace.

www.ingramcontent.com/pod-product-compliance
Lightning Source LLC
Chambersburg PA
CBHW020322180626
46812CB00001B/16